SPARTAN RUN

"I'll cover you, Blade," Teucer said. "Get in!"

A half-dozen soldiers were racing to stop them from escaping. There was no time to lose. Blade vaulted up into the van, then slid over the console to the driver's seat. Blade beckoned urgently. "Let's go!"

"Just getting some air," Teucer quipped, and let fly, his right hand a blur as he fired one, two, three arrows in rapid succession. The shafts sped true, and three Spartans toppled. "The natives are a bit restless. I suggest we haul butt."

MADMAN RUN

As the aircraft arced into the heavens, a small spherical object dropped from the right wing directly toward the three youths. Blade's intuition flared, and he gave his friends a shove. "Into the forest! Move!"

Confused, Geronimo and Hickok nonetheless trusted the giant's judgment enough to obey him instantly. They darted to the northwest.

When the spherical object was 15 feet from the soil, Blade threw himself to the ground and bellowed, "Get down!"

Again the pair complied, and when they hit the ground, a blast with the force of a quarter ton of dynamite rent the air and rocked the ground....

BETTIE'S BOOKS
1445 D WEST MAIN
LEBANON, TN 37087
444-6303

The *Endworld Double* Series:
**YELLOWSTONE RUN/NEW ORLEANS RUN
BOSTON RUN/GREEN BAY RUN
CINCINNATI RUN/DALLAS RUN
ATLANTA RUN/MEMPHIS RUN
NEVADA RUN/MIAMI RUN
ANAHEIM RUN/SEATTLE RUN
LIBERTY RUN/HOUSTON RUN
CAPITAL RUN/NEW YORK RUN**

SPARTAN RUN/ MADMAN RUN

DAVID ROBBINS

LEISURE BOOKS NEW YORK CITY

*Dedicated to...
Judy,
Joshua,
and Shane.*

A LEISURE BOOK®

August 1993

Published by

Dorchester Publishing Co., Inc.
276 Fifth Avenue
New York, NY 10001

If you purchased this book without a cover you should be aware that this book is stolen property. It was reported as "unsold and destroyed" to the publisher and neither the author nor the publisher has received any payment for this "stripped book."

SPARTAN RUN Copyright © MCMXCI by David L. Robbins
MADMAN RUN Copyright © MCMXCI by David L. Robbins

All rights reserved. No part of this book may be reproduced or transmitted in any form or by any electronic or mechanical means, including photocopying, recording or by any information storage and retrieval system, without the written permission of the Publisher, except where permitted by law.

The name "Leisure Books" and the stylized "L" with design are trademarks of Dorchester Publishing Co., Inc.

Printed in the United States of America.

SPARTAN RUN

PROLOGUE

"If one of their patrols spots us, we're dead."

"At least we'll have died trying."

The two men ran at a steady pace to the northwest, angling across a wild field, the landscape surrounding them brightly illuminated by the radiant full moon overhead. Both men were in superb physical condition due to their grueling daily toil, and both breathed easily as they silently ate up the distance to the next stretch of woods.

Off to the east an owl hooted.

"What if we don't make it, Ansel?" asked the shorter of the pair. He cast repeated fearful glances to their rear, clearly far more nervous than his companion.

"How many times must I tell you, Merle?" responded the other. "We'll escape if we keep our wits about us. You must calm yourself. We've gone fifteen miles already and there's been no sign of them."

"Their patrols cover a thirty-mile radius," Merle noted apprehensively.

"Then only fifteen more miles and we're free men," Ansel stated. "Free for the first time in our lives."

"Freedom," Merle said softly, pronouncing the word

with exquisite delicacy, as if the very term was too fragile to withstand its utterance.

For two minutes they jogged onward, until ahead loomed a dark wall of foliage typical of the lush vegetation found in the former state of Iowa.

"Can we rest when we reach the trees?" Merle inquired hopefully.

"If you must."

"I'm sorry, Ansel. I know I'm slowing you down."

"Don't be ridiculous. I'm glad you came along. I don't know if I would have had the courage to try alone."

"You would. You're naturally brave. Even they knew that."

"How do you figure?"

"They picked you to be an overseer."

"They picked me because I followed their orders better than most. No other reason."

Merle scrutinized the forest and licked his thick lips. "I hope we haven't made a mistake we'll live to regret."

"Isn't freedom worth the price?"

"Yes, but what if we're wrong. What if there isn't any place better? What if the outside world is even worse? It's been one hundred and six years since World War Three. Who knows what we'll find?"

Ansel regarded his friend for a moment. "It's too late to turn back now. They've undoubtedly discovered we're missing and have sent trackers after us."

"Do you really think we have enough of a head start to outrun the dogs?"

"I hope so."

Merle ran a little faster.

Soon the fleeing pair reached the treeline. Scarcely slowing, they plunged into the forest, swatting at branches that lashed their bodies and plowing through undergrowth that tried to snare their legs. The heavens were harder to discern, but every now and then they spotted the North Star and knew they were still on course. Twenty strenuous minutes elapsed, and at last they emerged from the oppressive gloom to find a seemingly limitless expanse of open plain ahead.

"I could use a break," Merle commented, puffing from the exertion.

"I guess a rest can't hurt," Ansel said, and halted.

Expelling a breath in relief, Merle stopped and placed his hands on his knees. "I'm glad I didn't eat much supper."

Ansel glanced at his companion. "So am I."

"Do you still think it was wise not to bring a food pouch along?"

"Yes. The less we carry, the better we run. That's the reason I insisted on taking nothing except the clothes on our back." Ansel looked down at his sweaty, torn T-shirt and his tattered jeans. "If I was one of them, I'd strip off all my clothes and run naked just as they do during the contests and processions."

"If you were one of them, you wouldn't need to run at all," Merle said.

Ansel cocked his head, listening.

"Did you ever wish you were?" Merle inquired.

"Were what?" Ansel replied absently, still listening.

"One of them?"

The question distracted the taller man and he gazed at his companion. "Did you?"

"Every damn day. I'd love to have someone grow all my food for me. I'd love to be able to lord it over Helots and have them do all my bidding. Most of all, I'd love to wear one of those flowing red cloaks, bronze helmets, and short swords," Merle said dreamily. "I'd love to have it easy like they do."

"You really think they have it easy?"

"Sure. Don't you?"

"Not at all."

"I don't understand."

"Do you think it's easy for them to be taken from their

parents at the age of seven and forced to live in a barracks? Do you think it's easy for them to devote almost all of their time to perfecting the arts of war? Do you think not being permitted to marry or have children until the age of thirty is easy?'' Ansel asked. ''I don't. I don't envy them one bit.''

Merle uttered a light laugh. ''You almost sound as if you pity them.''

''In a way, I do.''

''Amazing.''

''Why?''

''Because if you don't hate them, if you sympathize with them, then why the hell are we out in the middle of nowhere running for our lives?''

Ansel cocked his head again. ''I might sympathize with them, but that doesn't mean I condone the status of the Helots. I'd rather be free. If I can't be, then I might as well be dead.''

Merle opened his mouth to speak.

''Hush!'' Ansel cautioned, motioning for silence with his right hand.

''What is it?'' Merle blurted anyway.

''Listen.''

Merle did, and for several seconds he heard nothing out of the ordinary. Then his ears registered the distant barking, and goose bumps broke out all over his skin. ''Oh, God!''

''The dogs,'' Ansel declared angrily.

''How far away?''

''I don't know. Maybe a mile. Maybe less.''

''What should we do?''

''Keep going,'' Ansel suggested, and suited action to words by racing to the northwest.

''Wait for me!'' Merle bleated, and hastened to catch up, his short legs pumping furiously.

''Our only hope is to find a stream or a river,'' Ansel said. ''They can't track our scent through water.''

"Are there any in this area?"

"Not according to the old-timer I talked to, the one who drew us the crude map."

"We're doomed!"

"Don't give up yet. Where there's hope, there's life."

Onward they sprinted, oblivious to everything except the barking of the canines to their rear. Both their forms became caked with sweat, their shirts drenched. The plain was unending.

"We're doomed," Merle repeated forlornly.

"Keep going."

"Maybe we should give ourselves up."

"Be serious."

"I am," Merle stated, breathing heavily. "If we stop now and let them capture us, they might decide to go easy on us."

"Don't be ridiculous. You know the law. The Lawgivers stipulated that any Helot who tries to flee should be put to death."

The reminder sparked Merle to increased effort. He looked over his shoulder every ten strides or so, dreading the moment when he would spot the lanterns. Three quarters of a mile later he finally did. "Look!"

Ansel glanced back and frowned. "Evidently I miscalculated."

"Miscalculated? Damn, man, we're about to die and you act like you made a mistake on a math problem."

"We're not dead yet."

"I'm open to any bright ideas."

"Let me think."

"We're doomed, doomed, doomed."

Five minutes went by. The lanterns drew ever nearer, the barking ever louder and louder.

Merle wheezed air out and gasped air in, his entire body strained to limits he never imagined he could withstand. But he refused to slack off. Surrendering *was* a stupid idea, a desperate step of last resort. He imagined how it would feel to have a pack of dogs tear into his flesh, and his terror of such a gruesome death eclipsed his fear of their pursuers.

"Trees!" Ansel suddenly stated.

Hope welling within him, Merle stared ahead and saw sprawling woodland. "If we can make it . . ." he began, and wasn't able to complete the sentence for want of breath.

"We'll make it."

Their feet pounding on the ground, their limbs constantly in motion, they covered the thousand yards to the forest, and paused before entering to ascertain the exact location of the patrol after them.

"Look!" Merle cried.

The lanterns were now less than five hundred yards away, and the dogs were yapping excitedly.

"Come on," Ansel urged, and dashed into the woods.

Panic-stricken, Merle followed, parting the brush with his forearms and ignoring the branches that tore at his skin. He focused on his friend's back and nothing else, because to dwell on anything else might inadvertently cause him to slow down and he couldn't afford to slacken the pace for an instant, not if he wanted to live, which he most definitely did. At that moment life was the sweetest, headiest nectar he'd ever known, a priceless treasure he would never relinquish. If he could help it.

How soon would the dogs be released?

Merle knew the routine. The patrol would close to within a hundred yards or so, then the officer in charge would give the command and the four dogs would leap clear of their leashes to chase down the targets with unerring, instinctual precision. He knew there were four dogs because there were always four dogs. Four big black dogs, any one of which could hold its own against a bear or a cougar or even a mutation.

The thought almost made Merle stumble.

Mutations!

What if they stumbled on a mutant in the darkness? They wouldn't stand a prayer without weapons. Mutations were not only extremely aggressive, they were hard to kill, as if the radiation or chemical warfare toxins responsible for the genetic deviates conferred a feral hatred of life and an astonishing capacity for brute endurance.

Please, God!

Don't let there be mutations abroad tonight!

More minutes went by. Not a creature stirred in the woods. Every living thing seemed to be aware of the tableau unfolding under the starry canopy and none made the slightest sound.

Merle glanced behind them and saw the flickering lanterns moving through the trees, the lights appearing to blink on and off as the men carrying them were briefly obscured by tree trunks or dense thickets.

The dogs were in a frenzy.

With his eyes rearward, Merle didn't realize his fellow Helot had halted until he accidently collided with Ansel, ramming the taller man in the back.

"Watch it!" Ansel snapped, almost falling.

"Sorry."

"Do you hear it too?"

"Hear what?"

"Listen, damn it."

Merle did, and almost shouted in delight when he heard the distinct gurgling of rushing water. "A stream?" he queried hopefully.

"Let's find out."

They moved forward, the sound increasing in volume, and covered only 15 yards before they came to the bank of a shallow creek. It was only three feet wide, the water five or six inches deep at most, and then only in the periodic pools.

Merle stood above one such pool and surveyed the flow in both directions. "Which way?"

"You go right. I'll go left."

"I don't want to split up," Merle said, horrified at the very notion.

"We have a better chance if we do."

"Please, Ansel. Don't make me do it."

The former overseer took but a second to decide. "All right. We'll go to the right. Stick close."

"You don't need to tell me twice," Merle stated, smiling, starting to turn. Out of the corner of his eye he detected movement, something coming from their rear, and his mind belatedly perceived the reason a second after the charging Doberman pinscher hurtled into Ansel and bowled him over.

A throaty snarl rent the night, becoming a sustained bestial snapping and growling as the canine sank its white teeth into its prey again and again and again.

Merle took a step toward his friend, his terror rendering his movements sluggish.

"Run!" Ansel yelled, fighting the Doberman, rolling and punching.

Unwilling to desert the man he considered his best friend, Merle took another stride, his eyes casting about for a potential weapon.

"Run, Merle!" Ansel shouted. "Please!"

Loud barking came from 20 yards away.

The other dogs! Merle realized, and suddenly there was no question of staying, of sacrificing himself needlessly. Ansel was as good as dead. Why should he die too? He pivoted and stepped into the creek, then ran to the right, splashing noisily. What if the dogs came after him? He had to pray they concentrated on Ansel and failed to pick up his scent in the water. The creek abruptly curved to the left. He stayed right in the middle, terror lending him speed, and ran, ran, ran.

CHAPTER ONE

The giant clasped the steering wheel loosely, his seven-foot tall frame relaxed as he skillfully threaded the huge van he was driving through a gauntlet of gaping potholes and wide cracks that marred the crumbling surface of the aged highway. A comma of dark hair hung above his penetrating gray eyes. His bulging muscles threatened to burst the seams of his black leather vest and his green fatigue pants. Combat boots covered his feet. Strapped around his lean waist were two big Bowie knives, a matched set, snug in sheaths on either hip.

"We should be there within a few hours," commented the small, wiry man in the front passenger seat. He was dressed all in black, his features revealing an Oriental heritage. He rested his right hand on the hilt of the sword propped between his legs and draped his left arm on the console between his seat and the giant's. His eyes and hair were both dark.

"At least we'll be in the general vicinity, Rikki," responded the driver.

"If the man spoke the truth."

"Why would he have lied?"

"Who knows, Blade?" answered the man in black.

"Maybe he concocted the whole story for the benefit of the Cavalry, to make them feel sorry for him so they'd permit him to stay in their territory."

Blade smiled and studied the small man's features. "Becoming cynical in your young age, huh?"

"Realistic. Honor and truth are dying ideals in the Outlands. Out here people live by their wits or their brawn. The survival of the fittest is the unwritten law of the land."

A chuckle came from behind them. "Don't let him fool you, Blade. He's a grump because Lexine got on his case about doing this."

The giant glanced over his right shoulder at the man occupying the seat running the width of the vehicle. Six feet in height, the speaker wore forest-green apparel. His hair and beard were both blond. The former was tied into a ponytail with a thin strip of leather. The latter had been neatly trimmed and jutted forward on his pointed chin. His green eyes perpetually danced with an inner mirth, an unrestrained zest for life. Propped on the seat to his right was a Ben Pearson compound bow. Lying next to his left leg was a quiver filled with arrows. "How do you know, Teucer?" Blade inquired.

"I overheard part of their conversation when I was waiting at the SEAL for you to arrive," the bowman said. "Lexine told him he's going on a wild-goose chase."

"Your ears are quite keen," Rikki remarked. "It would be a pity if you were to lose them."

Teucer laughed. "You've been hanging around Hickok too much. Now you're beginning to sound like him."

The small man looked at Blade. "I trust you had a good reason for bringing him along?" he asked dryly.

"Teucer is one of the few Warriors who hasn't been on a regular run yet. This trip will be an invaluable training experience, a chance to hone his skills."

"Just so he hones his tact."

Blade stared at the diminutive martial artist for a

moment, then concentrated on his driving. He'd never seen Rikki-Tikki-Tavi so tense before, and he realized how much the trip must mean to the Family's perfected swordmaster. He thought of the 30-acre compound located in the extreme northwest corner of the state once known as Minnesota, the walled retreat constructed by the wealthy survivalist just prior to the nuclear holocaust and dubbed the Home. He also thought about the descendant of the Founder and his companions, the friends and loved ones Blade knew as the Family, and in particular he dwelled on his wife and young son, Jenny and Gabe. A twinge of guilt gnawed at his conscience for leaving them yet again to venture into the hostile Outlands, the vast regions not under the jurisdiction of any organized faction.

But how could he have turned Rikki down?

As one of the martial artist's best friends, and as the one Warrior who had gone into the Outlands time and time again and knew the savage domains better than anyone, he could hardly refuse to help.

And there was another reason. Out of the 18 Family members selected to be Warriors, to defend the Home and protect the Family, Blade was the leader. He had a responsibility to those under him. Plus there was the fact Rikki would have gone by himself if no one else went along, and even the highly seasoned Warriors found surviving in the Outlands a strenuous task. What with scavengers, the crazies, mutations, and assorted cutthroats roaming all over the countryside, a sole Warrior could easily be slain.

Blade didn't want to lose Rikki.

He recalled the recent death of another Warrior, a novice named Marcus, who had perished in the Outlands while on a rescue mission, and he inwardly vowed that none of them would die on this run.

"Where exactly are we?" Teucer inquired.

"Rikki has the map," Blade noted, skirting yet another yawning pit in the center of the road. Although the highways were in deplorable condition, having suffered over a century of neglect and abuse by the elements, they were easier than going overland, even for the SEAL.

The Solar-Energized Amphibious or Land Recreational Vehicle had been the brainchild of the Family's Founder, Kurt Carpenter. He'd wisely foreseen that conventional cars and trucks would become largely obsolete after World War Three; fuel would be scarce and spare parts virtually impossible to obtain. So he'd spent millions to have the SEAL developed by automotive experts who believed they were creating the "recreational vehicle of the future." Carpenter had never revealed his ulterior motive.

Eventually the experts had produced a remarkable prototype. Green in hue and van-like in configuration, the SEAL incorporated a number of unique features. The body was composed of a special heat-resistant, shatterproof plastic that had been tinted so no one could see inside. The floor was an impervious metal alloy. A powerful air-cooled, self-lubricating engine enabled the transport to attain speeds in excess of one hundred miles per hour. The tires were immense.

Especially unique was the power source: the sun. A pair of solar panels attached to the roof of the SEAL collected the sunlight, and the energy was then converted and stored in a bank of six revolutionary batteries housed in a lead-lined case under the vehicle. So long as the solar panels weren't damaged or the battery casings weren't cracked, the SEAL would have a constant source of energy.

Kurt Carpenter had taken the innovations a step further. After the prototype was completed, he'd brought the SEAL to other specialists, to mercenaries versed in the art of war, and instructed them to transform the vehicle into an armed dreadnought. This they'd readily done.

Four toggle switches on the dashboard activated the armaments. There were two 50-caliber machine guns hidden in recessed compartments mounted on the roof above the driver's seat with others in reserve. Called

Stingers, the missiles were heat-seeking and had a range of ten miles. The mercenaries had also outfitted the SEAL with a flamethrower positioned at the front, behind the fender. When the proper toggle was thrown, a portion of the fender lowered and the flamethrower's nozzle extended six inches and engaged. Finally, secreted in the center of the front grill was a rocket launcher.

Without the SEAL, Blade reflected, the Family would never have been able to send the Warriors out from time to time to make contact with other outposts of civilization.

Like they were doing now.

"We're in northeastern Iowa," Rikki stated, the map spread open on his lap. "The road we're on is State Highway 76." He gazed out his open window at the rugged terrain. "This region was the least inhabited part of the state. They called it the Switzerland of America because of all the hills and cliffs. East of us is the Mississippi River, twenty or thirty miles away at the most. West of this region is prime farming land. Three glaciers leveled that area ages ago and left fertile topsoil in their wake."

"Been doing some studying, I take it?" Teucer remarked.

Rikki nodded. "Once the Cavalry told us about the man they found and relayed his tale, I decided to do some research."

Blade listened attentively. He'd also conducted background research after being contacted by the leader of the Cavalry, Kilrane. Occupying the Dakota Territory, which embraced the former states of North and South Dakota, the Cavalry was one of six factions allied with the Family in the Freedom Federation. They lived much as did their frontier ancestors, and they were renowned for their superlative horsemanship.

"Are there any towns nearby?" Teucer asked.

"A few. Not far ahead we should find a secondary road that leads to the small town of Dorchester. If we go straight, in six or seven miles we should come to the Upper Iowa River."

"But there's no mention on the map of a town named Sparta?" Teucer asked.

"No," Rikki answered, and sighed.

"Maybe your wife is right," Teucer said. "This *is* a wild-goose chase."

"Perhaps."

"Do you mind if I ask you a question?"

Rikki twisted in his seat to stare at the bowman. "Be my guest."

"Why is this so important to you? What does it matter to you if a new Sparta has arisen?"

Blade waited expectantly for the martial artist's answer. When the message from Kilrane had arrived at the Home, he'd been surprised at Rikki's reaction. The normally cool-headed Warrior had been all set to take off immediately to ascertain the truth. Blade suspected Rikki's enthusiasm had something to do with the time they'd been in Memphis. Rikki had mentioned meeting a man who claimed to be from Sparta, a new city-state that had arisen since the war, but he'd never disclosed the details of that meeting.

"I made a promise to a dying man once," Rikki said. "And I intend to keep that promise."

"Mind if I ask who?"

"A man who went by the name of Thayer, a former Spartan who was exiled for abandoning his post."

"Where'd you meet this guy?"

"In Memphis."

"How'd he die?"

"I killed him."

"Oh."

Blade looked at Rikki's inscrutable face, then at the highway. This was news to him. He resolved to get to the truth of the matter at the earliest opportunity. "I hope we do find these Spartans," Blade mentioned. "We could always use another ally in the Federation."

"If they'll join," Teucer said.

"I don't see why they wouldn't. It would be in their best interest to sign the mutual defense pact. They'd be able to trade with the Civilized Zone and the Free State of California for goods impossible to find in the Outlands. And they'd have friends they could rely on should they be attacked," Blade stated.

"Everyone should have friends," Teucer observed philosophically, and as was his habit, launched into a poem. "He who gets and never gives will lose the truest friend that lives; he who gives and never gets will sour his friendships with regrets; giving and getting, thus alone, a friendship lives—or dies a-moan."

"Who wrote that?" Blade queried.

"A poet named Alexander MacLean."

"Cute," Blade said.

Teucer sat up. "Cute? Poetry is more than merely cute. Poetry is an expression of the soul, an attempt to reach out for spiritual values. Poetry is language at its most beautiful." He paused. "Poetry is artistic expression."

"Excuse me for living," Blade muttered.

"Why do you like poetry so much?" Rikki asked the bowman.

"I've been hooked on it since I was a kid. My mom read me a poem every night when she tucked me into bed. I guess I learned to appreciate it fully," Teucer responded, and glanced at the giant. "Unlike some people I can think of."

Blade knew the remark was directed at him and grinned, then turned serious. "Rikki, what do you know about these Spartans?"

"Not a great deal. Apparently their society is patterned after ancient Sparta. Like their namesakes, they're a war-oriented culture."

"This Spartan you knew. What was he like?"

"One of the best fighters I've ever encountered. He was

my equal at hand-to-hand."

"Really?" Teucer interjected. "You're the best martial artist in the Family."

"I wouldn't say that," Rikki replied. "Blade and Yama are as talented as I am."

"Blade maybe," Teucer agreed. "But as good as Yama is, he's not quite in your class."

Rikki smiled for the first time in hours. "Tell that to Yama."

"No way. I'm not about to commit suicide."

For a minute they rode in silence. The condition of the highway improved marginally.

Blade idly surveyed the trees lining both sides of the road, his left elbow resting on the window, the air stirring his hair. He estimated the temperature to be in the seventies. Not bad for the first week in November. The weather had been exceptionally mild for weeks, and all of the trees still bore their leaves.

A slight curve appeared ahead.

Slowing marginally, Blade negotiated the curve with ease, alert for the cutoff to Dorchester and debating whether they should check out the town. A flutter of wings to his left drew his attention to five crows flapping into the air, and when he faced front again his eyes widened in alarm and he went rigid.

Not 30 feet distant, racing directly toward the SEAL, terror showing on her face, was a young woman.

CHAPTER TWO

Blade frantically spun the steering wheel to the left and tramped on the brake pedal. The SEAL slewed violently, straight at the woman, who had halted in her tracks and was gaping at the vehicle in stark astonishment, and for a moment he thought the transport would plow right over her. Then the rear end swung back again, and the SEAL shot past her, missing her body by inches. The huge tires squealed in protest as the green van lurched to a stop.

All three Warriors were whipped forward; all reacted instantly. Blade merely gripped the steering wheel harder. Rikki pressed his hands to the dash. And Teucer caught himself by bracing his arms against the front seats.

"Warn a guy, why don't you?" the bowman quipped.

Blade threw the gearshift into Park, shoved the door wide, and leaped out. He ran around the rear of the transport and found the woman still rooted in place, gawking. Her luxuriant shoulder-length hair was black, her eyes brown. A blue shirt and brown pants, both of which were faded and worn, clung to her shapely body. "Hello," he said, and held his hands out to indicate his peaceful intentions. "Are you okay?"

"Yes," she said softly.

Rikki and Teucer joined the giant.

"Why were you running?" Blade asked. "Are you in danger?"

The question snapped the woman out of her daze. She looked past them, back the way she had come from, and the terrified aspect returned. "Yes," she stated.

"From what?"

"From that!" she cried, and pointed.

Blade spun, his hands dropping to his Bowies, not knowing what to expect, but certainly not expecting the monstrosity that was charging toward them, a monstrosity that vented a tremendous roar.

"Dear Spirit!" Teucer breathed.

The creature was a mutation. Six and a half feet in height, with a thick body and stout limbs, the thing vaguely resembled a bear in its general shape, but there the comparison ended. Where bears spent most of their time on all fours and only rose on their hind legs for brief intervals, the onrushing beast ran on two legs just like a human, although with a shuffling, awkward gait. Instead of hair it had reddish, lumpy skin. Its elongated mouth contained wicked, tapered teeth. A pair of triangular ears crowned a rounded head. Most horrible of all were the eyes. They were oversized, as big as apples, and had tiny red pupils.

"Run!" the woman screamed.

The Warriors had no intention of doing so.

Rikki-Tikki-Tavi moved to meet the deviate, gliding gracefully, his long black scabbard wedged under his belt and slanted across his left hip. He assumed a back stance, both hands on the hilt of the sword he could wield with unparalleled precision, and waited for the creature to reach him.

Blade drew his Bowies and went to aid his friend, wishing he had taken the time to retrieve his Commando submachine gun from the rear storage section of the SEAL. The creature sported five-inch claws on each front paw, which combined with its size and ferocity made it a formidable adversary. The Commando could slay the genetic deviate in seconds, whereas with the Bowies the task would be much more difficult. He saw Rikki's arm move, saw the martial artist's gleaming katana streak from the scabbard, and with the mutation only 20 feet away he braced for the onslaught.

Only the monstrosity never reached them.

A swishing sound arose behind them, and a long green shaft sped into the creature's chest with a pronounced thud. The thing roared again and paused to swipe at the object protruding from its flesh. Another swish sounded, and yet another, the second an instant after the first, and two arrows lanced into the mutation's eyes, one in each red pupil. For a moment the creature went rigid, snarling hideously, and then it toppled onto its left side, convulsed for a bit, and expired.

Blade and Rikki exchanged glances.

"Apparently we weren't needed," said the man in black.

"Don't you just hate show-offs?" Blade asked.

Teucer walked past them, another arrow already notched, and warily approached the beast. He nudged its head several times, and satisfied the thing was dead, he lowered his bow.

The woman ran over to them, staring at the mutation in disbelief. "You saved my life! That thing had chased me for half a mile!"

"Glad we could assist you," Blade mentioned, sliding the Bowies into their sheaths.

"I meant *him*," the woman stated, indicating the bowman. She stared at him with frank, adoring eyes.

"It was nothing," Teucer said, walking up to her.

"Are you kidding?" she replied. "You were magnificent."

The bowman grinned and slid the arrow into the quiver he had slung over his back while exiting the transport.

"I guess I was, wasn't I?"

"Oh, brother," Rikki mumbled, replacing the katana in a smooth, practiced motion.

"Who are you men?" the woman inquired, and looked at the SEAL. "And what is that vehicle of yours? I've never seen one like it."

"Our transport is unique," Blade disclosed. "As for our names, I'm Blade. This is Rikki," he said, and nodded at the man in black. "And the man who lucked out and hit the mutation named himself Teucer."

She stared at the bowman. "You named yourself?"

"Sure did, my dear. After a bowman in *The Illiad*. It's common practice at the place we're from to have a special Naming Ceremony on our sixteenth birthday. We're encouraged to select any name we want, from any source, as our very own."

"I never heard of such a thing."

"What's your name?" Blade questioned.

"Erica. Erica Johnson."

"Do you live around here?"

"Less than a mile away, on the outskirts of Dorchester. My dad has a farm." She paused. "I was out for a walk."

"Would you take us there?" Blade queried.

"No," Erica said, shaking her head.

"We'll give you a lift," Blade offered. "I promise no harm will come to you."

"It's not that. You're strangers. You must leave, and leave quickly."

"Why?"

"Just go, please," Erica advised, and began to head to the south.

"Wait," Blade said. "Explain the reason we should leave."

"I told you. You're strangers."

"So?"

The woman was almost abreast of the dead deviate. She looked back. "Please go. I feel I owe you for saving me,

SPARTAN RUN   25

and I'm trying to return the favor."

"Hold on, fair maiden," Teucer stated, and beckoned for her to return. "We need information and you're the only one who can provide it."

Erica stopped. "All right. But be quick about this. If they find you, you'll be taken into custody."

"If who finds us?" Teucer asked.

"The Spartans, of course."

Rikki-Tikki-Tavi took a step toward her. "Then we're near Sparta?"

"You're close. You have to go another ten miles on this highway, then take a gravel road to the east about four miles. But you don't want to go there."

"Yes, we do," Rikki informed her. "We've traveled a long distance to find the Spartans."

"Then you're crazy. They aren't very fond of strangers. If you're lucky, they'll escort you far, far away and tell you to never come back. If not, you could wind up in chains," Erica warned. "Please leave. Now."

"Are you a Spartan?" Blade inquired.

"I wish. No, I'm a Helot."

"What's a Helot?" asked Teucer.

"One of the farming class that raises all the food for Sparta. Each Helot is allotted fifty acres on which to grow the required quota. Any extra the Helot gets to keep."

"How many Helots are there?" Blade wanted to know.

"I'm not sure. Over two thousand, I think. Maybe three thousand."

"And how many Spartans?"

"There you've got me. Last I heard, about nine hundred. Probably more by now."

"Only nine hundred?" Rikki said.

"What did you expect?" Erica answered, and gestured at the van. "Please, for the last time, get out of here. A patrol could show up at any minute."

"We can't leave," Blade declared. "We're emissaries from the Freedom Federation, and we came to extend an invitation to the Spartan people and their leader."

"Leaders, you mean. The Spartans are ruled by two kings."

"Then we must present our message to them."

The woman shook her head. "You're just asking for trouble."

"It won't be the first time," Blade stated. "And since we're going no matter what, and we're heading the same direction you are, why not ride with us? You'll get home that much faster." He pointed at the mutation. "What if that thing has a mate? You wouldn't be safe by yourself."

Her brow furrowed in contemplation, Erica gazed at the carcass, then nodded. "All right. I'll let you take me to the farm. I can take the time to talk you out of visiting Sparta."

Teucer promptly stepped to the SEAL and held the door open. "After you, lovely one." He gave a little bow. "Your chariot awaits."

The Helot climbed inside, bestowing an affectionate smile on the bowman.

"Here we go again," Rikki said as he walked on Blade's heels toward the van.

"What do you mean?" the head Warrior responded.

"Do you realize how many of us have married women from outside the Home? Hickok married Sherry, and she's from Canada. Geronimo wed Cynthia, who hails from the Cavalry. Sundance popped the question to Bertha, who hails from the Twin Cities. And I took Lexine in eternal union. She's from St. Louis."

"Are you saying what I think you're saying?"

"Teucer could be next, which would be highly appropriate."

"How so?"

"Doesn't Cupid use a bow?"

Blade laughed all the way around the front of the transport. He clambered into the driver's seat, listening to the muted whine of the engine, and waited for Rikki to get in before resuming their interrupted journey, carefully bypassing the dead deviate.

"Wow!" Erica said excitedly. "I've never ridden in anything like this!"

"Does your family own a vehicle?" Blade probed.

"Heavens, no. None of the Helots do. Many years ago the Spartans allowed our ancestors to use tractors, but eventually the tractors wore out. So now we just use horses and oxen."

"Do the Spartans possess vehicles?"

"A few. They have a few jeeps that they only use on special occasions. I was told it's hard for them to obtain fuel. They receive a little now and then in trade with the Scarlet Clique."

Blade had heard of the Clique, a sophisticated network of smugglers and thieves who supplied anything a client wanted provided the price was met. He'd tried to learn more about them, where their headquarters were located and the identity of the party or parties running the operation, but so far he'd not uncovered the information. All he'd managed to discover was the fact that the Scarlet Cliques stole a substantial quantity of merchandise and military items from the Free State of California and the Civilized Zone, both allies of the Family. "What can you tell me about the history of Sparta?" he asked.

"Not a great deal. My grandfather claimed Sparta was formed about the time of the war. A bunch of college professors from back East came to this area to hide, to get away from the mobs and the looters. They were the ones who wrote the Spartan constitution and set up the system of government. They also forced some people to become Helots," Erica said, stressing the last word bitterly.

"I take it you don't like being a Helot?"

"What was your first clue?"

"Why not?"

"Would you like to be a second-rate citizen? Helots are good enough to grow food to feed the Spartans, but they're not considered good enough to have the right to vote or take control of their own lives. The Spartans are the lords and masters, and any Helot who doesn't toe the line winds up sentenced to work in the quarry for life."

"What quarry?"

"Where the Spartans mine the granite and marble for their buildings. No one sent there ever comes out alive."

Blade regarded her reflection in the rearview mirror. "Do all of the Helots feel the same way you do about the Spartans?"

"Some do. Some don't."

"Why do the Helots tolerate being inferior citizens? There are close to three thousand of them, you said, and only nine hundred Spartans. Why don't the Helots demand better treatment or rise in revolt?"

Erica snickered. "You don't know the Spartans very well, do you?"

"I've never met them," Blade confessed.

"Well, once you do you'll understand. The Spartans live for war. They're the best fighters on the planet. If the Helots ever rise in revolt, the Spartans will crush them just like they crush their enemies, like they crushed the early insurrections."

"There have been rebellions?" Blade inquired in surprise, his gaze on the mirror again, neglecting to watch the highway.

At that moment Teucer pointed at something up ahead and yelled, "Look out!"

CHAPTER THREE

Blade faced front, expecting to see another genetic deviate. Instead, stepping onto the highway from the forest to the west was a thin man wearing scruffy clothing, a lever-action rifle pressed to his right shoulder. Approximately 40 yards separated the SEAL from the rifleman.

"Oh, no!" Erica Johnson cried.

The thin man aimed at the van's windshield and fired.

Despite knowing the transport was bulletproof, Blade flinched when the round struck, the resounding smack and the shrill whine of the ricochet startlingly loud. He tramped on the gas and slanted toward the rifleman. "Let's teach this guy some manners," he commented.

The man had levered another bullet into the chamber and was taking aim again.

"Don't hurt him!" Erica declared. "Please!"

"Why not?" Blade demanded, and saw the man shoot. He heard a piercing screech as the slug was deflected and kept his foot down.

"I know him."

"Is he always this friendly to strangers?" Blade asked.

"Please! Slow down!"

The giant ignored her. He glanced at Rikki and said,

"Get ready," then closed on the rifleman.

"Please!" Erica pleaded.

Exercising commendable self-control, the thin man managed to get off one more shot. He stood in the highway until almost the last instant, working the lever, then leaped to the side.

Which served as Blade's cue. He applied his right foot to the brake and held onto the wheel with all of his strength to prevent the SEAL from swerving. Out of the corner of his eye he glimpsed Rikki opening the passenger door, a small silver object in the martial artist's hand. A moment later the man in black vaulted from the vehicle.

Blade glanced in the mirror and witnessed the brief confrontation. The rifleman never stood a chance.

In a fluid, acrobatic movement Rikki landed and rolled, sweeping erect as the thin man tried to get a bead on him. His right arm flashed downward and the glittering metal object, a seven-pointed shuriken, whizzed through the air and ripped into the rifleman's left forearm. The man uttered an agonized expletive, dropped the rifle, and held his wounded arm next to his chest, gaping at the imbedded throwing star and blood seeping from the laceration.

The SEAL came to a halt. Blade shifted and killed the engine, then turned. "Teucer, give me the Commando."

About to leap out, the bowman nodded and shifted so he could reach back to the rear storage, where their provisions were piled, and grab the Commando Arms Carbine. "Here," he said, and gave the weapon to the giant.

Blade slid out, working the cocking handle and verifying the 90-shot magazine was securely in place. Somewhat resembling the ancient Thompsons, the Commando had been modified by the Family Gunsmiths to function on full automatic. Although rather heavy as submachine guns went, in his massive arms the Commando was as light as the proverbial feather. He strolled around the SEAL.

Rikki-Tikki-Tavi was standing close to the rifleman, the katana out and pointed at the man's chest.

The thin man was doing a marvelous imitation of a tree.

"Who are you?" Blade demanded, cradling the Commando in his right arm.

"I can answer that," volunteered Erica to his rear. "his name is Rick Grennell. He's a neighbor of ours."

"A real friendly sort, I take it?"

Johnson didn't respond.

The giant walked to within a yard of the man. He noticed blatant fear in Grennell's eyes and his estimation of the rifleman lowered.

Teucer and the woman joined them.

"Erica!' Grennell exclaimed. "How did these bastards capture you?"

"I'm not their prisoner, Rick."

"You're not?"

"No. These men saved me from a mutation. They were giving me a ride to the farm."

Grennell looked at each of the Warriors in evident perplexity. "They were?"

"Why did you shoot at us?" Blade inquired.

"I heard Erica scream and was coming after her. When your vehicle came into view, I naturally assumed you must be responsible. I figured you had harmed her."

"What were you doing in this area?" Blade asked.

"Hunting."

"Did you know Erica was nearby?"

"I didn't."

"Then how did you know she was the one who screamed?"

Gennell blinked a few times. "I, uh, I've known her since we were kids. I'd know her voice anywhere."

"Do tell," Blade said, and nodded at the man's arm. "We'll bandage that for you."

"No. It's not necessary," Grennell responded. "I'll walk home and let my sister take care of it."

"We insist," Blade stated, and turned to Rikki. "Would you get the medicine bag from the SEAL?"

"Certainly." The martial artist returned the katana to its scabbard and ran off.

Grennell winced and stared at his arm. "What is this thing?"

"A shuriken," Blade said.

"Never heard of it. The damn thing flew too fast to follow. Where did the runt learn to throw like that?"

"He's practiced for years," Blade revealed. "And I wouldn't call him a runt to his face if I were you."

"Why not? Will he kick my ass?" Grennell replied caustically.

"No," Blade said softly. "I will."

Teucer picked up the rifle. "This is a Marlin 30-30," he commented.

"Where did you find the gun, Rick?" Erica asked. "You know as well as I do that owning a firearm is an offense punishable by death. Our Spartan masters don't permit Helots to own guns."

"It's been in my family for generations. Usually we keep it hidden in the root cellar and only take it out on very special occasions."

"And you were hunting with it?" Erica asked, her tone conveying marked doubt.

"We wanted some venison," Grennell said.

Blade regarded the man coldly. Although he lacked proof, he suspected Grennell was completely untrustworthy. An indefinable aura of deception and menace lurked just below the man's superficial exterior. He noticed the way Grennell's shifty dark eyes lingered on Erica's form, and he deduced a possible motive for the man's behavior and presence. The thought angered him. "You say this guy is a neighbor of yours?" he asked the woman.

"Yeah. His family lives four miles southwest of us."

"How trustworthy is he?"

"In what respect?"

"If we were to let him go, would he run to the Spartans and inform them about us?"

Erica glanced at the thin man, her brow knit. "I don't think so."

"You know I wouldn't," Grennell asserted.

"But there is a reward for any information about strangers," Erica divulged. "Any Helot who tells the Spartans will receive an extra food ration for a year."

"Now there's incentive if ever I heard it," Teucer joked.

"It is," Erica stated. "Most Helots have a hard time meeting their alloted quota, so there's very little grain, vegetables, and fruit left over for their own consumption. An extra food ration can mean the difference between going hungry and a full stomach."

Blade watched Grennell surreptitiously stare at the woman's prominent breasts, and experienced a keen loathing for the man. He was tempted to slug Grennell in the mouth on general principles, but footsteps signaled the timely arrival of the Family's preeminent practitioner of the martial way of life.

"Here's the medicine bag," Rikki announced, and stepped in front of the thin man. Slung over his left shoulder was a brown leather pouch. He gingerly inspected the wound. "The blood flow is already diminishing, which is a good sign. It means the shuriken didn't slice a major artery or vein."

"Are you a doctor?"

"I'm a Warrior, not a Healer. But I have considerable experience in administering herbal remedies and treating the types of injuries sustained in battle. On many an occasion I've assisted the Healers so I could hone my medical skills."

"But you're not a doctor?"

"No."

"Are these Healers doctors?"

"Not in the sense you intend. Our Healers don't rely on artificial substances."

Grennell glanced at the giant. "I'd really prefer to have my sister take care of my arm. She's a whiz with peroxide and a bandage."

"We'll bandage you," Blade insisted. "Go ahead, Rikki."

The man in black lightly touched his fingertips to the exposed part of the shuriken. Three of the silver points stuck out an inch above the skin. "This will sting for a bit," he cautioned.

"What will?"

Rikki suddenly gave a sharp wrench, pulling the shuriken loose. Blood dripped from the throwing star.

Gernnell stiffened and gasped, his mouth opening to screech, but he caught himself and scowled. "Damn! Sting, my ass! That hurt like hell."

"You must learn to control discomfort. Use your pain to mold your character."

"What the hell are you talking about?"

The small man knelt and deposited the medicine bag in front of him. He lifted the flap and rooted inside. "I'm talking about self-control, the acme of human virtues. For a person who has perfected self-control, all things are possible. For a person lacking self-control, all pursuits of spiritual consequence are impossible. When persons have self-control, they are the masters of their destiny." He paused to remove a handful of large leaves. "Pain, for instance, can be dominated and channeled. Instead of resisting it, you can use self-control to embrace the discomfort and subdue it."

"I don't have the slightest idea what you mean," Grennell said.

"Cultivate genuine faith and give yourself a few hundred years. The answer will come to you."

"You're downright weird."

Blade chuckled and rotated to scan the woods lining the

highway. "Hurry up, Rikki," he directed. "I want to get moving."

"As you wish."

Teucer surveyed the forest. "What's the rush?"

"I don't like standing out in the open like this," Blade responded. He didn't bother to add that deep down he felt uneasy, felt as if unseen eyes were gazing upon them. After so many years of living on the edge, of constantly confronting the enemies of the Family and the Federation, he had learned to rely on his instincts, and his instincts now told him that something was amiss.

"Is anything wrong?" Erica asked.

"No," Blade said.

Rikki-Tikki-Tavi was busy grinding the leaves into powder using a small bowl and pumice stone he'd removed from the pouch.

"Were you alone?" Blade queried, his flinty eyes on Grennell.

The thin man hesitated, then nodded vigorously. "Yep. Sure was."

Blade took hold of the woman's elbow. "Come with me."

"Where are we going?" Erica inquired as the giant pulled her away from the others.

"It's best if your neighbor doesn't hear us," Blade said, and led her a distance of 12 feet. He looked at Grennell, who stared suspiciously at them, and spoke in a hushed tone. "Tell me the truth. Is he a close friend of yours?"

"I wouldn't say that."

"Do you even like him?"

"I wouldn't say that either."

"Then why did you stop me from running him down?"

"He's a neighbor. My parents and his parents are best friends. I never liked him much because he's always been more interested in my body instead of me. Once, about seven years ago, I went to a barn dance with him to please my folks. He spent the whole night trying to slip his fingers under my dress. The man is a crud," Erica stated with obvious sincerity.

"Does he have any brothers or sisters?"

"Yep. Two brothers. Both younger than him."

Blade observed Rikki adding water from a canteen to the crushed leaves. "Do you buy his story about being out here hunting?"

"It's possible."

"It's also possible he saw you leave your farm."

"What are you implying?"

"You're no dummy. You figure it out," Blade commented.

The woman gazed thoughtfully at her neighbor.

"One more thing," Blade said. "Why would you go for a walk without a weapon? Isn't that a bit risky with mutations roaming about?"

"The only weapons Helots are allowed to use are knives, and I just forgot mine. Besides, I wasn't planning on going more than a mile or two. And the Spartans have done a fine job of killing off most of the monsters in this region. They slay every mutant they come across."

"I see," Blade responded. Now he knew they were both lying. He had to decide whether to turn around and leave before the trouble began or to carry the mission through to the end. As the head Warrior and an official representative of the Federation he had no choice. He must contact the Spartans.

Damn.

Just *once* he'd like to be sent on an easy run!

CHAPTER FOUR

The two-story farmhouse and the barn were in need of a fresh coat of paint. A narrow dirty driveway led from a pitted, cracked secondary road up to the front lawn, which was bordered by a small picket fence, and a narrow cement walk ran from the drive to the front porch. Meticulously tended flowers bordered the base of the fence.

The wide door to the barn stood open. A black horse was visible in an inner stall, and a dozen chickens were walking about near the entrance and pecking at the ground.

Blade climbed from the transport, the Commando held at the ready, and stepped to the picket fence. "Where is everyone?" he inquired when the others emerged.

"My dad is probably out in the fields," Erica said. "My mom might be in the kitchen."

"Can I go home now?" Grennell asked, holding his bandaged left arm against his side.

"No," Blade responded.

"When, then?"

"When I say you can."

Rikki-Tikki-Tavi took hold of the waist-high gate. "Do you want me to check the house?"

"Go," Blade directed. "Teucer, you take the barn."

"On my way," the bowman said, and jogged toward the structure.

"You guys certainly are professionals," Erica commented.

Blade looked at her. "Know a lot of professionals, do you?"

A crimson tinge spread across the woman's cheeks and she answered in a flustered manner. "Well, no, certainly not. But I know true professionals when I see them. I mean, I've seen the Spartans on parade and the like. In a way you guys remind me of them. You know. The Spartans and you are both military-like."

"Are we?" Blade said with an air of casual innocence.

"Most definitely."

Suppressing a grin, Blade watched Rikki enter the house. Moments later Teucer went into the barn.

"I don't see why you can't let me go home," Grennell groused.

"I can bind and gag you if you don't keep quiet," Blade stated.

The thin man shut up.

The Warrior kept an alert eye on the windows of the farmhouse, particularly the second floor. Nothing stirred, though, and within a minute Rikki escorted an elderly woman out the screen door.

"Mom!" Erica declared anxiously.

"Let's go," Blade commanded, and motioned for the Helots to precede him along the walk. He gazed at the fields to the south and spied a lone figure far off. The father, perhaps?

"I demand to know what's going on?" the mother said angrily, glaring at the giant. "This little man waltzed into my kitchen and told me to come outside. Ordered me out of my own house! You're not Spartans. What gives you the right to boss us around?"

Blade hefted the Commando. "This does."

"Well, I never!"

Erica hastened to her mom's side. "Don't be too hard on them. They saved me from a mutant."

"Why did they save you?" Mrs. Johnson responded suspiciously.

"What?"

"Perhaps they have an ulterior motive."

"We have no intention of harming any of you," Blade assured her while staring at the barn.

Mrs. Johnson nodded at Grennell. "And what happened to Ricky? I suppose he did that to himself?"

"He tried to shoot one of us," Blade explained.

"I can't say as I blame him," the mother said arrogantly.

A moment later Teucer walked from the barn and gave the hand signal for "all clear."

Blade stepped onto the porch and indicated three chairs arranged next to the wall, to the left of the door. "Why don't all of you take a seat?"

"And if we'd rather stand?" Mrs. Johnson rejoined.

"Sit anyway."

"Such rudeness. I hope the Spartans skin you alive."

"We don't want to be impolite, but we must take certain precautions," Blade explained. "We don't know if we can trust you yet."

"Trust us?" Mrs. Johnson said tartly. "Haven't you got the shoe on the wrong foot?"

"Please take a chair."

"You must be a barbarian," the mother stated. She moved to the nearest chair and sat down in a huff.

Erica and Grennell followed suit.

"I have a family of my own," Blade said in an attempt to pacify the older woman. "A wife and a son, both of whom I love with all my heart. Rikki, here, is also married," he said, and indicated the martial artist. "None of us are barbaric. We were all reared at a place called the Home, where we were taught to revere the Spirit and respect others. We're not any threat to you whatsoever. Believe me."

"I'll believe anything you tell me," Mrs. Johnson replied. "I make it a point never to argue with a giant holding a submachine gun."

Grinning, Blade shook his head and turned as Teucer hurried up the walk. "What did you see?"

"Animals. A horse. Two cows in stalls at the rear of the barn. All those chickens outside. And in a small pen attached to the side of the barn on the west are seven pigs," the bowman detailed.

Blade glanced at the mother. "Was that your husband I saw out in the fields?"

"Maybe it was, maybe it wasn't."

"Please, Mom," Erica interjected. "Can't you be nice to them?"

"I can, but I won't," Mrs. Johnson snapped. "For all we know these men are scavengers or worse. The Spartans have told us about the conditions outside our territory. Every stranger is to be considered an enemy until our masters decide otherwise."

Rikki-Tikki-Tavi cleared his throat. "Is any person truly master of another? Aren't we all equal in the eyes of the Eternal Source?"

Mrs. Johnson peered at the man in black as if studying a peculiar insect she had never seen before. "Are you religious?"

"All of us are," Rikki answered politely. "Everyone at the Home is encouraged to develop a spiritual consciousness, to seek spiritual answers to the fundamental questions all of us eventually ask. Who are we? What are we doing here? What is our destiny? These are questions every thinking person views as supremely important."

"What religion are you?"

"Myself, I practice Zen. But there are many Christians at the Home, as well as Moslems and those of other faiths.

The religious books in our library are among those most frequently checked out."

"There might be hope for you after all," Mrs. Johnson said. "I'm a firm believer in the Holy Bible."

"And where in the Bible does it say that you should call other men your masters?"

"Render unto Caesar the things that are Caesar's and to God the things that are God's."

Blade stepped to the west end of the porch and peeked around the corner. The figure he'd spotted earlier was approaching slowly, evidently unaware of the situation at the house. Blade leaned against the wall and waited, idly listening to Rikki and Mrs. Johnson discussing the importance of religion. He admired the way in which the martial artist had verbally disarmed the woman and gotten her to open up. Engrossed in their conversation, he didn't realize several minutes had elapsed until he heard the steady tread of someone who was almost to the front of the house, and he quickly swung out, the Commando leveled.

Not eight feet off a tall man abruptly froze. He wore jeans and a patched flannel shirt. His face was rugged, distinguished by a square jaw. Blue eyes stared fearlessly at the giant. "Who are you? What do you want?"

"Mr. Johnson?"

"That's right."

"My name is Blade. Kindly step onto the porch. Your wife and daughter are both here."

"Martha and Erica?" Johnson stated, and hurried forward. He took one look, relief washing over his countenance.

"Harry!" Mrs. Johnson declared.

"Are you all right?" her husband asked.

"Fine. These men claim they won't harm us."

"That's right," Blade threw in. "If you'll give me your word that you won't cause us any trouble, we won't need to keep you under guard."

Johnson stared at the giant. "How do you know you can trust us?"

"You impress me as being an honest man."

The declaration seemed to surprise the farmer. He smiled and nodded. "Fair enough. I give you my word none of my family will be a problem. Satisfied?"

"Yes," Blade said, and slung the Commando over his left shoulder. "Now why don't we all go inside where we can talk?"

"Hey, what about me?" Grennell queried. "Can I go home now?"

"No."

"But you said you wouldn't keep us under guard."

Blade shook his head. "I said I wouldn't keep the Johnsons under guard. You're a different matter. Where we go, you go."

Grennell glowered, but had the presence of mind not to reveal his innermost thoughts.

"Martha, why don't you make some tea for our guests," Johnson proposed, coming onto the porch.

"Gladly. And Erica can help," the mother said, with a glance at the giant. "If it's all right with you, of course."

"Go ahead," Blade agreed. He let the Johnsons and Grennell enter, then turned to the bowman. "Stay out here and keep watch."

"Will do. You never know when those chickens might decide to jump us."

Blade ignored the crack and went in, Rikki right behind him. The living room was sparsely but comfortably furnished. Grennell sat in a chair on the left, Harry Johnson in a rocker on the right. The women were moving about in the kitchen, which was connected to the living room by a doorway situated at the southeast corner.

"Have a seat," Johnson said, gesturing at a sofa along the east wall.

"Thanks," Blade said, and did so.

Rikki-Tikki-Tavi remained near the doorway.

"So what can we do for you?" the farmer inquired. "We've never had the opportunity to talk to outsiders before. You're different than I expected. The Spartans tell us that most outsiders will slit our throats in a minute and steal all of our possessions. Yet something tells me you're not the throat-slitting type."

"I'm not," Blade said. "I'd like to talk about the Spartans, if you don't mind. We've traveled hundreds of miles to present an offer to them, and I'd like to know a little more about them before we make contact."

"What kind of offer?"

"To join the Freedom Federation, an alliance of seven factions dedicated to fostering the remnants of civilization."

Johnson sat forward, his forehead furrowed. "Really? I had no idea there was such a thing. We've always believed the rest of the country is in ruins, and that savage bands roam the countryside killing everyone they meet."

"It is that bad in most of the country," Blade admitted. "But the leaders of the Federation hope to eventually turn things around, to eliminate all the scavengers and the raiders, to make the country a safe place to live in once again. The goal won't be achieved overnight. Decades might be required, but one day peace will reign again."

The farmer smiled wistfully. "Listening to you, I almost believe it's possible."

"Your daughter told us the Spartans might try to put us in chains. How do you think they'll react to our proposal?"

"There's no telling. I'm just a Helot, mister. I farm for them. Affairs of state are way out of my league," Johnson said, resting his elbows on his knees. "I can tell you that one of the kings might be receptive to your offer. King Dercyllidas is a reasonable sort. At least he doesn't like to lord it over the Helots as King Agesilaus does."

"Dercylliadas and Agesilaus? I'm not an expert, but those names sound Greek."

"They are. The Spartans all have Greek names, just like the ancient Spartans. In fact, they take their names from a list compiled by the Lawgivers who founded Sparta during the war. If a Spartan should fall into disgrace, he is stripped of his rank, his name, and his cloak and barnished from Sparta for life."

"Fascinating," Blade said. "And it's encouraging to learn one of the kings will listen to us. All I want is a chance to present our case, and then we'll leave."

"I'll be honest with you. You're taking a great risk."

"It can't be helped. And I doubt the Spartans will harm us once they learn the Federation would take appropriate action. They wouldn't want a war on their hands."

Johnson made a snorting noise. "You don't know the Spartans, friend. They live for war."

Blade was about to respond when a loud thump came from outside. He glanced at Rikki.

The martial artist promptly went out.

"Is something wrong?" Johnson asked.

"I don't know," Blade said. He rose and stepped to the doorway, staring through the screen at the empty lawn. "Rikki? Teucer?"

There was no reply.

Alarmed, Blade shoved on the door and took a stride, and as he did a sharp object touched his neck and a low voice growled a warning.

"Don't move, big one, or you're a dead man."

CHAPTER FIVE

Blade froze. A muscular arm came around his left side and the Commando was pulled from his shoulder. A man stepped into view, moving in front of him, a strapping man attired in the most unusual military garb he'd ever seen.

For starters, the man wore a burnished bronze helmet completed with a dyed horsehair crest. A one-piece outfit snugly covered his sinewy physique. Boots adorned his feet. And clasped at the neck, flowing over both broad shoulders, was a light cloak that reached almost to his knees. Strangest of all was the fact that the crest, outfit, boots, and cloak were all red. A black belt encircled his waist, and from it dangled the scabbard to the short sword he held in his right hand. Slung over his left shoulder was an Uzi.

The Warrior glanced to the right and saw Teucer prone on the ground, unconscious. At the edge of the porch stood Rikki-Tikki-Tavi, hands in the air, covered by two more men in red bearing Uzi submachine guns. Blade looked to the left and discovered three more men with their weapons leveled.

"What's your name, big one?" demanded the man

who'd taken the Commando.

"Blade."

"I'm Captain Chilon of Spartiate Company C. You will consider yourself my prisoner until such time as may be decreed otherwise."

"We come in peace," Blade said.

"That has yet to be established. Kindly place your knives on the porch."

Without a moment's hesitation, Blade responded in a firm tone. "No."

"You will place your knives down now," Captain Chilon directed. "When I give an order, I expect to be obeyed."

A sharp retort almost issued from Blade's mouth, but he decided to try diplomacy instead of antagonizing the Spartan. "With all due respect, I must decline. Warriors are duty-bound to retain their weapons at all costs."

The captain's eyebrows knit. "But I took your submachine gun."

"Correction. I let you take the Commando, to buy time until I could ascertain the situation. Had you grabbed one of my Bowies, it would have been a different story. And now that I know all of you are Spartans, I have nothing to fear by refusing to turn them over."

"You don't?" Captain Chilon asked in surprise.

"No. Not if everything I've heard about the Spartans is true. Your people are fearless fighters, renowned for their discipline and dedication. Such men wouldn't kill others in cold blood," Blade stated with somewhat more assurance than he felt. He hoped subtle flattery would have the desired effect. If not, his next move would be to employ his Bowies.

The officer smiled and lowered his sword. "Your wit, big one, has disarmed my objections. By your bearing I can tell you're a brave man, and Spartans respect bravery." He paused. "But tell me. What are you doing in our domain?"

"I'm an official representative of the Freedom Federation," Blade explained yet again. "I've been sent to present a proposal to your kings."

"You're ambassadors of some sort? Very well. We'll escort you to the palace. You may keep your other weapons, but not any guns."

"Thanks," Blade said, glancing at Teucer. "I must check on him."

"He's fine," the Spartan stated. "One of my men gave him a tap on the head." He glanced at the two soldiers on the right. "Simoeis, revive the bow carrier."

"Immediately, Captain."

The screen door opened and out stepped Harry Johnson. "Hello, Captain," he said. "It's been a while."

"Mr. Johnson," the officer replied, sliding his sword into its scabbard. "Have these men harmed your family in any way?"

"No. They've treated us decently."

Rick Grennell materialized in the doorway, hatred contorting his visage. "They damn sure didn't treat me decently! The bastards cut me!" He stormed outside and pointed at Rikki. "That one there used a fancy spiked thing."

Captain Chilon stared at the bandaged arm, then at Blade. "Attacking a Helot is a serious offense."

"He attacked us first," Blade explained. "We had no choice. Afterward, we treated his arm."

"You applied the bandage?"

Blade nodded at the martial artist. "Rikki-Tikki-Tavi did. He's quite skilled at rendering first aid."

"Let me get this straight," Captain Chilon said. "First the small one wounded Grennell, then he took the time to bandage him?"

Blade nodded.

"It doesn't matter whether the son of a bitch helped me or not," Grennell snapped. "The important point is that he cut me in the first place. I want to press charges."

"I'm not certain of your legal standing in this respect," Chilon stated. "These men, being outsiders, fall under the special laws set down by the Lawgivers."

"I know my rights," Grennell insisted. "I demand that charges be pressed against these men. I'll gladly testify against them." He sneered at the giant. "I'll even accompany you to Sparta."

Blade recalled the information Erica had imparted concerning the possession of weapons by Helots. "If you're going to Sparta with us," he said calmly, "you'll need your rifle."

Grennell's mouth slackened and his eyes widened.

"Rifle?" Captain Chilon repeated.

"Yes. He tried to shoot us with a Marlin 30-30. It's in our transport," Blade revealed.

The Spartan officer's features hardened. "Is this true, Grennell?"

"No," the Helot answered. "It's a lie. They're just trying to get your sympathy. It's a lie, I tell you."

"No, it's not," interjected a newcomer to the conversation, and Erica emerged from the house.

Blade noticed a curious reaction by the officer. Chilon's stern expression shifted, becoming instantly friendly, almost regarding her with open tenderness and affection. The Spartan's eyes seemed to drink in her beauty like a thirsty man quenching a parched throat.

"Ms. Johnson," Chilon said formally.

"Captain," Erica responded with equal formality.

"Are you saying these outsiders are telling the truth?"

"I am. They saved me from a mutation and were giving me a ride home when we ran across Mr. Grennell. He tried to shoot them."

"You were attacked by a mutant?" Chilon asked, momentarily indifferent to the matter of the rifle.

"I'm fine, really," Erica said softly. "The bowman over there shot it."

Captain Chilon looked to the east, where his men were

busy reviving the man in green. "Then we owe him a debt of gratitude. I'm almost sorry we had to knock him out." He turned to Grennell. "So not only did you break the law about owning firearms, but you lied to me as well."

"I didn't lie to you," the Helot said. "I'd never lie to a Spartan officer. She's lying, just like them."

"And why would Ms. Johnson lie?"

"Because she has the hots for that bowman."

No one, least of all Grennell, anticipated what would happen next. Captain Chilon abruptly clamped his right hand on the Helot's shirt and lifted, actually raising Grennell into the air with just one arm. He spun and hurled the Helot from him, causing Grennell to sprawl onto the cement walk. "Take this man into custody," he bellowed.

The three Spartans on the left side of the porch promptly ran around to the front. Two of them seized Grennell and rudely hauled him erect.

Blade checked on his companions. He was relieved to find Teucer awake and standing. Rikki stood next to a window, his arms at his sides, his eyes not missing a thing.

"Your fate is now in the hands of the Ephors," Chilon was telling Grennell. "And you know the usual punishment for violating the firearms law."

"But I'm a loyal Helot!" Grennell said. "I've never used the rifle against a Spartan. My family has owned a gun for decades, and not once have we used it to violate the law."

Captain Chilon smiled grimly. "So your family has possessed an illegal gun for decades?" He faced to the west and called out, "Martin, get out here!"

Blade was surprised to behold another Helot appear. The man resembled Grennell enough to be his brother.

"Your older brother has informed me of the rifle your family owns," the officer declared.

Martin Grennell gulped and wrung his hands together. He cast a despairing look at his sibling, gnawed on his lower lip for a few seconds, then blurted out, "The rifle belongs to him, not the whole family."

"You lying sack of manure!" Rick Grennell shrieked. "Tell them the truth!"

"It is the truth, sir," Martin told Chilon. "I don't know where he got the gun. But as the Lord is my witness, the gun is truly Rick's."

"Leave the Lord out of this," Chilon snapped.

"Martin, you scum!" Rick shouted. "You'll pay for this! You always were worthless, you know that?"

Captain Chilon looked at the pair of soldiers restraining the older Grennell. "Shut him up."

One of the Spartans whipped his right fist straight up, catching the prisoner on the jaw. Grennell's eyelids quivered and he slumped in their arms.

"And as for you," Chilon said to Martin, "you can run home and tell your parents the Crypteia will be paying them a visit soon."

"But we're innocent!" Martin wailed.

"I'm a soldier. It's not my responsibility to evaluate innocence or guilt. I simply report to my superiors, and once they learn of this incident you can be sure the Crypteia will be dispatching men to your farm."

Martin took an anxious step backwards.

"Go!" Chilon barked.

Like a frightened rabbit, Martin Grennell whirled and raced off.

"Miserable cowards," Chilon muttered.

"Where did Martin come from?" Erica spoke up. "I didn't realize he was here."

The officer's anger evaporated once he gazed at her. "We were on patrol on Highway 76 when we ran into him. He claimed he'd been out hunting with his brother, although he never mentioned anything about a rifle. Told us that he'd witnessed his brother being captured by strangers in a green vehicle. Said he hid in the woods when they jumped Rick. He also claimed you had been taken by the same strangers." He paused. "Naturally, my first thought was to come here and investigate whether or not you were missing."

"Naturally," Erica said, her lips curling in a curious little grin.

Blade listened to the narration, able to piece together the missing pieces of the puzzle. Rick and Martin Grennell hadn't been out hunting, as they asserted. Rather, they'd been following Erica, and he could readily imagine the reason. For now it would be better if he kept the secret to himself. Such information might prove valuable later on. He abruptly became aware of someone next to his elbow and glanced down at Martha Johnson.

"Captain, all this nasty business is very distressing. Would you care to come in for a cup of tea?"

"Thank you, but no. We must be on our way," Chilon answered courteously.

"I have some already on the stove," Martha said. "It wouldn't be a bother. And we do so enjoy your visits."

"I wish we could stay for a while," Captain Chilon stated. "Our duty dictates otherwise. Perhaps next time we pass this way on patrol."

"We'll look forward to it," Martha remarked.

"Excuse me," Harry interjected.

"Yes?" Chilon responded.

"The Grennells are good friends of ours. What will happen to them?"

"I wouldn't go around bragging about your friendship, were I you," the captain advised. "As far as their punishment is concerned, Rick will either be put to death or sentenced to the quarry for life. Martin might receive a lesser sentence. Their parents may be placed on probation."

"Thank goodness," Harry said. "The parents are decent folks, not like their boys."

"Perhaps," replied Captain Chilon. "But it's been my experience that inferior genes are responsible for breeding inferior offspring." He gave a courtly bow to Erica, and walked from the porch.

Blade followed, Rikki a few feet behind. "How do you propose traveling to Sparta?"

"We'll walk," the officer answered.

"Why not drive in our van?" Blade suggested.

Chilon halted and studied the transport. "How do I know you're not trying to trick me?"

"As one Warrior to another, I give you my word. There's room inside for three of your men and Grennell. The rest can ride on the roof. There's plenty of room to set next to the solar panels. I also promise I'll drive slowly."

"It would save time," Chilon mentioned thoughtfully. "All right. But we'll have you and your men covered the whole time."

"I understand," Blade said.

"Then on to Sparta," Captain Chilon commented, and motioned for his soldiers to move toward the transport.

On to Sparta, Blade thought, and hoped his diplomacy wouldn't result in their deaths.

CHAPTER SIX

Blade had no idea what to expect when they reached Sparta. Although he entertained no preconceptions, he was nonetheless astounded by the awe-inspiring spectacle that unfolded before his wondering gaze as he drove the SEAL along the gravel road into the heart of the city. He couldn't bring himself to regard Sparta as a town, even though there were only 900 or so inhabitants, not when he beheld the marvelous architectural wonders situated in a narrow valley lined by steep cliffs. "This is incredible," he breathed in amazement.

"A century of labor has gone into Sparta," Captain Chilon stated proudly. He sat in the front passenger seat, his Uzi trained on the giant.

From the wide seat came a pertinent comment. "Spartan labor or the labor of the Helots?" asked Rikki-Tikki-Tavi.

Chilon glanced at the man in black. "Spartans aren't laborers. We're soldiers. Yes, the Helots built our city, assisted by criminal conscripts." He paused. "What's wrong with that?"

"Did the Helots do so willingly?"

"Most did. Not all Helots are dissatisfied with their

status, as your tone implies."

Blade was concentrating on the marble and granite structures. He felt as if he'd gone through a portal in time and somehow wound up in ancient Greece. During his schooling years at the Home he'd studied the history and culture of that country, and he remembered being impressed by photographs of the Parthenon, the Erechtheum, the temple of Poseidon, the temple of Apollo, and many others. Now here they were again, rising right before his eyes, resplendent in the bright sunlight, every bit as magnificent as the originals after which they were obviously patterned.

At the very center of the city, surrounded by a public square, sat an enormous Doric structure, its colonnades glistening, rearing ten stories high.

"That's the Royal Palace," Captain Chilon disclosed.

Blade simply nodded.

Spartans were everywhere, easily distinguished by their red clothes. Even Spartan women wore red: red blouses, red skirts, red dresses, red shoes. Red ribbons or bows adorned their long hair. In contrast, the Helots in the city wore drab hand-me-downs or homemade clothing.

"Park in front of the Palace," Chilon directed.

There was no need to ask exactly where to stop because a portion of the public square served as a parking area. Four jeeps were aligned in a row, each with a Spartan seated behind the wheel, apparently ready to depart at a moment's notice.

Chilon noticed the direction of the giant's gaze. "Only our most skilled drivers are assigned to the Transportation Squad. Usually only the Kings, the Ephors, or one of the high-ranking officers in the Crypteia use the jeeps."

"You mentioned the Crypteia before," Blade noted. "Is it a branch of your army?

"The Crypteia are our secret police."

"What purpose do they serve?"

Captain Chilon, who had his window down, waved at

SPARTAN RUN

a Spartan strolling along the sidewalk. "The Crypteia help keep the Helots in line. I don't know if you're aware of it, but the Helots outnumber us Spartans by a substantial margin. If it wasn't for the secret police, the Helots might be inclined to revolt." He paused. "They've tried in the past, and always without success."

"Makes you wonder, doesn't it?"

"About what?"

"About whether or not there might be a flaw in your system," Blade said.

"The Lawgivers designed a perfect government. Our system of checks and balances has served us well for over a century. There aren't any flaws," Chilon declared snobbishly.

Blade pulled the transport in alongside the nearest jeep and turned off the engine. He looked back at Rikki and Teucer, who were seated between Spartans, and smiled, only he smiled in a certain way, a very precise smile in which he touched the tip of his tongue to his lower lip while at the same time he tapped his right forefinger on his chin. To a casual observer the smile and the tap were innocent enough, but to the martial artist and the bowman they conveyed a secret message.

Because of the nature of their work, because the Warriors were frequently placed in life-or-death situations where verbal communications were impractical, a series of hand and facial gestures had been developed to enable them to convey messages without anyone else being the wiser.

Blade stared at each of them, and although neither Warrior reacted he knew they understood his instruction: STAY ALERT. FOLLOW MY LEAD.

"Everyone out," Captain Chilon said, and opened his door. He extended his left arm toward the giant. "I'll need those keys."

"I'd prefer to keep them," Blade said, debating whether to turn them over or put up a fight. The mission must come first, he reminded himself. Reluctantly, he dropped the keys into the officer's palm.

"Thanks. I'll take good care of them," Chilon said, and slipped them into his left front pocket.

"I hope so," Blade responded. He slid out and moved around in front of the grill, studying the Royal Palace. A flight of ten steps led up to the first floor. Stationed at regular intervals all around the perimeter were Spartans armed with the traditional short swords and nontraditional M-16's.

In short order Captain Chilon had his men lined up by twos. In front of them, bound at the wrists, was Rick Grennell. The officer indicated that the Warriors should walk ahead of the Helot, then he took the lead and headed toward the steps.

"Shouldn't our vehicle be locked?" Blade asked.

"Why?"

"What if someone steals our provisions?"

Captain Chilon laughed. "No one will steal a single article. Petty thievery doesn't occur in Sparta."

"Never?"

"Not ever."

"How did you Spartans accomplish that miracle?"

"It's really very simple," Chilon responded. "The penalty for stealing is to have both hands chopped off at the wrists. Since the law went into effect approximately ninety years ago there hasn't been a single incident."

"I wonder why," Blade commented wryly.

"We also have a very low homicide rate," the officer bragged. "The last murder in Sparta occurred seven years ago."

"What's the punishment for that? Beheading?" Blade joked.

"How did you guess?"

Blade glanced over his right shoulder at the six Spartan troopers. One of them had his Commando slung over a shoulder. Another had Rikki's AR-15, which the Spartans had appropriated from the rear section of the SEAL. At least Rikki still possessed his katana, Teucer his bow, and he had his Bowies. If they weren't accorded a friendly reception, they stood a fighting chance of reaching the transport. Once they were inside the virtually impervious van there was no way the Spartans could stop them from leaving.

Which reminded him.

The Founder had left only one set of keys for the SEAL. Blade had recently learned from an acquaintance in the Free State of California that machines existed capable of duplicating any key ever made. He wanted to have spares of the transport's set produced at the first opportunity.

Captain Chilon made for a huge door at the top of the steps. He returned the salute of a guard, which consisted of pressing his clenched right fist to his left breast. "Are both kings in attendance?"

"Yes, Captain," the guard replied.

"Good," Chilon said, and paused while the trooper rapped loudly three times.

Blade heard a faint click. The door swung slowly inward, pulled from within.

Chilon motioned for them to proceed and entered the Royal Palace.

Inadvertently tensing, Blade stayed on the officer's heels. The three soldiers who had opened the door stood at attention as the party passed. Ahead was a great hall, all polished and grand just like the exterior, with Spartans lining both walls.

"These men are part of the Three Hundred," Captain Chilon mentioned proudly.

"The Three Hundred?" Blade repeated.

"The three hundred best soldiers are selected to serve as bodyguards to the kings. To be picked for the Three Hundred is a special honor. Any Spartan warrior would give his right arm to be chosen."

"Are you part of the Three Hundred?"

"Not yet. All candidates must be at least thirty years old. I still have six months before I'm eligible, but I have every hope of being nominated when the time comes."

"Wait a minute," Blade said, doing a few mental calculations. "How many men are there in the Spartan army counting the Three Hundred?"

"Approximately five hundred and fifty. There are also fifty police."

"Which means there can only be about three hundred women and children in Sparta," Blade said.

"Yes. You're remarkably well informed about our population."

"How can this be? The ratio of males and females is all wrong."

"True, and through no fault of ours. I'll be honest with you. There has been a chronic shortage of women for many years. No one knows why, but most of the female babies die. So do a lot of the males, but not quite as many. The doctors speculate there might be some form of contamination in the area, either radiation or a chemical toxin. They can't isolate the source, however."

"What about the Helots?"

"What about them?"

"Are they also afflicted?"

"Yes, but not to the same degree."

"Then I'd guess Spartan men must take a fair number of Helot women as wives."

"You'd guess wrong," Captain Chilon responded, his voice lowering slightly, almost sadly.

"Why?"

"Because it's against the law for a Spartan to marry a Helot. Even for a Spartan to show interest in a Helot is to flirt with banishment or worse."

"The law makes no sense," Blade stated.

"It did years ago when the Helots were always making trouble. And too, the Lawgivers wanted to keep the Spartan bloodline pure."

"How do the Spartan men feel about the situation?"

"What we feel is unimportant. Our duty is to serve our kings and safeguard our city-state. This we will do no matter what the cost."

Blade fell silent, contemplating this new revelation. Now he understood the game Chilon and Erica Johnson played, and realized the consequences should he reveal the officer's secret. Another thought occurred to him, the real reason Rick Grennell had been in the same area as Erica, carrying a rifle no less. What would happen if Grennell told Chilon's superiors?

They had advanced for over 40 yards along the corridor, passing many doors en route. Directly in front of them loomed another enormous door, only this one hung open. Beyond was an incredibly immense chamber packed with Spartans, both men and women, as well as a few children and Helots. A dozen soldiers were posted just outside, all at attention.

"This is the audience chamber," Captain Chilon disclosed.

One of the soldiers stepped forward, blocking their path, and saluted. "Halt, please, Captain Chilon."

The officer saluted. "Captain Tyrtaios. Is there a problem?"

"You have strangers with you."

"Yes."

"They're armed. You know the law as well as I do. Armed outsiders may not be admitted to the audience chamber under any circumstances whatsoever."

"I take full responsibility for them," Chilon stated.

Captain Tyrtaios pursed his lips and studied the Warriors. "This is most irregular. I trust you have an excellent reason?"

"Of course."

"Then they will be permitted to enter, but six of my men will accompany you."

"Take whatever steps you deem necessary."

Tyrtaios moved aside and pointed at six of his detail. As Chilon started forward again, Tyrtaios leaned closer and whispered, "I hope you know what you're doing."

"So do I."

Blade scanned the chamber. A red carpet covered the floor except at the far end. There, on the east side, on a spacious dais, were a pair of matching gilded thrones on which sat men wearing full red robes and golden crowns. Behind the thrones, in a line from north to south, were ten more soldiers. Unlike the Spartans Blade had encountered so far, these ten carried bows, powerful longbows, and on their backs perched quivers containing red shafts.

Captain Chilon walked toward the dais, his shoulders squared, his horsehair crest swaying.

Every man, woman, and child stopped whatever they were doing to stare at the newcomers.

The two men on the thrones reacted differently. On the left sat a blond man who sported a full beard and bushy brows. He regarded the party intently, yet calmly. Not so the other king. An exceptionally lean man with black hair down to his shoulders and dark eyes, he leaped to his feet and jabbed his right hand at them.

"Chilon, what's the meaning of this? You dare bring armed outsiders into the audience chamber?"

The officer saluted and halted a few yards from the base of the dais. "King Agesilaus, I beg your indulgence. These men are here on a peace mission. Please hear them out."

"Have you taken leave of your senses? I won't tolerate a threat to my royal person." Agesilaus shifted and glanced at the ten archers. "Kill them!"

CHAPTER SEVEN

For a moment Blade expected to have to fight for his life. He saw three of the Spartan archers step forward, notching arrows to their bows, and he draped his hands on the hilts of his Bowies.

"Wait!" thundered the other king, Dercyllidas, who stood and gestured to the archers. "I say we should listen to the strangers. Captain Chilon wouldn't have brought them before us without due cause."

King Agesilaus cast a hostile gaze on his fellow monarch. "And *I* want them slain immediately."

The blond king stepped to the edge of the dais and studied the three Warriors for a bit, then faced Agesilaus. "As a favor to me, agree to let them speak."

"And what will I get in return?"

"I'll owe you a favor, and you know I always make good on my debts."

"True," King Agesilaus said, the corners of his thin lips curling upward. "May I claim this favor at any time?"

"Of course."

"No matter what it might be?"

"If it's within my power to accomplish it, then I'll do it."

"Fine. You may question the strangers," Agesilaus stated, and gave a contemptuous wave of his hand as he sat down.

The blond king placed his hands on his hips and regarded the giant critically. "Who are you and where are you from?"

"My name is Blade. I'm here as an official representative of the Freedom Federation. Perhaps you've heard of it?"

"I recall an outsider who made mention of such a name once," King Dercyllidas said.

"The Federation is an alliance of seven factions that are trying to salvage what's left of civilization from the ruins of World War Three. Each member has signed a mutual defense treaty, agreeing to aid any other member whenever the need arises," Blade related. "I'm here to extend an invitation to Sparta to join."

King Agesilaus came out of his chair again. "What? Sparta has no need of allies. What presumption! Perhaps we should send your head back to this Federation as a symbol of our indepedence and strength."

"Let's hear him out," King Dercyllidas suggested. "I'm interested in the offer. We should learn all we can before we dismiss it out of hand."

Agesilaus sighed. "Very well. Suit yourself."

"What are these seven factions?" Dercyllidas inquired.

"The faction I'm from is called the Family. The others are the Free State of California, the Civilized Zone, the Cavalry, the Clan, the Moles, and the Flathead Indians," Blade disclosed.

"So the state of California survived the war?" King Dercyllidas said. "We've heard about the Civilized Zone, but not the others. Where are they located?"

"I'd rather not say."

"Why not?"

"The exact locations of the Federation factions must

remain a secret until we're satisfied we can trust your people."

King Agesilaus took a stride and glared at the gaint. "Trust us? Why, you miserable swine! Who are you to sit in judgment on Spartans? You're not fit to tie our shoelaces."

"Calm down," Dercyllidas told the co-ruler. "I'm certain he meant no offense, and I admire this Federation for possessing the foresight not to trust anyone blindly."

"You would," Agesilaus snapped.

"As Captain Chilon explained, we've come here in peace," Blade went on. "As official emissaries we expect to be treated accordingly. If we should be harmed, the Federation will respond accordingly."

"Is that a threat?" Agesilaus demanded sternly.

"No, a promise," Blade responded, refusing to be intimidated by the pompous chief of state. "The Federation has successfully withstood attempts by the Russians, the Technics, the Superiors, the Peers, the Doktor, and many others to destroy it. We can field a combined army of over ten thousand troops, plus tanks and aircraft, on short notice. If need be, twice that number could be conscripted into service." He paused and surveyed the chamber. "I reveal these factors not to threaten you or to try and put fear into your hearts, because I've learned that Spartans fear nothing. Rather, I tell you this so you can appreciate the gravity of the situation should you decide to oppose the Federation. Sparta might boast the bravest army on the planet, but bravery is no match for tanks and vastly superior odds. Consider these facts. Consider that the Federation would be honored to have Sparta as a member. And bear in mind that once you've joined, your enemies would be our enemies. Anyone who would try to crush you must first crush us."

"Tanks and aircrafts?" King Dercyllidas said, sounding impressed by the news.

"I bet they don't have a single measly tank," King Agesilaus stated. "He's just making these absurd claims so we'll agree to his proposal."

"And what if you're wrong?" Dercyllidas replied. "Would you sacrifice Sparta on the altar of your vanity?"

Agesilaus turned livid and clenched his fists.

Blade held up his right hand. "Please, I don't want to be the cause of contention between you. Would king Agesilaus be satisfied I speak the truth if I provided proof?"

The dark-maned monarch glowered at the Warrior. "What sort of proof? Did you bring a tank with you?" he asked, and laughed.

"We brought something better than a tank," Blade stated. "And if you're willing, we'll provide a demonstration that should convince you of our sincerity."

King Dercyllidas smiled. "I, for one, would like to see this proof."

At least ten seconds elapsed before King Agesilaus spoke. He was deep in thought the whole time. Finally he nodded and said, "All right. I'd like to see the proof also. But mark my words, Blade. Should this be a trick, you'll live to regret it."

Captain Chilon cleared his throat. "My lords, before we conduct the demonstration there is another matter that must be brought to your attention."

"Haven't you done enough for one day?" King Agesilaus quipped.

The officer pointed at Grennell. "This Helot has been arrested for possessing a firearm."

"Did you confiscate the weapon?" King Dercyllidas inquired.

"Yes, sir," Chilon responded, and snapped his fingers. The last soldiers in his squad brought forward the Marlin 30-30. "Here it is. He'll be turned over to the Ephors for disposition of his case."

King Agesilaus swaggered to the rim of the dais and

bestowed a mocking gaze on the bound Helot. "Planning a little insurrection, were you, scum?"

"No, your lordship," Grennell responded in a pathetic whine. "I'd never think of rebelling against our wonderful masters."

"Did you use the rifle for target shooting, then?" Agesilaus taunted.

"My family used it for hunting, that's all, your lordship."

"Of course, my dear Helot."

Grennell looked at the rope binding his arms, then at Captain Chilon. His expression transformed into a mask of hatred and his lips twitched. He impulsively took several steps, until a Spartan stopped him, and blurted out, "Would you grant me leniency, good kings, if I tell you the truth?"

"Do you really think we care?" Agesilaus rejoined.

"Your fate is in the hands of the Ephors," Dercyllidas said. "We can't influence the verdict of the judges."

"But I have important information," Grennell insisted.

"Sure you do," declared King Agesilaus, and pressed his left palm to his forehead. "Your prattling is giving me a headache. Will someone shut him up?"

Grennell cried out shrilly, "But I do have information you'd want. I know the name of a Spartan who is breaking the law by—"

Acting more in impulse than logical judgment, Blade spun and delivered an arching haymaker to the Helot's chin. The punch lifted Grennell from his feet and sent him sailing for two yards before crashing to the floor.

No one else moved. Everyone appeared bewildered by the startling development.

Captain Chilon stared at the unconscious Helot, then at the Warrior.

"Why did you do that?" King Agesilaus demanded.

"You wanted him to stop prattling," Blade noted.

"Yes. But what was that business about a Spartan who

has broken the law?"

"I have no idea," Blade answered, lying to save the officer. "And I'll confess, I've wanted to lay him out ever since he tried to kill us."

King Dercyllidas came halfway down the steps. "You say this Helot attempted to take your life?"

"Yes. He tried to shoot us."

"I can substantiate that," Captain Chilon interjected. "I spoke with a witness to the attack."

"This is most serious," King Dercyllidas said. "I trust you realize, Blade, that the Helot's action wasn't sanctioned by the Spartan government. Helots aren't permitted to own firearms. Do you know the reason he attempted to kill you?"

"No."

"Well, the Crypteia will get the truth out of him," Agesilaus stated, and nodded at two Spartans standing at the base of the dais. "Take him to General Agis. Inform the general he is to use every means at his disposal to wring this Helot dry, then turn the wretch over to the Ephors. I want to be informed of every word he utters. Understood?"

"Yes, your lordship," one of the soldiers said.

In moments the troopers had hauled Grennell away.

Blade noticed Captain Chilon gazing at him, and deliberately focused on the kings. "I apologize if I stepped out of bounds. As a Federation emissary, I should be on my best behavior at all times."

"You're forgiven, this once," King Agesilaus said. "Now about this demonstration of yours. What does it entail?"

"I'd like to show you some of the capabilities of our vehicle," Blade explained.

"Where is it?"

"Parked outside."

"Then let's get this over with."

The two kings descended the dais, and were promptly

surrounded by two dozen Spartans. As they made for the doorway, the crowd parted.

Captain Chilon waited until the royal guard passed, then led the Warriors and his own squad out. He walked alongside the giant, and when they were going through the doorway he spoke in a hushed voice. "I don't know why you saved me, but I thank you."

"You're welcome."

"How did you know about Erica and me?"

"I can add two and two."

"Was it that obvious?"

"Afraid so."

"Damn," the officer said. "Well, I've only myself to blame for what happens after the secret police finish interrogating Grennell. They'll arrest me."

"What about Erica?"

"Helots are rarely punished for having romantic relations with Spartans. Since Spartans are required to be perfect models of self-control and discipline, we're the ones whom the Ephors punish," Chilon said. "At most, you've bought me some time. I only wish I could see Erica at least once before I'm taken into custody."

"Perhaps I can help there."

"How?"

"Leave it to me."

Rikki-Tikki-Tavi nudged Blade's left elbow. "When can I address the kings?"

"After we're done with the demonstration," Blade answered. "Sorry. As soon as we've proven ourselves to them, go ahead."

They passed along the corridor to the outer door, which had been opened well in advance by the three soldiers assigned to the task, and the two kings led the way down the steps. At the bottom they halted and studied the SEAL.

"What type of demonstration did you have in mind?" King Dercyllidas asked.

Blade surveyed the open area. At the north end

construction was under way, and a huge mound of dirt had been piled next to the foundation for a new building. "With your permission, I'd like to show you the firepower of our transport."

"Be our guest," Agesilaus said.

"Perhaps you should clear the pedestrians away from that dirt mound," Blade suggested.

King Agesilaus merely motioned with his right hand and instantly six Spartans hastened off to do his bidding.

"And I'll need the keys," Blade told Captain Chilon.

The officer handed them over.

Blade turned to his friends. "Let's go." He walked to the van with Rikki and Teucer on his heels.

"What gives?" the bowman queried. "Why are we doing this?"

"The Spartans only respect power. If we give them a taste of the SEAL's armaments, they might be more inclined to take the Federation's offer seriously."

"Convincing Dercyllidas won't be hard," Rikki commented, "but the other one is unpredictable. I don't trust him."

"Neither do I," Blade concurred. "We must try to persuade him, though, and this might do the trick." He unlocked the door, then climbed in and unlocked the passenger side.

"What was going on with Chilon and you?" Teucer asked as he took his seat.

"Chilon and Erica Johnson are in love," Blade revealed, inserting the key. He started the engine, waited for Rikki to close the door, then backed up and drove to within 20 feet of the dirt mound. The soldiers were moving all citizens from the immediate vicinity.

"What do we do if Agesilaus isn't impressed?" Teucer questioned.

"We'll get the hell out of here," Blade said.

"Good. I don't relish the notion of being thrown in a prison or forced to work in a quarry."

Blade watched the last of the pedestrians reach a safe distance from the SEAL. "Here goes," he declared, and flicked the silver toggle switch that activated the 50-caliber machine guns. Almost immediately the big guns cut loose, thundering in unison, the rounds boring into the mound, dirt flying in all directions. The SEAL vibrated slightly for the duration of the ten-second burst. Blade switched the toggle off.

"Think that's enough?" Teucer asked.

"No," Blade responded, and activated the flamethrower. He saw a red and orange hissing tongue spurt from the front fender and strike the dirty with a sizzling crackle. He counted to three, then shut the flamethrower off. There was no sense in wasting the fuel.

"Let's use the rocket launcher on the Royal Palace," Teucer suggested. "That should really impress them."

Rikki glanced at the bowman. "Have you been hanging around Hickok a lot lately?"

"No. Why?"

"Just asking."

Grinning, Blade returned the transport to its original position and killed the engine. Both kings, and many of the soldiers, were regarding the van in amazement. Agesilaus, oddly, abruptly smiled slyly and whispered a few words to the Spartan on his left.

"Did you see that?" Rikki asked.

"Yep," Blade replied.

"See what? See what?" Teucer wanted to know.

"Do you want us to stay in here?" Rikki queried.

"You took the words right out of my mouth. I'm leaving the key in the ignition," Blade said, opening his door. He looked at both of them. "As soon as I step around the front of the SEAL, all eyes should be on me. Roll up the windows and lock the doors. If everything is all right, I'll give the proper signal."

"Why not simply stay put?" the martial artist mentioned.

"We'll give our hosts the benefit of the doubt," Blade stated, and slid to the ground. He whispered his final instructions. "Rikki, you've had driving lessons. If we're right, get the SEAL out of here."

"We won't leave you."

"That was an order."

"As you wish," Rikki said, frowning.

Blade slammed the door, plastered a fake smile on his face, and strolled toward the kings.

"An astounding display of firepower!" King Agesilaus exclaimed, and clapped his hands together.

"Evidently the Federation is every bit as strong as you indicated," King Dercyllidas added. "Spartan might would avail us little against such mechanized dispensers of death.'

"The Federation has no intention of attacking Sparta unless you give us provocation," Blade said. "We'd rather join hands in friendship and become allies."

"Sparta can take—" Agesilaus began, then glanced at the transport. "Why are your companions still inside?" He did a double take. "And why have they just rolled up the windows?"

"They're making ready to depart."

"Depart!" Agesilaus practically bellowed. "I didn't give them permission to leave."

"There's no need for them to be present during our further talks," Blade said.

"I want them out of there this second!"

"I'm afraid that's not possible."

King Agesilaus took a step forward. "Don't tell me what is and isn't possible! You're addressing a Spartan king, not some miserable cur of a Helot."

"What different does it make whether they stay in the vehicle or not?" King Dercyllidas said, interceding.

The thin monarch whirled on his blond peer. "It's a trick. They're up to no good."

"You're making a mountain out of a molehill," Dercyllidas said. "Why do you persist on blowing everything out of proportion?"

"I do, do I?" Agesilaus rejoined, his right hand casually easing under the folds of his robe.

"Most definitely. These men would hardly have risked their lives to come here merely to indulge in petty tricks. They're offering us a wonderful opportunity, a chance to expand our horizons, to enter into a political alliance that will reap untold benefits. Think of the possibilities! Why, we might be able to trade for ammunition and other necessities that are currently in short supply."

"Sparta has managed quite well for over a century without outside aid. There's no reason to change our policy now."

"But there is. For far too long has Sparta existed in isolation. We've had no contact with the world beyond our boundaries for decades. We don't know what's out there. And we owe it to ourselves and our people to find out."

"The Lawgivers instructed us to be extremely cautious in making contact with outside influences."

"True, but they wrote those words a century ago when the world was in turmoil, when hordes of looters and crazies were scouring the countryside, slaying everyone they met." Dercyllidas paused. "Now the world is different. The presence of these three men is proof of it. We must keep our minds open to their words or we'll run the risk of suffering another century in a self-imposed quarantine."

Agesilaus stared at the ground. "Then I gather you've already decided Sparta should join the Federation?"

"Yes. But the final decision isn't up to us. The Ecclesia must vote on such a monumental issue, and I fully expect they will agree once they hear about the benefits to be derived from such a venture."

"The general assembly will never hear about the benefits."

"Oh? And why not?"

"Because they'll be too busy discussing your heinous plot to betray Sparta into the hands of her enemies," Agesilaus declared harshly, and the next moment he whipped a dagger from under his robe and plunged the keen point into King Dercyllidas's chest.

CHAPTER EIGHT

All hell broke loose.

King Agesilaus raised the dagger for another strike as Dercyllidas staggered backward and fell to his knees.

"No!" Captain Chilon cried, and stepped between the monarchs, giving Agesilaus a shove that propelled the thin ruler onto the ground.

The two dozen Spartan soldiers leaped forward, some surrounding King Dercyllidas, the rest encircling Agesilaus. In a flash swords appeared, and the two sides promptly clashed. Three men perished in the opening seconds of combat.

Shocked by the unexpected turn of events, Blade saw an Agesilaus partisan charge Chilon. He automatically darted to the officer's side, drawing his Bowies as he did, and braced for the onslaught.

The soldier swung his short sword in a tremendous overhand clash, intending to cleave the giant's skull.

Blade blocked the blow with his right Bowie, the clanging impact jarring his arm, then stabbed his left knife into the soldier's side. The man crumpled, and Blade jerked the Bowie free and glanced at Captain Chilon.

The officer was supporting King Dercyllidas. "We've

got to get out of here!" he told the Warrior. "There's no time to explain."

Blade didn't need to be persuaded. A quick look showed him the Agesilaus partisans outnumbered the Dercyllidas defenders by two to one, and despite the brave resistance of the defenders they were about to be overrun. "Get him to the van!" he shouted to be heard above the clashing of the swords.

Captain Chilon nodded, looped both arms around the wounded king's torso, and hastened toward the SEAL.

Three troopers moved to intercept him.

What had he gotten himself into? Blade wondered as he dashed to Chilon's defense. Since all the Spartans were dressed alike, he had a difficult time determining which side they belonged to. The trio, however, left no doubt of their intentions. He parried the sword of the foremost soldier, then dodged when another tried to impale him in the groin.

Nearby a defender went down fighting, blood spurting from his ruptured throat.

The three Agesilaus backers converged on the giant in concert, their expressions set in grim determination.

Blade backed up, his eyes flicking from Spartan to Spartan, knowing he was at a decided disadvantage. Not only was he outnumbered, the short swords were six inches longer than his Bowies and double-edged. The swords had also been forged with heavier steel. He couldn't expect to hold them off indefinitely.

All three lunged at the same instant, each one spearing his weapon at a different part of the giant's anatomy.

A side step enabled Blade to avoid a thrust aimed at his legs, and his Bowies deflected the other swords. Almost immediately the trio tried again, two slashing high, one going low. Blade threw himself rearward, evading the high strikes, but an intensely painful stinging sensation in his left shin made him aware the third soldier had scored. He didn't dare glance down to see how bad it was or the threesome would finish him off. He blocked two swords, still backing up, and glimpsed a fourth foe racing toward him.

Damn.

Blade knew he had to put at least two of them out of action and do it swiftly or he would be overwhelmed. He dodged to the right, and when the nearest Spartan tried to slice open his abdomen he swung his left Bowie straight down, cutting into the soldier's wrist and almost severing the man's sword hand.

Incredibly, the soldier simply grabbed the sword with his good hand and renewed his attack.

The Warrior skipped to the left this time, just as another Spartan aimed a terrific swipe at his neck. Blade ducked under the sword and lanced his right Bowie into the man's stomach, then wrenched the razor-sharp blade upward, ripping the Spartan from the navel to the sternum. The man doubled over and toppled forward.

There were still three adversaries remaining, counting the man whose split wrist gushed forth a crimson spray.

Blade countered a series of swings, his superior size and strength enabling him to temporarily keep them at bay. One of the soldiers came at him from the left at the same moment a second came at him from the right. He parried the latter and spun to confront the other one, but someone else beat him to the punch.

A diminutive black-clad figure seemed to streak out of nowhere and a gleaming katana arced into the Spartan's neck. Red drops splattered in all directions. Not slowing for an instant, the martial artist swung his cherished sword in a figure-eight pattern, the blade cutting through two foes, downing both.

For a moment they were clear.

"Took you long enough," Blade said, backing toward the transport.

"I helped Captain Chilon and the king climb in," Rikki-Tikki-Tavi explained, his body coiled in a ready stance.

"Then let's get out of here," Blade proposed, and was about to turn when three more soldiers came at them.

Nearly all of the Spartans who had come to Dercyllidas's aid were dead. Off to one side, well out of range, stood King Agesilaus. He shrieked the same command over and over again: "Kill them! Kill them! Kill them!"

Blade braced to meet the charge of the new trio. An object suddenly flashed past his left shoulder. Three objects, actually, one right after the other, making a slight swishing noise.

All three green shafts struck home with unerring accuracy. Each hit a soldier in the eye, penetrating deep into the cranium, slaying the target in midstride.

"Kill them! Kill them!" Agesilaus raged.

Blade whirled and sprinted to the vehicle.

Standing next to the open door, another arrow already notched to the green bow, was Teucer. "I'll cover you!" he said. "Get in."

A half-dozen soldiers were racing to stop them from escaping.

There was no time to lose. Blade vaulted up into the van, then slid over the console to the driver's seat. Both Chilon and Dercyllidas were in the wide seat behind him, the king unconscious. Blade beckoned urgently at his companions and shouted, "Let's go!"

Rikki entered next, moving back to sit beside the Spartan officer.

Teucer hadn't budged.

"Get in here!" Blade bellowed.

Several of the soldiers were in the process of unlimbering their automatic weapons.

"Just getting some air," Teucer quipped, and let fly, his right hand a blur as he fired one, two, three arrows in rapid succession. The shafts sped true, and the Spartans in the act of employing their guns toppled. Teucer rotated and quickly clambered into the passenger seat, pulling the door shut just as a soldier ran from the east and swung a sword, the steel edge glancing off the virtually indestructible plastic. "The natives are a bit restless. I suggest we haul butt."

Blade started the SEAL and threw the gearshift into reverse. Outside, King Agesilaus raved insanely and more soldiers poured from the palace. Some opened fire, their rounds ricocheting off the van with high-pitched whines. Blade tramped on the accelerator and the SEAL hurtled rearward. Spinning the wheel, he executed a semicircle, then shifted again and made for the gravel road.

"We must reach the barracks," Captain Chilon stated urgently.

"Why?" Blade asked. "What's going on?" He gazed into the rearview mirror and saw Spartans piling into the four jeeps.

"You and your friends have been caught in the middle of a power grab. Agesilaus is trying to take complete control of Sparta."

"Tell me something I don't know," Blade said, scanning the pedestrians crowding the sidewalks that lined the square. So far none had displayed any hostility.

"This has happened twice before, many years ago. Each time the would-be dictator was defeated," Chilon disclosed. "Frankly, I expected Agesilaus to make his move a long time ago. He probably decided to act now because he wants to prevent Sparta from joining the Federation at all costs."

"What difference does joining make?" Blade asked while exiting the square and speeding westward, the huge tires spewing gravel and dust in the SEAL's wake.

"I'm just guessing, but I'd say he's afraid the Federation would intervene if he tried to take control afterward."

"Then the joke is on him. A clause in the treaty prevents Federation factions from interfering in the internal affairs of other members."

"Really? Well, whatever his reason, Agesilaus has gone

over the brink and blood will flow until he's stopped."

"What will you do now?"

"I must get King Dercyllidas to the barracks where his bodyguard contingent is housed. They'll protect him."

"His bodyguard contingent? I thought there are three hundred Spartans assigned to safeguard both kings," Blade said. He took a curve as tightly as possible and glanced in the mirror.

The four jeeps, intermittently visible through the swirling dust, were roaring in pursuit.

"True, but each king selects one hundred and fifty men for the royal bodyguard. In effect, each king controls half of the contingent. Those who were picked by Agesilaus will back him to the death, and the same goes for those who owe their position to King Dercyllidas."

"What about the rest of the army and the Spartan people? Which king will they help?"

"Neither."

"What?"

"The regular army and the populace at large won't intervene. Custom dictates that the kings decide this between themselves."

"And what about the judges everyone keeps talking about, the Ephors? Do they have any power? Can they influence the outcome?"

"In a word, no. The Lawgivers tried to improve on ancient Sparta's constitution by incorporating certain changes into ours. Unlike the Ephors in the early Sparta, ours have only judicial powers. Even though all five might prefer Dercyllidas over Agesilaus, they won't attempt to intervene. Agesilaus is crazy enough to have them slain on the spot."

Blade passed an intersection, narrowly missing two Helots who were scurrying to get out of the SEAL's path. "Every Spartan must know that Agesilaus has gone off the deep end. Why haven't they deposed him?"

"Such an act would be unthinkable. Spartans are raised

from infancy to be loyal citizens. They pride themselves on their dedication to Sparta and the principles underlying the foundation of our city-state. For a Spartan, even the mere thought of disobedience is unconscionable."

Frowning, Blade glanced at the pedestrians on both sides of the road. "Are you telling me they'd rather be ruled by a madman than revolt?"

"Essentially, yes."

Blade shook his head in astonishment. What manner of people were these Spartans? He looked in the mirror once more and spotted the jeeps, now less than 40 yards behind the transport and slowly gaining. "Where are the barracks you mentioned?"

"Almost on the outskirts of the city. The troops are billeted there in case of an attack, so they can be called up and into formation at a moment's notice," Captain Chilon said. "Look for a side street on the left. There will be a long, narrow building adjacent to the street."

"Are Agesilaus's men in the same barracks?"

"No. They're in a building on the other side of this road."

"So the contingents are right across from each other?"

"Yes."

"Terrific," Blade muttered, and checked on their pursuers again. Only 30 yards and closing.

Unexpectedly, King Dercyllidas coughed and spoke. "Blade, I want to thank you for your aid."

Captain Chilon bent over the slumped monarch. "Don't talk, my liege. You must stay still until I've summoned a doctor."

"I'm a Spartan king," Dercyllidas stated, straightening slowly. "I won't be coddled."

"These guys give new meaning to the word tough," Teucer interjected.

"All of you must leave as soon as you can," Dercyllidas said. "Drop me off here, if you like, and depart in safety."

"No can do," Blade responded.

"Why not?" the ruler asked weakly, his left hand pressed to his chest.

"Because I intend to drop you off at the barracks where your bodyguards are housed. You wouldn't be safe anywhere else."

"You must leave," Dercyllidas insisted. "If anything happens to you, the Federation will blame us. For the sake of my people, this mustn't happen. I don't want to jeopardize Sparta's chances of joining."

"I can appreciate your concern," Blade noted, his eyes on the road ahead, seeking the barracks. "But look at this situation from my perspective. I believe the Spartans would make great allies. But if Agesilaus prevails, he'll never sign the treaty. Sparta won't be able to join the Federation until after he dies. I'd prefer to hasten his demise." He paused. "It's in the Federation's best interests if we help you out."

"This isn't your fight."

"Wrong. It became our fight the second Agesilaus tried to have us killed. If he wants us for enemies, he's got us."

King Dercyllidas glanced from the giant to the man in black, then at the bowman. "I am deeply in your debt."

"Save your gratitude," Teucer said. "If you're not alive when this is all over, you won't owe us a thing."

Blade looked in the mirror at the thick cloud of smoke behind them. Where were the jeeps? he wondered, and moments later received an answer.

The dust briefly parted, revealing a jeep not ten yards off. A Spartan was leaning out the passenger side, his arm extended.

It took Blade a second to realize the soldier held a hand grenade.

CHAPTER NINE

Blade turned the wheel sharply to the left, causing the SEAL to slew wildly. He regained control and saw the jeep still ten yards away, riding on the right side of the road. Apparently the driver planned to draw closer and then the other soldier would throw the grenade. Sixty feet beyond the first vehicle was the rest of the pack.

"Too bad we can't get behind them," Teucer remarked.

"Who says we can't?" Blade said, and slammed on the brakes, holding on tightly as the van screeched to an abrupt stop. He saw the lead jeep shoot past and floored the accelerator, hoping the other three jeeps wouldn't smash into the rear of the transport.

Loud, shrill noises came from the rear, the squealing of brakes applied roughly, too roughly as the subsequent crash signified.

Blade concentrated on the jeep dead ahead, slanting the SEAL in directly behind it. He promptly flicked the silver toggle to the machine guns, and the twin big-fifties blasted and bucked, the rounds punching into the jeep's tail and stitching a pattern of holes all over it.

Not a heartbeat later the jeep swerved to one side, then the other. The driver appeared to have lost his grip. For a full five seconds the vehicle veered back and forth until finally leaving the road entirely, angling up and over a sidewalk and ramming into a building. The gas tank ruptured, flames shot from under the hood, and a fireball engulfed the jeep and its occupants.

Blade gazed at the mirror. The dust completely obscured the road so he had no way of knowing if the remaining vehicles were still chasing the van.

"The barracks shouldn't be too much farther," Captain Chilon said.

"What will you do once we get there?"

"How do you mean?"

"Will you lead King Dercyllidas's backers against the Agesilaus contingent?"

"I can't. I'm not a member of the Three Hundred. The officer in charge will make the decision if the king is unable," Chilon answered. "And he's out again."

Blade glanced back and found the monarch sagging against the captain. "Who is the officer in charge of Dercyllidas's men?"

"That would be General Leonidas, one of the most widely respected of all Spartans. He was instrumental in staving off a large force of raiders a couple of years ago."

"Then you trust him?"

"With my life."

They rode in anxious silence for less than a minute.

"There's the side street!" Chilon cried.

Blade had already spotted it and the long structure, which was surrounded on three sides by a wide field. Spartan soldiers were everywhere; some were engaged in gymnastics; some were sparring; some were sharpening their swords; and some were simply conversing. He started to slow and looked to the right.

Almost an identical scene was on the other side of the road. The barracks building had been constructed a bit farther from the junction, and the level ground around it wasn't quite as spacious, but there were scores of soldiers involved in similar activities.

"Neither contingent must know about the fight at the palace," Rikki observed.

"No, Agesilaus hasn't had time to inform his men and General Leonidas will hear the news from us," Chilon stated.

Blade took the turn much faster than was safe, the tires sliding, the SEAL threatening to tip over.

"I'm glad I didn't eat much breakfast," Teucer said.

Twisting the steering wheel, Blade eased up on the brakes and drove toward a pair of wide doors situated at the north end of the barracks. The Spartans were all gazing in consternation at the transport. He brought the van to a full stop within 15 feet of the double doors and rolled down his window. "Is General Leonidas here?"

A nearby Spartan, who held a freshly sharpened sword in his right hand, answered curtly. "He is, stranger. What's your business with him?"

"Get him," Blade directed.

"A Spartan doesn't take orders from an outsider."

"Would you rather that your king died?"

"What?" the Spartan responded, taking a step.

"*Get General Leonidas!*" Blade commanded in a voice that carried to all corners of the field.

Despite the soldier's aversion to taking orders from outsiders, he'd been conditioned since early childhood to respond automatically to authority. That conditioning now compelled him to hasten into the barracks. He instinctively recognized a genuinely authoritarian person when he met one, and the giant impressed him as being a man accustomed to being obeyed.

Blade glanced at the scores of Spartans all around, who were now moving toward the transport, then at Captain Chilon. "Stay put until I see what kind of reception we get."

"Don't you trust me?" the officer responded.

"You I trust. But I don't know this Leonidas. Until I

meet him, we'll sit right where we are."

Chilon smiled. "If I didn't know better, I'd swear you were a Spartan."

"I'm a Warrior. So are my friends."

"Is that a title of some kind?"

"Yes. Eighteen Family members are selected to serve as guardians of the Home."

"Blade is the head Warrior," Teucer commented.

The officer nodded. "I would have expected as much." He regarded each of them. "I saw all three of you in action back there, and I never thought I'd see the day where three outsiders could hold their own against Spartans. Each of you is extremely skilled."

"We've had lots of practice," Blade said, gazing at the barracks. No one had yet appeared. He checked the road, but there was no sign of the jeeps. "There are a few things I need cleared up. What part will the secret police, the Crypteia, play in the power struggle?"

"None. Like the regular army, the police won't interfere. You see, the Crypteia are recruited from the ranks of the army and the bodyguard contingent. Some favor King Dercyllidas, while others prefer Agesilaus. And the man who controls the Crypteia, General Agis, toes a fine line of neutrality. He believes in maintaining a balance of power between the monarchs. There isn't a man alive more devoted to Sparta than him."

"Tell me this. During the fight the soldiers relied almost exclusively on their swords. They didn't resort to their automatic weapons until we were getting into the van. Why?"

"They didn't use their assault rifles or submachine guns on each other because it's against the law for one Spartan to shoot another."

"But the men who were defending Dercyllidas might have won if they'd used their guns."

"Possibly. But none of them wanted to be permanently banished from Sparta should they do so. When Spartans have disputes, they're required to settle their differences with swords or in hand-to-hand combat. Guns are strictly forbidden."

"They tried to shoot us," Blade noted.

"The three of you are outsiders. It's perfectly legal so shoot outsiders and Helots."

Teucer chuckled. "Figures."

"Wait a minute," Blade said. "Does this mean the two sides will only use swords if they engage in a pitched battle?"

"Swords and spears."

Blade looked at the barracks again, annoyed at not seeing anyone emerge. Where was General Leonidas? "Something else has been nagging at me. When Agesilaus attacked Dercyllidas there were twenty-four bodyguards with us. Yet almost two thirds sided with the madman. Why weren't the soldiers evenly divided?"

Captain Chilon frowned. "They should have been. The law specifically calls for an equal number of bodyguards from each contingent to be on duty at all times. I suspect treachery. Agesilaus is renowned for his devious nature."

"Do tell," Blade said dryly, and at last saw several Spartans step from the barracks. He immediately took a liking to the soldier in the lead, a muscular man four or five inches over six feet in height and endowed with an imposing physique. The man's helmet shimmered in the bright sunlight.

"I'm General Leonidas. Who are you and why do you want to see me?"

"Are you loyal to King Dercyllidas?" Blade asked bluntly.

The Spartan studied the giant. His features were rugged, his eyes and hair both dark. "If you knew me well, stranger, you'd know that my life is the king's to do with as he pleases."

"And would you protect him with your dying breath?"

Leonidas smiled. "What a stupid question. I would walk

through hell barefoot for my liege."

"Good," Blade said, and opened his door. "Because King Agesilaus has tried to kill him and he needs a doctor badly."

The general stiffened. "How do you know? Where is King Dercyllidas? And who the hell are you?"

"I'm Blade," the Warrior disclosed, and jerked his right thumb to the rear. "Dercyllidas is in here. He's been stabbed. Do you have a stretcher?"

Leonidas turned to another soldier. "Get one immediately."

"Yes, sir," the Spartan said, and ran into the barracks.

"Do you know Captain Chilon?" Blade queried.

"Yes."

"Good. He can explain everything. He's right behind me with your king."

"What's your—" Leonidas began, then stopped when the metallic rumble of racing engines came from the east.

Blade twisted and saw a rising cloud of dust drawing steadily nearer. The remaining jeeps were back in action. He shifted into park and stepped out of the SEAL. "Hurry and get Dercyllidas out. Those jeeps are filled with Agesilaus's men."

The general turned and pointed at four approaching soldiers. "Over here on the double."

They raced to the transport.

"Climb in and assist Captain Chilon in removing King Dercyllidas. And be gentle," Leonidas instructed them.

Blade admired the precision with which the Spartans went about their business. No one pestered the general with meaningless queries. In half a minute they had their monarch out and lowered him to the ground. "We'll be back," Blade said, and vaulted into the driver's seat.

"Where are you going?" Chilon inquired. He stood next to the general.

"It's payback time."

"You're going to try and take out the jeeps?"

"We'll buy Leonidas the time he needs to get organized," Blade said. He backed up, then drove to the side street and took a right.

The jeeps were 50 yards distant and going over 70 miles an hour.

"Teucer, be ready," Blade directed, and swung the SEAL onto the gravel road. He promptly braked and reached for the toggle switches.

Predictably, the soldiers in the three jeeps opened up, their weapons chattering, the drivers holding the vehicles steady so the gunners could aim with a reasonable degree of accuracy. Two jeeps were speeding abreast of one another while the third trailed by three vehicle lengths.

Blade waited, letting them get within range, listening to the slugs zing off the windshield.

Thirty yards separated the jeeps from the transport.

"When?" Teucer asked, his right hand poised to roll down the window, the bow in his left hand with an arrow already notched.

"I'll let you know," Blade replied, still waiting.

Twenty yards and closing.

Rounds were smacking into the SEAL in a continual hail of lead, peppering the van and the puncture-proof tires, buzzing like angry hornets.

Fifteen yards.

Blade's right index finger flicked the switch to activate the rocket launcher. The SEAL shook as the conical projectile shot from its launch tube, a tendril of smoke and flame marking its level trajectory.

The rocket struck the right-hand jeep in the left headlight.

A tremendous explosion shook the very earth and a blistering fireball swirled skyward. All three jeeps were totally shrouded in a cloud of flame, smoke, bits of gravel, and dust.

The concussion buffeted the SEAL, actually sliding the transport backwards a half-dozen yards. Blade was tossed from side to side and front to back, gritting his teeth as he struggled to retain his hold on the steering wheel and his foot on the brake. Out of the corner of his right eye he glimpsed the bowman being thrown into the door. He glanced behind him and saw Rikki gripping the top of the back seat, his face composed, unaffected by the bucking motion.

As quickly as it occurred, the concussion force of the explosion expended itself. The fireball took a little longer to subside, and the murky cloud persisted for minutes.

Blade placed his hand near the toggles again, his narrowed eyes probing the roadway. With any luck, the rocket had taken out a pair of jeeps. Conceivably, but not likely, even the third vehicle had been caught in the blast.

"You cut that a bit close, didn't you?" Teucer asked.

"I've cut them closer."

"Glad I wasn't along at the time," the bowman cracked.

"Traveling with Blade is always an educational experience," Rikki threw in. "Each time I return to the Home, I seem to have more bumps and bruises than the last trip."

"Then why do you volunteer to go on so many runs?" Teucer inquired.

"Bumps and bruises build character."

"Remind me to hear all about your philosophy of life sometime."

Blade leaned over the steering wheel, striving to detect any sign of life in the cloud of death and destruction. Nothing appeared, and just when he leaned back, almost convinced the rocket had blown up all three jeeps, the roar of an engine proved his assumption to be wrong. He tramped on the accelerator and backed up, striving to put as much distance between the SEAL and the cloud as he could, vexed at himself for not doing it sooner.

A jeep barreled into the open, its windshield cracked but otherwise unscathed. Leaning out the passenger side was a Spartan, an assault rifle resting on his right shoulder.

On his shoulder?

Blade looked again, and this time he recognized the contours of an Armbrust 700 anti-tank portable missile launcher. A tingle ran along his spine. If he remembered his Warrior training on ordnance and armaments, the Armbrust 700 could penetrate up to 12 inches of armor plating. Even the SEAL might not withstand such firepower.

The soldier was tracking the front of the van.

Instantly Blade swerved, attempting to throw the Spartan's aim off. If he recalled correctly, the primary blast radius for a 700 was 50 feet. If he could only get more than that distance from the jeep, the SEAL might not be damaged. All he needed was a few more seconds.

He didn't have them.

A heartbeat later the soldier fired.

CHAPTER TEN

Blade had only a split second to react, and his response was automatic. He already knew the SEAL hadn't covered enough ground to be safe from the missile. He already knew the transport would be caught in the blast radius. And he already knew evasive tactics would be unavailing at such short range. So instead of trying to evade the missile he committed an act of desperation. His right hand hit the switch to the machine guns.

In a staccato burst of the twin devastators a barrage of lead zinged toward the jeep. With so many rounds filling the air, and with the SEAL and the jeep facing each other when the 50-calibers opened fire, the inevitable occurred. The missile was hit in mid-flight, halfway between the two vehicles, and detonated with an explosion that rivaled the earlier one in intensity.

Again Blade withstood the harsh buffeting. During those precious seconds he had a chance to think, to recollect every fact he knew about the Armbrust 700. One fact, in particular, gave him a glimmer of hope. When the buffeting ceased, he was ready. Instead of continuing in reverse, he put the van into drive and put the pedal to the metal.

"All right!" Teucer exclaimed. "Let's waste these suckers!"

Blade's eyes were riveted on the jeep. He had to get within 20 feet of the enemy. If his memory was right, the strategy would win the day. If not, Jenny would soon be a widow.

The Spartan in the front passenger seat was visible through the bullet-riddled windshield, calmly yet quickly endeavoring to reload the missile launcher. To his left the driver was slumped over the wheel.

Blade realized some of the rounds must have struck the soldier doing the driving. He kept the accelerator all the way down, rapidly closing the range. "Get set," he told Teucer.

Nodding, the bowman rolled down his window and leaned out, the compound bow extended.

"Wait until I give the word," Blade admonished.

"Understood."

In the space of seconds the SEAL drew within 40 feet of the jeep. The soldier suddenly popped into view again, in the act of raising the launcher to his shoulder.

No! Not yet! Blade mentally counted off the yardage and recalled the critical information concerning the Armbrust 700. The state-of-the-art weapon had been developed just prior to World War Three and widely distributed to U.S. forces. Intended for use against enemy tanks, the 700 had been designed with a unique safety feature. To prevent an accidental detonation as the missile was being fired, which sometimes occurred with conventional launchers, the manufacturers of the 700 had incorporated a computerized chip, a smart chip as they were known, into the hollow-charge missile. The projectile actually armed itself after 20 feet of flight. Prior to that range and the 700 wouldn't explode.

But the SEAL wasn't close enough yet.

They needed a few more seconds.

"Shoot!" Blade ordered, knowing the angle wasn't

right, knowing the bowman couldn't possibly score, but banking on the reflex action of anyone who found an arrow headed toward them.

Teucer already had the string pulled back to just below his right ear. He sighted and released the shaft in the twinkling of an eye, then grabbed another one.

The Spartan ducked back the instant the arrow cleared the bow, his aim spoiled, and nearly lost his life then and there when the shaft struck the windshield a few inches to his left, punctured through the glass in a shower of shards and fragments, and thudded into the edge of the seat. He swung out again and swept the Armbrust 700 onto his shoulder.

Blade slammed on the brakes and turned the wheel briskly, slanting the SEAL, intending to pass the jeep on the passenger side.

The Spartan let the missile fly.

Blade saw the projectile leap toward the transport, and the next sequence of events transpired so swiftly they were over in an instant. The missile struck the SEAL's grill and bounced off without detonating, its smart chip thwarted because the two vehicles were only 15 feet apart.

Teucer loosed his second shaft simultaneously, and this time he had a clear shot.

A lightning streak of green sped from the bow into the soldier, the arrow penetrating his flesh at the base of the throat, the three-edged hunting tip tearing clean through his neck and bursting out of his body next to his spine. He clawed at the shaft, his lips curled in a snarl, then sagged onto the dashboard.

The SEAL narrowly missed the jeep. Blade drove around the smaller vehicle and brought the van to a stop. He looked in the mirror, gratified to see there wasn't a soul stirring, then faced forward and scrutinized the damage caused by the SEAL's rocket. Both of the first pair of jeeps had been obliterated. Now that the dust had settled, the smoldering wreckage and twisted frames lay like rotted carcasses in the middle of the road.

Teucer eased inside and rested his bow on his lap. "We cut that one close," he commented.

"At least we took care of their only vehicles," Blade said. "Dercyllidas's troops will have a fighting chance."

"Evidently you spoke too soon," Rikki spoke up.

"Why?"

The martial artist nodded to the north. "Get set for round two."

Blade shifted, surprised to behold a pair of motorcycles, large dirt bikes actually, roaring from the direction of the barracks where Agesilaus's bodyguard contingent lived. "No one said anything about them," he said, and gunned the engine, bearing to the east.

"Both the riders are holding objects in their right hands," Rikki announced. "Hand grenades, I believe."

"Teucer, try to nail one," Blade directed.

"Where's a cannon when you need it?" the bowman muttered.

The Spartan bikers raced onto the gravel road and took off in pursuit of the van, their red cloaks billowing, their helmets gleaming.

Teucer eased out the passenger window once more, twisting so he could watch the dirt bikes approach. He nocked another hunting arrow to the string, straightening his left arm, and hugged the transport's side, keeping his body flat in the hope the Spartans might not notice him until it was too late.

On they came, their tires kicking dirt into the air, the bikes growling as they shifted.

The bowman forced himself to relax, to stay loose. One of the first courses taken by every Warrior was entitled Elementary Combat Psychology, and the Elder responsible for teaching the material had continually emphasized the fundamental importance of remaining calm in a crisis. Adrenaline might add strength to panicked limbs, but the hormonal rush could also cloud the reasoning process and impair overall effectiveness. A calm state of mind, therefore, was critical to Warrior survival.

As the Elder had repeatedly emphasized, self-control and self-composure were the keys to becoming an exceptional fighter and a valued defender of the Home and the Family. Of the two traits, the Elders stressed self-control the most. Without it, self-composure was impossible to attain. "Know thyself" had been carried one step further. "Master thyself" became the basic precept for novice Warriors, and only those who achieved a supreme degree of self-mastery were placed on the active-duty roster.

Even then, the diversity among the Warriors surprised Teucer. The range of personalities ran the full spectrum. There was Blade, the devout Family man, a natural leader of men if ever there was one, whose steely body reflected the steely mind within. There was Rikki, a man who lived and breathed the martial arts, who spent every waking moment honing his skills, who dedicated his entire being to becoming the prefected swordmaster. There was Hickok, the Family's preeminent gunfighter, who had a reputation as a consummate killer, the man who faced trouble with a smile on his lips and a pair of blazing pearl-handled revolvers. And there was Yama, the Warrior who had taken his name from the Hindu King of death, the Warrior considered by his peers to be the best all-around fighting man at the Home, the Warrior who could do virtually everything exceptionally well and who had transformed his personal combat techniques into a fine art.

Then there's me, Teucer thought. The Warrior who is a poet at heart. The man who would rather spend an afternoon reading Byron than slaying scavengers. The man who had almost decided not to become a Warrior because he disliked the spilling of blood. Oh, sure, Teucer loved archery, and no one else could handle a bow with such skill and finesse. But his lifelong devotion to archery stemmed from his keen appreciation of the craft's aesthetic qualities; he shot a bow for the mere sake of shooting. To him, the flight of an arrow qualified as poetry in motion. And striking a target dead center was akin to a religious experience. Back when he'd been twelve years old he'd read *Zen in the Art of Archery* by Eugen Herrigel, and his life had never been the same.

On his sixteenth birthday, at his Naming, he'd selected the name of the famous Greek bowman who had fought so valiantly during the siege of Troy. He'd been tempted to pick the name of several other famous bowmen; Robin Hood, especially, had appealed to him. But since *The Iliad* had always been one of his favorite books, and since he'd always been fascinated by the exploits of the best bowman in the Achaean force, he'd finally settled on Teucer.

Now he was about to demonstrate once again the expertise that had earned him the respect of every other Warrior, the archery skill few men could ever hope to match. He saw one of the Spartans bearing down on the rear of the SEAL, evidently planning to race in close and toss a grenade, and he forced himself to stay still until the soldier came within 15 feet of the bumper. At the moment the Spartan pulled the pin and lifted the grenade overhead to toss it, Teucer leaned out, pulled the string on the 75-pound pull compound bow back to his ear, and loosed the shaft.

The green arrow was a blur as it flew straight and true, the hunting point boring into the Spartan's chest, the impact jerking him backwards. He lost his grip on the handlebars and toppled off the bike. At the very moment he struck the gravel the grenade detonated with a brilliant flash. By then the transport had traveled another 40 feet.

The whomp of the concussion blasted a gust of hot air and stinging dirt particles into Teucer's face, and he squinted and held on tight to the edge of the window.

One down, but where was the other rider?

Teucer knew the second Spartan could toss a grenade at any second. He also knew he couldn't finish the man off if the soldier stayed on the far side of the van. With the Commando and the AR-15, the Warriors had no way of nailing their foe. So there was only one thing to do. He slung the bow over his left arm, twisted, and reached overhead, straining his arms to the limit until his probing fingers touched the narrow, thin railing that ran around the entire roof. He gripped the rail, took a deep breath, and hauled himself out.

"What are you doing?" Blade called out.

As much as he would have liked to respond, Teucer had more pressing concerns. His legs dangled and banged against the SEAL's body, and his shoulders were focal points of sheer torment. He must reach the roof, and rapidly.

"Teucer?" Blade shouted.

The bowman grunted and pulled his body gradually higher. While he possessed a muscular build, he wasn't anywhere near as powerful as Blade. Nor, for that matter, could he match Rikki in strength. The martial artist might be small, but he was *all* muscle.

"Teucer!" Blade roared.

Unable to respond, gritting his teeth against the pain, fighting the wind and the bucking of the transport, the bowman inched high enough to put his feet on the bottom of the window. The added support elicited a sigh of relief, and for a few seconds he clung there, gathering his energy.

From the rear rose the roaring of the motorcycle.

Teucer resumed his climb, bracing his elbows on the top and using his arms for added leverage. In moments he succeeded in drawing his legs onto the roof, and he simply slid onto his stomach and rose to his knees. To his immediate left was one of the solar panels.

The noise of the dirt bike grew louder and louder.

Turning carefully, Teucer rose to a crouch and made his way to the back of the van. He kept low and risked a peek, unslinging the bow as he did.

Thirty feet away rode the second Spartan. From the grim set of his features, it was obvious he intended to ram the grenade right down the SEAL's exhaust pipe.

Teucer slid an arrow from his quiver and notched it. He counted to three, calming his nerves, then straightened and in a fluid motion whipped the bow up, pulled the string, and released.

The Spartan spotted the man in green at the last instant. He looked up and automatically tried to swerve to the right. The cycle had just started to turn when the arrow caught him in the mouth, the metal point drilling through his front teeth, through his tongue, and deep into his throat. He grabbed at the protruding shaft, lost all semblance of control, and went down in a crash with the bike.

Almost immediately the SEAL began to slow.

Teucer grasped the rail and waited until the van came to a halt before he hastily climbed down the metal rungs at the rear. He hastened around the corner and almost bumped into a peeved giant.

"Were you trying to get yourself killed?" Blade demanded.

"I needed the exercise."

"Don't you ever pull a stunt like that again without ample cause."

"Don't worry. I won't."

"Let's get out of here," Blade proposed. "We'll return to the barracks and consult with General Leonidas."

"Not yet we won't," stated a soft voice behind him.

Blade pivoted to find Rikki standing near the open door, the katana already out. "Why not?"

"See for yourself," Rikki replied, and nodded to the north.

Dreading the worst, Blade looked and discovered eight Spartans bearing down on them.

CHAPTER ELEVEN

"They're coming out of the woodwork!" Blade snapped, and drew both Bowies.

"At least these are on foot," Rikki noted.

All eight soldiers had their short swords drawn. None carried a firearm. They charged in ranks of twos, and one of the men voiced a challenge when they drew within 30 feet. "Who are you? What's the meaning of this?"

Blade stepped forward, hopeful further bloodshed could be avoided once he explained the situation. These eight must have been en route either to or from the barracks, and must have witnessed the battle with the troopers on the dirt bikes. Blade mustered a smile and motioned for them to halt.

The speaker held up his sword arm and the Spartans stopped. "I'm Sergeant Thoas. You will lay down your arms and place yourselves in our custody."

"We will not," Blade responded.

"Then we will take you by force," Thoas warned.

"At least hear me out. We were justified in killing those men."

"Since when is an outsider justified in slaying a Spartan?"

"Since the civil war started."

Sergeant Thoas cocked his head. "What are you talking about, stranger?"

"Then you haven't heard," Blade said. "King Agesilaus tried to kill King Dercyllidas a short while ago."

"What?" Thoas exclaimed, and glanced at the man next to him.

"I'm telling the truth," Blade asserted. "We were at the palace when the attack took place. Dercyllidas is now at the barracks where his bodyguard is housed. I have no idea where Agesilaus might be."

"And how do you fit into the scheme of things?"

"We're representatives of the Freedom Federation here to offer Sparta membership in our alliance. We've been caught in the middle of the dispute between your kings. We're just in the wrong place at the wrong time."

"You certainly are," Thoas concurred. "And will you remain neutral during the conflict?"

Blade pointed back at the last rider Teucer had slain. "Those were Agesilaus's men. Does that answer your question?"

"Yes, it does."

"Then you can see there's no reason for us to fight."

"Wrong," Sergeant Thoas stated.

"What?"

The noncom gestured at his companions. "We're Agesilaus's men also."

Teucer snorted. "When it rains, it pours."

"Please," Blade said. "We have no quarrel with you."

"Nor we with you."

"Then why go through with this? It makes no sense."

"It's clear you don't understand the Spartan way. We were personally picked by King Agesilaus to be part of his bodyguard. He bestowed a great honor on us. In return, we pledged our loyalty. We promised to defend him to our dying breath, to follow his orders implicitly no matter what they might be."

"But what if those orders are all wrong? What if you serve a madman?"

"It doesn't matter. We've given our word, and a Spartan *always* keeps his word."

Blade frowned. "It's not giving your word that's so important. It's *who* you give it to."

"Not for a Spartan."

"Why don't you just go your way and forget we ever bumped into each other?" Blade suggested. He'd already spilled enough Spartan blood for one day. In light of the rigid Spartan system, he tended to regard all their soldiers as mere pawns. They were superb warriors; of that there could be no doubt. But the Spartans had been conditioned to obey their superiors without question. Independent thoughts and actions were strictly forbidden. In the final analysis, the Spartan system bred perfect fighting machines.

One of those machines now shook his head a trifle wistfully. "I wish we could, but now that I know the situation I'm bound to my oath to slay you."

"Why not just report to your barracks? No one will ever know."

The sergeant tapped his chest with the hilt of his sword. "I'd know. And I couldn't live with the shame of knowing I'd failed my king and violated my vow."

Unexpectedly, Rikki-Tikki-Tavi took three strides and addressed the noncom. "I knew a Spartan once, a fine man who went by the name of Thayer. He told me that it wasn't his real name, that he'd lost the right to use his real name when he was banished from Sparta. Perhaps you knew him?"

"There have been a few soldiers who were banished in recent years," Thoas replied. "Most were men of distinction. Describe this man."

"He was a tall man, about six feet eight or nine."

"Ahhh," Thoas said. "Very few Spartans have been

that tall. You must be referring to Captain Sarpedon. He was an officer in the royal bodyguard, in King Agesilaus's contingent to be exact. One day a few Helots decided they were going to repay the king for the death of someone in their family. They gathered together about forty malcontents and tried to slay Agesilaus while he slept. Sarpedon was on duty at the time."

Rikki nodded. "The details of your story match with his."

"As I recall, Sapredon's son was also in the guard detail. When his son was killed, Sarpedon left his post at the king's door and ran to the boy's side."

"And for such a natural act, Sarpedon was banished from Spartan and his name removed from the plague of distinction that commemorates exceptional Spartans. He told me all about it."

"King Agesilaus banished him," Thoas disclosed. "Personally, I disagreed with the punishment, but there was nothing anyone could do. The judgments of the kings are final." He sighed. "King Agesilaus delights in banishing officers for the slightest of infractions."

"And this is the man you're willing to die for?" Blade inquired.

"I have no choice."

"Yes, you do," Rikki said.

Sergeant Thoas regarded the man in black quizzically. "Explain, please."

"I grew to know Captain Sarpedon very well before he died," Rikki said. "Thanks to him, I was granted certain insights into the Spartan character. I won't claim to comprehend the Spartan way completely, but I believe I know enough to make you a sound offer."

"What kind of offer?"

"You and I will fight, one on one. If I win, we'll be permitted to go our way without interference. Should you win, we'll let you take us into custody without resisting."

"We will?" Teucer interjected.

"This is a most unusual offer," replied Sergeant Thoas. "What makes you think I'll accept?"

"Because I know a Spartan never refuses a challenge and never tolerates an insult to his honor. So I challenge you, Thoas, here and now. And if you refuse, you will have shamed yourself in the eyes of all your men."

Blade took a step and placed his right hand on the martial artist's shoulder. "Now wait a minute. I haven't agreed to this."

Rikki looked over his shoulder. "Would you rather we take all of them on?"

"No," Blade admitted. He stared at the open SEAL door, estimating the odds of all three of them getting inside before the soldiers could reach them. The chances were slim. So either he agreed to his friend's proposal or they fought with all eight Spartans.

The noncom chuckled. "You present a most devious challenge, little one. You're pitting my personal honor against my duty to my king."

"This is a way for you to satisfy both," Rikki said.

"And I'm almost tempted to accept your challenge," Thoas responded. "But to a Spartan, duty must always come first." He turned to his fellows. "Slay them."

Without a moment's hesitation, the members of the patrol attacked.

His katana gleaming in the sunlight, Rikki moved forward to meet them. He held his sword in the middle position, the *chudan-no-kumae,* and braced for the onslaught of the two foremost Spartans, Sergeant Thoas and one other.

They never reached him.

An arrow whizzed past Rikki and struck the noncom in the throat, and a second shaft an instant later caught the other soldier in the center of the chest. Both men went down.

The next pair hardly missed a beat.

Rikki let them come at him, let them part and spring

at him from the right and the left, let them think they had the upper hand, the edge, as it were, of numbers and size, and then he showed them a different edge, the only one that mattered to a practitioner of *kenjutsu,* to a man who subscribed to the code of *bushido.*

Of all the Warriors, Rikki-Tikki-Tavi had always been the most devoted to the martial arts. His mild-mannered father, a former warrior who'd gone on to become a distinguished Elder, had been a black belt in karate. Naturally, his father had delighted in teaching the way of the warrior to him, and had encouraged his avid interest. By the time he turned six, Rikki could perform flawless kata. By the time he turned ten, he was regarded as the best martial artist in the history of the Family.

During his teens he worked diligently at increasing his knowledge and skills. Eventually, he qualified for Warrior status. One of the most memorable moments in his life came when the Elders decided to bestow the katana on him.

Out of the hundreds of hundreds of weapons in the vast Family armory, all of which had been personally stockpiled by the Founder prior to the war, there had only been the one genuine katana. There were firearms galore, as well as various miscellaneous weapons, racks upon racks of them: rifles, shotguns, revolvers, pistols, submachine guns, bows, spears, knives, and many, many more. None of them had interested Rikki.

He'd always wanted the katana.

Forged in Japan hundreds of years ago by a master craftsman, the sword had been initially owned by a famous samurai. Thereafter, from generation to generation, the sword had passed from father to son until, in the modern era, one of the samurai's materialistic descendents had sold it at an auction to a private collector. Years later, while making a film in Japan, Kurt Carpenter had bought the sword.

In ancient times, a katana had been considered an

extension of the heart and soul of its samurai wielder. After the collapse of Japan's feudal system, when the code of *bushido* had become discredited by those in positions of authority who were trying to force the Japanese people to adopt modern ideals and a "better" way of life, the samurai had supposedly died out. Although they were officially suppressed, many samurai had simply gone underground, and until World War Three there had been secret samurai societies in existence, practicing the honored precepts of their illustrious ancestors.

Although the samurai supposedly had ceased to exist, their cherished sword had not. The level of craftsmanship had ensured the katanas would last for countless decades. Made of high-carbon steel, each blade had taken months to be constructed. The skilled smiths had applied layer after layer of carefully forged metal until the weapons they produced could cut through heavy armor. Such a sword rarely broke, rarely even became nicked, and retained its razor-sharpness indefinitely.

Rikki-Tikki-Tavi felt supremely honored to possess his katana. As a man who believed in the code of conduct of the samurai, the way of bushido, he exalted ideals largely abandoned by the descendants of the original proponents. As a Warrior, he lived the way of the warrior.

Now, as the pair of Spartans came at him, their short swords arcing at his body, Rikki demonstrated the peerless swordsmanship that had earned him the right to carry the katana. He moved and shifted with deceptive ease and economy of movement, parrying a swipe by the trooper on his left that would have taken off his leg, then pivoting to counter a swing at his neck.

Even as he countered the neck stroke, Rikki took the offensive. He slid the katana off the short sword and executed a hidari-men, an oblique slash at the Spartan's left temple. The katana's edge bit into the man's bronze helmet, and the softer metal parted as readily as butter. Rikki drove the blade several inches into the head, then pulled it out and spun, reversing his grip on the hilt, and spearing the tip under his left arm straight into the chest of the first soldier, who was about to aim a blow at the nape of his neck. Still in motion, Rikki yanked the katana free and skipped backwards, ready to continue if necessary.

It wasn't.

Both Spartans crumpled.

The remaining four were trying to overwhelm Blade.

Rikki went to the giant's aid, wondering in the back of his mind where the bowman might be, and called out to attract attention. "Try me!"

Two of the soldiers whirled and instantly came at him. Like all of the Spartans, their swordsmanship was superb. Had they been confronting a typical foe, they would surely have prevailed.

But the martial artist wasn't typical.

Eager to end the fray, Rikki terminated the shorter of his foes with a throat cut. He turned to confront the other man, and at that moment the unforeseen occurred. His left foot slipped on a patch of blood, throwing him off balance, exposing his chest and head. He saw it coming.

The second Spartan's sword whistled through the air at his face.

CHAPTER TWELVE

Blade had downed one of his adversaries, and was blocking a terrific blow aimed at his abdomen, when he glimpsed Rikki's predicament out of the corner of his right eye. He leaped backwards and whipped his right arm overhead, about to throw the knife, but he was already too late.

An arrow caught the Spartan about to slay Rikki squarely in the center of the back, and the soldier arched his spine and stiffened, his arms flinging outward. Before he could hope to recover, to continue fighting, another arrow struck him within an inch of the first. He turned slowly, his mouth set in a defiant snarl, and fell.

The distraction almost cost Blade his own life. His opponent tried to take his legs off at the knees, and he barely deflected the short sword in time. The blades clanged loudly and continued to clang as Blade parried more strikes. The greater reach of the short sword compelled him to retreat as he fought, and in just a few long strides he bumped into the SEAL.

The Spartan drove his weapon at the giant's stomach.

Blade countered with his right knife, then sliced his left Bowie across the soldier's extended wrist, severing tendons and muscles and drawing a spurt of blood.

Grimacing, the Spartan backpedaled.

The Warrior wasn't about to close again. Why risk impalement when he finally had the opening he needed? His arms a blur, he raised both hands above his head and surged them down again, releasing both hilts at the proper moment.

The twin knives covered the intervening space in a millisecond, and both sank into the soldier with distinct thuds. His face contorted in agony, the Spartan made one last effort to stab the giant, but collapsed in mid-stride.

Rikki-Tikki-Tavi was standing over the soldier who'd taken the arrows in the back, his features reflecting sadness.

"Are you okay?" Blade asked, moving to his fallen foe and wrenching the Bowies out. He proceeded to wipe them on the trooper's cloak.

"This man was brave," Rikki said. "All Spartans are brave. It's not fitting for such courageous fighters to be shot in the back."

"It was him or you," Teucer declared. He stood next to the open door. "I didn't have time to ask him to turn around."

"I know," Rikki responded, and frowned. "You did what you had to do."

Blade rose and slipped the Bowies into their sheaths, then regarded the dead Spartans for a moment. "I take no joy in killing them," he commented.

"Is there ever joy in slaying others?" Rikki inquired.

"Sometimes."

"Oh?"

"When I killed a drug dealer in Miami, I felt a certain joy. There have been other instances, and I'm not about to list them all now. But I've learned we can't always remain detached from our work. Sometimes the act of exterminating evil can be personally gratifying," Blade observed.

"But these Spartans weren't evil. They were simply

misguided," Rikki stated.

"More's the pity," Blade agreed, and walked over to the bowman. "How did you get over here? The last I saw, you were next to the rear bumper."

"A bow isn't much use at infighting. I needed to put a little distance between those short swords and me, so I scooted to the front as they charged," Teucer detailed and grinned. "Besides, someone had to prevent them from getting inside after someone else conveniently left the door wide open."

"You did well. This might be your first official mission away from the Home, but you're performing as well as any of the more experienced Warriors," Blade said.

"Thanks."

Blade gazed to the north and saw several citizens near an ornate building. They were staring at him in transparent hostility. "Let's get going before more soldiers show up."

"You don't need to tell me twice," Teucer said, and climbed inside.

"Perhaps we should simply leave Sparta," Rikki suggested, moving toward the front of the transport. "After all, do we really have the right to interfere in their internal affairs? Wouldn't the wise course be to stay neutral and let them decide the outcome?"

"And what if Agesilaus wins? We lose any chance of Sparta joining the Federation."

"I know," Rikki said, and paused. "We're caught between a rock and a hard place, as the saying goes."

Blade studied his friend. "You admire them a lot, don't you?"

"Yes," Rikki confessed.

"So do I. And because I respect them, I'm not about to run off and leave them at the mercy of Agesilaus. They deserve better than to be ruled by a petty dictator," Blade said.

Rikki simply nodded and hurried to the far side of the van.

So now what? Blade asked himself as he took his seat.

He intended to offer his services to General Leonidas. Would the Spartan accept? If so, defeating Agesilaus would be easy. The SEAL's firepower could devastate the madman's bodyguard contingent. He doubted, though, whether Leonidas would agree to such a proposal. If the general was anything like Captain Chilon, he would insist on conducting the battle the traditional way, using swords and spears instead of guns and other armaments.

"Look," Teucer declared, and leaned forward to point to the east.

Blade looked up.

Not 60 yards away was a lone Spartan, a lean man naked except for a red loincloth. He was running at breakneck speed along the grass bordering the road, heading in their direction.

"What's his big rush?" Teucer wondered.

"Who knows?" Blade replied absently. He started the engine and performed a tight U-turn.

"Let's hope King Dercyllidas is still alive," Rikki remarked.

The reminder prompted Blade to floor the accelerator. They rode in silence until they came within sight of the two barracks, and then it was the bowman who shattered their individual reflections.

"Dear Spirit! Will you look at that!"

Facing each other across the road, approximately 50 paces separating them, were the respective royal bodyguard units, each arrayed in phalanx formation.

Blade slammed on the brakes.

"They're getting set to go at it," Teucer said. "We could mow down Agesilaus's men before they knew what hit them." He didn't sound too enthused by the idea.

Scrutinizing both contingents, Blade saw that neither displayed any movement. They were just standing there, either waiting for orders or for the other side to make the first move.

"We mustn't be hasty," Rikki advised.

"Keep your eyes peeled," Blade stated, and picked up speed, glancing from unit to unit. None of the Spartans bore firearms. Each soldier carried a long, glittering spear and something new, a large circular shield that covered each man from mid-thigh to the shoulder. On the front of every shield was depicted a strange symbol that vaguely resembled the capital letter A, but lacking the center line.

Neither formation broke ranks as the transport drove between them. The Spartans might as well have been statues.

Blade took a left at the side street and drove to the barracks of Dercyllidas's contingent, stopping near the north doors. No sooner had he turned the ignition off and left the SEAL than two Spartans emerged.

General Leonidas and Captain Chilon walked side by side, both with grave expressions. Each, perhaps unconsciously, had a hand on the hilt of his sword.

"We saw part of your fight," Chilon said. "Did you destroy the two motorcycles?"

"Agesilaus won't be using them against you," Blade replied as Rikki and Teucer joined them.

"How is King Dercyllidas?" the martial artist inquired.

"Stable," General Leonidas disclosed. "The doctor is with him now. Our liege was fortunate. The dagger came close to puncturing a lung, but he'll live."

"Your physician got here quickly," Rikki commented.

General Leonidas pointed at a cluster of buildings to the east of the training field. "He lives in one of those. Each king selects a doctor who agrees to serve as the offical Aesculapian for the bodyguard and is housed at government expense nearby. We sent a runner for him the minute you departed." His gaze strayed to the gravel road. "And here comes another runner now, only he's not heading here."

Blade shifted and spotted the same lean man in the red loincloth he'd seen earlier approaching from the east. "How do you know?"

"All runners wear a red loincloth. And since he's on the opposite side of the road, he's undoubtedly delivering a message to General Calchas, the commander of Agesilaus's contingent."

"You should stop him," Blade suggested.

"Whatever for?"

"He could be bearing an order for Calchas to attack."

Leonidas shrugged. "So be it. The sooner the battle is over, the sooner all Spartans can breathe easier. I would rather engage Calchas now while my men are prepared."

"Is that why your troops are in formation near the road?"

"Yes. Both sides are awaiting the command to attack. King Dercyllidas is unconscious and not to be disturbed until morning or we would have done so by now."

"Why can't you lead your men?" Blade asked.

"I will when the king instructs us to wipe out Agesilaus's forces."

"And in the meantime you stand around and do nothing? Haven't you heard that the best defense is always a good offense?"

"I believe in the same strategy, but my hands are tied. Unless attacked, I must await Dercyllidas's directions."

Blade opened his mouth to tell the Spartan he was being foolish, then changed his mind. Antagonizing the man would be counterproductive. Instead, he decided to make his offer. "We could rout Agesilaus's men for you."

General Leonidas glanced at the giant. "Using your vehicle, I assume?"

"Yes."

"No."

"Why not?"

"Need you ask? Spartans have a code of honor, and I won't violate that code under any circumstances."

"Not even if doing so would save the lives of your own men?"

"A Spartan has no fear of dying. To be slain in combat

is the ultimate honor, and those who perish on the field of battle have their names duly enshrined on the plaque of distinction to commemorate their bravery and loyalty for all eternity," Leonidas said.

"I wish you would reconsider."

"Never. And I formally request, man to man, that you don't interfere once the battle is joined."

"And if your side is defeated?"

"Then such is the will of the Creator. But don't count us out yet. My troops are every bit as skilled as those under General Calchas."

Blade frowned and placed his hands on his hips, annoyed at the senior officer's obstinate attitude. While he found much to admire in the Spartan character, their stubborn persistance in adhering to tradition at all costs was extremely aggravating.

"Don't look so upset," Leonidas said. "Surely a fighting man such as yourself can appreciate our military philosophy."

"Yes and no."

"Where do we fall short?"

"You won't take advantage of all the forces at your disposal. As a result, if Agesilaus triumphs, Sparta will be thrown back into the equivalent of the Dark Ages. The leaders of the Federation will be severely disappointed."

"Ah, yes. The Federation. Captain Chilon has been telling me about it. I think the idea has merit, and I'll push for Sparta to join once this conflict has been resolved."

"Excuse me," Teucer interjected. "I'd like to ask a question."

"Go ahead," General Leonidas said.

"I couldn't help but notice all those archers on the dais at the Royal Palace, and as a bowman I'm naturally interested in such things," Teucer mentioned. "Why were there archers guarding the kings? Why not soldiers armed with machine guns?"

"Years ago there were men posted in the audience room

who were armed with automatic weapons. Then one day three Helots tried to assassinate one of the kings. The guards opened fire, and in the act of slaying the Helots they accidentally hit a half-dozen bystanders. A machine gun is impossible to control in a crowd. No matter how good a marksman a man might be, he can't prevent stray rounds from striking those who are standing near the target," Leonidas said. "After that regrettable incident, the decision was made to employ archers on the dais. There are also riflemen concealed behind the walls."

"There's something I'd like to know," Blade said. "Who started Sparta?" He hoped to elicit more information about its origin.

"There were seven men, all college professors, who worked at the same prestigious university back East before World War Three. When all hell broke loose, they gathered their families and fled. Eventually they met up with the remnants of a National Guard unit and they all decided to hide out in this secluded area," General Leonidas related. "After the U.S. government collapsed, there were hordes of looters and killers roaming the land. The only safe place for the professors and the Guardsmen was right here, so they resolved to start over, to build new lives for themselves."

"But why did they select a system of government similar to ancient Sparta?" Blade asked.

"One of the professors, a history teacher, suggested the idea. They realized only the strong would survive in the postwar era, and there were few people as strong as the Spartans. They held meeting after meeting, and finally agreed to start their own town and to form their own government. Using the Spartan constitution as a model, the professors created a book of laws for all their followers. Inevitably, I suppose, the seven became known as the Lawgivers."

"And the town has continued to grow over the past century."

"We no longer refer to Sparta as a mere town. It's a city-state in every sense of the word."

"What about the Helots? Where did they come from?"

"There were many farmers in the outlying territory, and most of them balked at turning over part of their crops to the invaders, as they regarded the Spartans. So they were subjugated and forced to turn over a portion of their yields whether they liked it or not. In due course they became an entirely separate class, just like the Helots of old."

"And you approve of such a system?"

"Why not? It works out for the best for everyone. The Helots feed us and we protect them. What more could they want?"

"Their freedom."

"The Helots are as free as they need to be."

Just as Blade was about to respond, a harsh musical blast sounding very much like a trumpet shattered the stalemate. "What was that?"

"The signal!" Leonidas exclaimed, running toward his troops. "Agesilaus's men are going to attack!"

CHAPTER THIRTEEN

"What do we do?" Teucer asked.

"Technically, this isn't our battle. We've been told in no uncertain terms not to use the SEAL. And since they're fighting in formation, there's no place for us," Blade said.

"I'd still like to view the clash," Rikki remarked.

"So would I," Blade stated. "This is a once-in-a-lifetime opportunity."

"Where the two of you go, I go," Teucer declared. "Count me in."

Blade grinned at both of them. "Okay. We're all agreed. Back in the SEAL." He clambered into his seat, waited for them to get in, then started the engine, backed up, and drove along the side street to the junction with the gravel road.

Neither contingent had moved. General Leonidas stepped around to the front of his men, a sword in his right hand, a shield in his left. Across the way a similar figure stood at the head of Agesilaus's troops.

"That must be General Calchas," Blade deduced, and killed the engine once more.

"He waited for Leonidas to arrive," Rikki said in a respectful tone. "He could have attacked sooner if he wanted."

The bowman leaned between the buckets seats and braced his hands on the console. "I've never known men like these Spartans."

"And you never will again," Rikki responded.

Both generals now addressed their contingents.

"Roll down your window," Blade suggested to the martial artist. "Let's hear what they have to say."

Nodding, Rikki complied, and the deep, booming voice of General Leonidas clearly reached their ears.

"—what happened to King Dercyllidas. I need not remind each of you about your oath to him. All of you have taken a solemn vow to defend him with your lives, and now is the time to prove the worth of your word. Stand shoulder to shoulder and fight bravely as Spartans should. And remember that you fight not for yourselves, but for the common good of Sparta and all her people, for your families, friends, and even those you don't know." The general paused.

"The man has a way with words," Teucer observed.

Leonidas continued. "We face the prospect of death today, but what is death to a Spartan? Death is simply the way we get from this life to the next. And should you fall, you know that you'll be honored as a valiant soldier. Your name will be engraved on the plaque of distinction in the palace for all to see. Your wives and children will receive the praise and gratitude of the whole city. And the marker on your grave will bear not only your name, rank, and age, but will include a list of your accomplishments and mention you fell heroically. Only soldiers slain in combat receive the special markers. Think of the glory you'll have won!"

"Big deal," Teucer said. "I don't see what difference a fancy headstone makes."

"Shhh," Rikki said.

General Leonidas raised his sword on high. "Above all, you are Spartans. Above all, you value duty and discipline. Get ready for both to be put to the supreme test. Remember the instructions you were given the day you received your shield." He touched his sword to his own shield and declared, "With this or on it. Either return from battle victorious with your shield or dead on it. That is the simple creed by which we live, the creed that sums up our existence. Let's show Agesilaus's men the courage in our hearts. Let's carry our swords to victory and not stop until the enemy has been routed."

"Say, what happened to Captain Chilon?" Teucer absently queried.

"Maybe Leonidas let him join the formation," Blade speculated.

Further conversation was cut short when the two generals assumed their positions in the first rows of the soldiers, each in the very center. The two officers lifted their swords overhead, then swept the blade down, and at the signal both formations moved forward.

"I wish we could aid Leonidas," Rikki said wistfully.

Blade simply nodded, his gaze riveted on the Spartans. The phalanxes presented veritable walls of shields and long spears on three sides. He imagined how he would feel if he faced such a line himself, and shook his head in amazement. Only a truly courageous soul could perform such a feat. He'd rather take his enemies on one by one instead of in a packed mass where the element of chance figured so prominently in deciding the victor.

The phalanxes neared the gravel road slowly, every Spartan moving at a set pace, every man holding position, the glittering tips of the spears held perfectly steady. Red boots marched in precision order.

"Why do they wear all red?" Teucer asked no one in particular.

"I read that the ancient Spartans wore red cloaks so those they fought wouldn't know if they were hurt. They didn't want their enemies to see them bleed," Blade answered.

SPARTAN RUN

"A lot of them are about to do just that," the bowman said.

As the twin phalanxes drew closer to the road they moved faster, yet still retained their formations. Soon they broke into a headlong charge, running in rhythm, their horsehair crests bobbing.

Blade scarcely breathed as the two sides converged. The clash, when it came, resounded to the heavens, a tremendous crash of metal against metal, and a mighty shout added to the din. Spears flashed in the warm air. Neither side gave way, and the battle became a grim, intense struggle for survival.

The leading ranks of both phalanxes were on the gravel road, and their strenuous exertions raised choking dust that gave the air a powdery aspect.

Blade had yet to see a Spartan fall, and he marveled at their prowess and stamina. More than ever he wanted to persuade them to join the Federation. They would be invaluable in times of war and their military counsel would be priceless.

The fighting devolved into a mad melee of thrusting spears, slashing swords, and countering shields. Soldiers finally fell on both sides, and whenever a man in the first rank went down, another moved forward to take his place. At such close quarters all the spears of those in the front were soon shattered or rendered useless by the press of combat, compelling the Spartans at the forefront to rely exclusively on their swords.

Locked in savage conflict, neither phalanx made any headway. The men fought toe to toe, shoulder to shoulder. Those Spartans who were slain died without uttering a cry. Except for the banging of sword on sword and sword on shield, the battle was conducted in an eerie silence. None of the combatants yelled or cursed, as so often happened in mass engagements. Their discipline was superb.

"Just think," Teucer remarked. "One machine gun

would turn the tide."

"The man who used one would be ostracized if he lived," Rikki noted. "Not one of them would violate their code of honor." He paused. "In a way, their code of honor is a lot like ours, only stricter. Perhaps even better."

"If you like them so much, maybe you should become a Spartan," Teucer joked.

"No thanks."

"Why not? I thought you were big on codes of honor."

"I am," Rikki admitted. "On bushido. But the real reason I won't become a Spartan is because I'd have to give up my katana." He looked at the bowman. "And the only way anyone will take my sword from me will be to pry it from my cold, stiff fingers."

Teucer frowned. "You're becoming morbid in your young age, my friend."

Blade listened to their conversation with only half an ear. He was absorbed in the battle, noting the ebb and flow, amazed at the swordsmanship displayed on both sides. A crick developed in his neck, and to relieve it he places his hand on the nape, squeezed, and turned his head to the right. His gaze happened to sweep the field in the general direction of the barracks, and he was puzzled to observe ten Spartans approaching the building from the southeast. "Where did they come from?" he wondered aloud.

Rikki and Teucer both looked.

"They must be Dercyllidas's men," the bowman commented.

The ten were running toward the barracks with their swords drawn, their cloaks billowing behind them. They did not have shields.

"If they're Dercyllidas's men, why are they heading for the barracks instead of the battle?" Rikki questioned.

"Who knows?" Teucer responded. "Maybe they're going to protect Dercyllidas."

"What if they're not?"

"What are you getting at?"

"Could they be some of Agesilaus's soldiers?"

Blade had been thinking the same thing himself. He wouldn't put it past the madman to try and finish the job. If Dercyllidas was assassinated, Agesilaus would win. And what better time to send in an assassination squad than while most of the bodyguard contingent was embroiled in the battle? It would have been easy to send a squad around the long way and have them sneak into the barracks at the proper moment. Acting on a hunch, he started the SEAL and performed a tight U-turn.

"Where are we going?" Teucer asked.

"Three guesses," Blade replied, watching the squad. They were almost to the building. He raced to the south, driving onto the field and angling straight toward them. If he was wrong, no harm done. But if he was right, he must save King Dercyllidas at all costs.

Four soldiers suddenly emerged from the barracks. Without hesitation, as if they'd seen the squad approach through the windows, they drew their swords and formed a line facing the newcomers, blocking the entrance.

Blade had the answer he needed. He pushed the speedometer over 50.

The squad never slowed. At a word from one of the soldiers in the lead, they fanned out and bore down on the quartet. In moments they engaged, and although the four men fought bravely and downed two of the squad, the fight was hopelessly one-sided. All four defenders perished.

"We're too far away," Rikki said anxiously.

The SEAL was 40 feet from the building. Barring a miracle, Blade couldn't prevent the squad from entering and slaying Dercyllidas. He needed a distraction, and he did the first thing that came into his mind. His right palm pressed on the horn.

At the unexpected blaring to their rear, the eight

Spartans spun. The leader barked orders, and four of the men ran toward the van while the rest went into the barracks.

Blade brought the van to a slewing stop. "Stay with the SEAL," he instructed Teucer, then vaulted to the grass, drawing his Bowies as he landed. He ran to meet the four assassins.

Out on the road the battle attained a furious metallic crescendo, the dust becoming thicker by the moment.

The four members of the squad halted, hefting their weapons, and regarded the giant coldly.

"This doesn't concern you, stranger!" one of them barked. "Leave immediately."

Slowing, Blade studied each of them, then focused on the speaker. "I'm going inside."

"Care to bet?"

Before Blade could reply, a black-clad whirlwind hurtled past him.

Rikki-Tikki-Tavi's katana was a blur as he tore into the Spartan on the right, and his graceful movements belied his lethal intent. The Spartan executed a single thrust, then staggered when his neck was nearly severed, blood pumping from his throat. Rikki slipped around his foe while the man was still swaying and dashed inside.

"Get him!" cried one of the soldiers.

Blade leaped forward to prevent them from chasing Rikki, forcing them to deal with him first, his Bowies flashing. He took on the soldier in the middle, wielding his knives ambidextrously, his initial swings deftly blocked.

The remaining pair came to the aid of their comrade.

Three against one were uncomfortable odds. Blade opted to reduce them immediately by faking an overhand swing with his right arm, then following through with an underhand left thrust when the Spartan lifted his sword in a reflex action. The thrust took the soldier in the chest and the man stiffened and let go of his short sword. Blade yanked the Bowie free and moved to the right, his back to the transport, both knives extended.

Only steps away, the last two abruptly halted, wary now. Each glanced at his fallen buddies and gripped his sword a bit tighter.

"There's no need for this," Blade told them. "Surrender your weapons and you can live."

"A Spartan never surrenders," responded the thinner of the pair, and they both pounced.

Blade backpedaled to gain a few precious seconds. From behind him there was a familiar swishing noise, and an arrow struck the thin Spartan in the right eye, jerking the trooper's head around. He dropped where he stood.

The last soldier was game to the last. He leaped at the giant and swung his sword furiously, seeking to batter the big knives aside and revenge his companions.

Hard-pressed to parry the flurry, Blade resorted to an ingenious ploy. At the very instant the Spartan's sword hit his left Bowie, he deliberately released the knife. For a fraction of a second, as the Bowie arced to the grass, the soldier's eyes were on the knife, and at the moment of distraction Blade dropped to his right knee and sank his other knife into the Spartan's stomach.

Unwilling to admit defeat even with a Bowie sticking in him, the soldier delivered a swipe at the giant's head.

Blade caught the man's wrist in his left hand, pulled the Bowie out and reversed his grip, then smashed the hilt into the Spartan's jaw.

Four up, four down.

And now to check on Rikki. Blade took several strides, when a sharp shout drew him up short.

"Blade! Look!"

Whirling, Blade saw Teucer standing next to the SEAL and pointing toward the road. He glanced at the site of the battle and couldn't believe his eyes.

King Agesilaus's men were winning!

General Leonidas's phalanx had buckled in the center

and their foes had breached the outer ranks, forcing a wedge deep into the heart of the formation. Dercyllidas's bodyguards were resisting gallantly, but the break in their lines created gaps in their defensive wall of shields, gaps the enemy poured into, causing even more casualties in the process.

Blade hesitated, torn between wanting to go help Rikki and the necessity of determining the outcome of the battle. If Leonidas and his men were routed, Agesilaus's contingent would undoubtedly pursue them to the barracks. The SEAL could fall into enemy hands. General Calchas might decide to destroy the van using grenades or dynamite. Blade couldn't allow that to happen. The SEAL was essential to the safety and future of the Family.

A mighty shout of triumph from the throats of Agesilaus's men signified the worst had occurred.

With their ranks in complete disarray, General Leonidas's troops broke and raced in retreat toward the Warriors and the transport.

CHAPTER FOURTEEN

Blade was forced to make a snap decision. Would it be Rikki or the SEAL? As if there was much choice. As the top Warrior, he had to constantly regard the Family's welfare as his paramount responsibility. And since every Warrior was expendable, but the SEAL wasn't, he had but one option.

Damn.

"Get in the van!" Blade instructed the bowman, then stepped to the doorway and shouted into the barracks. "Rikki! Can you hear me?"

There was no response.

"Leonidas has lost! We've got to leave!"

Still no reply.

Frustrated, Blade cupped his hands to his mouth. "We'll be back! Count on it!" He scowled, and quickly reclaimed his other knife, then wiped both on his pants.

The retreating contingent was still 40 yards distant.

Casting a last glance at the barracks, Blade ran to the transport and took his seat. He slammed and locked the door, then gunned the engine and drove to the side street.

Teucer sat in the front passenger seat, his countenance glum. "I don't like leaving Rikki behind."

"Do you think I do?" Blade snapped.

"No, of course not. But what do we do now?"

"We keep the SEAL from falling into General Calchas's hands and figure out a way to reach Rikki."

"Why don't we just mow Calchas and his men down?"

"You made the same suggestion before. Since when did you become so bloodthirsty?"

"I'm not, ordinarily. But we shouldn't hold back any longer, not with Rikki's life on the line."

"General Leonidas requested that we not intervene. So we won't." Blade braked and stared at the Spartans sweeping across the field.

Despite being routed, Leonidas's men were fighting as they retreated, covering their flanks and inflicting heavy losses on their overeager adversaries. Calchas's men had broken their own phalanx to give chase, a mistake that was costing them dearly. Bodies littered the road and the grass, dozens of them, lying in pools of blood.

"We couldn't help Leonidas now even if I wanted to," Blade mentioned bitterly.

"Why not?"

"How would we know which Spartans are on our side?"

The bowman gazed at the conflict, his forehead furrowed. "Beats me. I never thought to ask. They all look alike in those helmets and red cloaks, but there must be a way to tell them apart."

King Dercyllidas's contingent reached the building and poured inside, fighting a rearguard action all the while.

Blade expected General Calchas to order an all-out assault on the building, to crush the opposition while his forces enjoyed the initiative, but to his surprise Calchas's troops began to pull back.

Teucer was equally perplexed. "What in the world is going on?"

"I don't know," Blade admitted. "But we shouldn't look a gift horse in the mouth. Rikki is somewhere in the

SPARTAN RUN 127

barracks, and as long as Calchas doesn't try to overrun the Spartans inside, he should be safe."

"You hope."

The last of Dercyllidas's troops retreated inside and the wide doors were slammed shut.

Outside, a stocky Spartan was organizing the victorious contingent into proper order, commanding them to fall in, his crimson coated sword waving in the air.

"That must be General Calchas," Teucer guessed.

"What's he up to now?" Blade wondered.

In pratically no time at all General Calchas had his men formed into ranks and issued further instructions. A third of his men were deployed to the right, a third to the left, and they hastened in practiced order to do his bidding, aligning themselves in a row from north to south and linking up at the rear of the building, completely surrounding the structure.

"No one will be able to get in or out," Teucer said bitterly. "Rikki is trapped in there."

"We'll find a way to rescue him."

"We'd better," Teucer replied, and smacked the dashboard in anger. "First we're captured, then we have to contend with a psycho, and now this. Nothing has gone right since we got here."

"Which is par for the course," Blade said. "Try and look at the bright side."

"What bright side?"

"For whatever reason, Agesilaus's men seem to be ignoring us."

The bowman nodded at the Spartans. "Looks as if you spoke too soon."

Blade looked and saw a dozen soldiers racing toward the SEAL. None, as far as he could tell, carried grenades or other explosives, but he drove toward the gravel road anyway, easily outdistancing them, and stopped at the junction.

"What's the plan?" Teucer inquired.

"I wish I had one. We've been playing it by ear so far, letting the madman and his bodyguard make all the moves. I think it's about time we turned the tables."

"How?"

"We carry the fight to Agesilaus," Blade proposed, staring at the barracks. "Rikki should be safe for the time being, a few hours at the least, which is more than enough for us to locate Agesilaus and kill him."

"We're going to drive off and leave Rikki?"

"Can't be helped. Agesilaus is the key to the conflict. Without him, his bodyguards aren't obligated by their oath of loyalty. His death will bring peace."

"And how do you propose we take care of him? He's not going to let us anywhere near his royal person," Teucer said, emphasizing the last two words sarcastically.

"There has to be a way," Blade stated. He cast an anxious glance at the barracks and the ring of soldiers encircling it, then took a right and headed toward the center of the city. If his scheme succeeded, scores of lives would be saved and Sparta's admittance to the Freedom Federation was virtually assured. If he failed, not only would the Federation lose a potential ally, he'd likely lose one of his best friends.

There were few pedestrians in sight. The smoldering jeeps and the smashed motorcycles were still where they had been destroyed, and the eight dead members of the Spartan patrol still lay where they had fallen.

"Odd that no one has removed those bodies," Teucer mentioned as they drove past.

"My guess would be that most everyone has taken shelter indoors for the time being. The average person wouldn't want to be abroad in the midst of a civil war. Even the regular army troops and the secret police are staying out of the way."

"Just so they stay out of our way."

The farther they traveled, the fewer people there were. By the time they came to the center of Sparta, the city resembled a ghost town.

"This is spooky," the bowman said.

Blade nodded in agreement and focused on the Royal Palace. Not a single guard was in evidence. Even the public square was deserted. He stopped just outside it and scanned in all directions.

"If King Agesilaus is in the palace, why aren't there any guards?" Teucer queried.

"They could be inside." Blade drove the transport to the base of the steps, parked, and palmed the keys.

"I still don't see anyone."

"There must be someone home," Blade said, glancing at the spot where they had fought the guards. "All the bodies are gone." He cautiously opened his door.

"Am I going with you this time?"

"No."

"Are you sure it's wise?"

"No, but we can't risk both of us being captured or worse. You stay with the SEAL until I get back. If I'm not back in half an hour, take the SEAL and go bail Rikki out of the jam he's in."

"All by my lonesome?"

Blade's expression hardened. "If I don't make it back, then all agreements are off. Use the full firepower of the van if you have to, but save Rikki."

The bowman nodded. "All right. But you know I've only had a few driving lessons. I'm liable to wreck the SEAL."

Smiling, Blade handed over the keys. "Take care."

"May the Spirit be with you."

Slipping out, Blade depressed the lock and closed the door. He crouched alongside the front fender, scrutinizing the colonnades, then dashed up to the huge door. Suspicion flared when he found the door slightly ajar. His every instinct told him to turn around and get out of there, but he disregarded the feeling and pushed. Ever so slowly, and without making the slightest sound, the door swung inward.

Blade tentatively stepped into the great hall. Once again there were no Spartans. Had the entire palace been evacuated? He moved toward the audience chamber. He went by several closed doors and eventually came to an open one. A sideways look riveted him in place.

Lying in two rows within the room, their red cloaks used to cover their bodies, were the Spartans who had been slain during the fight outside. What about their weapons? He entered and lifted the cloak of the first corpse to discover an empty scabbard hanging from the man's belt.

Too bad.

He could use a submachine gun, preferably his Commando.

Blade let the cloak fall and turned to leave, his eyes straying to the left wall, to the rack in the corner, and he smiled.

Bingo!

The rack contained M-16's, UZIs, and assorted other automatics. He went over and inspected the collection, and was disappointed to find the Commando and Rikki's AR-15 weren't among them. Selecting an M-16, he checked the magazine, which turned out to be empty, then noticed a drawer under the rack. A quick tug exposed enough ammunition to start a war, and he picked up a box of 5.56-mm bullets. Working swiftly, he inserted 20 into the magazine, cocked the rifle, put the selector on safe, and slid the magazine back into the feedway until he heard a distinct click.

Voices suddenly sounded outside.

Blade quickly pulled the charging handle all the way to the back and released it, then flicked the selector to semi. He moved to the doorway and stood to the left of the jamb, listening.

"—be mad as hell because we're so late."

"It couldn't be helped."

SPARTAN RUN   131

"Try telling him that."

The Warrior estimated the speakers were drawing close to his position. He waited, hearing their footsteps, and when they walked past he slid from concealment and trained the M-16 on the backs of two Spartans. "Hold it!" he ordered. "Drop your swords!"

Both men whirled, their shock almost instantly controlled and replaced by reserved defiance. They reluctantly obeyed.

"Who are you?" one of them demanded.

"I'll ask the questions," Blade growled. "Are you two with King Agesilaus's bodyguard?"

"No," answered the first man. "We're not with either unit. I'm Major Xanthus." His green eyes narrowed. "And you, if I'm not mistaken, are the outsider named Blade, the one who appeared before the kings earlier today."

"Yes. Little did I know I'd become embroiled in a power struggle. Whose side are you on?"

"Neither," Xanthus answered. "The issue will be settled by our two monarchs."

Blade looked from one to the other. "If only I could trust you."

"We won't try to harm you," Major Xanthus said.

"Not unless you interfere in the confrontation between our kings," the other one stated.

Blade studied the man, who stood a shade over six feet and sported a full brown beard tinged with streaks of gray. "And who might you be?"

"My name is unimportant, but my advice is critical. You mustn't interfere or you'll lose important support from many who believe Sparta should join your Federation."

"You know about that?"

"All Sparta knows about the offer."

"Surely you know that if Agesilaus wins, Sparta won't be able to join."

The bearded man nodded. "Sparta's fate is in the hands of God."

"We have a saying at my Home: Never presume to rely on the Spirit to do that which you're too lazy to do yourself. Relying on God is all well and good, but don't expect Him to do your work for you."

"But that's my point. The struggle is Sparta's problem and will be decided by Spartans."

Blade sighed. "I wish I could afford to stand by and do nothing, but I can't."

"Why not?" the bearded man inquired.

"I take it you haven't heard the news. General Leonidas led his troops against General Calchas's men, and Leonidas came out on the losing end. Right this minute Calchas has the barracks where King Dercyllidas is being tended completely surrounded. It's only a matter of time before General Calchas mounts an assault on the building."

The officers exchanged startled glances.

"Leonidas lost!" exclaimed Major Xanthus.

"Are you certain of this information?" asked the bearded man.

"I was there," Blade informed them grimly, and was about to elaborate when he saw the major look past his shoulder. From behind Blade came a harsh shout.

"You there! Don't move or we'll shoot!"

CHAPTER FIFTEEN

Rikki-Tikki Tavi raced into the long barracks and saw the four soldiers he was chasing 30 feet in front of him. On each side extended a row of double bunks, dozens upon dozens of them. At the foot of each rested a red footlocker. In racks mounted on both walls were scores of weapons, primarily guns.

"Someone is after us!" shouted the last soldier in line.

"Stop him!" came the command from the front.

Immediately, the Spartan spun and blocked the aisle, his sword held at chest height.

Rikki never slowed. He was determined to stop the assassins before they reached King Dercyllidas, and he raised his katana in the ready posture as he closed. "Surrender!" he declared.

The Spartan laughed.

There was no time for fancy swordplay, no time for elaborate thrusts and parries, no time to go easy on the trooper, no time for anything but the exquisitely deadly art of kenjutsu. Rikki approached to within five feet of the Spartan, feinted to the left, and when the soldier blocked the strike, speared his katana under the sword and deep into the man's chest.

Complete astonishment filled the Spartan's face. His lips curved upward and he gave a slight nod. "Well done," he said in appreciation, and died.

Rikki yanked the katana out and hastened along the aisle. A doorway appeared ahead, and he raced to it as fast as his legs would fly. In the next long room was more of the same: bunks, footlockers, and racks of weapons. The three Spartans were halfway to the next door, and one of them glanced back and abruptly halted.

"He got past Deiphobus! I'll take care of him!"

The Warrior closed the gap. If just one of the death squad reached the king, the result would be disastrous. As much as he would like to match his katana against the next soldier's short sword, he couldn't waste a single precious second. He transferred the katana to his left hand and reached behind him with his right, his slim flingers opening the brown pouch he always kept strapped to the small of his back. In it he carried his yawara, kyoketsu-sgogei, and four shuriken. He extracted one of the throwing stars, drew to within two yards of the soldier, and threw it.

The glint of whirring metal alerted the Spartan to the fact an object was streaking straight at him, although he had no idea what the thing might be. Automatically he brought his sword up to deflect whatever it was, but he misjudged both the object's size and speed.

Unerringly on target, the shuriken struck the soldier at the base of the throat and sliced several inches into his soft flesh, severing vessels. Blood sprayed out, splattering on his chin and chest. He gagged, released his sword, and clutched at his neck. His eyes acquired a bewildered quality as he sank to his knees, wheezing.

Rikki finished the Spartan without stopping, using the katana to finish the job the shuriken had started.

The last two Spartans were almost to the next door.

No! Rikki almost yelled, his arms and legs pumping. The door was closed, and he intuitively perceived that

King Dercyllidas lay behind it. He couldn't possibly prevent the soldiers from reaching the ruler first.

He'd failed!

One of the soldiers shoved the door wide and both men dashed inside.

Rikki frowned in disapproval of his performance and chastised himself for not trying harder. A flurry of activity took place within the next room, and he detected the swinging of swords and the sounds of a struggle. A moment later one of the men he'd been chasing staggered out, his face split, his mouth moving soundlessly, then pitched to the floor. Rikki halted.

More Spartans poured through the doorway, ten of them in all, and they warily approached the man in black. The soldier leading them held up his right hand and they all stopped.

"You're one of the outsiders," he stated bluntly.

"Rikki-Tikki-Tavi, at your service."

The soldier looked past the Warrior at the slain assassin. "You've been trying to protect our king. Why?"

"My friends and I want King Dercyllidas to live."

At that moment, from the north end of the building, came a shout diminished by the distance. "Rikki! Can you hear me?"

"Who is that?" the leader asked.

"My friend Blade."

The giant shouted again. "Leonidas has lost! We've got to leave!"

"Leonidas has lost?" the man at the front repeated, and the Spartans began talking among themselves, expressing their disbelief at the news.

Rikki opened his mouth to reply to Blade when he heard another yell.

"We'll be back. Count on it!"

His friends were leaving? Rikki turned and called out, "I'm coming!"

"Hold it!" the lead soldier snapped.

The Warrior halted.

"I can't let you leave just yet, not until I'm certain you can be trusted. I'm Captain Pandarus, and I must ask that you surrender your sword and place yourself in my custody until our superiors decide your fate."

Rikki pointed at the trooper he'd disposed of. "What does it take to earn your trust? If I wasn't on your side, would I have tried to prevent your king from being assassinated?"

"No," Pandarus conceded. "But I still can't permit you to depart. I have my duty to perform."

"And I must rejoin my companions," Rikki stated, and began to retrace his steps. He heard the soldiers pounding in pursuit and increased his speed, confident in his ability to outdistance them. He was the fastest runner at the Home and he had yet to meet his match.

"Stop!" Captain Pandarus cried.

Rikki had no intention of obeying. He drew closer to the dead assassin and tensed in preparation for leaping over the body instead of skirting it.

"Stop or else!"

Or else what? Rikki wondered, and glanced back to see if they were about to shoot him or hurl a spear. Neither was the case, so he faced front an instant before he leaped. Under ordinary circumstances he would have cleared the corpse with ease, but in his haste he neglected to look down at the floor. He jumped, and didn't realize he'd stepped on slick blood until his legs swept out from under him and he crashed onto his back.

The Spartans!

Rikki shoved to his feet, his left palm contacting a sticky, slippery substance, and he was almost erect when it seemed as if a two-ton section of the ceiling slammed onto the top of his head. The room danced and he sagged, struggling to retain his awareness. Another chunk of ceiling crashed onto him, and an inky vertigo engulfed his senses. He was only barely conscious of his head striking the floor.

The excruciating pain awakened him.

Rikki lay still, flat on his back, his eyes closed, and took stock of his condition. Waves of agony pounded at the inside of his skull. He gritted his teeth and inhaled softly through his nostrils, endeavoring to compartmentalize the anguish. But the pain resisted and tried to swamp his consciousness, almost like a living creature that was trying to devour him from the inside.

Remember the Zen teachings, Rikki reminded himself. All created beings knew pain and grief at one time or another. Humankind only learned wisdom from tribulation. One of the greatest of afflictions was never to know hardship. The one who knows that pain is universal is at peace even though adrift in a world of pain.

Embrace the pain.

Become one with it.

And in the process, dominate it with the sheer force of indomitable human will.

Rikki relaxed his body and accepted the pain, allowing his consciousness to adjust to its presence. Slowly he came to control the sensation, to master the agony instead of letting it master him. As he did, he perceived sounds all around him, the murmur of muted conversations.

One in particular stood out.

"—food in the barracks?"

"You should know better. It's against the law for our unit to eat anywhere but in the public mess. We don't have so much as a crumb."

The Warrior recognized the first speaker as Captain Chilon, and he believed the second to be Captain Pandarus.

"We can hold out for three or four days at the most," stated another person in a forceful tone. "After that, our bodies will be too depleted of energy to withstand the rigors of combat."

"How are we fixed for water, sir?" Chilon asked.

"We have a faucet in the small room at the rear of the barracks," replied the forceful one. "But General Calchas knows about it, and I have no doubt he'll cut off our water supply. He won't waste the lives of more good men when he can simply wait us out, then pick up off easily when he ventures from the barracks."

Rikki finally identified the third speaker as General Leonidas. He opened his eyes and glanced to his right. Sure enough, there they were: Chilon, Pandarus, and the general. Leonidas sported a wide bandage on his left shoulder. Rikki discovered he was lying on the top bed of one of the double bunks, and next to his right arm lay his katana in its scabbard.

"Go check on the progress of the casualty count," Leonidas directed Pandarus.

"Yes, sir," the captain said. He did a smart about-face and departed.

The general stared down at the floor and sighed. "Damn my luck! If I hadn't taken a spear we might have won."

"You shouldn't blame yourself, sir," Chilon stated.

"And why not? If the men had let me lie there instead of trying to protect me, our line wouldn't have broken and Calchas wouldn't have breached our phalanx. The fault is mine for being careless."

"The men were doing their duty by safeguarding you at all costs," Captain Chilon remarked. "You're the best officer King Dercyllidas has under his command. If anything happened to you our cause would be bleak."

"Our cause *is* bleak," Leonidas stated. "Dercyllidas is at death's door. General Calchas has us trapped. We have no food, and soon the water will undoubtedly be cut off. And to top it all off, the outsiders and their van are unaccounted for."

Blade and Teucer were missing? The revelation upset

Rikki, although he took comfort in knowing his friends wouldn't desert him.

"Not all the outsiders are unaccounted for," Chilon commented.

Rikki saw both men look at him, and smiled. The mere movement of his lips intensified his discomfort. "I take it you're talking about me."

"Rikki!" Chilon declared, and stepped over to place his hand on the Warrior's shoulder. "Thank God you've revived. The doctor told us you would be all right. How do you feel?"

"Where's the debris?" Rikki responded, and rose onto his elbows to survey the room in which they had placed him. He spied the north doors 30 feet away, closed and barred and guarded by six soldiers.

"The debris?" Chilon repeated quizzically.

"From the part of the roof that came down on my head."

The captain grinned. "If it's any consolation, Captain Pandarus feels very bad about knocking you out."

"Not half as bad as I feel."

General Leonidas moved up to the bunk. "I'd like to extend my apology for what has happened. My subordinate believed he was doing his duty."

"He does it very well."

"Can we get you some water?" Leonidas inquired. "I'm afraid that's all we can offer."

"Water would be nice." Rikki placed the katana in his lap, then swung around and draped his legs over the edge of the bed.

"Get him a glass," the general instructed Chilon, who promptly hurried off.

There were Spartans standing at every window, and scores of them seated on the bottom bunks, most sharpening their swords or talking quietly.

"I heard you mention my friends," Rikki said. "What happened to them?"

"I don't know," Leonidas answered. "I was injured during the battle and carried back to the barracks, so I didn't note where they went. Some of my men reported that your vehicle was last observed heading into the city. Do you have any idea why Blade would go there?"

"No, but he must have an excellent reason."

"King Agesilaus is still in the city. He'll never let them return."

Rikki grinned. "If you knew Blade as well as I do, you wouldn't be worried."

"And if you knew Agesilaus as well as I do, you would be."

"I understand you're trapped in here," Rikki noted, staring out the nearest window. Beyond stood a row of soldiers holding their shields in front of them. Only their heads, necks, and legs from mid-thigh down were exposed to view.

"General Calchas has us surrounded, yes. I suspect he intends to simply wait us out. Hunger will drive us into his hands."

"Perhaps you won't mind if I offer a suggestion?" Rikki tactfully said.

"Be my guest."

But before the Warrior could elaborate, a loud crash shattered the hushed atmosphere in the confines of the room as a heavy spear smashed through a window on the west side.

"They're attacking!" someone cried.

CHAPTER SIXTEEN

Blade crouched, spun, and threw himself to the right, his finger on the trigger. Four soldiers were rushing toward him, each with an assault rifle they were bringing into play. He squeezed off a burst, sweeping the M-16 from right to left, his rounds taking them at chest height.

All four were jerked rearward by the impact, and all four went down without getting off a single shot.

The Warrior whirled again, anticipating the bearded one and Major Xanthus would be coming at him, but neither of them had moved. Confused, he straightened and tried to read their inscrutable expressions. "Why didn't you try to stop me?"

"We told you we're not backing either side," replied the man with the beard. "Those were Agesilaus's men."

Blade glanced at the bodies, at the bronze helmets and the red cloaks worn by every Spartan soldier. "How could you tell?"

"Do you see these?" the bearded one asked, and reached up to touch the large metal clasp that fastened his cloak at the neck.

"Yeah. So?"

"Look at it closely."

Suspicious of a trick, Blade studied the clasp briefly. "It's made of copper."

"All of the troops in the regular army wear such clasps, as do a few others. But the men assigned to King Agesilaus's bodyguard wear ones of gold, while those in King Dercyllidas's contingent wear clasps of silver."

"So that's the secret."

"It's no secret, actually. Every Spartan is aware of the difference. You're the first outsider to know."

"Thanks for filling me in."

The bearded man smiled. "I wouldn't want you to kill a soldier from the wrong unit by mistake."

"Where's Agesilaus now?" Blade inquired.

"In the audience chamber, I believe."

"Then let's pay him a visit," Blade suggested. "The two of you can go first."

"Do you still intend to interfere in Sparta's internal affairs?" asked Major Xanthus.

"I plan to eliminate the madman, yes."

"Why not let the struggle take its natural course as we advised?"

"Because one of my men is trapped in the barracks with King Dercyllidas. The only way to guarantee his safety is to terminate the egomaniac responsible for your civil war. If Agesilaus dies, it's all over."

The bearded man sighed. "Isn't there anything I could say to convince you to change your mind?"

"No."

"Very well."

The two Spartans turned and walked toward the enormous door at the end of the hall.

Blade stayed a few feet behind them, his eyes darting from side to side, mystified by the absence of guards. Were they in the audience chamber? Even if they were, someone should have heard the blasting of his M-16. Yet the palace resembled a tomb.

"I do wish you would listen to us," Major Xanthus said over his shoulder.

"I can't."

"Suit yourself."

The door to the throne room, like the entrance door itself, hung open a crack.

"Open it," Blade directed. "Slowly."

The pair complied, pulling the portal a few feet out from the jamb.

"Do you prefer us to go in first?" asked the bearded man.

"Go ahead."

Blade walked on their heels and hunched down. He planned to open fire the second he laid eyes on Agesilaus. All it would take was a single shot. He stared between the Spartans, braced for the worst. Instead, to his consternation, he beheld an empty chamber: no king, no guards, no audience, nothing. "Stop," he commanded the two men.

"Leave now before it's too late," Xanthus said.

"Be quiet." Blade straightened and regarded the vacant thrones. "Since he isn't here, we're going to check out every floor from bottom to top."

"You have no idea what you're getting yourself into," the major stated.

"Let me worry about that." The Warrior shifted so he could cover the entrance. "Where are the stairs?"

The bearded Spartan pointed at the southeast corner of the chamber. "Through that door."

"After you."

Their faces reflecting resignation, the pair of soldiers complied.

Blade noticed other doors rimming the room and wondered where they led. He wouldn't put it past the madman to have a secret passage out of the palace for use in emergencies or a hidden room no one else knew about. Agesilaus was a narcissistic power monger, true, but he was also a *clever* narcissistic power monger. Not the kind of man to leave anything to chance.

So far Agesilaus had stayed one step ahead of everyone else. The monarch must have been planning to do away with Dercyllidas for a long time, and the opportune arrival of the Warriors with their offer for Sparta to join the Federation had given Agesilaus the pretext he'd needed to save Sparta from a detrimental alliance and come off as the hero who slew the wicked Dercyllidas.

The assassination attempt was also a testimony to the man's cunning. Agesilaus had deliberately drawn Leonidas's troops away from the barracks so the hit squad could terminate Dercyllidas. And by having the soldiers in the squad carry nothing but swords, Agesilaus had stuck to the letter of the law.

The man never missed a trick.

But it was time to do to him as he'd been doing to others.

Blade thought of Rikki, and hoped the martial artist was all right. His weapon leveled at the Spartans, he came to the middle of the room and idly gazed at the magnificent vaulted ceiling.

"Don't move!"

The stern command seemed to emanate from the very walls.

Crouching, Blade swung from side to side, searching for the source.

"Drop your gun!" the voice directed.

Unwilling to relinquish the M-16, Blade was confounded by the lack of a target until he abruptly recalled a statement made by General Leonidas. "There are also riflemen concealed behind the walls." He'd automatically assumed the marksmen wouldn't be there when the chamber was empty, and his carelessness had cost him. In his understandable zeal to eliminate Agesilaus and save Rikki, he'd committed a cardinal blunder, a basic mistake even a novice Warrior knew to avoid: Never take *anything* for granted.

"This is your last warning!" the concealed man stated. "If your weapon isn't on the floor in three seconds, we have orders to open fire in four." He paused. "One."

Blade wanted to smack himself in the head with the stock for his stupidity.

"Two."

His broad shoulders slumping, Blade eased the M-16 to the floor and lifted his hands into the air. "Satisfied?" he snapped.

"Quite," responded a different voice, and a section of wall behind the thrones slid aside to reveal King Agesilaus and a dozen soldiers.

Scowling, the Warrior faced the dais.

Other hidden panels all around the chamber opened and disgorged a score of Spartans armed with high-caliber rifles.

"Isn't this grand?" Agesilaus asked, and pranced to his throne. "Isn't this positively wonderful?"

"It would be more wonderful if you'd go take a long leap off a short cliff," Blade stated.

The monarch tittered. "Now, now. Where's your sense of fair play? You outsmarted me earlier and escaped. Now I've outsmarted you and lured you into my trap."

"I did it to myself," Blade said bitterly.

"Where are your two companions?"

"I have no idea."

Agesilaus gestured, and all the soldiers in the chamber converged on the giant with their weapons trained on him. "I trust you won't try anything foolish?"

"Not if I can help it."

Smiling contentedly, the dark-haired ruler descended the dais and approached the Warrior. He glanced at the bearded man, then the major. "And what have we here? How did you manage to get yourselves captured?"

"He took us by surprise," replied the Spartan with the

beard.

"Am I to understand, my dear General Agis, that this barbarian took the head of the Crypteia unawares?" Agesilaus inquired, his tone reeking of sarcasm. He gazed at the general's empty scabbard. "Look at this! No wonder he took you by surprise. You apparently left your sword at home this morning." He laughed uproariously.

The leader of the secret police controlled himself with a visible effort, his cheeks acquiring a scarlet hue.

Major Xanthus glanced at Agis, then at the monarch. "You sent for us, your lordship?"

The question had an immediate sobering effect. Agesilaus frowned and placed his hands on his thin hips. "Yes, I did. You were supposed to be here an hour ago."

"We were unduly delayed, your highness," Xanthus said.

"What could possibly be more important than an appointment with me?"

It was General Agis who answered. "I'm the one to blame. I was in the middle of a meeting when your messenger arrived, and I felt it wiser to finish the meeting before coming here."

"What was the nature of this meeting?"

"I called together every member of the Crypteia and impressed upon them the need to remain totally neutral during the dispute between King Dercyllidas and yourself."

Agesilaus grinned. "How wise of you."

"Many of my younger recruits might have been tempted to take sides. The Crypteia must always remain above petty politics if we're to survive as an institution. Our first loyalty must always be to Sparta."

"Wise and noble," the ruler stated, smirking. "I wonder if the good people of our illustrous city-state know how fortunate they are to have such a dedicated protector."

"Service is its own reward. I don't want the gratitude

of the people."

The major cleared his throat. "About the reason we were sent for, sir?"

"Be patient, Xanthus," Agesilaus said. "I'm getting to that." He regarded them both for a moment. "What would you say if I told you I plan to reorganize our armed forces after I've defeated Dercyllidas?"

"You must defeat him first," General Agis said.

"And I will," Agesilaus declared passionately. "Once I do, and since I will be the sole king in Sparta, there will be no need for the royal bodyguard to include three hundred men. I intend to muster any of Dercyllidas's men who live through the conflict into the regular army. Naturally, Major Xanthus, since you're the officer in charge of the regular forces, these men will come under your command. I fully expect you'll have four hundred men at your disposal by tomorrow evening."

"How interesting," the major said.

"Interesting? I should think you'd be delighted at the opportunity to increase your command."

"Of course I am, sir."

"But you realize this will only be achieved if I prevail?"

"Yes, your majesty."

Agesilaus turned to the general. "And as for you, dear Agis, I've decided the Crypteia should be permitted to increase their number by fifty. How would you like a hundred secret police to ferret out traitorous Helots and other rebels?"

"There are currently fifty, your highness, and they do the job admirably."

The king appeared flustered. "What is the matter with the two of you? Here I offer you the greatest gift imaginable, more power, and you both treat my generosity in a cavalier fashion. Don't you realize that power is the only thing that matters in life? You're Spartans. You're military men. You, better than anyone else, should appreciate the sublime feeling that comes from knowing you have unlimited authority over others."

"We realize it fully, your lordship," General Agis stated.

"Then I fail to understand your attitude."

"Forgive us. But being military men, we know better than to let our hopes soar when your victory hasn't been assured."

"It will be. A messenger is on his way at this very minute to General Calchas with the orders that will enable me to triumph."

"We've heard that Calchas defeated Leonidas," Major Xanthus commented.

Agesilaus blinked. "Where did you hear the news?"

"From him," Xanthus said, and indicated the giant.

"Ahhh, yes. Well, he told you the truth. Leonidas and his men were no match for my bodyguards. By sunrise his forces will be crushed."

General Agis looked at Blade. "And what about this man, your majesty?"

A sly grin curled the ruler's lips. "I have special plans for our honored guest."

"May I ask what kind of plans?"

"Certainly. He's going to run the Marathon of Death."

CHAPTER SEVENTEEN

Rikki-Tikki-Tavi dropped to the floor and quickly slipped the scabbard under his belt, slanting it over his right hip.

"To your posts!" General Leonidas bellowed, and the Spartans on the bunks rose and dashed to nearby windows, their swords out and ready. He walked to the shattered window and peered out at the row of troops, none of whom had moved. "Who claimed we were being attacked?" he asked.

"I did, sir," a soldier responded.

"A Spartan must never lose his head, Lieutenant Idomeneus. You are hereby reduced in rank to sergeant and you'll consider yourself on report."

"Yes, sir."

Surprised at the general's strict judgement, Rikki stepped to the left of the broken glass. "Why was the spear thrown?" he wondered.

As if in reply, a hearty shout came from outside. "Leonidas! Are you still with us or has your guardian spirit ferried you to the far side?"

Leonidas chuckled. "I'm still alive, Calchas. You should give your men lessons on spear throwing. They can't seem to hit what they aim at."

"I know you were hit. I saw you being carried inside. Perhaps it's you who needs more exercise. You're not in the best of shape."

Many of the soldiers surrounding the barracks laughed.

"I got your attention so I can make a proposal," General Calchas went on. "I don't want to see more men die needlessly. You're beaten and you know it. If you try to break out, my troops will cut your men down as they try to get through the doors and windows. We have the advantage."

"You think you do," Leonidas stated.

"Save your false bravado for another time. The lives of your men are at stake, and I can't believe you'd sacrifice them for a lost cause."

"Who says our cause is lost?"

"I do," replied Calchas.

Rikki spied the enemy general walking along the line of soldiers, a stocky man sporting a large gold clasp on his cloak. That was when he noticed all of Calchas's troops wore gold clasps; Leonidas's wore silver.

"Then you must be aware of some fact I'm not," Leonidas called out. "The cur you serve won't win unless my liege dies, and King Dercyllidas is very much alive."

"Not for long," Calchas predicted, and stared at the broken window. He gave a courteous nod to Leonidas. "I'm a patient man, as you well know. I can wait out here until you become desperate with hunger or Dercyllidas dies, whichever occurs first. But I'd prefer to spare your men from such acute suffering. Surrender now. Lay down your arms and turn Dercyllidas over to me. I promise he'll be treated with proper respect."

General Leonidas gripped the hilt of his sword. "I've always regarded you as an honorable man, Calchas, until this very moment. You've insulted my king, my men, and me." He paused. "You imply that my men aren't willing to make whatever sacrifices are necessary to perform their duty. You say you would spare them from suffering, but Spartans are bred to endure suffering. And you demand that we turn over the man we have pledged to serve with our dying breaths, if need be. Well, here's my answer. Never!''

A spontaneous cheer rocked the barracks.

Rikki scanned the relaxed, smiling Spartans and marveled at their composure in the face of imminent death. Their attitude was almost Zen-like in their acceptance of the inevitable, whatever it might turn out to be.

"You're a fool, Leonidas!" Calchas cried.

"Perhaps. But I'm a loyal fool."

"Prepare yourself, my former friend. I've a strategy or two up my sleeve that will make you realize how foolish you're being." Calchas spun and stalked to the north, out of sight.

"I imagine he does," Leonidas said softly.

"He was your friend?" Rikki queried.

"We were inseparable at one time."

"What happened?"

"I was appointed by King Dercyllidas to take charge of his bodyguard. Calchas was still an officer in the regular army. My promotion upset him immensely. He'd always wanted to be in the Three Hundred. Later, when Agesilaus offered him a post equal to mine, he gladly accepted," Leonidas detailed. "I never did understand the reason Agesilaus selected him. They'd never gotten along very well." He scowled. "Only later did I realize Agesilaus took advantage of Calchas's jealousy to set him against me."

"How long ago did this occur?"

"About four years ago. Why?"

"It means Agesilaus has harbored the idea of becoming sole ruler of Sparta for a long time. Where I come from, we refer to such persons as power mongers. Men and women who crave power for power's sake. Our Founder warned us in his journal against allowing such people to live among us. Whenever power mongers are discovered in our midst, they are banished from the Family or terminated."

"Terminated?"

"Yes. But only if they refuse to mend their ways or leave peacefully."

"Have you had many such power mongers?"

"Only one. A Warrior named Napoleon. About six years ago he attempted to seize control of the Family."

"Was he exiled?"

"No. I killed him."

"Oh."

Rikki gazed at the soldiers standing like statues 30 feet away. "So what are your plans?"

"To wait until King Dercyllidas revives and follow his orders."

"And if he doesn't revive soon?"

"I'll wait as long as I can."

"Doing exactly as Calchas expects."

General Leonidas studied the man in black. "Do you have a better idea?"

"Yes."

"Tell me."

The Warrior nodded at the row of enemy troopers. "Attack now, when they'd least expect it."

"Don't think I haven't considered the idea. But we're outnumbered. They could leisurely pick us off if we tried to escape."

"I'm not talking about escaping," Rikki elaborated. "I mean *attack*. Calchas expects you to send men out every door and window. In that case, he would have a numerical advantage. So do the unexpected. Lead all of your men out at one point, say the north doors. Bear in mind that Calchas has his unit stretched thin. How many soldiers has he posted opposite the doors?"

"Four rows of ten men each. The rest of his forces are deployed in a single row around the building."

"Then you see my point? Pour all of your men out of the doors at the strongest part of his line. I know your losses will be high. Those in the vanguard will undoubtedly be slain, but as more and more of your soldiers press into the open the tide will turn. His forty men at arms can't possibly hope to contain all of your men. And by the time the remainder of his line rushes to the north, it will be too late."

Leonidas scratched his chin and regarded the Warrior respectfully. "A commendable plan. It might work, but the losses, as you've noted, would be large."

"I'll understand if you decide against it. The cost might be higher than you're willing to pay. Losing men is always a distressing experience."

"You've lost a few, I take it."

Rikki nodded, sadness etching his features. "Friends of mine, fellow Warriors, have died in the line of duty. I mourned their passing, even though I have faith they'll survive this earthly life."

The general turned and scanned the room full of Spartans. "I care for each and every one of them. After all the hours I've spent training and drilling them, I hate to see any of them die. But to die in combat is the dream of every Spartan from boyhood on, and we view death as the crowning glory of a life of service." He nodded at the doorway on the south side of the room. "Come with me."

"Where are we going?"

"To check on King Dercyllidas. I'd like to present your proposal to him."

"And if he isn't awake yet?"

"Then the final decision will be mine, and depending on the outcome the praise or blame will fall squarely on my shoulders." The general started off.

Rikki kept pace with the officer. "Did you know a man named Sarpedon?"

Surprise registered in Leonidas's face. "Captain

Sarpedon? I knew him well. He was an honorable man, even if he did have the distinct misfortune of being in Agesilaus's bodyguard."

The Warrior grinned. "He was the first Spartan I met. And, as you say, he was a man who put honor before all else. I admired him greatly."

"Where did you happen to meet him?"

"In Memphis. He wound up there after he was banished from Sparta."

"Is he still in Memphis?"

"No, he's dead."

Leonidas glanced at the small man. "Did you see him die?"

"I killed him."

The general abruptly stopped. "I seem to detect a trend here. Why did you slay him?"

"We found ourselves on opposite sides. I didn't want to fight him, but he left me no choice. He did his duty to the very end."

"A true Spartan," Leonidas said, and smiled. He resumed walking.

They went into the next room, which was likewise filled with soldiers.

Rikki saw Captain Chilon approaching with a glass of water, and halted once again when the general did.

"Here you are," stated the junior officer. "Calchas hasn't cut off our water yet."

"Thanks," Rikki responded, taking the glass. He swallowed eagerly, grateful for the opportunity to quench his thirst.

"Have you seen Captain Pandarus?" Leonidas inquired.

"Yes, sir. He's finishing the casualty count."

"Good. Let's proceed. Fall in, Captain."

"Yes, sir."

The three of them moved briskly along the aisle to a closed door. Leonidas rapped once and opened it.

Within was a modest-sized office containing a desk, a chair, a file cabinet, and along the east wall, a green cot. Across the room was another door, partly open, revealing more bunks. There were already eight Spartans crammed into the office. King Dercyllidas was resting on the cot. Kneeling next to him, a stethoscope in his hands, was a man with a worried look. The rest were all guards who snapped to attention the instant the general entered.

"How is he, physician?" Leonidas asked without ceremony.

The kneeling man frowned. "He's asleep, and I wouldn't advise waking him. He's lost far too much blood for my liking."

"I need to talk to him."

"Now?"

"I wouldn't ask if it wasn't urgent."

The doctor, clearly displeased, laid his hand on the monarch's arm. "I'll see if I can rouse him. I gave him an herbal remedy to bolster his immune system and make him sleep. He might not wake up."

"Try."

The door on the south side suddenly swung open and in came Captain Pandarus. Like the guards, he stood at attention. "I have the casualty count as you requested, sir."

"At ease, Captain," Leonidas said. "Give it to me straight."

"We lost sixty men, sir."

"And I'd estimate that Calchas didn't lose more than thirty," Leonidas stated. "Damn."

"Excuse me," Rikki interjected, "but is that sixty men killed or sixty counting your injured?"

"There are no injured men," the general replied.

"How can that be? Surely, in a battle like you fought, there must be dozens of injured on both sides?"

"You don't understand," Leonidas said patiently. "Spartans would rather die than be taken prisoner. If a Spartan is injured on the battlefield, he'll fight to his dying breath instead of surrendering." He paused. "We have no injured men because they were all slain in combat."

Now it was Rikki's turn to voice a simple, "Oh."

The physician was gently shaking the monarch's arm. He looked up at Leonidas. "I'm sorry, General. Our liege won't respond."

"Keep trying."

Rikki placed the empty glass on the desk and scrutinized the Spartans. They were riveted to the cot, anxiously waiting for their king to revive, as if their very existence depended on it. In a way, he reflected, that was the case. As much as he admired their bravery and devotion to duty, there was a certain flaw in the Spartan system, an ingrained dependency on higher authority that bordered on the fanatical. Spartans followed orders with the single-minded determination of zealots. They never questioned a command, even when it might be issued by a potential dictator like Agesilaus. The Warriors, by contrast, would never follow an order that was unethical, immoral, or given by a power monger. The Family's protectors enjoyed a latitude of freedom and individual responsibility never known by the Spartans.

"The king is coming around," declared the doctor.

An air of tension permeated the office. The soldiers watched Dercyllidas intently. General Leonidas stepped to the cot and knelt next to the pillow. "Can you hear me, my lordship? It's Leonidas."

A fluttering of the ruler's eyelids was the only reaction.

"King Dercyllidas?" the general persisted.

For a second nothing happened, and then with startling abruptness the monarch's eyes snapped wide open. "Leonidas?" he said weakly.

"Right here, your highness."

Slowly, grimacing in pain, Dercyllidas twisted his head to stare at the officer. "What has happened?"

Leonidas bowed his head in shame. "We engaged General Calchas and he broke our phalanx. We're now trapped in our own barracks, surrounded by his troops."

"You must break out at all costs."

"There is a way, but the cost will be very high."

Dercyllidas's eyes closed for a moment. When he opened them again his voice was even weaker. "At all costs, Leonidas. Do you hear me?"

"I hear and obey."

Sighing, Dercyllidas nodded once, a barely perceptible bobbing of his chin. "Good. And Leonidas?"

"Yes, your highness?"

"Once you've defeated Calchas, as I know you will, kill Agesilaus."

"None of your bodyguards will rest until his head has been brought to you on a platter."

Dercyllidas smiled. "I can always rely on you . . ." His voice trailed off and he lapsed into unconsciousness.

General Leonidas stood. "You heard our king." He turned to Rikki. "We'll put your plan into effect immediately. Would you care to take part?"

"Yes," the Warrior answered. "And I have a favor to ask you."

"Anything."

"I'd like to be the first man out the doors."

CHAPTER EIGHTEEN

"Do you have any idea what this is?" King Agesilaus queried imperiously.

Blade refused to give the man the satisfaction of a reply. He stared at the field in front of him, which extended to the east for 300 yards, then glanced over his right shoulder at the Royal Palace. He'd been escorted, under tight security, from the audience chamber and out a door at the rear of the structure. Now he stood at the edge of the field, with Spartans on both sides and to his rear, all Agesilaus's soldiers except for two.

Both General Agis and Major Xanthus had insisted on accompanying the king. They'd told him they wanted to witness the Marathon of Death, and Agesilaus had gladly assented.

"This is a training field," the ruler was saying. "When those assigned to palace duty aren't required for specific tasks, they come out here to hone their skills. During the midday meal break dozens work out instead of eating."

Blade surveyed the field. A gravel track ringed the outer boundary, evidently for jogging and foot races. There were bales of hay set up at one point, stacked three high, to which targets had been attached. There were also practice dummies dangling from wooden scaffolds. Each dummy was the size of a man and had white circles painted on its cloth surface to signify human vital points.

"Do you see the men I sent out?" Agesilaus asked.

The Warrior couldn't miss them. Eight riflemen were positioned along the outside of the track, spaced equal distances apart. Between them they covered every square inch of the field.

"If you try to flee, you'll be shot," the monarch stated gleefully. "If you break the rules, you'll be shot. And if you don't follow my instructions to the letter, guess what happens?"

Blade glared and clenched his fists.

"Allow me to explain about the Marathon of Death," Agesilaus went on. "Occasionally a Spartan fails to perform his duties as required, or exhibits inferior ability in combat. If the violation is serious enough, as in a case of suggested cowardice, the offender is given the opportunity to prove himself by running the Marathon. If he survives the tests, he's redeemed. If he doesn't, then it's taken as an omen that he wasn't fit to be a soldier, that the charges against him were true."

Curiosity compelled Blade to speak. "What kind of tests are you talking about?"

"Ahhh. I have your undivided attention at last," Agesilaus said sarcastically. "The tests are very simple, actually. Your primary goal will be to run around the entire track."

"What else?"

The ruler took a few steps and pretended to be studying the field. "Now let me see if I can remember all of them." He chuckled. "Yes. I think I do."

"Impossible," Blade said.

"What?" Agesilaus said, his train of thought disrupted. He glanced at the giant, clearly puzzled.

"It's impossible to think unless you have a brain," Blade elaborated, and indulged in a self-satisfied smirk.

The monarch glowered. "Is your petty witticism supposed to anger me? A man of my stature is above such trifling insults." He turned to the field again. "Now where was I? Oh, yes. Your tests."

"Have you ever run the Marathon of Death?" Blade interrupted him again.

Agesilaus, his resentment transparent, pivoted. "Don't be absurd. Why should I submit to a lowly test of courage?"

"I figured as much," Blade said. "In fact, I'll bet you've never even been in combat. You're a coward, the kind who hides behind his royal office and lets others do his dirty work."

At the word "coward," Agesilaus went livid. He hissed and took a step toward the prisoner, his hands upraised, about to strike.

Blade braced for the attack, his plan of action already thought out. If he could get his arm around the would-be tyrant's neck, he might be able to reach the SEAL. None of the Spartans would do anything to endanger their ruler's life, and a simple threat to snap the power monger's neck should do the trick.

Suddenly Agesilaus halted, a crafty gleam lighting up his eyes, and lowered his arms. "Damn, you're good. You almost tricked me."

"I have no idea what you're talking about," Blade said innocently.

"Sure you don't," Agesilaus snapped, and pointed at the targets 50 yards distant. "You can see that bales of hay have been arranged in a row from north to south as backing for the targets used by our archers and shooters. Your first challenge involves a test of speed. You'll run along the track until you are even with the bales, then move off it and wait for the signal. When I give the word, you'll race from one end of the bales to the other, passing directly in front of the targets. Should you survive, you will return to the track and continue."

"Will I be dodging automatic weapons fire?" Blade asked caustically.

"No. Arrows," Agesilaus said, and glanced at a nearby Spartan. "Lieutenant, move your squad into position."

The officer nodded and promptly led nine other soldiers, each armed with a bow, out onto the field. They jogged to within 30 feet of the bales and arranged themselves in a corresponding row, each archer standing directly in line with one of the targets.

"After the test of speed comes the test of skill," Agesilaus went on. "You'll run until you reach the area where the dummies are set up for the soldiers to practice their swordsmanship. Four men will be waiting for you there." He indicated a quartet standing to his right and and they sprinted off. "Should you vanquish each and every one, then you'll return to the track and complete your circuit."

"Pardon me, King Agesilaus," General Agis interjected. "Isn't it traditional for the test of skill to pit the runner against only two opponents?"

"Yes, but I'm making an exception in this case. I wouldn't want our huge friend to become bored."

Agis frowned but said no more.

"And now we come to the last test, the test of endurance," the ruler said. "You see, not only must you complete a circuit of the track, but you must do so without being wounded."

"And if I am?" Blade inquired, surveying the track solemnly.

"Then the riflemen posted around the perimeter will open fire and riddle you with bullets," Agesilaus stated, grinning maliciously.

The Warrior glanced at a soldier who was holding his Bowies. "Am I permitted to carry weapons? I'd like to take my knives."

"You must be joking."

General Agis and Major Xanthus looked at one another,

and the head of the secret police voiced an objection. "It's traditional for the runner to be permitted to carry a sword, your highness."

Agesilaus stared coldly at the officer. "I had no idea you were such a stickler for tradition, my dear general."

"More than you know, sir."

"In any event, the traditions you desire to uphold apply exclusively to Spartans, not to outsiders."

Agis jerked his right thumb at the giant. "He should at least be given a fair chance. That's the decent thing to do."

"Tradition and decency," Agesilaus said sarcastically. "You're a virtual pillar of moral behavior."

"Spartans are renowned for their fairness, my lord," Agis noted. "We wouldn't want word to get around that we had put an outsider to a rigged test, would we?"

The king's nostrils flared and his lips compressed. "Rigged? Who would dare accuse me of such an act?"

"Certainly not I," General Agis said with a slight bow. "But you know as well as I do how tongues can wag. Even if the accusation was untrue, the story might still spread." He paused. "Why add fuel to the fire, if you get my meaning?"

"I get it, all right," Agesilaus stated harshly. He stared at the Warrior for a moment, nervously gnawing on his lower lip. "Very well!" he spat. "The prisoner may take his knives. Never let it be said I'm an unjust man."

The soldiers holding the Bowies took a pace toward the giant, intending to hand them over.

"Not yet, you ninny!" Agesilaus barked. "You'll wait until he has gone ten yards on the course, then give them to him. Understood?"

"Yes, sir."

"Aren't you forgetting something?" Blade queried.

Agesilaus's brow knit. "Not that I know of."

"If I survive this Marathon of Death, what do I win?"

"Your life."

"Not good enough."

The monarch snorted. "Don't presume to dictate terms to me."

"I want your promise of safe passage out of Sparta for my friends and myself."

Agesilaus cocked his head and made a show of squinting up at the sky. "The sun must be affecting your judgment."

Blade folded his arms across his chest. "I'm not budging until I have your word."

"I'll have you shot where you stand."

"Go ahead."

Bewilderment and anger fought for dominance on the ruler's visage, and anger won. "Don't think I won't! Are you prepared to die right here and now?"

"Yes."

Agesilaus did a double take. "You're bluffing, outsider."

"Try me," Blade said, and he meant every word. He wasn't about to run the course simply to provide sadistic amusement for the monarch. A pledge of freedom, given in front of witnesses, would be an ideal incentive to see it through. Besides, he told himself, if Agesilaus did give the order to have him shot, he'd try and reach the bastard before the slugs brought him down and snap the man's neck.

"What harm can such a promise do, your majesty?" General Agis commented. "The odds of him surviving are extremely slim. And even if he does, good riddance to him and his intervention in Sparta's internal affairs."

"You have a point," Agesilaus said, although his tone betrayed marked skepticism.

"Do I have your word?" Blade pressed him.

Hissing through clenched teeth, Agesilaus nodded. "Yes, outsider. You have my promise that you and your companions will be permitted to depart from Sparta should you survive the tests."

"I can't ask for more," Blade said sweetly, and glanced

at Agis. Why was the officer befriending him?

"Let's get this underway," Agesilaus declared. He clapped his hands once, then motioned for the giant to start running. "Off you go, and I hope I never have the displeasure of talking to you again."

Blade jogged slowly forward, the soldier bearing his knives keeping pace on his left. He glanced at the archers, the swordsmen, and the riflemen, and wished he could use the Commando instead.

What to do?

What to do?

Teucer repeated the same question over and over again in his mind. Blade had been gone over half an hour. He was under strict orders to leave and go find Rikki. But how could he just up and drive off, leaving Blade to an unknown fate? What if the giant was in trouble? He'd never forgive himself if Blade died.

What the hell should he do?

He'd slid into the driver's seat as soon as Blade disappeared inside the palace, and now he anxiously tapped his fingers on the steering wheel and stared apprehensively at the keys in the ignition. There was another reason he didn't like the idea of driving off; he lacked confidence in his ability. As part of Blade's new policy to give every Warrior going on a run lessons in how to handle the transport, he'd spent several hours familiarizing himself with the operation of the SEAL. He'd even taken the van on several hour-long chaperoned practice jaunts and learned the basics of steering, braking, and negotiating rugged terrain. But he still got a case of the willies at the mere thought of driving any great distance by himself.

Damn these Spartans!

Teucer leaned back in his seat and closed his eyes. He could use a few hours of sleep, but he dispelled the urge. First things first. The way he saw the situation, he had three choices. He could obey Blade and go rescue Rikki. He could defy the head Warrior and try to find Blade. Or he could sit there and do nothing.

What wonderful options.

He opened his eyes again, then stiffened.

Spartans were pouring from the palace. Ten, 15, 20 of them in rows of two. They quickly descended the steps and fanned out around the SEAL, training their M-16's and UZIs on the tinted plastic.

Teucer knew he was safe. It would take an industrial diamond drill to penetrate the transport's nearly impregnable body, and he doubted very much that the Spartans possessed such a device. Once before, about three years ago, the nefarious Technics had used just such a drill to bore a small hole in the side so they could slip a hanger in and unlatch the lock. That was the only time the SEAL had ever been breached.

Two more soldiers emerged, one of them holding an object in his right hand.

Teucer leaned forward, trying to get a good look at the item. The pair were halfway down the steps before he succeeded, and recognition caused him to clutch the steering wheel in dismay.

The Spartan held a bundle of dynamite.

CHAPTER NINETEEN

"I positively refuse."

Rikki-Tikki-Tavi did not allow his frustration to show. Instead, he persisted in his attempt to convince the general. "I accept full responsibility for whatever happens."

"Which is all well and good for you," Leonidas stated while watching his men organize into rows four deep down the entire length of the center aisle. "But your safety is in *my* hands. King Dercyllidas would be upset if harm were to befall you. Part of the reason for this struggle, as Captain Chilon explained it to me, is Sparta's opportunity to join the Freedom Federation. Dercyllidas very much wants to join. Agesilaus, the isolationist, doesn't. If you were to be injured or killed, the blame would fall on Sparta and King Dercyllidas's dreams of joining would be ruined." He paused. "I can't allow that to happen."

The Warrior glanced at the north doors, not 15 feet away. "Isn't there anything I could say that would change your mind?"

"No," Leonidas stated emphatically. "You'll remain in here when we launch our attack."

"But the plan is my idea."

"For which I sincerely thank you."

"Allow me to talk to Dercyllidas."

"You heard the physician. The king isn't to be disturbed unless it's an emergency. An extreme emergency," Leonidas stressed.

Their conversation was punctuated by the arrival of Chilon and Pandarus, both of whom stood at attention to report.

"A guard of twenty men has been designated to stay with the king, General," the former stated.

"And the troops are almost ready, sir," chimed in the latter.

"Excellent," Leonidas said.

Rikki pointed at a rack of automatic weapons on the east wall. "You could win the day easily if you used those."

"You know better," the general responded, gazing out a window. "We'll do this the Spartan way or not at all."

"Will you be leading your men?"

"Of course."

"In your condition?"

"I sustained a slight injury, nothing more."

"You took a spear in the shoulder."

Leonidas gingerly moved his left arm. "This scratch won't keep me out of the battle. And the way I look at it, I'm living on borrowed time anyway."

"How so?"

"Remember our discussion about injured Spartans? My men should have left me on the battlefield. I failed them, failed my king, and failed myself." Leonidas frowned. "I have much to atone for."

Rikki stared at the ranks of soldiers. The last of the men were taking their positions in the assault column. He rested his left hand on the hilt of the katana and bided his time.

General Leonidas stepped in front of the first row. "We lost once today," he stated in a firm but not overly loud voice. "Now we have a chance to make amends and demonstrate to our king that we're worthy of his trust."

He slowly drew his sword. "Let's acquit ourselves as only Spartans can. Your new orders for the day are simple: Give no quarter. Once we are outside, we will not retreat. Either we triumph or we all die as Spartans should."

The two captains took positions directly behind their superior officer.

Leonidas faced the doors, where two soldiers were awaiting the command to fling them open. "Spartans! Swords!"

As one, in a ringing display of precision, the troopers drew their weapons.

"Now!" Leonidas cried.

An instant later the doors were flung wide. Thirty feet away was the 40-man formation Calchas had posted to guard the entrance.

"Charge!" Leonidas shouted, and started forward.

The moment Rikki had been waiting for arrived. None of the Spartans were paying attention to him. He could do as he pleased without intervention. The katana leaped from its scabbard as he darted over and joined the column, stepping into place next to Captain Chilon.

The officer glanced at him and smiled.

With Leonidas at the forefront, the column poured out the doorway and charged the formation.

Rikki heard one of the enemy soldiers shouting, but the words were indistinct in the rush of the moment. His total attention was focused on the formation, on the spears and shields toward which he raced at full speed. Lacking a shield of his own, he would have to counter the long lances of his foes in another manner. In mere seconds he was close enough to see the pupils in the eyes of Agesilaus's men, and he raised his katana.

Two spears swung toward him.

The Warrior's arms were a blur as he swung the gleaming katana down, first slashing to the left, then reversing direction and swinging to the right, the steely edge of his ancient weapon cleaving both spears in half. Knowing he would be at a disadvantage if he attempted to batter through their shields, he automatically opted to force them to lower their guard by angling his compact form downward in an overhand cut, aiming at their legs. The katana bit into their flesh below the knees.

Both Spartans buckled, their shields dropping as their legs gave way.

Rikki had them. He slew both with a single horizontal cutting motion that sliced open both their throats. They fell, spewing their life's blood, and he waded into the thick of the formation. There were Spartans in front of him, Spartans to the right, and Spartans to his left. He swung and parried, thrust and stabbed, fighting by instinct, pressed on all sides. Crimson drops splattered his face and clothes, but he paid no heed. He mustn't think, mustn't allow himself to be distracted for a millisecond, because distraction meant instant death. He had to swing and swing and swing. Up and down. From side to side. Slicing through spears and foes alike. Never stopping, never permitted the luxury of a breather, transformed into an emotionless killing machine.

Cut to the right.

Cut to the left.

Sweat caked his brow, but he paid no attention. His clothes became damp, but he hardly noticed. His shoulders ached and his hands stung from the impact of metal on metal, but he ignored the discomfort.

In all his years, in all the combat he had seen, Rikki had never known anything like this. Unlike individual clashes, where the fighters could take a measure of each other and their personalities figured as prominently in the outcome as their expertise, in a mass battle there was no personalities, only automatons who fought and fought until they lived through the conflict or lost their lives. There was no middle ground.

The katana became coated with blood. Blood dotted Rikki's martial arts uniform, custom-made for him by the Family Weavers. Blood formed in puddles on the earth, and drenched the red uniforms of the slain Spartans. Blood was everywhere, as if the universe itself had sprung a crimson leak at that particular spot. The tangy aroma of blood filled the air, and the salty taste of blood touched the lips.

Rikki downed five of the enemy. Eight. Ten. He lost count early, and still the battle waged. For the most part the Spartans died in grim silence. A few gasped. One or two cried out, more in surprise at their own demise than out of fear.

On and on it went.

And abruptly, to his amazement, Rikki found himself in the clear, temporarily free of soldiers. He looked around and saw bodies littering the field, piled in heaps. Spartans were still fighting, many in man-to-man contests. He realized that all of Leonidas's men were out of the barracks, and that all of Calchas's men had converged on the north end of the barracks to do battle.

Calchas.

Even as he entertained the thought, Rikki saw a stocky soldier bearing down on him. The man had a dent in his helmet and blood dripping from his sword. Somewhere along the line he'd lost his shield.

"Outsider!" Calchas bellowed, halting several yards off.

"General," Rikki responded.

"You and your friends are to blame for this!" Calchas declared bitterly. "You and your accursed Federation."

"I don't know what lies Agesilaus has been feeding you. We came here in peace."

"You're the liar! And you shouldn't have come here at all, because you're never going to leave."

"That remains to be seen."

The general drew himself up, his eyes flashing sheer spite, and attacked.

Rikki never gave ground. He met the assault calmly, dispassionately, his katana matching the officer's short sword blow for blow. The Spartan's anger worked in Rikki's favor. After half a minute the officer struck in a frenzy, apparently frustrated by his failure to penetrate Rikki's guard, the swings much wider than were prudent. Rikki countered three of them. On the fourth swipe he made as if to block it, then let the short sword swish past his head as he reversed his own stroke and buried the katana in the general's chest.

Calchas stiffened and released his weapon, then staggered backwards, pulling loose from the Oriental blade. "Damn you!" he snarled defiantly, and pitched onto his face.

Rikki glanced at the melee all around him and discovered the conflict was winding down. There were fewer Spartans fighting. Someone nearby, he didn't know who, began to yell stridently.

"General Calchas is dead! General Calchas is dead!"

More of the somber struggles ceased. Soldiers stopped their deadly contests to gaze in the direction of the slain officer and the man in black standing over him.

From out of the intermingled forces came General Leonidas, his features a study of fatigue, the bandage on his shoulder stained red. He walked over to his dead nemesis, then stared at the Warrior. Finally, he turned and raised his sword. "Hear me, men on both sides! With General Calchas gone, there is no longer any reason to continue our conflict. I call on all of those who have served so valiantly under him to sheath your swords and convey his body back to your barracks. Those under my command will not interfere. I give you my word."

Rikki waited hopefully for a sign that Calchas's troops would accept the offer. He'd had enough of blood and gore for one day; for many days, in fact. But a rabid shout from a member of the opposing contingent dashed his hopes on the uncompromising rocks of reality.

"For Agesilaus! Victory or death!"

And suddenly the battle was joined again.

The Warrior turned to confront a new foe, knowing he'd been unduly optimistic. For a moment there he'd forgotten who these men were.

Spartans.

"You can take them now," the soldier announced, his arms extended to hand over the Bowies.

Blade grabbed his knives on the run. Almost immediately the soldier dropped behind him, and he stared at the site of the first test, studying the placement of the bales and the positions of the archers. How could he possibly hope to evade ten skilled bowmen? Given his size, he'd be hard to miss.

There were two factors working in his favor, though. First, the archers were 30 feet from the targets. Arrows weren't like bullets. They couldn't travel such a distance almost instantaneously. If the bows were as powerful as they appeared, then the shafts would cover the span in a second and a half to two seconds. Not much of a margin, but it would have to suffice.

The second factor was his speed. None of the Spartans were aware of how fast he could run. Next to Rikki, he was the fastest man in the Family. He slid the Bowies into their sheaths, glad to have them back. Soon he came in line with the bales and veered from the track to take the required position. He stood next to the last target in the row and glanced to the west at the monarch.

The archers all nocked arrows and prepared to fire.

King Agesilaus didn't waste any time. He cupped his hands to his lips and bellowed, "Begin the first test!"

Taking a deep breath, Blade sprinted forward.

CHAPTER TWENTY

The sight of the dynamite galvanized Teucer into action. He twisted the key and the engine purred to life. Simultaneously, from the Spartans ringing the transport poured a hail of lead, the rounds striking the bulletproof plastic and zinging off.

In their attempt to shatter the green body the soldiers made a grave mistake. With so many of them so close to the SEAL, and all firing from such short range, the inevitable transpired. Three of them were struck by ricochets and went down.

By then the bowman had the transmission in reverse. He saw the Spartan bearing the dynamite racing down the steps and floored the accelerator. There was a thump behind him, and the transport bounced into the air, as if going over a curb. Instead, when he glanced foward, he spotted the crumpled form of a crushed trooper who hadn't moved out of the way fast enough.

The withering fire from the remaining Spartans persisted. they ran after the van, the man with the explosives shouting instructions.

Teucer had them all in front of him. He slammed on the brake pedal, reached over to the toggle switches, and activated the machine gun.

The big fifties made mincemeat of the soldiers. They were perforated repeatedly, thrashing and jerking, then flung to the ground. The man carrying the dynamite made a futile effort to light the fuse, but several slugs bored through his skull and dropped him on the spot.

Teucer turned the SEAL about and exited the public square, bearing to the west, finally having made up his mind. He could take a hint as well as the next guy. Since Blade had explicitly commanded him to seek out Rikki, that's exactly what he would do. The gravel road was deserted and he made good time. After a smile he spotted a solitary figure far ahead, a lone man in a red loincloth running on the north side of the road.

A messenger.

The bowman recalled the comments made by General Leonidas, and slowed. If he was right, the runner must be in the act of conveying a message from General Calchas to Agesilaus. Obviously the communication must not get through.

Should he blow the man up?

No, Teucer decided, shaking his head. Such a drastic step would be a waste of firepower. Discretion called for taking the runner prisoner and conducting an interrogation to discover the message. But how should he accomplish the task? Simply pulling over and pointing an arrow at the guy might work; it also might make the runner take off. He had to be clever.

What to do?

Only 40 yards later the answer came to him, and he abruptly pulled over to the side of the road and switched off the engine. Next he leaned across the console and extended his arm fully so he could unlock the passenger door and open it a crack.

Now he was all set.

The messenger came on at a strong clip, arms and legs

pumping, his gaze riveted on the ground in front of him in total concentration.

Grinning, the bowman slid into the passenger seat and waited, placing the compound bow in his lap. The information the man bore might be critical to Dercyllidas's cause. He thought about the runner he'd seen earlier and wondered if this was the same man. Because he foolishly hadn't paid all that much attention, he didn't know for sure. Another fact about the messenger struck him.

Strange people, these Spartans.

Since General Leonidas knew that orders and other information were relayed from the Royal Palace to the barracks by means of professional runners, and since the officer knew Agesilaus would undoubtedly use such a means during the course of the civil war, why hadn't Leonidas simply posted troopers along the road to ambush the messengers? Was it another of their strange traditions, like only using swords and spears against other Spartans?

The bowman's musing was disrupted by the approach of the runner, who now had only 50 feet to cover. He calculated the man in the loincloth would pass within a foot or two of the SEAL, close enough for him to get the job done.

Keep on coming, speedy.

Teucer gripped the handle and tensed his right arm, gauging the distance carefully. He froze when the runner glanced up and stared at the van. Would he stop? Were his suspicions aroused? But the man never slowed down.

Perfect.

Sprinting at full speed, his body coated with sweat, the Spartan came alongside the transport.

Teucer was ready. He shoved the door wide at just the right moment, causing the runner to crash into the steel-like plastic with a resounding thud. The door swiveled on its hinges, and the messenger was knocked flat on his back, dazed, the breath forced out of him by the impact.

Clutching his prized bow, Teucer jumped down and notched an arrow. He stepped up to the stunned runner and aimed the tip of the shaft between the Spartan's eyes. "Surprise, surprise, friend. I wouldn't move if I were you."

"You fool!" the man snapped, shaking his head to clear his thoughts. "It's against the law to interfere in any manner with a royal messenger."

"Those laws only apply to Spartans. And in case you haven't noticed, I'm wearing all green, not red."

"Who are you? What do you want?"

"I want answers."

The Spartan scowled and glanced at the SEAL. "I knew I should have given that vehicle a wide berth, but I was anxious to get back to the palace and report. My shift is almost over."

"Spare me your sob story. And don't change the subject," Teucer admonished. "I want to know the message you carry."

"I'm not carrying any."

Teucer leaned over the runner, holding the arrow point a fraction of an inch from the other man's nose. "At this distance the shaft will penetrate all the way through your head. Which is it going to be? Answers, or your death?"

"I prefer to die."

"Suit yourself," Teucer said, and shrugged for effect. He pulled the bowstring back a quarter-inch farther.

The prospect of imminent death brought a worried look to the messenger's face. "If I were to reveal the information you want, King Agesilaus would have me shot."

"Who's to know?" the bowman rejoined.

"I can't," the man said, although his tone lacked complete conviction.

Teucer frowned. "I haven't got all day. Either tell me now or die."

Conflicting emotions caused by the messenger's sense of

duty and his desire to live fought an abbreviated war on his countenance. "I have a wife and children," he blurted out.

"I'm sure your widow will be gratified to know that you were thinking about her at the very last."

The contending emotions intensified, the Spartan's lips a thin line of frustration, when suddenly he blurted out, "All right!"

"You'll talk?" Teucer said, wary of a trick.

"Why not? I don't owe Agesilaus a thing after he assigned me to this lousy detail over my objections."

"You didn't want to be a messenger?"

"Hell, no. I was content in the regular army. Then he spotted me at the Games, taking part in the foot races, and decided he wanted me as a runner."

"It sounds like something Agesilaus would do," Teucer tactfully observed. "He's treated you like dirt. Here's your chance to get even. Tell me the message you're supposed to relay."

"I was sent from the Royal Palace with orders for General Calchas, and now I'm taking his reply back."

"What were the orders?"

"To burn down Dercyllidas's barracks within the hour."

Teucer thought of Rikki. "And the response from General Calchas?"

"He intends to try and convince Leonidas to surrender. If that doesn't work, Calchas will torch the barracks."

The bowman slowly let up on the string and took a stride backwards. He had to reach the barracks and warn the martial artist and Dercyllidas's men. "All right. Stand up and continue on your way. And don't worry. I'll never tell a soul about this."

"Thanks," the messenger stated gratefully, rising with an effort. He skirted the door and made toward the east without so much as another look at the Warrior.

So there were a few dissidents in the Spartan ranks,

Teucer reflected as he quickly climbed into the SEAL and slammed the door. He moved behind the wheel, deposited the bow and arrow on the console, and started the vehicle. He'd begun to think of all the Spartans as infallible machines. The discontented runner had been the proverbial exception that violated every rule.

Concern for Rikki's safety dominating his mind, the bowman peeled out and raced off. There was no longer any doubt about his decision. Rikki needed help. Blade would have to wait until after he rescued their companion. Then, and only then, would he return to the palace and seek the head Warrior. He just hoped that in the meantime the giant stayed out of trouble.

How long had it been?
An eternity?
Two eternities?
Rikki-Tikki-Tavi stood alone on the blood-drenched battlefield and surveyed the carnage in disgust. What a waste of brave men! He wearily shifted his attention to the two figures approaching from the east.

"It's over," General Leonidas declared wearily. "We've won."

"But at what a cost!" Rikki responded, sorry he had ever suggested the plan.

Captain Pandarus gazed at a nearby body. "Every last one of Agesilaus's bodyguard has been killed. They fought valiantly to the very end."

Rikki knelt and went to work wiping his katana clean on the cloak of a dead adversary. "I've never known men who died so willingly in the name of duty. They let themselves be slaughtered without a single request for mercy."

"They were Spartans," Leonidas stated proudly.

"Have you seen Captain Chilon?" Rikki asked.

Pandarus nodded. "We were fighting side by side when he took a sword in the chest. He managed to slay the man who had killed him with his dying breath."

SPARTAN RUN   179

Sadness softened the Warrior's face. "I'm sorry to hear that. I liked him." He looked up at the general. "What will you do now?"

"Carry out King Dercyllidas's orders. We'll regroup and march on the Royal Palace. I won't rest until Agesilaus is dead."

Rikki straightened and stared out over the crimson sea of corpses. "You're not the only one."

Blade heard an arrow thud into a bale behind him as he bounded toward the far end of the row. He passed another target and felt a slight tugging sensation on the back of his black leather vest a fraction of a second before a second shaft smacked into the hay.

Two down, eight to go.

He abruptly dived and rolled, and narrowly missed being impaled by the third shaft. The archer had shot low, aiming for his waist. Surging erect, he weaved and dodged, his legs flying.

Another shaft nearly clipped his nose.

Blade wrenched rearward at the last instant, then ducked under the arrow and sped onward.

Four down, six to go.

Inspiration struck, and he abruptly halted. The fifth shaft whizzed by his chest and sank several inches into a bale. He went around it, going all out, knowing he was only halfway to safety.

The remaining five bowmen were all aiming carefully.

Blade leaped into the air, sailing in a graceful arc as if diving from a high rock into a lake, his ears registering the clean hit of the sixth arrow somewhere below him. He tucked his arms to his chest and his chest to his legs and flipped, a gymnastic feat he had performed many times in his youth.

The seventh shaft brushed his hair.

Uncoiling, his body a streak of motion, Blade landed lightly and dashed to the south.

Three more to go.

Again he threw himself to the grass, expecting to hear yet another arrow strike the bales, but nothing happened. He rose and hurtled toward the final bales, glancing at the archers as he did, and was astonished to discover that none of them were paying the slightest attention to him. They were all staring in the direction of the palace. Mystified, he continued to the very end of the row before he halted. Only then did he face in the same direction. A second surprise greeted his gaze.

King Agesilaus and his bodyguards were hastening toward the bales, the ruler gesturing angrily and shouting, "No! No! No!"

Now what? Blade wondered, waiting patiently and conserving his energy. He inhaled deeply, grateful to be alive.

The archers lowered the bows. From their expressions, it was evident they were as perplexed as their intended target.

Agesilaus merely glared at the bowmen as he brushed past them, and drew to within a dozen feet of the giant before he halted. "I knew it!" he declared bitterly. "I knew you would cheat!"

"Cheat?" Blade responded in bewilderment.

"Don't deny it, outsider! You cheated, and now I have every legal right to carry out your execution."

CHAPTER TWENTY-ONE

"How did I cheat?" Blade demanded. "Or is this a charge you've trumped up so you can kill me and be done with it?"

"You dare!" Agesilaus snapped. "You insolent swine. No one accuses me of being a liar. You did violate the rules and you know it. My instructions were to race from one end of the bales to the other."

"Which is exactly what I did."

"Like hell! You were supposed to run, moron, not indulge in all that leaping and diving and spinning."

"You should have been more specific. How was I supposed to know?"

"Don't plead ignorance. You were well aware of the rules," Agesilaus stated.

"Perhaps he wasn't, your highness," interjected a familiar voice.

Blade glanced at the Spartans on both sides of the ruler and saw General Agis to the right. Strangely, Major Xanthus had disappeared.

The king pivoted, his countenance radiating spite. "Are you presuming to disagree with me *again*?" he asked the head of the secret police.

"Not at all, sire. I merely point out that he might not have realized he had to run the whole distance. As you wisely noted, he's an outsider. He's completely ignorant of our customs, laws, and general rules of conduct."

"Are you saying I should forgive him?"

"Why not, your majesty? The greatest Spartan kings have always been renowned for their compassion. The ability to wield power is only one of the many attributes a wise monarch cultivates," General Agis said.

"I know all that," Agesilaus spat. "You don't need to lecture me on the proper demeanor of a monarch."

Agis smiled. "Of course not, sir."

The power monger studied the Warrior for a moment. "Perhaps I was a bit rash. It would be foolish to expect someone who possesses inferior mental capacity to comprehend Spartan ways."

"Then we can simply continue with the Marathon?" Agis asked.

"Not quite."

"Your highness?"

"Since he failed to adhere to the rules, he can start over."

Blade stiffened. "Start at the beginning?"

Agesilaus smirked and nodded. "You're not as dumb as you appear to be."

"But is that fair?" Agis queried.

"Don't try my patience with the same implied accusation twice," Agesilaus said. "He opened his mouth to speak again, then stopped when he saw someone coming through the cluster of soldiers. "What is the meaning of this?"

Blade looked and discovered Major Xanthus returning. The army officer carried a golden goblet in his left hand and an opened bottle of wine in his right.

"What the hell are you doing with the victory goblet?" Agesilaus demanded angrily.

SPARTAN RUN

"It was my idea," General Agis said. "It's customary to toast those who survive the tests, and I thought it would be appropriate to have the goblet on hand should Blade succeed in doing so."

The ruler scowled in displeasure. "Only Spartans are entitled to be honored with a victory toast. I'll be damned if we're going to give this outsider such a privilege."

Major Xanthus held out the bottle of wine. "But what about this, your lordship? I just took it out of the root cellar under the palace, and the wine is still chilled. Do you want me to replace the cork and return the bottle to the cellar?"

King Agesilaus licked his lips. "The wine is cold, you say?"

"Yes, sir."

"Then we shouldn't let such a superb beverage go to waste," the ruler stated, and grabbed the bottle. He raised it to his mouth and swallowed greedily several times.

Blade noticed General Agis and the major exchange cryptic glances.

"Ahhhh, this is delicious," Agesilaus commented, lowering the wine and grinning contentedly. "I believe I'll finish the rest while the giant runs the course again."

"Is that wise, your highness?" Agis inquired.

"What do you mean?"

"That wine has been fermenting for decades. It must be quite potent. What with all the excitement and this heat, you could become drunk very fast. And we both know that it's against the law for a Spartan to be inebriated."

"I'm beginning to wonder how you've managed to last so long as head of the Crypteia," Agesilaus stated coldly. "Especially since antagonizing your superiors seems to be your forte."

"I meant no disrespect, sir."

"For your sake, I hope so." Agesilaus took another swig of wine. "And for your information, General, I can hold my wine better than most." He gulped even more.

"My apologies, your highness."

The ruler gestured with his hand. "Apology accepted. Now let's conclude the Marathon. I have other business to attend to, you know."

"Certainly, sir."

Agesilaus tramped eastward, but he went only six feet or so when he suddenly halted, placed his right palm to his forehead, and swayed slightly.

"Is something wrong, your majesty?" General Agis queried.

"Perhaps you were right. It's much hotter than I realized. I've broken out in a sweat."

"You should sit down and rest."

"After the Marathon." Agesilaus took one more step, then unexpectedly sank to his knees before anyone could catch him. He groaned loudly.

General Agis, Major Xanthus, and other Spartans closed in about their leader.

"Are you all right?" the general asked solicitously.

"I feel dizzy. Never felt this way before."

"Perhaps we should carry you inside, sir," Major Xanthus proposed.

"I'm fine," Agesilaus snapped, and tried to rise. Instead, he pitched onto his face.

General Agis gently turned the monarch over. He glanced at one of the nearby soldiers and issued an order. "Go find the doctor. Have him hurry."

The soldier saluted and raced off.

Perplexed by the turn of events, Blade stood near the bales and observed the tableau unfold. He could see the power monger's wide, unfocused eyes and hear ragged intakes of breath.

"What is happening to me?" Agesilaus declared, seemingly directing his question at the azure sky. "I feel so weak."

"I've sent for your personal physician," Agis told him.

"Who said that?" Agesilaus asked, his brow knitting, perspiration coating his skin. "I can barely hear you. Speak up!"

"I spoke, your majesty," Agis said. "I'm right here beside you."

Agesilaus swung his head from side to side. "Then why can't I see you or hear you very well?"

"I have no idea, sir. Please, don't exert yourself. Stay quiet until the doctor arrives."

"I'm suddenly very cold."

"Perhaps it's your heart, sir."

"Don't be ridiculous. I'm as healthy as a horse."

"What else could it be?" Agis commented innocently.

Blade suddenly perceived the truth, and the insight shocked him. He looked at the bottle of wine lying on the grass, then at the ruler. The plot had been flawless. He now knew exactly how Agis had lasted so long.

King Agesilaus arched his back and gasped. "Oh, God!" he cried pitiably, and abruptly broke into violent convulsions, his entire body rocking and bouncing.

Agis and three troopers tried to restrain the monarch, to keep him still. They almost had him pinned down when he screeched in torment, gurgled, and went limp.

"What's happened to him?" Major Xanthus remarked in concern, playing his part to the hilt.

General Agis felt for a pulse, and for five seconds no one else uttered a word or moved. Finally he straightened and shook his head sadly. "The king is dead."

"Do you really think it was his heart, sir?" asked one of the soldiers.

"I do. But you can be certain my office will investigate his death carefully." Agis stepped over and retrieved the wine bottle. "The first step will be to have this wine tested."

Blade was tempted to laugh. How convenient, he

thought, that the general should be the one man responsible for the oversight of such investigations.

General Agis scanned the assembled Spartans. "I believe all of you can fully appreciate the significance of Agesilaus's death. As of this moment, the civil war is ended. I'll personally convey the news to King Dercyllidas."

"But what about those of us who were assigned to Agesilaus's bodyguard?" queried a soldier.

"You'll report to your barracks and wait there until further notice. Agesilaus has a distant relative, a cousin I think, who is next in line to assume his throne. The Ephors will call this relative before them and formally inauguarate him. Whether he retains the current contingent of the Three Hundred will be up to him to decide."

"Yes, sir."

The head of the secret police turned to the Warrior. "You'll be happy to hear that you won't need to finish the tests."

Blade grinned. "Thank you. I am very relieved."

"I'll be leaving for the barracks housing King Dercyllidas's bodyguards in a few minutes. Would you care to come along?"

"I'd be delighted."

"Good. You may bring your knives."

"There's another favor you can do for me."

"Name it."

"I'd really like something to drink."

"Anything you want is yours. We want our new allies in the Freedom Federation to feel right at home here." Agis grinned. "What would you like?"

"It doesn't matter. Whatever you have," Blade said, then quickly corrected himself. "Just so it isn't wine."

"You're not much of a wine drinker, I take it?"

"Now and then. At the moment, I'm just not in the mood."

SPARTAN RUN 187

General Agis stared at the royal corpse. "I don't blame you one bit."

The SEAL was parked at the base of the steps, both doors wide open. Gathered to give the three Warriors a proper send-off were all the important political officials and military officers in Sparta: King Dercyllidas, General Agis, General Leonidas, Major Xanthus, the Ephors, Captain Pandarus, and many others. Packed into the public square were the citizens of the city-state.

"These last four days of discussions have been most productive," Dercyllidas said. "How soon do you think we can expect to hear the decision?"

"The Federation leaders will hold a special conclave and vote formally on Sparta's admission. As soon as they decide, a delegation will be sent to establish diplomatic relations. I'd imagine that most, if not all, of the leaders will come here for the signing of the treaty."

"The date the treaty is signed will become an annual Spartan holiday. Unfortunately, we can never fully express our gratitude to you personally."

"I don't deserve special recognition," Blade said.

"Yes, you do. All of you do. You acquitted yourselves nobly," Dercyllidas said, and glanced at the small man in black. "Leonidas told me about your participation in the battle. You slew more opponents than any of our own men. He rates you as the best fighter he's ever laid eyes on."

"The general exaggerates," Rikki responded.

"Spartans never exaggerate," Dercyllidas said.

"We'd better be going," Blade stated, casually slinging the Commando over his left shoulder.

"As you wish. But please remember that if we can ever be of assistance to you or your Family, you have only to say the word. After all the three of you have done for us, we'll always be in your debt."

Rikki-Tikki-Tavi cleared his throat. "If it's permissible, I'd like to make a request."

"Name it and it's yours."

"There was once a Spartan by the name of Sarpedon, a brave, loyal man devoted to Sparta. He was unjustly banished from your city and forced to wander the Outlands. I knew him well, and I can safely say that no Spartan has ever been more worthy of the name."

"I'm familiar with his case," Dercyllidas mentioned.

"Then perhaps you'll see fit to grant my request. Sarpedon's name was deleted from the plaque of distinction after his banishment. I came here specifically to ask that it be restored to the position of honor it deserves."

The king stared at the martial artist, a tinge of melancholy etching his countenance. "As you wish, so shall it be done."

"Thank you."

Dercyllidas gazed at the bowman. "And what about you, archer? You seldom speak. Is there anything we might do for you?"

"No," Teucer answered.

"No honor would be too great or too small," the ruler said, and added partly in jest, "Perhaps a statue would be in order."

Teucer chuckled. *"Even This Shall Pass Away."*

"I don't understand."

"That's the title of a poem by one of my favorite poets, a man who lived a couple of centuries ago, Theodore Tilton."

"And what did this poet have to say?"

Teucer surveyed the assembled Spartans, feeling uncomfortable at the idea of quoting poetry in front of so many people he didn't know. But what difference did it make? he reasoned, and responded to the king's question. "Once in Persia reigned a king, who, upon his signet ring, 'graved a maxim true and wise, which, if held before the eyes, gave him counsel at a glance, fit for every change and chance. Solemn words, and these are they: 'Even this shall pass away.' "

MADMAN RUN

Dedicated to...
Judy, Joshua, and Shane.
To everyone who remembers
those scary Saturday afternoon matinees.

Oh. And to the memory of
H.G. Wells. His imagination
has inspired so many.

Dear Plato:

Hi.

Enclosed is the file you requested. I had to go into the basement to find it. No one has read this particular one in many years, and I was extremely surprised when you asked for it.

Although you are probably as familiar with the facts as I am, I thought it might help to refresh both our memories and provide some background.

All three of them were in their midteens at the time. Blade had just turned 16, according to the records. This was the fourth of their little adventures and the one that affected Blade the most.

As usual, I employed a subjective style instead of an objective narrative. History should be vibrant, not dull.

Knowing you as well as I do, I took the liberty of going through the archives for the other files related to Blade's travels during the same period. If you desire to see them, I'll be happy to send them over.

By the way, does Blade know you're doing this? He doesn't take kindly to anyone prying into his past without a good reason. I know the files are official records open to every Family member, but it's a privilege that should not be abused, even by our esteemed leader.

Does this have anything to do with the recent incident involving Blade's son Gabe and that mutated black bear? If so, I understand your motive. Will you give this to Blade before or after you read it? Heh-heh.

Well, I've rambled enough. Stop by and visit me sometime. I get lonely with no one to talk to.

Respectfully,
RLD

The Chronicler

CHAPTER ONE

The scorching July sun was perched at its zenith above the northern Minnesota landscape. A slight breeze provided scant relief from the heat, occasionally stirring a leaf in the verdant forest. Birds sang gaily and insects buzzed, indicating there were no predators abroad.

Three youths were hiking to the southeast at a brisk pace, despite the temperature. All three carried backpacks, and all three were armed to the proverbial teeth.

In the lead walked a teenager whose features revealed his Indian ancestry. The blood of the Blackfeet flowed in his veins, and perhaps it was due to his biological inheritance that he had always excelled at hunting and trapping. He wore torn jeans and a faded blue T-shirt that fit his stocky frame snugly. Tucked under his brown leather belt were two tomahawks, one on either hip. He held a Winchester 30-30 in his left hand.

"Whose bright idea was this, anyway?" he asked while swatting a fly the size of his thumb.

"It wasn't mine, pard," replied the second youth in line. His hair was blond, and a thin moustache just beginning to take shape on his upper lip was the same color. He wore buckskins that served to accent his alert blue eyes. Strapped around his slim waist were a pair of Colt Python .357 Magnum revolvers sporting pearl handles. "Blame this on Mikey."

"The new name is Blade, remember?" stated the third member of their party, a giant standing six-feet eight-inches tall and endowed with a herculean physique. A black leather vest and jeans scarcely contained his bulging muscles. Around his waist were two matched Bowie knives, while slung over his left shoulder was a Marlin 45-70. His hair was dark, his eyes a penetrating shade of gray.

"Well, excuse me for living," the blond gunman said. "I've been calling you Mikey since we were knee-high to a grasshopper. Just because you had your Naming last week doesn't mean I'll automatically stop."

"You will if you know what's good for you," Blade declared.

The gunman halted and turned. "Was that a threat?"

"It was a promise," the giant said.

"Oh, brother. Here we go again," the Indian interjected, looking at the gunman. "Hickok, he's right and you know it. You don't like us to call you Nathan any more, so have the decency to call Mikey by his new name." He grinned broadly.

"I reckon you have a point, Lone Elk," Hickok said. "Too bad your Naming isn't for a couple of months yet. Have you picked the one you want?"

"I've decided to take the name Geronimo."

The young gunfighted cackled. "Leave it to you to pick the name of a bloodthirsty Injun. Why couldn't you select something civilized?"

Lone Elk straightened indignantly. "Like what, for instance?"

"Oh, I don't know. How about Percival or Barney?"

"If they're such great names, why didn't you pick one

for yourself?"

"Because I like a handle with class."

"You know what you can do with your class."

Hickok pretended to be offended. "Why are you being so touchy? It was the Founder who said a person's name should reflect their personality. I can't help it if you're more the Percival type than a Geronimo." He glanced at the giant. "What do you think, Mikey?"

"Leave me out of this," Blade responded. He walked past them and took the lead, refusing to become embroiled in yet another senseless argument over their names. Although the three of them were the best of friends, they still found plenty to bicker about, especially after they'd been hiking for miles through dense woodland in 100 plus degree weather.

Blade was proud of his new name. He'd spent countless hours narrowing down a list of those he liked the most and had finally chosen the one that best described his outlook on life and his preference in weapons. Ever since the age of four or five, he'd entertained a fascination with edged arms of every type, and over the years he'd become extremely proficient in the use of all the knives, swords and daggers in the huge Family armory. So it was only natural for him to take a name that typified his passion.

The way he saw it, he owed a debt of gratitude to the long-deceased Founder of the Home, Kurt Carpenter, the man who had constructed the 30-acre survivalist retreat in northwestern Minnesota shortly before the outbreak of World War III. A wealthy film maker who realized the inevitability of nuclear conflict after the liberal Russian president was deposed by militant hard-liners, Carpenter had spent millions on his pet project. It was he who first dubbed the compound the Home and designated his select band of followers as the Family, and for 92 years they'd survived in a world deranged by radioactive and chemical toxins.

Carpenter had instituted many unique social reforms

designed to stabilize the new society, and among them was the ceremony known as the Naming. Because he had worried that subsequent generations would lose sight of their historical roots, he'd encouraged all parents to have their children search through history books and choose the name of any historical personage they admired as their very own, a name they were formally christened with on their 16th birthday. The practice was later changed to allow those undergoing such a special event to select the name from any source they liked or even to adopt one of their own devising, as Blade had done.

The young giant suddenly halted and cocked his head. He belatedly realized that all the birds and insects were quiet, which could only mean trouble. Unslinging his Marlin, he surveyed the forest but saw nothing to arouse alarm.

Hickok and Lone Elk were 20 feet away, still going at it.

Blade shrugged and continued trekking in the direction he hoped to find the castle mentioned in the Founder's diary. Carpenter had meticulously noted every item of interest in a daily log, and one of those items talked about a mysterious castle belonging to an eccentric recluse who lived 15 miles from the Home. The cryptic reference had aroused Blade's curiosity, and he'd persuaded his friends to do a little exploring with him to see if the castle still stood.

"Hey, Mikey!" the gunfighter yelled. "Wait for us."

Halting, Blade turned and regarded them critically as they jogged up to him. "This isn't the time or place for your petty squabbles," he said.

"Whoa! Who died and made you boss?" Hickok quipped.

"As you pointed out, this was my brainstorm. So by rights I should take charge," Blade noted.

"We're both Warriors. I don't see why you should lord it over us just because you had an idea for once."

MADMAN RUN

"What about me?" Lone Elk interjected. "I can lead, too."

Hickok snorted. "You don't count. You're not even a Warrior yet."

"But I will be soon," Lone Elk pointed out.

Blade smiled. "I bet you can hardly wait."

"You don't know the half of it."

But Blade did have an excellent idea of the excitement his friend felt. After all, he'd felt the very same way when it came time for the Family Elders to decide on his nomination.

The Warrior class consisted of twelve Family members who were carefully screened not only for their ability as fighters, but for their temperament and intelligence as well. They were diligently trained under the tutelage of a retired Warrior in everything from the martial arts to combat psychology. Because of a recent mishap, three vacancies had developed. Blade and Hickok had applied and were accepted, and shortly it would be Lone Elk's turn.

"If you ask me, we don't need someone in charge," Lone Elk stated. "It's not like we're on official Family business. All we're doing is taking a day to goof off."

"Speak for yourself, twinkle-toes," Hickok responded. "I'm a Warrior now. I never goof off."

Lone Elk unexpectedly leaned down and inspected the grass at their feet.

"What the blazes are you doing?" Hickok demanded.

"Making a note of this spot. I want to return next week and see how well you've fertilized it."

Blade chuckled and marched onward, eager to reach their destination. If they didn't spot the castle soon, they'd have to head back to avoid being abroad after dark—not that they were afraid—but at night the predators and mutations were out in force, and anyone foolish enough to roam around courted death or risked being maimed.

The eerie stillness persisted. Not so much as a bee buzzed.

"Have you guys noticed how quiet it is?" Blade asked.

"Yeah. And I don't like it," Lone Elk said.

"What's the big deal?" Hickok wanted to know. "We'll blow away anything stupid enough to mess with us." His hands hovered near his Pythons.

Lone Elk stopped. "Did you hear that?"

"I didn't hear nothing," Hickok said. "Your mind is playin' tricks on you."

As if deliberately trying to prove the gunfighter wrong, howls and snarls erupted from a dense thicket to the west, and a moment later a feral pack of mutations burst from cover and charged.

CHAPTER TWO

They resembled coyotes in shape and size, but there any resemblance ended. Hideously transformed by an unknown agent, the nine creatures loping toward the three humans lived purely to kill. Their bodies were hairless and covered with sores that oozed a yellowish-green pus. Their teeth were bared, their eyes blazing like miniature beacons of blood-crazed insanity.

Blade had seen such horrors before. The Family referred to such creatures as mutates. None of the Elders knew what caused them to exist, although Blade's father and another man who was called Plato had often speculated the chemical weapons employed during the war were somehow responsible. If radiation was the culprit, so the reasoning went, then there would be humans similarly affected, and there wasn't a single report in the entire Family history of a human mutate. As far as anyone knew, only reptiles, amphibians and mammals were mysteriously altered. Never had anyone observed a mutated bird or insect. Since the war, the mutate population had grown dramatically to the point where they were a serious threat to all travelers, day or night. Plato, the wisest member of the Family, believed the mutates were increasing by geometric progression, and he was eager to secure a live juvenile specimen for analysis. Unfortunately, the only way to get one was to kill it.

The young giant pressed the Marlin to his right shoulder, sighted on the foremost mutate, and fired.

Struck in the head, the lead coyote was flipped backwards by the impact of the slug. Other members of the pack collided with it, causing momentary confusion.

Lone Elk opened up with the Winchester, levering off two shots in rapid succession, the sharp retorts producing two dead beasts.

Leaving six.

Blade was aiming at another onrushing form when Hickok moved around him. He held his fire, the Marlin still raised to provide cover if need be, but as he anticipated, his help wasn't required.

The blond youth's hands streaked those gleaming Colts from their holsters and twin shots sounded as one. Three times the gunman stroked each hammer, and after the six shots there were six twitching, dying mutates stretched out on the grass. Each one had been shot in the head between the eyes. Dead center between the eyes. Grinning, Hickok ambled toward the pack, ready to finish off any that tried to rise. None did.

Lone Elk glanced at Blade and said softly, "If he gets any faster he'll have to change his name to lightning." Then he looked at the gunman and declared, "You could have saved some for us."

"I can't help it if you're as slow as molasses," Hickok retorted, in the act of prodding each coyote with a toe.

"Don't get smart with us, ding-a-ling. We know your secret," Lone Elk said.

"What secret?"

"Your so-called quick draw is a trick done with mirrors."

"Anytime you feel inclined to try and outdraw my mirrors, feel free to let me know."

Lone Elk stepped forward to help check the bodies. "You'd shoot little ol' me?" he asked innocently.

"Of course not. Oh, I might crease your head, but it's so swelled up you'd never notice the difference."

Blade surveyed the woods in case there were more mutates in hiding. Nothing moved, and he relaxed a bit. "We'd better get going," he urged. "If there are scavengers in the area, they're bound to have heard the shots."

Hickok looked up and smirked. "There you go again, trying to take charge."

"You can't blame him," Lone Elk said. "It's in his veins. His dad is our Leader, after all."

"And one day Mikey might follow in daddy's footsteps," the gunfighter joked.

"I have no intention of becoming the Leader of the Family," Blade asserted stiffly. "How many times do I have to tell you?"

"You can tell us until you're blue in the face, pard, but we won't believe you."

"Why not?"

"Because we know you," Hickok said. Satisfied the mutates were all dead, he began to reload the Magnums.

"And what does that mean?" Blade demanded.

"It means you're a rotten liar. Deep down you really do want to become Leader some day."

"You're nuts."

"Hey, Lone Elk agrees with me," Hickok said, glancing at the Blackfoot. "Don't you?"

"Are you talking to me?" Lone Elk rejoined.

"No, I'm talkin' to one of the blamed critters," the gunman muttered, then raised his voice. "Of course I'm talkin' to you, mutton head."

"If you care to address me, from now on you'll call me by my new name."

"You want me to call you Geronimo?"

"Yes.'"

Hickok paused, a cartridge in his left hand. "But you haven't had your Naming yet."

"So? I will, soon. And since Mike and you already have your new names, I want you to call me by mine."

"Forget it, dimwit."

"What harm can calling me by my new name do, yo-yo?"

"Technically you don't have a new name until after the ceremony, and I aim to abide by the rules until then."

"Suit yourself, Nathan," the stocky teen said, using the name bestowed on the gunman by his parents, and walked off.

"Of all the childish antics," Hickok protested. He swung toward the giant. "What do you say?"

"I say we humor him. If he wants to be called Geronimo, it's fine with me."

"Some attitude for a future Leader."

"If you keep bringing that up, you won't have a future," Blade chided and followed Geronimo.

Hickok trailed after them, still reloading. "Well, don't expect me to break the rules. As far as I'm concerned, Lone Elk is Lone Elk until the Naming is over."

"Do whatever you think is best," Blade said.

"Besides, I still figure he'd make a better Percival."

They traveled another mile and neared a hill with a bald crown. A hawk soared on the air currents to their right, and a pair of deer fled at their approach.

"I sure do like the outdoors," Hickok remarked, his thumbs hooked in his gunbelt. "Don't you, Lone Elk?"

There was no answer.

"You're serious about not talkin' to me, aren't you?" Hickok inquired.

There was still no answer.

"Fine. Suit yourself. See if I ever speak to you again."

Blade grinned and stared at the crest. It would be a good spot to take a break and decide whether to continue or turn back. The heat was getting to him, and he wouldn't mind heading for the Home with their goal unaccomplished. Once back, he could take a refreshing dip in the moat.

Minutes later they stepped from the trees and halted just below the rim.

"Let's rest a bit," Blade proposed.

"Sure, fearless Leader, whatever you want," Hickok said, sitting down on a log. He studiously refrained from gazing at Geronimo.

"I'd like to take a vote. Do we head on or head home?" Blade asked them.

"It makes no difference to me," Geronimo said.

"I couldn't care less," Hickok added.

"So the decision is mine," Blade declared and moved toward the top of the hill for a view of the country beyond. If there was no sign of the castle, he'd return to the compound. Perhaps, after consulting the Founder's diary once more and pinpointing the exact location, he might try to find it again one day—on a cooler day.

"Hey!" Geronimo suddenly yelled. "What's that?"

Blade spun and saw his friend pointing skyward. He tilted his neck and spied something flying far overhead. At first he thought it was a hawk, until the glint of sunlight off a metallic surface demonstrated otherwise.

"It's not a bird," Hickok stated, rising.

"The thing appears to be made of metal," Geronimo mentioned.

Stunned, Blade watched the object perform a tight circle hundreds of feet above them. Could it be an airplane? he wondered. Thinking of all the books dealing with aviation in the Family library and all the plane photographs he'd admired, he decided the object was far too small to be an aircraft.

"I hear a strange buzzing," Geronimo announced.

Blade heard the sound, too, as if a million angry hornets were in flight en masse, and his brow knit in bewilderment.

"Maybe we should try to shoot it down," Hickok suggested.

"Why? It's not trying to harm us," Blade replied. "Unless it attacks, we leave it alone."

"Yes, *sir*."

The alien device swooped lower, revealing its shape.

With a start, Blade realized he'd been wrong. He distinguished a set of long, thin wings and the unmistakable contours of a tail assembly; he realized it was a plane, but the smallest one he'd ever seen. One of the books he'd read came to mind, a volume detailing how to construct and operate tiny aircraft known as model planes. If he wasn't mistaken, the thing in the sky was a model plane. But it couldn't be.

"It looks like a baby plane," Hickok noted, apparently having the same train of thought as Blade.

"Such things don't exist any more," Geronimo said.

"Peepers don't lie," Hickok stated.

Buzzing even louder, the diminutive aircraft angled to the southeast and flew off.

Eager to see where it went, Blade hastened to the top of the hill and stared after it. His gaze strayed to the valley below and every fiber of his being tingled at the sight of the structures less than half a mile off. "Bingo," he said. "We've hit the jackpot."

Hickok and Geronimo were on the crest in seconds.

"It's the castle!" the gunman exclaimed.

"Or what's left of it," Geronimo amended.

From a distance, the castle appeared to be in a severe state of disrepair. Windows were missing. One of the four turrents was damaged. Vines grew in profusion up the slate gray walls. A flock of starlings was flying above it, bearing eastward.

"I vote we check the place out," Blade said.

"Count me in," Geronimo agreed.

Hickok nodded. "I've always wanted to see a real castle."

The three of them hastened down the far side of the hill into yet more forest, revitalized by their discovery.

Blade took the point, selecting the easiest route, bypassing the thickest brush and skirting clusters of large boulders. After traversing 50 feet, he looked at the ground and halted in astonishment.

Hickok almost bumped into the giant. "What the heck did you stop for?"

"This," Blade said, indicating a well-worn trail leading deeper into the valley. The path wound past them to the northwest.

"So you found a game trail. Big deal."

"Take a closer look," Blade advised.

The gunfighter squatted and peered at a strip of bare earth, his eyes widening when he recognized the distinct impression of a shoe. "Someone has used this trail recently."

"Within the past day or two," Geronimo said.

"Stay alert," Blade instructed them. They followed the path until they arrived at the border of a spacious meadow. Blade stopped short again, shocked by the unexpected.

Corn, wheat, oats and other crops covered the eastern half of the meadow, aligned in separate plots. From the hill, the meadow had been partly obscured by the trees, and the crops tended to blend into the surrounding vegetation. No one would ever suspect the land had been tilled unless they came right up on it.

"Someone lives in this valley," Hickok said.

"In the castle," Geronimo speculated.

"There's enough there to feed a hundred people," Blade noted. "Maybe we've stumbled on a pocket of survivors."

"Let's hope they're friendly," Hickok stated.

Blade led them across the meadow. Halfway to the other

side ther trail broadened, becoming a grassy road. Ruts formed by heavy wagon wheels lined the soil, and there were many more footprints in the intermittent bare spots. Except these prints were of naked feet.

"What do you make of it, pard?" Hickok asked when they halted to examine the tracks.

"Beats me," Blade said. He glanced at Geronimo, who was kneeling and lightly touching the impressions. "You're the tracking expert. What can you tell us?"

"It's hard to determine precise numbers because so many have passed by, but I'd guess that ten to twenty people use this road on a regular basis, at least once a day. And the freshest wagon ruts were made this morning."

"This morning?" Blade repeated, scanning the meadow. "Then they must still be close by." He had the oddest feeling that the three of them were being watched, but by whom was anyone's guess.

"We'd be smart to take cover," Hickok suggested.

"No. If we did, these people might get the wrong idea and think we're here to harm them. We'll stay out in the open and demonstrate they have nothing to be afraid of."

"And what if they're the ones who want to harm us?"

"We'll cross that bridge when we come to it."

The gunman sighed. "Don't take this personal, but you're too trusting sometimes. Not everyone is as kind and decent as the folks at the Home."

Suddenly, from the woods to the south, arose harsh, mocking laughter.

CHAPTER THREE

Blade and his friends crouched and swung to the south, probing the trees for movement. After a minute Geronimo spoke.

"There's no one there."

"Go double-check," Blade said.

The youthful Blackfoot glanced at the giant, then nodded. "Whatever you want." He was up and off in a flash, weaving as he ran, the Winchester at the ready.

"Givin' orders just comes naturally to you, doesn't it?" Hickok asked.

"Don't start," Blade warned. "Someone has to check, and he's more skilled at moving stealthily than the two of us combined."

"Speak for yourself. Geronimo's good, but he has a long way to go before he's in the same class as Atilla."

Blade said nothing, his eyes on the forest. Attila was the current head of the Warriors, an extremely popular, extremely deadly man whose mastery of the martial arts, marksmanship and combat tactics bordered on perfection. His partisans believed he was the best Warrior the Family ever produced, a sentiment Blade shared.

Geronimo had disappeared, melting into the foliage without disturbing a leaf.

"That hombre better be careful," Hickok commented.

"Do I detect a note of concern?"

"Me worried about that no-account Injun? Don't make me laugh."

"Why don't you just admit you love him like a brother?" Blade asked without taking his gaze from the woods.

"Sure I care about him. I care about you, too. But that doesn't mean I'll get all misty eyed if he gets himself killed. I just don't want him to lose the rifle, is all."

"Uh-huh."

"Don't you believe me?"

"In a word, no."

Hickok made a hissing noise. "You're gettin' real sarcastic in your young age, you know that?"

"Think so?"

"I know so. You're changing, Blade. You're not the carefree kid you used to be"

"Are any of us?" Blade responded. "And thanks."

"For what?"

"For calling me Blade instead of Mikey. If you don't stop, I'm liable to lose control and haul off and bust you in the chops."

"Sarcastic *and* mean. I liked you better when your main interest in life was catchin' crayfish."

"We all have to grow up sooner or later. Back in the old days, before the Big Blast, some people went through their whole lives without acquiring an ounce of maturity. It's not the same now. We don't have that luxury."

"You've been listening to Plato again, haven't you?"

"What's wrong with listening to the wisest philospher in our entire history? Even my dad looks up to him. Hearing Plato speak is like having the mysteries of the universe unraveled right before your eyes."

"Oh, brother."

Blade was about to elaborate when he saw Geronimo returning on the double.

"Find anythiung?"

"I didn't see anyone," Geronimo reported, "but I found a network of trails and a garden."

"A what?" Hickok asked.

Geronimo looked at Blade. "Kindly remind that know-it-all that I'm not talking to him until he calls me by my name or the earth plunges into the sun. Whichever occurs first."

Hickok glared. "Enough is enough, already. Come on, Geronimo, give me a break."

In two swift strides Geronimo reached the gunman and gave his startled chum a bear hug, actually lifting Hickok off the ground. "You did it! You called me by my new name!"

"It slipped out," Hickok exclaimed, flustered by the embrace. "Now put me down, you cow chip, before somebody sees us!"

Geronimo let go and beamed. "I knew you wouldn't let me down. For a White Eyes, you're not half bad."

"Yeah, well, let's not get all mushy about this. Show us the garden."

Nodding happily, Geronimo led them down the road through a narrow tract of woodland to a cleared area where flowers grew in profusion, neatly arranged in trimmed rows. There were roses, columbines, geraniums, violets, marigolds and more.

Hickok shook his head in astonishment. "I never would've believed it if I hadn't seen this with my own eyes."

"There must be someone living in the castle," Geronimo reiterated. "As far as I know, there aren't any towns nearby."

Blade thought of the laugh they'd heard and nodded. "Let's go see." He led them along the road, which wound past the garden, through yet another strip of forest, and angled directly at the castle.

The farther they went, the more obvious the damage became. The glass panes in those windows still intact were all cracked or splintered. Inch-wide cracks marred those sections of the outer wall where the vines had yet to get a purchase. And two other turrets were missing portions of their sides.

"I don't get it," Hickok said as they crossed a narrow field toward the medieval edifice looming in front of them. "Why are the crops and the garden so well taken care of, but the castle hasn't been fixed up in ages?"

Blade was wondering the same thing. He spied a wide wooden door at the base of the building. "We'll ask the owner."

When they arrived at the closed door, a raven perched on the battlements vented a strident cry and flapped into the sky.

"I'll do the honors," Geronimo offered, and knocked loudly. His blows seemed to echo within, then fade.

A minute elapsed, and no one acknowledged the pounding.

"Let me," Hickok said, delivering several firm kicks to the bottom panel.

Again there was no response.

"Maybe no one is in," Geronimo stated.

Blade grabbed a large black handle and tugged, but the portal refused to budge. "It's locked."

"Kick it in," Hickok suggested.

"Be serious."

"I am."

"No," Blade declared. "I told you we must make a good impression on these people, and we won't if we barge into their home."

"Then what do we do? Twiddle our thumbs until someone shows up?"

The giant bore to the right. "No, let's have a look around." He craned his neck to view the top of the castle as he walked slowly to the corner. If he didn't know better, he'd swear the place was uninhabited. But how could that be when the garden and the crops indicated there were occupants?

Around the corner lay more of the same, more vines and a cleared space between the structure and the trees. The lowest windows were all a good 20 feet from the ground, too high to reach without a ladder.

"This dump is sort of spooky," Hickok remarked.

"Don't tell me *you're* afraid?" Geronimo asked.

"No. I'm just bringin' up a fact is all."

Blade was halfway to the rear when he happened to glance at the grass near his feet. Lying within inches of his black combat boots was an apple core. "Look at this," he said and squatted.

The others moved in for a better glimpse.

"An animal, you think?" Hickok speculated.

"No," Geronimo said. "Animals eat cores. They don't care about ingesting a few seeds."

Blade jerked his thumb at the battlement. "My guess is that someone ate the apple up there and tossed the core over the side."

"I wish to blazes they'd show themselves," the gunman stated gruffly. "I don't like playin' cat and mouse, particularly when I'm the mouse."

Rising, Blade continued to the far corner. When he strode into the open, he couldn't quite credit the sight he beheld.

"Will you look at those!" Hickok marveled.

"What in the world are they?" Geronimo asked.

There were six small buildings situated in the middle of the yard, three in one row, three in another. Constructed from polished marble, they were one story in height and approximately 20 feet wide. They were ornately embellished with miniature columns and intricate engravings depicting elaborate scenes.

Blade scratched his chin, reflecting. He'd seen photographs of such buildings, but he couldn't recall where.

"They're too dinky to be houses," Hickok commented.

"Maybe they are memorials of some sort," Geronimo guessed.

An image flashed into Blade's mind, a picture in a book dealing with twentieth century social conventions and customs. "They're mausoleums," he informed his friends.

"Mauzi-what?" Hickok responded.

"Mausoleums. Places where the rich and famous were buried."

"Why would anyone want to be buried in a small house?"

"That was the custom before the war. Most people were buried in public cemeteries, and tombstones were placed over their graves. But those with money to spend could have a lasting monument erected in their honor."

"And I thought Geronimo has a swelled head."

Blade walked forward. "Loved ones visited regularly and deposited flowers in remembrance of those who died. Caretakers performed regular maintenance and upkeep to keep the tombs in top condition."

"I'll never understand the bozos who lived back then," Hickok said. "What good is buildin' a monument if you won't be around to enjoy it?"

They halted at the first mausoleum and studied the etchings. One scene displayed naked young men and women engaged in leaping over bulls by grabbing the horns and executing acrobatic flips.

"What the dickens is that supposed to be?" the gunman inquired.

"I believe it shows the bullfighters of ancient Crete,"

Blade surmised. "Don't you remember our classes on the subject?"

Hickok snorted. "I remember the paintings of the soldiers marching off to war or in battle, but I never paid much attention to those other pictures and drawings of men wearin' dresses and women in their birthday suits prancin' around trees."

"What a warped mind," Geronimo cracked.

The gunfighter disregarded the gibe. "Why would anyone want Cretan bullfighters on their tomb?"

Blade shrugged. "Maybe to show they were students of ancient history."

"Or to prove they were idiots," Hickok amended.

The giant moved to the recessed door and tried to open it, without success.

"You're not plannin' to go in there?" Hickok declared.

"I'm curious to see what's inside."

"I can tell you. An old wooden coffin and a bunch of moldy bones. Let's leave well enough alone."

Blade walked to the next tomb, which was slightly bigger than the rest, and stared at a pecular crest engraved near the top: A man in a suit of armor was holding the body of a child in one hand and the head in another.

"Disgusting," Geronimo said.

"Let me guess," Hickok stated. "This guy was tryin' to show that he was fond of the Middle Ages."

"Makes no sense to me," Blade chimbed in.

Geronimo dropped to one knee and ran his fingers over the grass. "This is strange."

"What is?" Blade prompted.

"A lot of people have been here within the past day or two."

"Standin' in front of this tomb?" Hickok said skeptically.

"No," Geronimo answered. "Going *into* the tomb."

Blade and the gunfighter exchanged bewildered expressions.

"You're crazy, pard," Hickok said.

"Which one of us is the tracker here? I know what I'm talking about. At least ten, possibly fifteen people entered this mausoleum."

"Did they come out again?" Blade asked.

"It's difficult to tell. Either they went in first and came out, or they came out, then went in."

"You must be sufferin' from heatstroke, pard."

Blade walked to the next tomb, thoroughly confused by the string of events. What connection was there between the tiny plane, the tilled plots, the apple core and the mausoleums? What was the significance of the laugh? And how did it all tie together with the castle?

He thought about the Founder's cryptic diary entry. Carpenter mentioned taking a hike and bumping into the castle's owner, a man named Edward, who had requested that he leave the estate at once. Although Carpenter tried to be friendly, the owner became angry and even threatened to club him with a walking stick. Rather than provoke the man further, Carpenter returned to the compound.

Blade realized the descendants of the recluse had been on their own for almost a century, completely cut off from the outside world. Perhaps they were simply afraid to make contact. He was more determined than ever to find them and convince them they had nothing to fear. If he practiced a little diplomacy, as his father was always stressing he should do, then he might persuade them to accompany him to the Home. The Family would be delighted at learning there were people living within walking distance, and friendly relations could be established. The Tillers would be very interested in learning the techniques these people used to grow such fine crops and flowers, and perhaps a system of trade could be set up.

The giant idly glanced at the castle and felt a prickling sensation run along his spine.

There was someone at one of the windows, staring back.

CHAPTER FOUR

She stood behind a shadowed pane crisscrossed with cracks, a vague, slim figure attired in what appeared to be a flowing white dress. Raven tresses cascaded over her shoulders. Unfortunately, the murky interior shrouded her facial features.

"Look!" Blade exclaimed.

Hickok and Geronimo spun, the gunfighter starting to go for his guns until he saw the reason for the cry. "It's a woman!" he blurted.

"What was your first clue?" Geronimo asked.

Suddenly, her white dress flowing, the phantom disappeared to the right.

"We've got to get inside," Blade said and ran to the rear wall. He scrutinized the vines, then reached out and tugged on one to test it. "These might hold our weight."

"Might?" Geronimo said, glancing at the nearest window.

"Let's give it a try," Blade said, slinging the Marlin over his shoulder and jumping with outstretched arms. He grabbed a stout vine and held on fast. "Let me go first. If the vines support me, we know they'll support the two of you."

"Good point," Hickok said. "You have been gettin' a mite big in the breadbasket."

"I'm all muscle, and you know it," Blade stated, commencing the ascent. "Keep me covered."

The gunman stared at the windows and the battlement, ready to fire at the slightest hint of a threat.

"At least now we know there's someone home," Geronimo noted. "I wonder who she is."

"The tooth fairy," Hickok quipped and stiffened at a loud crackling and snapping noise from above. He took one look and tackled Geronimo, bearing both of them backwards.

"What the . . . !" Geronimo declared.

Blade fell onto the ground, his powerful legs braced for the impact, and stumbled a few feet before he caught himself. "The vines won't hold," he informed them.

"No foolin'," Hickok said, rising to his knees. "You could have yelled or something. We were almost squished into pancakes."

"Sorry. It all happened so fast."

Geronimo stood. "No harm done."

The giant regarded the window, scowling, and walked to the right. "We'll keep searching until we find a way in."

"And what if we don't?" Geronimo inquired.

"Then I vote we stay here overnight and try again in the morning."

The gunman snickered. *"Now* you want to have a democracy, huh?"

"What do you guys say?"

"If you want to stay, it's fine with me," Geronimo said.

"Good," Blade stated. "I'd really like to get to the bottom of this."

"Where you guys go, I go," Hickok said. "Count me in."

They rounded the southeast corner, passing a compact jumble of vines, and worked their way back to the front entrance without discovering a means of getting in.

"Now what?" Hickok asked.

"We'll patrol the ground, then make camp," Blade answered.

"I have a better idea. There are a lot of big trees in these woods. Why don't we chop one down and use it as a battering ram?" the gunfighter submitted.

"How many times must I tell you that we're not going to damage the property?"

"Listen to you. You're the one who said we shouldn't go bargin' in on them, and yet you were all set to climb up to a window just because you saw a pretty woman."

"I have no way of knowing whether she was pretty or not," Blade responded.

"Listen," Geronimo interrupted.

"What is it?"

"The little plane."

Sure enough, Blade heard the unmistakable buzzing of the tiny aircraft and peered skyward to observe it flying in a wide circle above the castle.

"A woman in white, some horse's butt who likes to laugh to himself, tombs decorated with space cadets who fought bulls for a living, and a midget plane." Hickok listed their finds. "This is too weird for words."

"It beats fishing in the moat," Blade said. "Besides, look at the bright side. Except for the mutates, we haven't been in any danger."

"There's plenty of daylight left, pard."

Blade headed toward the trees, intending to prowl the area, and was halfway there when the buzzing grew in volume. He gazed upward and saw the plane sweeping toward him. Amused rather than disturbed, he watched the craft dive closer and closer, puzzled by its performance. What purpose did it serve? Was someone foolishly attempting to drive them off using such a toy?

"Can I plug that contraption?" Hickok requested. "It annoys me."

"No."

Geronimo raised his hand over his eyes and squinted. "What are those small things attached to the bottom of its wings?"

"Your guess is as good as mine," Blade said, as he saw the aircraft arc into the heavens again. As it did, a small spherical object dropped from the right wing directly toward them. Blade's intuition flared, and he gave his friends a shove. "Into the forest! Move!"

Confused, Geronimo and Hickok nonetheless trusted the giant's judgment enough to obey him instantly and without question. They darted to the northwest.

Blade raced on their heels, his gray eyes glued to the spherical object. When it was 15 feet from the soil, he threw himself to the ground and bellowed, "Get down!"

Again the pair complied, and not a moment too soon. For when they hit the ground, a blast with the force of a quarter-stick of dynamite rent the air and rocked the ground, sending a shower of dirt upward like an erupting geyser.

Blade was on his feet and running for the trees before the thunderous detonation died away. Clods of earth rained onto his head and shoulders. He glanced around for Hickok and Geronimo, but both were lost in the grimy cloud.

The miniature plane droned somewhere overhead.

Unslinging the rifle, Blade gazed upward, hoping for a shot. He emerged from the dust into the bright light, spied the aircraft off to the right, and snapped the stock to his shoulder.

Its wings tilting, the plane abruptly banked and flew toward the castle.

Blade tracked the craft, tempted to try even though the odds of hitting it were miniscule. In frustration he lowered the Marlin just as two hacking forms hurtled into the open.

"Where's the plane?" Hickok asked, his hands on the Colts.

"That way," Blade disclosed, pointing. "Follow me." Wheeling, he jogged into the woods and took shelter behind a trunk.

"What the dickens did that thing drop?" the gunfighter asked, halting next to an oak.

"A bomb of some sort," Geronimo said.

"A couple of feet difference and we would have been goners."

"I had no idea planes that size could do such a thing," Blade observed. "How did it know exactly when to release the bomb?"

"Someone must be controlling it," Geronimo said.

"Whoever it is, they're worm food when I catch up with them," Hickok vowed.

Blade didn't argue. Whoever lived in the castle clearly wanted them dead. By all rights he should hasten to the Home and report the incident to Attila. But he was a Warrior now, and it wasn't fitting for a Warrior to let someone else do his fighting. If he wanted to be worthy of the distinction bestowed on him by the Elders, he must prove their judgment to be sound.

Then there was another angle to consider. If the three of them departed, whoever lived in the castle would be free to conduct unwarranted attacks on others who might wander by. Because of the castle's remote location, such a likelihood was remote. He couldn't ignore the possibility, though, and still uphold his pledge to safeguard human lives.

"So what now, fearless leader?" Hickok inquired.

"We carry on as planned," Blade proposed. "First we'll scour the area, then make camp for the night far enough away to be safe."

"How far is that?" Geronimo asked.

Lacking a definite answer, Blade straightened and moved to the west, conducting a search of the forest. He didn't know what he was looking for, but he knew he'd recognize it when he saw it. When he bisected a well-worn trail, he nodded in satisfaction. There were many prints in the soft soil. "What do you make of these tracks, Geronimo?"

Again the Blackfoot youth examined the ground. "It's the same as before. Lots of footprints, most naked, indicating regular, daily travel." He paused. "Something else also uses this trail."

"An animal?"

"If it is, it's unlike any animal I know of. I'd say these belong to a mutation."

Blade stepped over to inspect the tracks in question, and one look sufficed to prove Geronimo correct. The tracks were immense, 15 inches long and five wide, and were further distinguished by having only three large, oval toes. From their depth in the soil, the creature must be extremely large.

"Imagine the size of that sucker," Hickok said.

"Let's hope we don't run into it," Blade commented.

"Makes no nevermind to me," the gunman responded. "I can always use a little target practice."

Turning to the lelft, Blade stuck with the trail, curious about where it might lead. He wasn't curious long. In no time at all the trail brought them to the edge of the yard, but from the west. He stayed in the trees and stared at the mausoleums, reflecting on their possible significance.

To the north, faint but distinct, was the buzzing of the tiny plane.

"It must still be huntin' for us," Hickok said.

"Let's keep looking around," Blade proposed and went deeper into the woods.

They hiked a mile to the west without finding anything of importance, then swung to the south, then east, and ultimately wound up back on the side of the castle in the forest near the flower garden. By then the sun hung above the horizon.

"We should think about where we want to make camp," Geronimo mentioned. "I don't want to be in the open if there are big mutations roaming this area at night."

"The only place we can hole up is the castle," Hickok said.

"We'll make a lean-to and build a fire," Blade suggested. "Even mutations are scared of flames."

"You hope, pard."

While Geronimo tended to gathering firewood, Blade and Hickok constructed a serviceable lean-to, positioning the open end to the east. Twilight had descended by the time they were done. Geronimo collected stones and formed a ring. Then he placed tinder he'd gathered earlier in the center and removed a flint from his right front pocket.

"Want me to do any huffin' and puffin'?" Hickok offered.

"No, thanks. I can manage."

Blade deposited his backpack inside the lean-to and opened the flap. Inside was ammunition, rope, an extra pair of pants, a whetstone for the Bowies, a canteen, and a brown leather pouch containing his food supply. He removed the canteen and several strips of dried venison.

In another minute Geronimo got the fire going, and all three of them sat around the blaze, munching contentedly.

"This ain't so bad," Hickok said. "At least I'm not pullin' guard duty."

"What's wrong with guard duty?" Blade asked.

"It's boring."

"You should take your responsibilities as a Warrior more seriously. Boring or not, guard duty is essential to the security of the Family."

"Lighten up, big guy. I'm not about to sleep on the job, but you have to admit walkin' the walls leaves a lot to be desired."

"I like guard duty."

"You would."

"What's your point?"

The gunfighter took a bite of jerky and grinned. "You're so gung-ho, you make Attila look like a goof-off."

"I'll let him know you said that when we get back."

Geronimo cleared his throat. "Say, did either of you happen to hear the latest rumor?"

"What now?" Blade asked. "The last stupid rumor was something to the effect that Plato had tried to talk my dad into sending an expedition out to discover what happened to the rest of the country after the Big Blast. I checked with my dad, and he said Plato did mention the idea but never formally submitted it to the Elders. Maybe one day he will."

"This latest rumor has nothing to do with Plato."

"What is it, pard?" Hickok asked casually.

The corners of Geronimo's mouth curved upward. "There's a story going around that a certain young lady has the hots for a certain young man."

Blade stopped chewing.

"Really?" Hickok said. "I haven't heard. Who's the woman?"

"She's not exactly a woman," Geronimo replied. "In fact, she's the same age as us."

"We don't want to hear it," Blade stated gruffly.

The gunfighter glanced in surprise at the giant. "Since when don't you like to hear juicy gossip? If my memory serves, you were the one who went out of his way to learn everything he could about Rikki-Tikki-Tavi and Tanya. Am I right or am I right?"

Blade gazed at the sky. "You're blowing everything way out of proportion, as usual."

The gunfighter laughed. "Am I?" He turned to Geronimo. "Ignore him. What's this latest gossip?"

"I was told that Jenny has fallen head over heels for a certain novice Warrior."

"Jenny?" Hickok snorted. "Some gossip. Everybody

knows she's warm for Blade's form."

The giant lost his interest in the heavens. "What do you mean everybody knows?"

"Everybody at the Home, that is. I can't vouch for the rest of the world."

Geronimo leaned foward. "Sure, everyone knows they're in love. But did you know Jenny wants to bind before the year is out?"

"Do tell," Hickok said, glancing at Blade. "You're a mite young to be gettin' hitched, aren't you?"

"Geronimo doesn't know what he's talking about," Blade declared testily, taking a bite of venison. In the process he accidentally bit his finger.

Hickok snickered. "Oh?"

"I heard the news from Betty, who heard it from Cathy," Geronimo said. "And we all know Cathy is one of Jenny's best friends. According to her, Jenny tried to talk our good buddy into tying the knot but he refused."

The gunman grinned at the giant. "This gets more and more interesting by the moment. Why don't you want to bind?"

"For the very reason you gave. We're too young to get married. Maybe in a few years, after I've established myself as a Warrior and Jenny has become a fully accredited Healer, we'll tie the knot. Marriage isn't a responsibility to be taken lightly."

"Sounds a lot like guard duty," Hickok said and cackled.

They ate in silence for a while. Stars blossomed in the firmament, and a full moon rose to the east. A cool breeze afforded refreshing relief from the day's heat.

"There's something I've wanted to bring up," Geronimo remarked at one point.

"It's not more gossip, I hope," Blade said coldly.

"No. It's about us. We've been best friends since we were in diapers. When we were kids, we adopted the motto of the Three Musketeers, remember? Well, I'd like to continue this way during our adult years."

"Get to the point," Hickok said.

"Okay. After I become a Warrior, why don't we ask Blade's father for permission to form our own Triad?"

Blade sipped at his canteen. The idea had merit. Since the Warriors were divided into combat units of three men apiece anyway, why not indeed? "I like the idea."

"Me, too," Hickok said. "It'll save me the trouble of havin' to break somebody new in to appreciating my refined sense of humor."

Geronimo chortled. "*You* have a sense of humor?"

"We would work well as a team," Blade stated. "I'm sure my dad would agree, and there's no reason the Elders would object."

"One for all, and all for one," Hickok said, grinning.

Geronimo suddenly stood and peered into the shadowy forest to the south. "Do you hear that?"

The gunfighter groaned. "Not again."

Blade was about to say he didn't hear a sound, when from off in the distance there came the distinct sound of a large animal—or something else—crashing through the undergrowth. It took him a few seconds to realize the thing was coming directly toward them.

CHAPTER FIVE

Hickok stepped from under the lean-to and straightened. "It sounds like a friggin' elephant."

"How would you know what an elephant sounds like?" Geronimo asked.

"I listen to you snore at night."

The crashing ceased as abruptly as it began.

"Maybe it's movin' off," Hickok said hopefully.

"And maybe it's spotted our fire," Blade stated. He moved next to the gunman and levered a round into the Marlin's chamber.

"I'll go out there and see," Geronimo offered.

"Not on your life. We'll stick together."

Hickok nudged the Blackfoot. "Sentimental cuss, isn't he?"

Without warning, the crashing resumed, growing louder and louder. A thumping noise became audible, mingled in with the breaking of limbs and the rending of brush.

"What's that?" Hickok whispered.

"Footsteps," Geronimo answered. He rose and joined them, the Winchester at his shoulder.

Blade peered into the dark woods. Although he knew an unknown creature was bearing down on them, he involuntarily stiffened when he detected movement at the limits of his vision. The thing's bulk was tremendous; a great, hulking mass of a brute almost as wide as it was tall, it appeared to be over ten feet in height.

"Dear Spirit," Geronimo exclaimed softly.

Reddish eyes the size of apples glared at them, and a rumbling, sustained growl issued from its throat.

"If it attacks, go for the head," Hickok recommended.

"I'd rather run," Geronimo said.

Blade agreed. An almost palpable aura of evil radiated from the beast, even at that distance, chilling him to the core. He tried to convince himself the sensation was all in his head, but couldn't. The size alone staggered him. Because of his own prodigious build, he'd rarely encountered any menace larger than himself. This thing dwarfed them all. Up close, it would even dwarf him.

"You guys have the rifles," Hickok said. "Why don't one of you take a shot?"

"I don't want to make it mad," Geronimo replied.

"Be serious, pard."

"I am."

The creature moved to the east, its red eyes fixed on their camp, plowing through the vegetation as if there weren't any. When it was nearly out of sight it vented a ferocious roar that caused every insect and animal within a mile's radius to fall silent. Then it departed, the thump of its feet receding to the southeast and finally fading away.

Geronimo expelled a sigh of relief. "That was too close for comfort."

"Didn't faze me none," Hickok claimed. "I could've taken it down, easy."

"Dream on," Geronimo said.

"Piece of cake."

Blade stared at the last spot he'd seen the thing, troubled

by his reaction. Rarely had he known the feeling of genuine fear, but while watching the creature he'd felt just that, a fleeting instant of stark panic. He shook his head to clear his mind of his apprehension.

Hickok glanced at the giant. "Are you okay, pard?"

"Fine."

"You sure? You look a bit peaked."

"I'm fine," Blade repeated sternly. He sat down in the lean-to, relishing the warmth of the flames.

"Why didn't it come after us?" Geronimo asked.

"The fire, maybe," Hickok said.

"A thing that big?"

"Maybe one of us has bad breath."

"Speak for yourself."

Blade swallowed water from the canteen and wiped the back of his hand across his mouth. "Do you want to draw lots to see which one of us pulls the first shift?"

"I'll take the first watch, if you don't mind," Hickok said.

"I'll take the second," Geronimo chimed in.

"Leaving me the third," Blade stated. "Fine by me."

The gunfighter took a seat, and after a minute Geronimo did likewise.

"This trip of ours is turnin' into quite an adventure," Hickok remarked.

Blade chewed on more jerky, engrossed in thought. When he'd expressed an interest in staying overnight, he hadn't foreseen they might have to take on a monster. He'd fought his share of genetic abominations in his time, but never anything as immense as the brute they'd just seen. If they were getting in over their heads, wouldn't the wise course of action entail returning to the Home? Sure, he was a Warrior, but he was new at his trade and had a lot to learn. The same with Hickok. He scanned the forest and realized they were stuck there whether they liked it or not, at least until morning.

"We should check the tracks that thing made at first light," Geronimo advised. "It might be the creature responsible for those strange three-toed footprints."

"If that critter comes back, let's offer it some grub and try to train it," Hickok said, smirking. "If it cooperates, we'll have it kick in the castle door."

The conversation drifted from the monster to a discussion of certain girls at the Home, with Hickok and Geronimo debating their assets and attractiveness for over an hour. Blade rarely spoke. His eyes darted to the woods whenever a noise was heard, and he kept the fire going high.

"Well," Hickok said at length, "I suppose the two of you will want to turn in soon."

"I'm beat," Geronimo commented.

"I'm not," Blade fibbed. "I'll stay up a while yet."

Hickok laughed. "Don't worry. I won't let the boogeyman slit your throat while you sleep."

"Not funny," Blade said sternly.

"Lighten up, Mikey. I was only kiddin'."

The giant leaned toward the gunfighter, his flinty eyes mere slits. "This is the last time I'll tell you. Don't *ever* call me that name again."

Shock registered on Hickok's face. He glanced at Geronimo, who shrugged, then nodded at Blade. "Sure, big guy, whatever you want. I didn't mean to get your goat."

"No offense taken," Blade said, although his tone contradicted the statement. He crossed his arms and hunched against the lean-to, glowering into the fire.

Geronimo spread out on his back and draped his left arm over his eyes.

For a minute Hickok regarded the giant intently, then he took a position on the east side of the fire where he could see in all directions and not have their makeshift shelter obstruct his view.

Blade idly gnawed on his lower lip, annoyed at himself for losing his temper over a trifle. He had no reason to jump down the gunfighter's throat, and he attributed his lapse to a bad case of nerves after the incident involving the monster. To cover his chagrin, he thought about other subjects—his dad, his budding friendship with Plato, his feelings for Jenny, and his new duties as a Warrior.

He appreciated his good fortune in having his dad as the Leader, but he disliked the extra attention directed his way because of it. The Elders all expected great things out of him. Plato claimed he possessed the spark of greatness within. Their compliments, however, fell on skeptical ears. As far as he was concerned, the only exceptional quality he possessed was size, which in itself hardly indicated any outstanding potential. On top of that, his whole goal in life was to serve as a Warrior until he reached retirement age and could sit on the council of Elders. Hardly a career that would result in terrific accomplishments.

Blade reflected on the comments his friends made about Jenny and recalled her asking him to bind. To say the least, he'd been surprised. Sure, they cared for each other. But they were only 16, and in his estimation they weren't mature enough yet to assume the awesome responsibilities of husband and wife. Jenny disagreed. She felt they were mature enough, but since girls invariably matured faster than guys, she was justified in making such a claim. He felt bad about disappointing her, but he wasn't about to say yes until he was certain they were both ready.

An image of Attila filled his mind—tall, lean, attired in black leather pants and a wolf's hide shirt, hair hanging to the small of his back and lively green eyes. There was a man! Of all the Warriors, of all the people at the Home next to his dad and possibly Plato, Attila impressed Blade the most.

The head Warrior possessed a carefree attitude that Blade keenly admired. Attila never lost his cool and always took everything in stride. Blade wished he could be the same way, wished others would refer to him as a man who lived life to the fullest and never got bent out of shape. Instead, everyone who knew him well claimed he was moody, an introvert, in a good frame of mind one minute and troubled the next. Maybe they were right. Ever since the death of his mom he'd been changed inside.

Blade's eyeslids drooped. He heard Geronimo snoring softly and saw the gunfighter staring at the fire. "Hickok," he said sleepily.

"Yeah, pard?"

"Sorry."

"For what?"

"For getting on your case."

"Don't sweat it. We all get cranky now and then."

"I seldom see you cranky."

Hickok grinned. "That's because I've naturally got a downright sweet disposition."

"I suppose you do."

"Why don't you grab some shut-eye, Mi—," Hickok began and caught himself, "—Blade. Geronimo will wake you when it's your turn to tend the fire."

"Thanks. Don't mind if I do." Blade sank on his side and felt the warmth of the flames on his face. Contented and comfortable, he drifted into dreamland.

When next his eyes fluttered open, Blade had to think for a minute to recall where he was. He spied Geronimo near the fire now and Hickok lying to the left, sound asleep. Inhaling loudly, he pushed up on his elbows and yawned. "Is it my turn yet?"

"No," Geronimo replied. "I just took over from motormouth a short while ago."

"I can pull my stint now if you like."

"There's no need. Go back to sleep."

Sighing, Blade settled down again and watched the flickering tongues of orange and red dance and writhe.

"Say, Geronimo?"

"Yes?"

"Would you say I'm moody?"

"Only during a full moon."

"I'm serious."

"Now and then. No more than the rest of us."

"Hickok is hardly ever moody."

"There's a reason for that."

"Oh?"

"Nathan is the only man alive who has a vacuum between his ears."

"He's sharper than most."

"True, but if you ever tell him I said so, I'll deny every word."

Grinning, Blade let his mind lapse into a disjointed state where his thoughts came in spurts. Finally, slumber claimed him.

What was that strange noise?

Blade didn't know if he were awake or asleep. He lay there, his eyes shut, and listened, positive something out of the ordinary had brought him around. Cracking his lids, he gazed at Geronimo, who was dozing while sitting upright, then at Hickok, who slept as peacefully as a baby.

He must have imagined the whole thing.

Just as Blade closed his eyes he heard the sound again, a peculiar, airy titter. Puzzled, he raised his head a few inches and gazed into the forest, astounded to behold dozens of things—moving about at the very edge of the firelight.

The vague shapes were thin and tall. They flitted about in the woods, prancing from tree to tree, giggling lightly all the while. Their skin had a pale cast, as if reflecting the moonlight.

Blade saw one of the things start to approach the camp. He sat up, grabbing the Marlin, and shouted, "Geronimo! Look out!"

In the fleeting interval between the instant the giant uncoiled and his bellowed warning, the creatures in the woods abruptly vanished, seeming to fade to nothingness in the blink of an eye.

Geronimo leaped to his feet, startled, the Winchester in his hands. "What? Where?" he exclaimed, looking in all directions.

A split second later Hickok came to his feet, both Colts drawn and cocked, bewildered but ready to fight. "What the dickens is going on?" he demanded.

Flabbergasted, Blade stood and stepped into the open. "Didn't you see them, Geronimo?"

"See what?"

"Those things in the trees."

The Blackfoot surveyed their surroundings again. "I don't see anything."

"They were there a few seconds ago. Dozens of them."

"Of what?" Hickok asked.

"I don't know. They were sort of like wood nymphs or fairies," Blade explained, unable to think of a more precise description.

"Wood nymphs?" Geronimo repeated.

"Fairies?" Hickok said.

"Yeah. You know. They were flitting around in the trees and laughing," Blade elaborated.

Hickok and Geronimo locked eyes, then the gunfighter twirled his Colts into their holsters and chuckled. "We'd better have the dried venison checked when we get back to the Home. They must be adding a new ingredient to it nowadays."

"Don't you believe me?" Blade asked.

"You've got to admit your tale is a mite hard to swallow."

"I saw them, I tell you."

"We believe you believe you saw them," Geronimo said, "but that doesn't necessarily mean they were really there."

"I *saw* them," Blade stressed.

Hickok made a show of turning in a circle while whistling and calling out, "Oh, little fairies? Where are you? Come out, come out, wherever you are."

Geronimo cackled.

"When have I ever lied to you?" Blade demanded, peeved at their attitudes. "One of those things was coming right toward us when I shouted. Somehow, they all vanished."

"Somehow," Geronimo said. "Like into thin air?"

"Yes. Exactly."

"Oh, brother," Hickok mumbled, laying back down. "Monsters with glowing eyes. Flittin' fairies. What I said before still goes. This place is too weird for words."

"I'd never doubt either of you," Blade said.

"Now don't get all upset over a bunch of wood nymphs," Hickok responded. "If you say they were there, then I'll go along with it. But let's be realistic. Even if there are a horde of fairies out there, I doubt they pose a danger to us. I can't see Peter Pumpernickel and his gang jumpin' our buns, can you?"

"That's Pan, dope," Geronimo corrected him.

"Whatever." Hickok stretched and closed his eyes. "If it's all the same to you, I've got to catch up on my beauty sleep. But be sure and wake me if Leapin' Leroy and his Killer Leprechauns attack."

Blade scanned the woods again and again, hoping for a glimpse of the creatures to redeem himself. None showed.

"Why don't you crash?" Geronimo suggested. "I'll keep watch for the nymphs."

"I'm not sleepy now," Blade said.

"Why waste the time staying up and waiting for those things to come back?"

"I can't honestly say."

Exasperated, Blade went under the lean-to and lay on his stomach. He began to wonder if he'd really seen them himself. His friends had never doubted him before. Maybe, because of everything that had happened in the past 24 hours, his imagination was playing tricks with him. He rested his chin on his forehead and patiently waited for his turn to pull guard duty, determined to stay awake. But after a while, despite his best intentions, he fell asleep for the third time and dreamed of rabid leprechauns in fairy suits swooping out of the sky to rend him limb from limb.

CHAPTER SIX

Leapin' Leroy was in the act of impaling him on a silver butter knife when Blade felt someone shaking his shoulder and sat bolt upright. He automatically reached for the Marlin, blinking in confusion, and only relaxed when he saw Geronimo kneeling at his side, regarding him as one might a lunatic.

"It's just me. Are you okay?"

"Yeah. Sure." Blade swallowed and gazed at the woods. "Is it my turn?"

"Yep. Nothing stirred the rest of my shift."

"Good," Blade said, retrieving the rifle and sliding out. "Get some sleep."

"I wouldn't mind pulling double duty."

"I'm fine. But you two clowns are beginning to give me a complex."

"Sorry. But I've never seen you so rattled before. What's wrong?"

"Nothing," Blade snapped.

Shrugging, the Blackfoot placed the Winchester near his chest and lay down. "Wake us at dawn."

"You got it." Blade stepped to the east side of the fire and squatted, shivering in the brisk night air. He stuck the rifle in the crook of his arm, rubbed his hands together, and feeling his stomach growl, resolved to hunt game for breakfast. Fresh roasted meat might do them all some good.

Sitting, Blade scrutinized the heavens, marveling at the celestial spectacle. There seemed to be a well-nigh infinite number of stars, a sea of cosmic creation aswarm with fiery beacons radiating light and life to countless worlds. He wished he'd been born before the war, for the sole reason of being able to witness the historic missions to Mars and the establishment of a lunar base in a joint venture of the United States, the Soviet Union and France. It was most unfortunate space exploration ground to a halt after the liberal Russian president was deposed and the hard-liners regained control. America and Europe devoted all of their attention to producing armaments instead of spaceships.

The sputtering fire snapped Blade out of his contemplation. He realized they needed more wood. Slinging the Marlin over his right shoulder, he walked into the forest, scouring the ground for fallen limbs. He loaded his arms and returned.

As Blade bent to set the wood on the ground, a faint rustling arose to his rear. He pretended not to notice, straightened slowly, and whirled.

The ruse worked.

One of the things was back, standing near a tree 20 feet away, watching him.

Instantly Blade took off, not bothering to yell to his companions because they wouldn't believe him anyway. He needed proof, and the only way to obtain it was to capture the creature. His legs pumping, he covered the ground in prodigious bounds consistent with his size. Only one other person in the entire Family had ever beaten him at a foot race—a martial artist named Rikki-Tikki-

Tavi—and he had no doubt he'd catch the nymph.

As quick as the giant was, the pale being was even quicker. It spun and took off like a frightened deer, moving with astonishing speed and seeming to fly over the terrain.

Blade breathed easily, adopting a natural rhythm, determined to stay after the thing until he dropped from exhaustion or caught it. In the back of his mind he wondered if the red-eyed monster might still be about, and he wavered for a few strides before reminding himself he was a Warrior and Warriors never let fear get the better of them.

The pale creature maintained a steady lead, never gaining or losing ground, bearing to the south.

If not for the full moon, Blade would have found the going extremely difficult. He tripped once on a root but righted himself quickly. Every now and then a limb snatched at his vest or gouged him in the cheek.

For several minutes the chase continued. The creature angled to the west, seldom looking back, apparently heading for a specific destination.

Blade lost all track of where he was. He guessed they were passing to the east of the castle. To his annoyance, the thing ran even faster and gained a wider lead. Even Rikki wouldn't be able to overtake it, he realized, but he stubbornly kept running.

The creature paused to look at its pursuer, then forged ahead, darting into a group of saplings and disappearing.

Not again, Blade reflected, sprinting to the stand and barging through the slender trees. Not until he broke from cover and saw the mausoleums did he realize he was at the border of the yard.

There was no sign of the thing.

Damn!

Furious at losing it, Blade walked into the open and looked in all directions. Where had the creature gone? Despite its demonstrated fleetness, the thing couldn't have crossed the yard in the time he took to reach the edge of the woods. Was it hiding behind one of the tombs? Unslinging the rifle, he moved to the nearest mausoleum and circled it.

Nothing.

Blade went to the next, then the next, and nowhere was there a clue to the creature's whereabouts. Mystified, he moved to the middle of the yard and halted. Now he didn't have any proof to show Hickok and Geronimo. All that effort had been wasted.

A sharp gust of wind from the north caused the trees to rustle and brought something with it—the faint sound of music.

Shocked, Blade gazed at the darkened castle. Were his ears playing tricks on him or did he really hear the soft strains of a melodious instrumental wafting through the air? As he strode toward the structure, the volume increased slightly. There could be no doubt. Somewhere in the bowels of the edifice someone was playing music.

He considered fetching his friends and letting them hear for themselves, but what if the music stopped before they came back? Neither of them would believe him. They'd laugh in his face and claim he was going off the deep end, and being humiliated once a night was more than enough for him.

Blade debated whether to investigate further, then thought of his friends slumbering unprotected back at camp. Reluctantly, he retraced his footsteps. At daybreak he would return to the castle and find a way in. Somehow, he intuitively knew the secret to the many mysteries they'd encountered lay within that foreboding monument from ancient times.

He covered half the distance when a guttural snarl off to his left drew him up short. Was it a mutation or a normal predator? His eyes roving over the murky vegetation, he proceeded warily. Between the 45-70 and his Bowies he should be able to handle anything that came along except for dinosaur-sized beasts with glowing red eyes.

Blade reached the camp without mishap and found his buddies still sleeping peacefully. He immediately fed fuel to the fire, and when the flames were high enough he sat back and draped his forearms on his knees. Jenny's beautiful image filled his thoughts, so he spent the next hour reviewing their disagreement over when to bind and another argument they'd had over what to name their first boy. She'd been so proud of him after his Naming, and a discussion about the importance of selecting the perfect name led to a consideration of the ones they'd want to bestow on their own children. Both of them liked Judy or Lisa for a girl, but they clashed where their future male offspring were concerned. Jenny wanted to call their first-born boy Gabriel. Blade wanted a more colorful name, but his wife-to-be absolutely refused to have any son of hers be called Tarzan.

The remaining hours until daylight were uneventful. Blade kept the fire roaring, making two additional trips to gather wood before the first streaks of light tinged the eastern sky. He rose and stretched, grateful the night was over.

Unexpectedly, from the direction of the castle, came a series of three strident, sustained musical notes.

Hickok and Geronimo were on their feet before the sounds faded. The gunman's hands hovered over his Colts as he swung from side to side, not yet fully awake but trying to identify the source of the noise.

"What the blazes was that?"

"Sounded like a bugle or a trumpet," Blade speculated.

"Who'd be playing music at this time of day?" Hickok asked grumpily. "They should have their head examined."

"This day begins as strangely as the last one ended," Geronimo commented.

"I'm glad both of you heard that bugle," Blade said.

"You are?" Geronimo responded.

"Yep. Because now you'll believe me when I tell you I heard music last night when I was standing near the mausoleums."

Geronimo was all interest. "What were you doing there?"

"I chased one of those nymphs."

A protracted groan issued from Hickok. "Terrific," he muttered. "I'm not up five minutes and already we're talking about the phantom fairies."

"Why don't we eat breakfast, then investigate the castle," Blade suggested.

"Do we get to kick in the door if no one answers our knock?" Hickok inquired.

"Yes. I get the feeling someone is playing us for fools, and I want to get to the bottom of this whole business."

"Okay. Then count me in, pard."

Blade picked up his rifle. "I'll go bag us some game."

"There's no need to go hunting on my account," Geronimo said. "I like to eat a light meal in the morning. Jerky and water will do me just fine."

"Same here. I'm not in the mood for stuffed pigeon with all the trimmings," Hickok added.

"Suit yourself."

They sat near the fire and munched on the venison while all around them the woodland came alive with the songs of birds and the rustling of animals.

"Tell me more about the thing you went after?" Hickok prompted.

"There's not much to reveal because I couldn't get a good look at it. All I know is the creature is light colored and runs faster than I do."

"Must be part cheetah," Geronimo quipped.

"Why didn't you shoot the critter?" Hickok asked.

"It didn't make a move to attack. Besides, what if the thing is part human?" Blade replied.

"Then it shouldn't be waltzin' around monster-infested

country in the middle of nowhere," Hickok declared. "Any lamebrain stupid enough to pull such a stunt deserves to have his fool head blown off."

Geronimo glanced at the buckskin-clad Warrior. "Need I point out that *we* are waltzing around monster-infected country in the middle of nowhere?"

"It's different with us."

"How so?"

"We know what we're doing."

Geronimo turned to Blade. "Did any of that make sense to you?"

"No."

"Good. For a second there, I thought it was me."

"Was that another cut?" Hickok wanted to know.

After finishing their meal, they doused the fire, donned their backpacks and tramped toward the castle. Geronimo took the lead. On all sides birds greeted the rising of the sun by joining in full chorus.

Breathing in the crisp air, Blade felt invigorated. Gone were the doubts and subtle fears of the night before. He was supremely confident they'd be able to deal with any threat, overcome any obstacle.

Geronimo constantly searched for tracks. When they reached the general area where the red-eyed monstrosity had been, he crouched. "Hey, take a look at this."

Butterflies fluttered in Blade's stomach when he laid eyes on more of the gigantic three-toed tracks.

"Now we know what makes those," Hickok remarked.

"These seem a bit smaller than the ones we saw yesterday," Geronimo mentioned.

"They look the same to me," the gunfighter said.

"What's your opinion, Blade?" Geronimo asked.

The giant pursed his lips thoughtfully. He honestly couldn't decide whether there was a size difference, but he did know he didn't like the idea of two of the brutes being abroad. "I don't know," he said.

"We're lucky none have shown up near the Home," Geronimo stated.

Hickok chuckled. "If we're lucky, maybe some of those wood nymphs will follow us back to the compound. We can set a snare and catch one of the rascals. I'm sure the rest of the Family will be tickled pink to see a genuine wonder in person. Or whatever."

"I can't wait until you see one yourself," Blade said.

"I hope you won't get upset if I don't hold my breath."

Geronimo took the point again, his eyes glued to the soil. "If there were other creatures here last night, they didn't leave a single footprint.

"*If?*" Blade repeated.

"You know what I mean."

"Certainly. You're a graduate of the Hickok school of blathering idiocy."

"Whoa!" Hickok exclaimed. "Now that definitely was a cut."

"Perish forbid."

The gunfighter snickered. "No doubt about it. You've definitely been spendin' too much time with Plato. You're startin' to use the same highfalutin words he does."

"At least he speaks English."

"Wow. Another cut. You're on a roll, pard."

A short while later they were close enough to distinguish the large individual stones composing the battlement. In anxious silence they neared the east side of the castle when they heard a familiar sound.

The buzzing of the miniature plane.

CHAPTER SEVEN

Warily the three youths neared the castle wall, using every available cover. At the edge of the forest, when they hid behind trees and scanned the blue sky, it didn't take long to spot their aerial nemesis.

The small plane was flying in a circle around the castle, just above the turrets, continually performing the same pattern.

"What do you reckon it's doing?" Hickok whispered.

"Looking for us," Geronimo guessed.

Blade regarded the aircraft solemnly. Whoever controlled the plane would employ it to try and stop them from entering. He'd made the mistake of letting the craft dive-bomb them yesterday; he wasn't about to let history repeat itself. "Gernimo, take it down."

"With pleasure," the Blackfoot replied, raising the Winchester to his right shoulder. He patiently aimed, tracking the craft's flight and waiting for the right moment.

"We don't have all day," Hickok said.

"Hold your horses," Geronimo retorted. The plane was

over the southeast turret, its tiny propeller a blur, moving faster than a bird in flight. He inhaled deeply, steadied the barrel and fired.

A shower of sparks and metal exploded from the center of the aircraft, and it went into a steep spiral, tendrils of black and white smoke trailing in its wake. Narrowly missing the rampart, the plane slanted toward the edge of the woods, diving straight at the trio.

Blade awoke to the danger first. Such a small craft posed little threat, but the load it undoubtedly carried did. "Scatter" he shouted, turning and dashing northward. He prayed the others were doing the same. Five yards he covered. Ten. A wide tree trunk on the right offered the sanctuary he needed, and he ducked behind it at the same second the aircraft hit the earth.

The resultant explosion was deafening. Trees buckled or shook. The very ground trembled as if from a quake. Dust and leaves and bits of wood formed a choking cloud vastly larger than the one before.

Hugging the grass, Blade felt the ground move under him. He held his mouth down low to avoid breathing in the swirling cloud and waited for it to disperse. Dirt and jagged pieces of timber rained down, covering him from head to toe. Impatient to learn the fate of his friends, he peered at the spot where the plane struck but saw no movement.

Gradually the cloud dissipated. Blade rose and moved closer to the impact point. "Geronimo! Hickok! Where are you?"

Silence greeted his cry.

Over a dozen trees had been toppled or shattered by the explosion and littered the ground in a jumbled mass. Falling leaves formed a carpet over everything.

"Hickok! Geronimo!" Blade called out again.

"Over here," the Blackfoot responded, appearing from behind an oak situated 20 yards to the south.

"Where's Nathan?"

Geronimo blinked. "I don't know. I thought he was with you."

"I haven't seen him since we took cover."

They walked slowly toward the center of the blast area, scouring the tangled trunks and branches.

"Hickok!" Geronimo yelled. "Answer us!"

Anxiety tugged at Blade's mind. If anything had happened to the colorful gunfighter, he'd never forgive himself. The idea to travel to the castle had been exclusively his; he was directly responsible for the fate of his friends. He shoved a busted section of limb aside and bent down to peer under a fallen tree resting on top of another downed monarch of the forest.

"Hickok! Hickok!" Geronimo kept shouting, turning every which way. "Quit playing games and tell us where you're at."

No answer was forthcoming.

Not until the two of them reached the middle of the flattened vegetation did Geronimo voice the concern uppermost on their minds.

"What if he's dead?"

"We won't stop searching until we find him."

"He must be buried under one of these trees," Geronimo guessed. "Maybe he was flattened like a pancake."

Blade scanned the ground, dreading the very thought. "We don't know that," he said gruffly. "Don't assume the worst."

"He might be a royal pain in the neck sometimes, but deep down he's one of the most decent guys I know," Geronimo lamented. "You couldn't ask for a more loyal friend."

"Will you quit talking like he's dead?" Blade snapped.

Geronimo began moving brush, his features downcast. "I'd never tell him to his face, but I'm proud to know him. To tell the truth, I even liked his sense of humor."

From ten yards to the east, from under a pile of shorn

branches and uprooted vegetation, came a triumphant bellow. "Aha! I heard that!"

"Uh-oh," Geronimo said.

Blade hastened over and got there just as the gunfighter succeeded in shoving the branches off and slowly stood. "Are you okay?"

"Oh, sure," Hickok replied, coughing. "I love being blown to smithereens."

"What happened?"

"I don't want to talk about it," Hickok stated, checking to ensure his prized revolvers were still in their holsters.

Blade brushed several leaves from the lean youth's left shoulder. "You had us worried to death. Why didn't you answer when we were shouting? The least you can do is explain."

Hickok bowed his head as if ashamed. "I tripped," he mumbled.

"You what?"

"Tripped. I was runnin' to beat the band when my foot got caught on this bush and down I went. Then the blamed plane hit, and I felt certain my number was up. The concussion must have knocked me out for a bit, because the next thing I knew I heard voices and there you guys were yakkin' about me."

"You were lucky," Blade said.

"Tell me about it."

Geronimo walked toward them, snickering. "Did I hear correctly, clumsy? You tripped?"

"And did I hear you say that you *like* my sense of humor?" Hickok countered.

"Me? Give me a break. The explosion rattled your brain."

"I heard you," Hickok stated. "Don't try to weasel your way out of this."

The Blackfoot straightened up indignantly. "Indians never weasel."

"Do they lie?"

"Definitely not."

"Then you're not an Indian."

"All right, already," Blade interjected. "We have more important things to concern us than Hickok's sense of humor."

"See?" The gunfighter beamed. "Even you admit I have one."

Sighing, Blade pivoted and started toward the castle. His gaze alighted on the base of the east wall, and surprise halted him in midstride. "Look!" he exclaimed.

The others focused on the building.

Where before there stood a solid wall, there was now a wide crack running from the ground to a height of ten feet. The force of the explosion had wrenched the very foundation, causing the massive stones to shift and split. A yard wide at the bottom, the crack tapered to a few inches at the top. Beyond lay impenetrable darkness.

Stunned by the discovery, the three of them converged on the wall.

"I don't see nothing movin' in there," Hickok commented.

"Are we going in?" Geronimo asked.

"I am," Blade declared. "You two can stay outside if you want."

"What's that crack supposed to mean?" Hickok demanded. "One for all, remember? Where you go, big guy, we go."

"I hate to say this," Geronimo said, "but Nathan is right."

The gunfighter chuckled. "Am I on a roll, or am I on a roll?"

Blade trained the Marlin on the opening and listened for strains of music or other sounds from within, but all he heard was the whisper of the breeze. He stopped at the wall and felt a cool draft on his face. A dank scent tingled his nostrils.

"Looks like the inside of Geronimo's noggin' in there," Hickok noted.

"Want me to make a torch?" the Blackfoot volunteered.

"Go ahead," Blade directed. He tentatively leaned into the crack and distinguished the outlines of a wide corridor but no sign of life. The interior resembled a tomb.

"I imagine whoever owned the flyin' contraption is a bit riled at us right about now," Hickok mentioned. "We'd best be extra careful."

"At least we won't have to worry about them using explosives on us when we're inside," Blade said.

"True, but who knows what other tricks these yahoos have up their sleeves?"

Blade leaned against the wall and waited for Geronimo to construct a makeshift torch.

First the Blackfoot selected a suitable length of straight limb, then chomped off the thin offshoots. Next he went to a pine tree and hacked away a section of bark, exposing the sap-coated trunk. Quickly he rubbed the thick end of the limb back and forth across the sap until it was caked with the sticky substance. Pivoting, he began collecting dried leaves into a pile. Once he had enough, he placed the end of the limb in the middle of the pile and used his left hand to pack the leaves onto the sap. Finally, he started a small fire with his flint, dipped the torch into the flames until it caught, then stamped out the fire.

"Here we go," Geronimo said, rejoining them.

Hickok feigned a yawn. "Is it still the twenty-first century?"

"Very funny."

"Let's go," Blade declared, easing through the crack. He moved a few feet and waited for the others. The moment Geronimo entered, the flickering torchlight illuminated the high corridor for a considerable distance, revealing stone walls and a stone floor.

"Reminds me of a cave," Hickok commented.

"Don't let your guard down for an instant," Blade cautioned, leading the way. He spied a recessed doorway on the right and stealthily headed toward it, bothered by the pervasive silence. There should be noise of some kind. He knew people were living there; he'd seen one of them. So where were they?

A large wooden door materialized in the shadows.

Holding the Marlin in his left hand, Blade reached for the black handle and paused when the latch clicked loudly. Anyone on the other side was bound to have heard. Standing to one side, he pulled the door open.

Within was a musty chamber as inky as the corridor.

Cautiously entering, Blade placed his back to the wall while his friends followed. Revealed by the torch was an enormous living room containing two sofas, a half-dozen chairs, and in one corner, incredibly, a grand piano.

"Wow," Hickok breathed.

"Everything is in perfect condition," Geronimo said.

Blade had noticed the same thing. He realized there must be countless treasures from the past on every floor. Walking through the castle was like taking a stroll back in time to the days before the war. "Stay close," he instructed them, as he moved out to the corridor. Taking a right, he proceeded deeper into the fascinating enigma.

For a good 20 yards there were only blank walls, then a stairway appeared on the left.

Stepping closer to investigate, Blade found there were steps leading upward and a flight going down. From below wafted a musty, moist smell.

"Which way, pard?" Hickok asked.

Before Blade could answer, they all heard a rustling noise and glanced up at the next landing. Standing in the open, her long, dark hair partially concealing her features, was the woman in the white dress. As soon as they laid eyes on her, she bolted.

"After her!" Blade cried, bounding up the stairs three at a stride and outpacing his companions before he took the first turn. Ahead was the mystery woman, fleeing as if her life depended on it, the lower half of her dress billowing behind her, already at the next landing. He saw her dart down a corridor and increased his speed.

"Wait for us," Hickok shouted.

But Blade had no intention of letting the woman escape. He attained the landing and spied her racing figure far ahead, her white dress making her easy to spot. "Wait!" he cried. "We won't hurt you."

Apparently she didn't believe him because she kept on running.

Blade took off, disregarding the fact that darkness now enveloped him. He thought he saw the woman dart to the left, possibly through a doorway, and he concentrated on the exact spot as he narrowed the gap. Sure enough, he found an open door and rushed recklessly inside, then halted. Not a trace of light broke the solid curtain of black, and he couldn't determine where the walls were or if there was furniture scattered about. Since he couldn't see her but suspected she was hiding nearby, he decided to try coaxing her out. "I know you're in here, lady," he declared in his most mature tone. "You have nothing to be afraid of. My friends and I have come in peace."

The black curtain mocked him with its silence.

"Please believe me," Blade urged. "We only want to talk to you, nothing more. Come out where I can see you."

That was when the net dropped over his shoulders.

CHAPTER EIGHT

Blade instinctively elevated his arms to ward off the clinging mesh, but he was too late to prevent the loops of rope from draping over his torso and falling almost to the floor. He took a step backwards, or tried to, and regretted his stupidity when his lower legs became entangled and he lost his balance. Down he went, toppling halfway through the doorway, his right shoulder bearing the brunt of the impact and making him wince as the stone floor jarred him to the bone. Rolling onto his stomach, he attempted to push erect, but the clinging net restricted his arms to the point where he couldn't move more than an inch.

Light thuds sounded to his rear.

Mystified, Blade tried to roll over again. Strong hands gripped his ankles and started to pull him into the room. Realizing he was helpless and anticipating he might be shot or stabbed at any second, he tilted his neck and yelled at the top of his lungs. "Hickok! Geronimo! They've got me!"

A hard object, perhaps a fist, rammed into the fledgling Warrior's back.

Blade arched his back, grit his teeth against the pain and renewed his struggle to turn over. He let go of the Marlin, which was flush with his body, and tried to force his huge arms outward, exerting all of his prodigious strength. More blows rained down, but he ignored them. The fact his assailants weren't using knives or clubs made him think they wanted to capture him alive, which was little consolation under the circumstances. He strained as he'd never strained before, every muscle bulging, and slowly, inch by inch, the net began to loosen.

A loud scraping sound suddenly punctuated the pounding of the fists.

Engrossed in breaking free at all costs, Blade thought nothing of the noise until a heavy object that felt like solid iron crashed down onto his head and shoulders. His consciousness swirled, and for a second he was on the verge of blacking out. He vaguely registered the drumming of footsteps, and then bright light engulfed him and familiar voices brought overwhelming relief.

"Here he is, Geronimo!"

"He's caught in a net!"

"What was your first clue?"

"Get him out, quick."

"You get him out. I can cover better than you can."

As the net was pulled off, Blade twisted his head and blinked up at his friends. Hickok stood with his Colts leveled, glaring into the chamber, while Geronimo was tugging on the net with one hand and holding the torch aloft with the other. "Took you long enough," Blade muttered, his shoulders and back throbbing, and then thought of his attackers. "Where are they?"

"Who?" Hickok responded.

"The ones who jumped me," Blade stated, sitting up.

"We didn't see anyone," Geronimo said.

"Impossible," Blade declared. "I think there were two of them, and they didn't go out this door." He clasped the Marlin and stood up. Nearby lay an overturned wooden chair. He realized one of his foes had used it to strike him and wished he could return the favor. Incredibly, there was no one else in the chamber.

But there were books, thousands and thousands of them, filling bookcases that lined all four walls from the floor to the ceiling. In the middle of the room was a large mahogany table and five chairs, brothers to the one lying near the doorway.

"It's a library," Blade said, stepping over to the table. His eyes made a complete circuit of the room, seeking an exit. There was none. He did discover how they'd managed to drop the net on him. The bookcases on either side of the door weren't completely filled, which led him to conclude his attackers had climbed up and perched there with the net taut between them until he came in. If so, it meant the woman in white deliberately led him into an ambush.

"Did you happen to get a look at the ones who jumped you?" Geronimo inquired.

"Nope," Blade replied. "It was too dark."

"How did the vermin escape without us spotting them?" Hickok asked.

Blade recalled a book he'd read several years ago entitled *The Complete Sherlock Holmes*. "There has to be a secret passage in here. Spread out and try to find it."

They each took a portion of wall and conducted a hasty search, moving books aside and thumping on the back panels in an effort to locate a concealed door. After several minutes each of them stopped and stared at the others.

"This is hopeless," Geronimo said. "There are too many shelves, too many books. It could take us a year."

"Then we'll keep going from room to room until we flush them out again," Blade proposed.

"What makes you think we will?" the gunfighter asked.

"They obviously don't want us in the castle. Why else did they pounce on me?"

Hickok shrugged. "They probably mistook you for that monster with the red eyes."

"Can't you be serious for one minute?"

"Okay. Maybe they figured you were one of the wood nymphs."

"You're hopeless."

"Yeah, but I've got style."

Blade walked into the corridor and glanced in both directions. There were more doors on this floor, including some he'd passed as he pursued the woman, and he nodded at the closest one. "Let's check it out."

"We're right behind you," Hickok said, replacing the Colts. "Just try not to get lost this time."

"Not funny," Blade said, leading the way.

The gunfighter leaned toward Geronimo and snickered. "Boy, a few bumps and bruises and he goes all to pieces."

Blade looked over his shoulder. "I heard that."

"Good ears. You must be part bunny rabbit."

Sighing, the giant opened the next door and peered in at a plush sitting room complete with thick carpeting, a half-dozen easy chairs, and a gold-gilded sofa fit for a palace.

Hickok whistled in appreciation. "Too bad we can't lug any of this stuff back with us. That sofa would look great in my cabin."

"You don't have a cabin yet," Geronimo noted. "Only married couples are alloted cabins."

"I'll be married some day."

"My condolences to your future bride."

"Clam up, you two," Blade snapped. He went to the next room, and the next, and in each found the same extravagant furnishings, the same immaculate conditions, the same evidence of greath wealth. The thought brought him up short.

Wait a minute!

Immaculate conditions?

Blade stared at the floor, then the walls. He ran his fingers over the stone and examined the tips. "Have you guys noticed something?" he asked.

"Do you mean other than you actin' weird?" Hickok rejoined.

"There isn't any dust," Blade informed them.

"Dust?" the gunfighter repeated.

"Yeah, you know. As in dirt and grime and all that. These walls and the floor are clean enough to eat off of, which means someone mops and dusts on a regular basis."

"You're right, pard," Hickok said, glancing around. "We must be up against a bunch of irate house cleaners. Or is that castle cleaners?"

Geronimo offered his rifle to Blade. "You're welcome to shoot him with my gun if you want."

"Why waste the bullet?" Blade said and resumed hunting for clues. They covered every room on the second floor, then went up to the third. Again they found chambers filled with furniture, ornaments and paintings that would have cost a small fortune prior to the Big Blast. But evidence someone lived there eluded them.

"How many floors are there in this place?" Hickok asked as they made toward the last doorway along the corridor.

"There must be six or seven in a building this size," Blade guessed.

"We can be here all day."

"If you have a better idea on how we can discover who's behind all of this, I'm open to suggestions."

"I was just thinkin' about Attila."

"What about him?"

"We're supposed to be on guard duty tomorrow night. If we don't show up, he'll be as mad as a wet cat."

Geronimo snorted. "You have such a wonderful way with words, Nathan."

"We'll be back at the Home by the time our shift

starts," Blade predicted. "Even if we stay over here tonight, we'll have all day tomorrow to make the return trip."

"Are you plannin' to stay over?"

"It depends on how things turn out."

Hickok chuckled. "You can't fool me. The real reason you want to stay another night is you're hopin' to see those fairies again."

"*Please* use my gun," Geronimo begged.

Blade turned to the door and reached for the knob when from somewhere far below, seeming to come from the very bowels of the earth, came a faint scream, a terrified shriek that lasted for a good 30 seconds and abruptly ended in awful silence. "Let's go," he barked and made a move toward the stairs.

"We can't," Geronimo stated.

"Why not?"

"The torch is going out."

Sure enough, the flames were much lower and might extinguish completely within the next couple of minutes. "There must be something we can use to make another one," Blade said, then he opened the door.

A music room unfolded before their wondering eyes, with a harp in one corner, a bass on a stand in another, a violin mounted in a case on the south wall, and another piano, this one smaller than its counterpart downstairs. the only furniture consisted of two chairs, a small sofa and a narrow cabinet against the rear wall.

"There doesn't appear to be anything we can use," Geronimo said.

Blade was about to close the door when his gaze fell on the polished piano. An idea occurred to him, and he hastened to the maple cabinet.

"What are you doing?" Hickok asked.

"Looking for whatever they used to polish the furniture and the piano."

"What in the world for?"

"It just might be flammable," Blade responded, opening the panel doors. There were four narrow shelves crammed with odds and ends—several bows for the violin, music books, a harmonica, three glass bottles partially filled with liquid substances, folded pieces of cloth and more. He raised one of the bottles and read its label: EVERLASTING WOOD POLISH. Unscrewing the cap, he raised the bottle to his nose and promptly regretted doing so. An acrid scent capable of gagging a horse made him turn aside and cough. On closer inspection of the label he found two words printed at the bottom: WARNING. FLAMMABLE.

"Bingo," he announced.

Geronimo had walked to the sofa and was examining the stitching in the smooth, pink fabric covering the upholstered seat and back. "Your knives can cut this easier than my tomahawks," he remarked.

Blade went over and handed the bottle to the Blackfoot, then crouched. Drawing his left Bowie, he proceeded to cut six-inch wide strips of pink fabric, each about a foot long, and draped them over the armrest. After accumulating four such strips, he slid the knife into the sheath and stood.

Hickok was standing guard at the door.

"The owners won't be very pleased at having their furniture destroyed," Geronimo mentioned.

"And I'm not overjoyed at having someone beat on me with a chair," Blade replied. "Which makes us even." He took one of the strips and poured the polish over it until the fabric was soaked, then did the same with the remaining three.

Meanwhile, the torch had sputtered down to a few lingering fingers of flame.

"Hold it out," Blade directed, clasping the drenched strips in both hands. He had to work quickly or suffer burnt fingers. Extending his arms to the side, he waited until the torch was almost out and he could barely see the limb, then he whipped the strips around and wrapped them tightly about the smoldering end. No sooner had he secured them and drew his hands back than the torch flared to life again with a sizzling sound and a puff of smoke.

"Pretty clever, pard," Hickok complimented him.

"Now let's go see where the scream came from," Blade proposed and hastened from the music room to the stairs, his companions right beside him. They paused at the landing to listen.

"Think it was the woman in the white dress?" Hickok wondered.

"No telling," Blade said, moving slowly downward. "But from now on we stick together no matter what."

"Shucks. Do you mean I can't go chasin' after any wood nymphs?"

"Will you stop already with the wood nymphs?"

"Sure. Just tryin' to cheer you up after the lickin' you took."

"Do me a favor."

"Anything."

"Try and cheer Geronimo up for a change."

"Hey, don't involve me," the Blackfoot said softly. "He's your problem."

"Who are you callin' a problem?" Hickok demanded.

"Quiet," Blade said sternly.

The gunfighter, of course, had to get in the last word. "Boy, what a couple of grumps."

In silence they descended to the ground floor and halted. Blade stood at the edge of the next flight of steps and peered into the inky domain below. The air felt cooler, and the dank scent was stronger. He gripped the Marlin and went down cautiously, carefully placing one foot after the other. Another stone corridor, narrower than those upstairs, appeared below, with branches running in four different directions. At the next landing they stopped to survey the lower level.

To Blade's amazement, they'd discovered a subterranean network of passageways and rooms. A half-dozen doors were visible along each branch. Even more surprising was the fact that the stairs continued down to yet another level. He speculated on how far down the levels actually went. If there were as many floors below ground as above, then trying to search every square inch of the castle was an impossible task.

The dank, cool air intensified, and a slight breeze caressed their faces.

"This place gives me the creeps," Geronimo said.

"How can there be a breeze down here?" Hickok asked.

"I don't know," Blade admitted, wrestling with the decision of whether to go lower or check this level first. He believed the scream came from farther down, but the idea of venturing into the castle's nether realms intimidated him. His vivid imagination created all sorts of horrid beasts waiting below for the chance to pounce on them. Before he could make up his mind, however, an unforeseen event occurred.

Hickok cleared his throat. "Excuse me," he said ever so politely.

"What is it?" Blade responded, turning to find the gunfighter staring up the stairs.

"We've got company."

Startled, Blade turned and couldn't believe his eyes when he saw the lady in white standing not ten feet away.

CHAPTER NINE

This time the woman didn't flee. She stood calmly in the middle of a step and regarded them with transparent curiosity. Her eyes were a striking green, her lips a rosy red, both contrasting sharply with her exceptionally pale complexion.

None of the three youths spoke. They were collectively mesmerized by her lovely presence, and not even the gunfighter thought to level a weapon at her.

After studying them for a moment, the woman smiled, exposing even rows of pearly teeth, and addressed them in a soft, oddly seductive voice reminiscent of a gentle breeze on a romantic, moonlight night. "Why, you're mere boys."

Hickok roused himself from the spell first, taking a menacing stride and wagging a Colt at her. "Who are you callin' boys, lady? I'll have you know two of us are Warriors."

The woman's composure was unruffled. "What, pray tell, is a Warrior?"

Nipping Hickok's response in the bud, Blade stepped

forward. "We'll ask the questions here, if you don't mind. Who are you? What is this place? Why were we attacked?"

"Such an inquisitive nature in so handsome a youngster," the woman responded.

"You're evading the question," Blade told her harshly.

"Aren't you being a bit presumptuous, young man?" she countered. "The three of you are the intruders, not me. You broke into our home, violated our sanctuary. If anyone should answer questions, it's you."

Blade didn't know what to do. Technically, she was right, and as someone who'd been trained since childhood to respect both his elders and the property of others, he felt acute guilt over his actions. Thankfully, Geronimo came to his rescue.

"We didn't break in, lady. We walked in after the plane you sent to bomb us crashed and opened a crack in the castle wall."

The woman stared at the Blackfoot for a few moments, her features inscrutable, then nodded. "Very well. Perhaps we both have some explaining to do." She gestured distastefully at the subterranean level. "But there's no need to question each other on these stairs. Why not come with me to the sitting room where we can converse like civilized adults?"

Blade wondered if her comment was a subtle slur. He decided to let it pass for the time being and nodded. "All right. We'll follow you. But don't try any tricks or you'll regret it."

Her eyes narrowed accustingly. "Is it customary where you're from to threaten an unarmed woman?"

"No," Blade promptly answered. "And it's not customary to throw a net over someone else and beat them to a pulp."

She viewed him from head to toe with an amused expression. "Funny. You don't look like pulp to me."

Motioning for his friends to stay close, Blade started to ascend the steps but managed only two strides when a strange thing happened. The woman recoiled as if in great fear and placed her forearms over her eyes.

"Stay back!" she blurted.

Bewildered, Blade halted. "What's the matter?"

"It's your torch," the woman disclosed. "The light hurts my eyes. Please don't get too close."

"Why does the light hurt?" Blade asked suspiciously.

She rotated so her back was to them and responded over her left shoulder. "Becuase I've spent my entire life in this castle, and the only time I venture outdoors is at night. Any bright light is terribly painful to me."

"We don't want to hurt you," Blade assured her. "You lead the way, and we'll stay far enough back to keep the light from bothering your eyes."

"Thank you," the woman said, climbing the stairs slowly.

Exchanging puzzled glances, the three of them trailed the woman to the ground floor. She led them down the corridor to an open door and paused at the jamb.

"Is it necessary for you to bring the torch into the room?"

"We can't see in the dark, lady," Hickok declared.

"You can't?" she responded, a hint of sarcasm in her tone. "In that case, I'll light several candles. Would that satisfy you?"

"Yes," Blade said. "We'll wait until the candles are lit before we extinguish our torch."

"Don't you trust me?"

"No."

She peeked at him and grinned. "Brutal honesty. I like that trait in a man."

Blade made no response. He watched her go into the room and looked at his friends. "What do you think?"

"I think we can trust her about as far as we can toss

this castle," Hickok said.

"This must be a ploy of some kind," Geronimo stated. "Why didn't she talk to us earlier when she had the chance? Why did she wait until we were about to investigate the underground levels? And what connection does she have to the scream we heard?"

"She has a lot to answer for," Blade conceded. "We'll play along with her game for the time being, but stay sharp. Let me do most of the talking."

"Why you?" Hickok inquired.

"What difference does it make?" Blade rejoined.

"Let Blade do it," Geronimo interjected. "He'll ask intelligent questions."

"And I wouldn't?" Hickok retorted.

A subdued glow filled the room. "You can come in now," announced the woman in white.

"Put out the torch," Blade said.

Geronimo lowered the burning end to the floor and moved it back and forth across the stones, gradually snuffing the flames. For added measure he tramped on the torch until smoldering red embers remained. "That should do it."

His rifle leveled, Blade walked into the chamber and halted. Seated on a sofa against the opposite wall was the woman. A fireplace stood to her right. Several chairs were positioned at various points, and he moved to one and sat down.

Geronimo took another chair, but Hickok remained standing near the door, his thumbs hooked in his gunbelt.

"You can sit down, too, young man," the woman addressed the gunfighter.

"I'll stand, lady, if you don't mind," Hickok replied. "And even if you do."

"There's no need to be rude."

"My apologies, ma'am," Hickok said, his mouth creasing in a grin that belied his statement.

The woman focused on the giant. "I trust you have better manners than your friend?"

"You'll have to excuse Hickok," Blade said. "He tends to get upset when someone tries to kill him."

"I haven't tried to kill him."

"We'll have to take your word for that," Blade said, staring at the two large candles on the mantle. How had she lit them so fast? Did she own matches? The Family still possessed a substantial portion of the dozens of cases Carpenter had stocked, although they were strictly rationed. Flints were the preferred means of starting fires, and by the time every boy and girl in the Family turned eight they were proficient at doing so.

"Why don't we start over again and try to get off on the right foot?" the woman asked. "My name is Endora, mistress of Castle Orm."

Blade had never known anyone called Endora before. "What an unusual name," he commented.

The lady misconstrued. "My great-grandfather named the castle after a legendary beastie believed to inhabit remote lakes in Scotland. He saw one of the monsters once, before coming to America, and read a book on them by a man named Holiday. Took the sighting as a sort of omen, he did."

"Your great-grandfather was Scottish?"

"Aye, he was. And stout Scottish blood flows in our veins still."

"My name is Blade." The Warrior introduced himself and pointed at his buddies. "Geronimo is the one with the tomahawks, and the rude one is called Hickok."

"I seem to recall reading those names somewhere," Endora said thoughtfully, then shook her head. "But no matter. Why have the three of you invaded our castle?"

"We didn't invade it," the gunfighter said. "We walked in through the crack in the wall. How many times do we have to tell you?"

For a moment Endora glared at Hickok. She recovered her composure quickly, though, and smiled at Blade. "Even allowing for the crack, is that any reason to walk into someone else's home without a by-your-leave?"

Blade pursed his lips. There she went again, playing on his guilt. He refused to let her tactic work. "After all the things that happened to us since we arrived, yes, we were justified in entering. We tried knocking, but no one answered the front door."

"Did you ever stop to think there might be a reason? Perhaps we don't like to be disturbed. Perhaps we want to be left to our own devices."

"Who is this 'we' you keep referring to?"

"I don't live here alone," Endora said.

"I know," Blade stated, rubbing a sore spot on his head.

Endora noticed the motion and appreciated its significance. "I'm sorry you were hurt. I truly am. But they thought you were trying to harm me."

"They?"

"My husband and my brother."

"Where are they now?"

"They had business to attend to. They'll be here shortly."

Blade glanced at Hickok, who nonchalantly strolled closer to the door and positioned himself so he'd spot anyone approaching. "Didn't you hear me call out to you? I promised not to harm you."

"How could we know whether you were speaking the truth?" Endora said. "You might have been trying to trick me."

The argument was valid, Blade had to admit. He studied her, trying to guess how old she was and to appraise her character. Her answers were honest enough, but he suspected she was hiding something. There was a trace of—panic?—in her eyes, detectable when he asked questions about the others living in the castle. Why? What did she have to be afraid of? Or was she hiding something?

"Granted," he said. "So I won't hold the beating I took against your husband and brother—for now."

"How gracious of you."

Blade decided to slip in a query she wouldn't be expecting. "By the way, do you happen to know who was screaming a while ago?"

The woman tensed, her hands clenched in her lap, and grinned. "Oh, that was me."

"You?"

"Yes. I bumped into my brother and mistook him for one of you. The shock made me scream my fool head off."

Blade didn't believe her for a second. "That was quite a scream."

She shrugged. "You know how it is when you're scared to death."

"No," Blade said, "I've never been that scared." No sooner did he finish speaking than an image of the red-eyed monster loomed in his mind, and he shook his head to dispel it.

"Then you must be very brave."

"We all are, lady," Hickok chimed in. "That's why you'd best not mess with us or you'll be eatin' lead."

Endora appeared shocked. "You'd threaten a woman?"

The gunfighter smirked. "Makes no nevermind to me who's tryin' to kill me. Anyone who does is history."

"Are there many like him where you come from?" Endora asked Blade.

"No. He's unique."

"Where do you come from, if you don't mind my asking?"

"Faraway," Blade lied. "In a small town northwest of here."

"Which town?"

"I'd rather not say at the moment."

"I see," Endora said, her countenance hardening.

"And why should I politely answer your questions if you're not going to answer any of mine?"

"You have a point," Blade said and gave the first name that popped into his head. "We're from Humboldt."

"How many people live there?"

What would be a reasonable number? Blade asked himself and made a guess. "About two hundred."

"Really? My husband will be interested in hearing that."

"Tell me something," Blade prompted. "I take it your great-grandfather built this place. Why? It's not every day you see a castle in the middle of the Minnesota countryside."

For the first time since they met, Endora laughed, her face relaxing and her hands unfolding in her lap. "Great-grandfather Moray was a wee bit of an eccentric. Before he came to America, he lived by himself on the moors in Scotland. He'd spend every waking minute hiking over those barren wastelands, and he developed quite a passion for them. Thought of the moors as his own private preserve. One day the government went and put a new highway right through the middle of his precious tract of nothing, and it sent him into a rage. He tried to stop them in court. When that failed, he vowed to leave Scotland and never set foot on her soil again." She paused. "Moray came to America and drifted west. Eventually he found this isolated spot and decided to build his new home here. He had all his funds transferred to an American bank and oversaw the construction of the castle. After that he settled down to the life of a country gentleman.

"I take it he survived the war?"

"Yes. The castle is built strong. He also foresaw the war coming and had the underground levels built to live in until the danger of radiation poisoning passed. Our family has lived here ever since."

"And you've had no contact with the outside world?"

"None."

"Why is that?"

The answer came from a totally unexpected source, courtesy of a gruff voice near the right-hand wall. "Because we don't *like* outsiders, boy. That's why."

Taken unawares, Blade swiveled in his chair and discovered two men standing 15 feet away, one with a double-barreled shotgun trained on his chest.

CHAPTER TEN

The newcomers were a bizarre, desperate pair.

Holding the shotgun was the shorter man, a lean, frail figure who was a mere five feet tall. An immaculàte, neatly pressed, baggy black suit hung from his frame like the oversized garments on a scarecrow. His head, in proportion to his body, was extremely large, a pumpkin on a broomstick as it were. A cruel slit of a mouth curled downward as he regarded the youths. High cheekbones and a slanting nose gave him an imperious aspect, complimented by his flashing green eyes and bushy brows, and a wild shock of black hair streaked with white crowned his cranium.

Only in one respect did the second man resemble the first. His brows were bushy, even more so, inch-wide strips of thick hairs that would have done justice to a gorilla. And in many respects he was like a huge ape. Seven feet tall, his broad, hunched shoulders gave him a perpetually stooped aspect. His brawny hands, possessing knuckles the size of walnuts, dangled next to his knees. Ill-fitting clothes scarcely contained his enormous arms and barrel chest, and his size 18 feet were naked. Dull brown eyes regarded the trio more in curiosity than in malice.

Blade saw the shotgun wielder pivot toward the doorway.

"Don't even think of it," the man snapped.

Shifting, Blade saw Hickok poised to draw.

"Drop the shotgun, mister," the gunfighter warned.

"No one dictates to Morlock in his own house," the shorter man snapped. "And if you go for those revolvers, I'll blow you in half."

Hickok smiled. "I've got news for you, chump. I'll put a bullet in your brain before you can squeeze the trigger."

"No one is that fast," the man scoffed.

"*I* am," Hickok stated.

Blade was going to admonish the gunfighter to wait when someone else intervened.

"Husband, no!" Endora cried, rising. "There's no need for killing. They've convinced me they have peaceful intentions."

The man called Morlock glanced disdainfully at her. "And you believe them, my dear?"

"Yes, I do. Look at them. They're just boys. They came here from Humboldt, where there are other survivors," Endora said. "And what about their families?"

A weird reaction occurred, and Blade didn't know what to make of it. Morlock perceptibly stiffened at the mention of other survivors, then slowly lowered the shotgun.

"Very well. We must do the proper thing, eh?"

"Please forgive my husband," Endora said, stepping to the man's side. Her shoulders were eight inches higher than his, and the contrast of her stately beauty to his malevolent mien was glaring. "Dearest, I'd like you to meet our guests. This is Blade, Geronimo and Hickok," she said, indicating each in turn.

"Guests, is it? More like intruders to my way of thinking," the husband snapped. He handed the shotgun to the apish man, who took it as if grasping an egg.

"We're sorry if we've upset you," Blade offered.

"Upset us, hell. You've put us to a lot of trouble, young man, and all because you don't know how to respect the rights of others," Morlock said. "This castle is our home. Don't they teach you any meaning of that word where you come from?"

"Of course they do," Blade said defensively.

"Then you'll be so good as to vacate these premises right now."

Endora cleared her throat. "Why don't we give them a spot of tea before they leave?"

"Why don't we ask them to move in?" Morlock responded sarcastically.

Blade had tolerated all the abuse he was willing to stand. He rose, being careful to point the rifle at the floor, and faced the spiteful owner. "Look, mister, we'll leave just as soon as we get answers to some important questions. For one thing, we'd like to know why you tried to kill us?"

Morlock sneered. "Don't be absurd. I never tried to kill you, boy."

"Someone did. First they used a toy plane carrying miniature bombs. And earlier, upstairs, I was attacked and beaten by two men. Tell me it wasn't you."

"I attacked you upstairs," Morlock said. "I freely admit as much. You and your friends broke into our home. Naturally, I took it as a hostile gesture and took appropriate measures."

"And the plane?"

"Was obtained by the man who built this castle long ago. He installed a surveillance camera in the nose and rigged the craft to carry miniature bombs, strictly for security purposes. The plane was programmed to spot interlopers and take appropriate action. Don't blame me if it came after you."

"Do you expect us to swallow that load of manure?" Hickok interjected.

"I don't care what you swallow, young man," Morlock said. "Just so you do it elsewhere."

"Husband, enough," Endora said.

"Enough!" The lord of the manor glanced at his brutish shadow. "Elphinstone, escort them outside. See to it that they depart immediately."

Nodding once, Elphinstone moved forward ponderously, his arms swinging at his sides, the shotgun clutched as if it was a club and not a gun.

"Put the shotgun down," Morlock commanded.

Obediently, like a puppy obeying its master, Elphinstone deposited the weapon.

Blade saw no reason to stay. Trying to interrogate Morlock would be an exercise in futility. "We must relight our torch first," he stated. "Then we'll go."

After a few seconds of deliberation, Morlock agreed. "Very well. But vacate these premises quickly or I won't be held responsible for the consequences."

"Are you threatenin' us?" Hickok asked.

"Take it any way you want, boy," Morlock said.

Motioning at Geronimo, Blade waited until the Blackfoot had touched the torch to a candle and reignited the strips before he walked from the room without a backward glance, his friends right behind him.

"I don't like runnin' with my tail between my legs," Hickok groused.

"We're not running," Blade said. "We're being diplomatic."

"Isn't that the same thing?"

They moved along the corridor toward the cracked wall, their apish escort dogging their heels.

Geronimo looked over his shoulder. "Elphinstone, is that your name? How do you like living here?"

The brute made no reply.

"Wonderful conversationalist," Geronimo quipped.

"Reminds me of you, Nathan."

Blade was pondering the implications of everything they'd learned so far, and he barely noticed when they drew abreast of the stairs. A wavering wail from below broke his concentration and brought him up short. "What was that?"

"Sounded like a woman," Hickok said.

"Let's go see," Geronimo proposed.

Suddenly Elphinstone moved, displaying surprising speed in one so massive, and blocked their access to the steps. He pointed toward the end of the corridor and uttered a raspy order. "Go."

Hickok bristled. "Who do you think you are tellin' us what to do, you overgrown sack of—"

"Enough," Blade stated, grabbing the gunfighter's left arm. "Whatever is down there is none of our business."

"Says you," Hickok responded. "I vote we go check."

"Not now," Blade said, pulling the gunfighter after him down the hall. He let go when Hickok quit resisting.

"Okay, pard, you made your point. But when we get back to the Home, I'm not tellin' a soul about this escapade of ours."

"Why not?" Geronimo inquired.

"Because I don't want anyone to learn I hang around with a pair of wimps."

"We'll talk outside," Blade stated and hastened his pace, grateful for the slash of bright light serving as their beacon out of there. They needed time to collect their thoughts and formulate a plan of action. Whether Hickok realized it or not, Morlock enjoyed a grave advantage, a fact he intended to explain shortly.

Seldom had a sunlit day radiated such beauty as the warm, tranquil setting into which they stepped after reaching the crack.

Blade squinted up at the blue sky, surveyed the lush green trees before them, spotted several sparrows flitting about in the undergrowth, and inhaled deeply.

"Thanks for seeing us out," Geronimo said to Elphinstone, who abruptly wheeled and stalked off. "Next time try not to bend our ears so much."

"Pitiful. Just pitiful," Hickok mumbled, marching into the forest, his posture consistent with his anger.

"Wait for us," Blade said.

"Why should I? I'm embarrassed to know you."

Geronimo still carried the flaming torch. He dropped it on the grass and stamped over and over on the lit end until it was out.

Hickok was still walking away.

"Come on," Blade said, jogging to overtake the cantankerous gunfighter. "I asked you to wait," he said when he caught up.

"No, you didn't. You *told* me to wait. This whole trip you've been actin' like you're top dog and Geronimo and me are common curs. I'm tired of it."

"I didn't mean to offend you."

"I know. But unless Attila appoints you as head of a Warrior Triad, or if some day—heh, heh—you become top Warrior, you've got no right to be bossing us around."

"I'm sorry," Blade said. "Now will you stop and listen?"

"Yeah," Geronimo added. "Try using your head for a change of pace instead of your heart."

Sighing, Hickok halted and swung toward them. "All right. Let me hear what you have to say. But it had better be good or I'm headin' on back to the Home, and nothin' you can say or do will stop me."

Blade nodded. "Fair enough. Try this on for size." He paused and glanced at the castle. "We're not leaving here until we discover the truth. I don't care what that pompous ass in there told us to do."

"Now you're talkin' my language," Hickok said, grinning. "But why'd you let him push us around?"

"Think for a minute. He wasn't about to reveal a thing, and we would have wasted our time trying to pry answers out of him. If we stayed we might have provoked him into using his shotgun and—"

"I could've taken him," Hickok interrupted.

"I know, but you're missing the point. We would have been in the wrong killing him without justification. Remember the course we took on the moral and ethical aspect of killing? A Warrior must never resort to violence unless there is no other alternative. We weren't in imminent danger. Sure, we suspect Morlock lied through his teeth and deliberately set the plane after us, but we can't prove it. And since we did enter their castle without permission, morally and ethically we were in the wrong."

"Only you could turn killin' a cow chip into a philosophy lesson."

"Do you see my point or not?"

"Yep," Hickok admitted begrudgingly. "You're right. But I don't like it none." He scratched his chin and cocked his head. "Even if we didn't have an excuse to blow Morlock away, we had every right to go into those lower levels and find out what was down there. It sounded like someone was sufferin' bad."

"It did," Blade agreed. "But if we'd tried to barge on down there, we would have played into Morlock's hand."

"How do you figure? That jumbo monkey couldn't have stopped us."

"Maybe. But Morlock certainly could have."

"Morlock?"

"Yeah, dummy. Think again. How did Morlock and Elphinstone get into the room where we were talking with Endora?"

"Beats me. I know they didn't come in the door because I was right there."

"Exactly. The only way they could have entered was through a secret passage. I was right. The castle must be honeycombed with hidden corridors enabling them to go anywhere and spy on anyone. And do you think for a minute that Morlock wasn't watching us leave? The moment we tore into Elphinstone, Morlock would have blasted us."

"Hmmmmm. I never thought of that."

"A warrior must keep sharp at all times, Nathan."

"Don't start with another lesson," Hickok stated defensively. "So I made a little mistake. No harm done."

"There could have been," Blade said.

"Okay. What's the plan?"

"We'll stay over another night."

"That's it?"

"Morlock will undoubtedly spy on us. When he learns we're not leaving, he might make a move against us."

"Then we nail the sucker?"

"Then we nail him, if need be."

Geronimo craned his neck to gaze at the battlement. "You know, I feel sorry for the woman. Can you imagine what it must be like for her to be married to Morlock?"

"There's another mystery," Blade said. "How old would you guess Endora to be?"

"I don't know. Twenty-five, maybe," Geronimo answered.

"Me, too. And how old do you think Morlock is?"

"Fifty. Fifty-five."

"Or older. Doesn't it strike you as strange that she would marry someone so much older?"

"Not really. Couples at the Home sometimes have a five or ten year age difference between husband and wife," Geronimo said.

"Yeah, but a thirty year difference?"

Geronimo shrugged. "Maybe there wasn't anyone else she could marry. They said they haven't had any contact with the outside world."

Blade nodded again. "Do you realize what that means?"

Sudden insight caused Geronimo to gape in astonishment. "Wow. I never thought of that."

"Thought of what?" Hickok asked.

"There can only be one explanation," Blade went on.

"Realize what?" Hickok inquired impatiently, looking from one to the other.

"This puts their relationship in a whole new perspective," Geronimo said.

"What the blazes are you two talkin' about?" Hickok snapped. "Would one of you kindly explain it to me?"

"Later," Blade said, staring off in the direction of their camp. "Let's go eat lunch and make our plans for tonight. I want to have everything ready before dark."

Geronimo and Hickok followed, the gunfighter nudging the Blackfoot.

"Would you mind explaining what in the world is going on?"

"We're going to eat lunch."

"That's not what I meant, and you know it."

Geronimo chuckled. "Sorry. There might be a skeleton in their closet."

"Did they bump somebody off?"

"Not that kind of skeleton."

"Then what kind?"

"The family tree kind."

Hickok hissed in frustration. "Skeletons. Trees. I'm beginning to think you've lost your marbles, pard."

"At least I had some to start with."

CHAPTER ELEVEN

The three of them were in position by nightfall.

Blade sat in the fork of an oak tree 30 feet from their camp and stared at the fire. Eventually one of them must creep out and add fuel to the flames, but for now, thanks to the strategic placement of their backpacks at the south end of the lean-to, the camp gave every impression of being occupied. It had been his idea to stack the backpacks at the one end to block the view of anyone, or anything, approaching from that direction. If he was correct in his hunch, if the creatures followed the same path tonight as last night, then his trap might work.

He glanced down at the ground 12 feet below and shifted to alleviate a cramp in his lower back. All day he'd been bothered by pain from his shoulders to his hips due to the beating he'd sustained. He guessed that Elphinstone had done the pounding. Only the hulking brute possessed the strength necessary to bruise his body even through the backpack he'd worn at the time.

Blade gazed off to his right at the thicket screening Geronimo and again to his left at the base of a tree where

Hickok lay hidden. Neither one was visible.

His simple plan called for staying concealed until either the mysterious wood nymphs or someone from the castle put in an appearance. If the former showed up, he'd try to capture one. If Morlock or Elphinstone appeared, he'd wait and see what they did before deciding on a course of action.

Cradling the Marlin in his arms, he settled down to spend the night if need be.

Blade mentally reviewed his performance in the castle and concluded he had a lot to learn yet about being a Warrior. He never should have gone after Endora by himself or let her lure him into an ambush. The mistake might have proven fatal.

And there was another mystery. Given Morlock's hatred of outsiders, and since, as Morlock claimed, he believed his wife was being attacked, why did Morlock use a net and a chair instead of a gun or knives?

There were so many questions and so few answers.

Another full moon arced above the horizon, a timeless celestial observer of the unfolding of human history.

An hour went by. Two.

Blade half-expected there wouldn't be activity of any kind until near midnight, so he was surprised when, idly glancing to the southwest, he spied pale figures gliding through the trees toward the camp.

The nymphs!

Excited, he tensed and watched the three or four dozen creatures rapidly near his position. They were tittering and prancing, the same as last night, remarkably light on their feet. He marveled at their grace and ghostly aspect, keeping as still as stone until they were almost to the oak tree.

Recognition brought shock. Blade's gray eyes narrowed as he realized they were human, near-naked men and women whose skin resembled the finest china. They were all over six feet tall but skinny as saplings. Members of both sexes wore skimpy leather shorts, nothing else, and the womens' breasts swayed as they ran. All were grinning or whispering excitedly.

Blade focused on a pair almost directly below him, a man and a woman standing a foot apart. He quietly looped the Marlin over his right shoulder, coiled his legs and leaped.

Somehow, the woman sensed his presence and looked up.

The youth landed behind them, bending at the knees to absorb his weight, and sprang, tackling both of them around the legs and bearing them to the ground. They felt incredibly light, as if they weighed a mere 90 or 100 pounds, and offered no resistance except for a startled cry from the woman.

At the same time Hickok and Geronimo rose from hiding and tried to capture others, but the rest of the band was already fleeing in stark panic into the forest.

Blade lay on top of the two he'd caught, neither of whom so much as twitched, astounded by their docile behavior. "I won't hurt you," he informed them. "Do you understand?"

There was no reply.

"Do you understand?" Blade repeated sternly.

"We do," the woman said in a high, musical voice.

"Shhhhh," said the man. "You know we're not allowed to talk to outers."

Perplexed, Blade eased his grip. "All right. You speak English. Good. Now listen closely. I'm going to sit up and let go of you. First I want your word that you won't try to escape."

"We can't give it, sir," the woman said.

"Why not?"

"Because our masts have told us we must get away if ever we're caught by outers."

The man looked at the woman. "Hush, Tabitha, you know better."

Blade clamped a hand on a wrist of each one and rose to his knees. "Okay. If you won't give your word, we'll do this the hard way." He stood, pulling them up, but being careful not to yank too hard for fear of yanking their arms from their sockets. "What's your name?" he asked the male.

The man said nothing.

"Tell me or else," Blade bluffed, glowering appropriately.

"Selwyn," the man blurted. "My name is Selwyn."

Blade glanced over his left shoulder and saw his friends returning empty-handed from the chase. "Come with me," he said, walking toward the camp.

Both prisoners abruptly walked, dragging their heels and tugging in vain to free themselves.

"Please, sir, no," Tabitha exclaimed.

"Not near the fire," Selwyn stated in sheer dread.

"Why not?" Blade demanded, stopping.

"The fire hurts our eyes terribly, sir," Selwyn said. "If we get too close, the brightness will damage our eyes."

"It's only a campfire," Blade noted.

"Our eyes are very sensitive, sir," Tabitha explained. "We can't even come out during the day."

Her plaintive tone impressed Blade. He studied their fine features, their straw-colored hair and almost colorless eyes, and realized the reason they were so pale. They spent their entire life in the dark, moving about only at night. But what did they do during the day? Where did they live? "Don't worry," he assured them. "I won't take you any nearer to the fire."

"Thank you, sir. You're very kind," Tabitha said.

The gunfighter and the Blackfoot halted and regarded the pair intently.

"I'm sorry, pard," Hickok said. "I'll never doubt your word again. These things are livin' fairies, just like you said."

"We are not things, sir," Tabitha declared. "We are serfs."

"Serfs," Hickok repeated. "Like back in the Middle Ages?"

"What are the Middle Ages, sir?" Tabitha asked.

"It was back in ancient times when men wore tin cans into battle and women went around throwin' their hair from balconies."

Tabitha and Selwyn were completely confounded.

"How did women throw their hair, sir?" she asked.

"Pay no attention to him," Geronimo interjected. "His grasp of history leaves a lot to be desired."

"Where did you acquire the name serfs?" Blade probed.

"I don't know, sir," Tabitha responded. "We've always been called serfs, I believe. My mother and her mother were both serfs. And for our lives we serve our masts loyally."

"There's that word again. Who are the masts?"

"Why, those who provide our clothes, our home and the food. They are the great ones who know all there is to know," Tabitha said, then added quickly, "sir."

"Do you mean masters?" Geronimo asked.

"Masts. Masters. They're the same thing, sir."

"It's slang," Blade realized, wondering what to inquire about next. "You say your people have been serving your masters for generations. Who are your masts?"

"Like I said, sir, the great ones."

"Where do the great ones live?"

Tabitha nodded at the castle. "Why, there, sir, in the great house."

The three youths exchanged meaningful looks.

"So Morlock, Endora and Elphinstone are the masters," Blade said slowly.

"Oh, yes!" Tabitha declared. "Master Morlock is the greatest of all."

Selwyn made a clucking sound. "And he will be very

mad if he learns you are telling these outers all about us."

The statement produced stark fear on Tabitha's face. "But what else can I do?"

"Don't worry about Morlock," Blade told her. "We'll make sure he doesn't do anything to you for talking to us."

"Do you know him, sir?"

"Yes. In fact, we were guests in the great house today," Blade stated, stretching the truth in order to elicit more information.

"You were, sir?" Tabitha said, delighted at the news. "Why, then, you must not be outers after all."

"What the dickens are outers?" Hickok asked.

"Outsiders, sir, such as yourself."

"You mean those who come from outside this valley?" Blade asked.

"Exactly, sir. Only we call this valley the Domain."

"Have there been outers in the Domain before?"

"Yes, sir. Every now and then some have shown up."

"Did they stay long?"

"I wouldn't know, sir. Usually they are invited into the great house, and we never see or hear of them again."

Blade frowned. Yet another sinister revelation to add to the growing body of evidence incriminating Morlock and his clan. How long had all of this been going on? Since the war? He now had proof that some force of slavery was being practiced, and slavery was abhorrent to every cherished principle of the Family. As a Warrior, he had a moral obligation to confront evil wherever it reared its wicked head, and from all he'd uncovered so far it was flourishing in Castle Orm.

"Now would you please let us go, sir?" Tabitha requested. "Our masts will be very upset with us if we don't get to work soon."

"Work?"

"Yes, sir. In the fields. Every night they let us out to till the crops and weed and water the garden."

Suddenly several mysteries were cleared up. All those naked footprints were left by the serfs as they went about their noctural business at the beck and call of Morlock and company. And so many crops were being cultivated because the food had to feed all the serfs, not just the freaky threesome in the castle. One of her comments, though, perplexed him. "Where do the serfs live during the day?"

"In the Underground, sir."

"Where might that be?"

"In the levels under the great house, sir."

Another puzzle cleared up, Blade reflected. The reason Endora confronted them on the stairs was to prevent them from descending farther into the levels where the serfs lived. "When we were in the great house today, we happaned to hear someone screaming and wailing. Do you know who that was?"

Sorrow etched the faces of both serfs.

"Yes, sir," Tabitha said. "That was poor Tweena. Master Elphinstone punished her for coming back here by herself last night."

"Explain."

"When we spotted your campfire last night, all of us came for a look when Grell went off to relieve himself. You saw us and we hid. Remember, sir?"

"I remember," Blade said. "But who is Grell? We haven't met him yet."

Selwyn shuddered and gazed into the surrounding darkness. "You don't want to meet him, sir. He's the immortal one."

Blade was confused again. "Skip him for the moment. Tell me about Tweena."

"She wanted to sneak back for a second look, sir," Tabitha explained. "We tried to talk her out of it, but she went anyway, alone. You spotted her and chased her to the portal, and Master Morlock caught her. Naturally, the great ones saw fit to punish her."

"They did, huh?"

"Oh, yes sir. They found out that all of us snuck away for a peek at you and decided to teach us the error of our ways by using Tweena as an example."

The statement rang false in Blade's ears. He suspected she was quoting words spoken by one of the great masters, probably Morlock. "What did they do to Tweena?"

Tabitha lowered her gaze and spoke in a whisper. "Horrible things, sir. Grell, Master Elphinstone and Master Morlock all took turns, beating and torturing her." She paused. "Tweena is in heaven now."

"They made us watch, sir," Selwyn said. "It was the most terrible thing I've ever seen, even worse than the time Grell ate Cathmor."

Blade wasn't certain he'd heard correctly. "This Grell ate one of the serfs?"

"Yes, sir. Cathmor tried to leave the Domain, and that's strictly forbidden by our masts."

"What the heck have we stumbled into?" Hickok spoke up. "Who ever heard of killin' a woman for takin' a look at strangers? And folks eatin' other folks is downright sick."

Geronimo fixed his eyes on Blade's. "You know what we have to do, don't you?"

"Yes."

"We can't let these atrocities continue."

"I know."

Hickok nodded. "Now you're really talkin'. Let's go find Morlock so I can shove both Colt barrels up his nose and see if his noggin is bulletproof."

"First things first," Blade said, turning to Tabitha. "There's something I don't understand. If Tweena was punished to keep the serfs away from our camp, why did all of you return tonight?"

The dainty woman's mood changed from sadness to giddy elation in the space of a heartbeat. She giggled and stated proudly, "We wanted to see you again. Grell heard an animal in the woods and went to check if it was dangerous. He protects us, you see, sir."

"And eats you," Blade reminded her. "But go on."

"As soon as he was out of sight, we dropped our tools and ran over here. We expected to be back before he returned. We're much faster than Grell, sir."

"And eats you," Blade reminded her. "But go on."

"And what about Tweena? Didn't her death impress you at all?"

"Yes, sir. It was horrible. I told you so."

"Yet all the serfs came anyway?"

Tabitha giggled again. "We like to break the rules. It's fun."

The inane smile creasing the woman's thin lips gave Blade cause for concern. "In other words, none of the serfs were fazed one bit by Tweena's death?"

"Not really, sir. No."

"When Cathmor was eaten, how did you feel about it?"

"Well, sir, the masts only did it to teach us a lesson. And they teach us lessons because they love us."

Hickok snorted. "Did I miss something here?"

Before anyone else could speak, a tremendous roar shattered the stillness of the forest, a roar the three youths had heard during their first night in the woods.

"It's Grell!" Tabitha screeched.

CHAPTER TWELVE

So stunned was Blade by the ferocious sound, he froze. In his mind's eye he saw the enormous creature with the glowing red eyes and felt again a tingle of fear ripple down his spine. He inadvertently released his hold on the serfs and gripped his Bowies.

Tabitha and Selwyn were off like panic-stricken antelope, bounding to the northwest in airy leaps.

"Run, sirs!" Tabitha cried.

"What *do* we do?" Geronimo inquired, the Winchester molded to his shoulder.

Blade wanted to answer, but couldn't. His lips wouldn't respond to his mental commands, and his body was frozen in place. Even his heart seemed to have stopped. He gaped in the direction of the roar, to the southwest, and experienced an almost overwhelming impulse to run.

"I say we show it who's boss," Hickok suggested, drawing the Colts.

"Are you crazy? Didn't you see how big that thing was last night?" Geronimo responded.

"Hey, the bigger they are, the harder they fall."

Sensation returned to Blade's limbs. He gulped and slid both knives from their sheaths. His heart hadn't stopped beating after all because now it was thumping in his chest and the veins in his temples were pounding, his entire body pulsing vibrantly, an adrenaline rush to end all adrenaline rushes making every nerve and muscle, every tiny cell, quiver expectantly. But this wasn't the pleasant rush brought on by intimacy with a loved one, nor the giddy rush of facing foes bravely in a battle to the death. This was a perverse rush, a rush he'd never known of outright cowardice. For the very first time in his young life Blade felt genuinely afraid of an adversary. Fear was an alien experience until that very moment, and being alien it tore down his psychological defenses and left him spiritually naked, his soul in supreme turmoil.

Hickok glanced at his giant friend and did an exaggerated double take. "What's with you, pard? You look sick."

Licking his dry lips, Blade opened his mouth to reply when he saw it, saw the monster, the thing moving directly toward them from out of the gloom. Ten feet high, its reddish eyes radiating malevolence, the creature effortlessly barged through the undergrowth, the thump-thump-thump of its feet growing louder and louder, matching the thump-thump-thump of Blade's heart.

"Are you okay, Blade?" Geronimo asked.

"Yeah," Blade mumbled.

"Since you want to be the boss on this expedition of yours, do we fight or what?" Hickok inquired.

The creature was close enough now to reveal its thick reddish coat of fur, its stout legs the size of tree trunks and its massive arms.

Blade couldn't stand to look into those red eyes any longer. "Let's take cover until it leaves," he proposed, backing up.

"You want to *run*?" Hickok declared in astonishment.

"We don't know what we're up against. Until we do,

let's play it safe."

"Some Warrior you'll turn out to be."

The monstrosity was only 30 feet away.

"We can argue later," Blade snapped. "Let's go." Whirling, he raced toward their camp, feeling deeply ashamed of his decision and suspecting his friends sensed the truth. He stopped at the campsite to grab his backpack. A glance over his shoulder showed the beast known as Grell lumbering in pursuit. Elation coursed through him, replacing the fear, when he saw it couldn't move faster than a ponderous walk. We can easily outrun it, he thought, and laughed.

"What's so funny, pard," Hickok asked, lifting his backpack.

"Nothing."

"If you don't mind my sayin' so, I think the beating you took rattled your brain. You're not actin' like your normal self."

Ignoring the comment, Blade started northward. "Come on. Let's get out of there."

"Why not?" Hickok grumbled. "We seem to be makin' it a habit to turn yellow at the first sign of danger."

Blade led them at a dogtrot for 40 yards, than halted and gazed at their camp.

The monster was nearly there. Grell stepped close to the fire, unaffected by the bright flames, and snarled in frustration. He proceeded to rip the lean-to into kindling with powerful swipes of his huge paws, then tramped on the broken bits for added measure. Finished, he glared at the youths and roared his defiance.

"*Please* let me plug the varmint," Hickok begged.

"Not yet."

"When? Next year?"

Blade saw Grell depart, heading toward the castle, and he was tempted to charge, to try and kill the thing in a hail of lead. But what if the bullets had no effect? To a creature that massive a gunshot might be equivalent to a bee sting, and if their guns proved useless, what then? Did he want to face it with just his Bowies? The answer was no. "Let's see if we can find the serfs," he suggested. "There are still a lot of questions they need to answer."

"Lead the way," Geronimo said.

Hickok vented a protracted sigh while watching the monster crash through the brush. "Sure. Whatever you want, pard."

Taking a few seconds to orient himself by using the stars, Blade hiked in the directions of the tilled field and the garden. He felt uncomfortable at leaving without making at least a token effort to slay Grell, but he couldn't bring himself to turn around and go back.

"That thing is the biggest mutation I've ever seen or heard of," Geronimo commented. "I wonder how Morlock exerts control over it?"

"Most likely with his charming personality," Hickok quipped.

"Why do you think Selwyn referred to it as the immortal one?" Geronimo wondered.

"Who knows?" Hickok rejoined. "I don't make it a habit of tryin' to figure out fruit loops and fairies."

"They're serfs, remember?"

"Serfs, smerfs, what's the difference?"

They walked in silence for five minutes, listening to the receding footsteps of the monster.

"I had no idea mutations grew so big," Geronimo said.

"Drop the subject, will you?" Blade snapped. "We have other things to consider."

"Like what, pard?"

"Like what we're going to do about Morlock, Endora and Elphinstone."

"What's to consider? We blow 'em away."

"I agree we must stop them from enslaving the serfs,

but how far can we go? Do we have the right to kill them, if need be?"

"Sure we do," Hickok said without hesitation.

"Oh? Even though they're not a threat to the Family?"

"What's that got to do with anything?"

"Everything," Blade said. "You and I are Warriors. We're pledged to safeguard the Home. Technically speaking, neither of us has jurisdiction here."

Hickok chuckled. "Why worry about a measly thing like jurisdiction when it comes to blowin' away a couple of lowlifes?"

"Because if we kill Morlock or any member of his family without proper justification, we're no better than common killers. Morally, we'd be in the wrong."

"Here you go with the morality business again. Why don't you forget being a Warrior and become a spiritual Teacher instead?"

The sarcastic comment stung Blade. A few years ago he *had* toyed with the idea of becoming a Teacher, as the Family designated those gifted individuals who possessed the capacity to teach truth and were in tune with the Source of all, but he'd decided his natural talents lay elsewhere.

Except for an occasional insect noise and once the hooting of an owl, an eerie stillness enveloped the forest.

Blade hoped his sense of direction was equal to the task and received confirmation when they broke from the trees and discovered the garden straight ahead. There was no sign of the serfs. "Where are they?" he absently mumbled.

"Probably off huggin' trees," Hickok said.

"They could have heard us coming and ran off," Geronimo guessed.

They skirted the garden until they came to the grassy road. Parked there was a crudely constructed, wooden wagon, six feet high and with immense wooden wheels and a thick beam for a tongue. Tilling implements were piled high inside.

"So now we know what made the ruts," Geronimo observed.

"Maybe they went to the castle," Blade said. "Let's check." Only when he uttered the recommendation did he recall Grell had headed toward the castle. Again he thought of the enormous brute and those eyes the color of fresh blood, and he involuntarily shivered as if from a chilling breeze. It was too late to change his mind without arousing suspicion, so he led them slowly along the road.

The front of the castle came into sight and with it the narrow field in front where dozens of pale forms danced and played in innocent abandon.

"Get down," Blade whispered, dropping to one knee.

"What the blazes are they doing now?" Hickok asked.

"Having fun," Geronimo said.

"With that hairy fart runnin' around loose? Those people ain't playin' with a full deck, if you get my drift."

"They're like children," Geronimo remarked quietly. "I'd say they have the emotional maturity of twelve year-olds."

"Should we try to capture one again?"

"Not yet," Blade answered. "They'd see us and take off. We're no match for them unless we can take them by surprise."

"Now I've heard everything," Hickok complained. "When you wouldn't let us tangle with Morlock and that great ape earlier, I held my peace. And when you beat a retreat without takin' on Grell, I figured you knew what you were doing." He gestured at the serfs. "But when you claim we're no match for a bunch of bimbos and dorks who like to traipse around in their underwear and who couldn't stomp a flea in a fair fight, I draw the line." So saying, the gunfighter rose and sped toward the serfs.

"Wait," Blade said. He tried to grab his friend's wrist and missed. He saw the pale figures collectively whirl around and gape at Hickok, then they fled en masse, giggling and running without really exerting themselves.

The gunfighter never slowed.

"Damn," Blade snapped and took off after him.

Geronimo kept pace on the giant's left. "You'll have to forgive Nathan," he commented.

"Why should I?" Blade responded testily.

"Because unlike the rest of us, he gets by with half a brain."

"When I'm done with him, he won't even have that."

Predictably, the serfs reached the castle well ahead of their puffing pursuer and ran along the base of the wall toward the yard in back.

The gunfighter was doing his best, but it was the tortoise and the hare all over again, and he wasn't the hare.

"Hickok! Stop!" Blade bellowed, and when his cry produced no result, added under his breath, "Idiot."

"You've got to admit there's never a dull moment with him around," Geronimo said proudly.

"For someone who's always on his case, you certainly stick up for him a lot."

"What are friends for?"

Blade increased his pace, annoyed that he wouldn't be able to overtake Hickok before the gunfighter reached the rear corner. He didn't like the idea of Hickok being out of sight, even for ten seconds. "Will you stop?" he shouted.

Incredibly, Hickok glanced back and grinned, his white teeth contrasted by the darkness. "I'm gainin'," he replied and kept going.

"Remind me to dunk him in the moat when we get back," Blade said angrily.

"Okay."

"Fifty or sixty times."

In graceful leaps and bounds the serfs went around the castle and disappeared.

"Hickok, don't—" Blade began and stopped in midcry

when the gunfighter took the corner. He pumped his arms and legs frantically, pulling ahead of Geronimo, and pounded into the rear yard with his mouth open to chew out Hickok for being such a blockhead.

But Hickok wasn't there.

Nor were the serfs.

Stunned, Blade halted so abruptly he nearly tripped over his own feet. He glanced to the right and the left. It was impossible, and yet it had happened. His intuitive dread had not been unfounded.

Geronimo came around the corner and stopped short. "Where's Nathan?" he blurted.

"You tell me," Blade said, gazing at the castle and the mausoleums, and jogged toward the latter when the thought occurred to him that Hickok might be behind one of the tombs.

Geronimo ran at his side. "He couldn't have just vanished," he declared in astonishment.

"He did."

They conducted a sweep of the mausoleums but found no trace of their rash companion. Winding up in front of the biggest tomb, they stood in mutual, baffled contemplation, trying to make sense of the inexplicable.

"Maybe they kept going around to the other side of the castle," Geronimo conjectured. "I'll go see." He sprinted off.

Blade idly stared at the Blackfoot, thinking they must stay there until daylight and scour the ground for tracks, expecting him to stop at the southeast corner. He never thought to advise Geronimo to stay in sight and was extremely upset when his friend pulled a Hickok and ran around to the east side. "Geronimo!" he called out, starting forward, his gaze straying to the castle.

Standing at a third floor window, her white dress impossible to miss, was Endora.

"Geronimo!" Blade repeated, louder this time, his

intuition flaring again, and when no response was forthcoming, he raced to the corner and stopped in breathless bewilderment.

The stretch of ground between the southeast and northeast corners was empty.

Geronimo, like the gunfighter, had disappeared.

CHAPTER THIRTEEN

He was alone!

Blade backed against the wall, the Marlin leveled, his heart beating wildly again, his temples drumming. He gulped and scrutinized the forest, half-expecting to see those savage red orbs glaring at him.

It couldn't be!

They couldn't both vanish.

He blinked and stepped into the yard, swinging the rifle first one way, then another, his nerves raw, itching to fire at anything that moved. His face was clammy with sweat despite the cool breeze. His mind was a blank slate. Dazed, he walked to the big mausoleum and crouched beside it. Endora was no longer visible in the window.

Get a grip, damn you!

Blade shook his head, confused by his reaction. He'd never been afraid of anything before, but the monster known as Grell had terrified him—and now this! What was happening to him? Maybe he wasn't cut out to be a Warrior. Maybe he didn't have what it took, didn't possess true courage. He'd never been tested in combat or faced such a grim predicament. This was his first real crisis, and he was cracking under the strain.

What should he do?

Breathing deeply, he willed himself to calm down and relax, controlling his emotions. A Warrior should always maintain strict self-control. That was the beginning lesson taught by the Elder responsible for training novice Warriors. Superb self-control was the foundation on which rested all other attributes essential to a Warrior.

Next came dedication, loyalty to a higher ideal, and in his case it was the ideal represented by the Home and the Family, the ideal of love and stability realized by the descendants of Kurt Carpenter. On a practical level, he was glad to be able to serve the Family by protecting them from any and all threats to their continued survival.

Also critically important to any Warrior was an acceptance of the inevitable. Everyone died. Sooner or later everyone passed on to the higher mansions. Death was simply the means of throwing off the earthly coil and ascending to the next level. Warriors, more so than most, must resign themselves to the fact they lived with a heightened prospect of death every single day. Dying was an ever-present consequence of living a life devoted to safeguarding others and confronting lethal dangers on a daily basis.

Was that his problem?

Hadn't he learned to accept the inevitability of death?

Why else did he fear the mutation so much?

The revelation sparked profound thought, and Blade leaned on the mausoleum, totally oblivious to the passage of time, while he pondered the ramifications. Sure, he didn't want to die, but then who did? By the same token, he didn't want his friends to die either. And if he didn't get his act together, they surely would.

What was the key to solving his problem? How could he find the courage to confront Grell? Where did true courage spring from, anyway? The heart? The mind? The personality? Or a combination of all three. What distinguished a man labeled brave from one branded a coward? Why were some men able to face death without flinching while others fled pell-mell? More to the point, which kind of man was he?

Which did he want to be?

Naturally, he wanted to be brave. Although only 16, he had adult responsibilities, and it was time he started owning up to them. He must conquer his fear and save his comrades.

Easier said than done.

How do you conquer fear? Blade asked himself. How do you overcome an intangible emotional state? Facing the object of one's fears was supposed to work, but he'd already faced Grell twice and quaked both times. If he could change his attitude, he'd be able to take on the mutation without flinching.

How did someone change their attitude?

The heart and mind alone couldn't do it, but the personality could through force of will. Was that the answer? Something so basic as willpower, the simple matter of making up one's mind? If a person wanted to be happy, all they had to do was will themselves to believe they were happy despite whatever external circumstances prevailed. Therefore, if someone wanted to be brave, all they had to do was believe they were brave.

Was that the way it worked?

Could so crucial a quality be so easy to obtain?

Shaking his head to clear his thoughts, Blade rose and scanned the yard and the castle. He'd worry about his problem later. Right now Hickok and Geronimo were more important. He took a step toward the castle, intending to start his search on the east side, when a scraping noise from the front of the mausoleum made him dart back. He peeked around the corner, his eyes widening in surprise.

The recessed front door was sliding open.

Elphinstone suddenly emerged.

Blade jerked his head from view, waited a few seconds, then risked another look.

The apish brute was pressing on one of the etched figures to the right of the door. Almost soundlessly the opening swung closed. Turning, Elphinstone walked to the northwest and disappeared around the corner.

Where was he going? Blade wondered. He stepped to the entrance and examined the walls on both sides. Carved into the marble near the right jamb was a reproduction of the crest engraved near the top of the tomb—the man in armor holding the head and body of a child. That had to be the one. Tentatively, he reached out and pressed on the cool surface, and to his delight the door moved inward on well-oiled hinges.

A quick check verified no one was watching. Blade ducked inside, then paused. There must be a way to close the door from within. He found himself on a spiral metal staircase that descended into the bowels of the earth. All below was pitch black.

Blade hesitated. Grell might be down there—but so might his friends. He felt the wall for a figure, switch or lever, but found none. Leaving the door open was his only option. Taking hold of the rail, he slowly headed down, treading carefully, wary of tripping and plunging to a hard floor far below.

Doubts assailed him. What good could he do if he couldn't see three feet in front of his face? He'd be easy prey for anyone—or anything—lurking in the lower levels. But if he turned back now he might as well keep going all the way to the Home. He'd never be able to look anyone else in the eyes again. Of all the shameful acts men committed, few rivaled deserting friends in an hour of need.

His soles scraped softly on the steps, and in his nervous state he was certain the noise could be heard for hundreds of feet. He breathed shallowly, straining his ears, and glanced upward every few seconds to see if he was being followed.

The staircase seemed to go on forever.

Blade estimated he'd desended 100 feet when he reached the bottom and discerned the outline of a corridor extending to the north, toward the castle. Stepping to the right-hand wall, he placed his palm on the smooth stone and continued onward. The familiar dank smell permeated the air.

For 20 yards the corridor ran straight without a break, and then a junction signified he'd arrived at the levels under the castle. Blade scanned each branch and elected to go forward. His eyes had adjusted to the murky conditions sufficiently for him to discriminate doorways on both sides.

All the doors were closed. He tried the first one on the left and found it locked. The next door on the right was likewise secure. But the third door opened at the twisting of its knob and revealed a huge storeroom beyond.

Blade slid in and surveyed shelves piled high with goods, stacks of crates and boxes, and tables laden with all kinds of articles. Conducting a closer examination, he discovered a stash of canned goods in the southwest corner, and by holding the cans up to his face he was able to read those labels bearing white print. There were peaches, fruit cocktail, string beans, lima beans, corn, several types of juice, zucchini and much more. From the dust covering them, he guessed the cans had been placed there almost 100 years ago by Moray, the first lord of Castle Orm.

He found tools, untouched medical supplies, piles of clothing, blankets, and even pots and pans. None of the goods gave evidence of use, which puzzled him. Why had Moray's ancestors let all this stuff go to waste? Perhaps for the very same reason the Family hadn't used all the supplies stockpiled by the Founder; it would take 1000 years to do so. Both men, apparently, provided more than their descendants would need for many, many generations to come.

A cabinet in a corner arrested his attention. He opened a door and found the equivalent of a gold mine in the form of three boxes of matches. Eagerly he scooped them up, placed two in his pockets and opened the third. Now all he needed to do—

What was that?

Blade stiffened at the faint patter of footsteps in the passageway. Crouching, he aimed at the doorway.

A pale figure appeared, then another.

"Pard, are you in here?"

Blade recognized Tabitha's voice. Flabbergasted, he rose and moved into the open. "Tabitha and Selwyn?"

"Yep," the woman replied happily.

"This isn't my idea, sir," Selwyn stated quickly. "She made me do it." He sighed. "The things brothers do for their sisters."

The youth walked over to them. "I don't understand. What are you doing here?"

"We've been following you, sir," Tabitha said.

"Following me?"

"Yes, sir. Ever since Grell came. We hid in the forest and watched him destroy your camp, then we followed after you."

"I thought you'd rejoined the other serfs."

"Not yet, Pard. We're having too much fun."

Blade looked into her pale eyes. "Why do you keep calling me pard?"

"Isn't that your name, sir? We heard the blond one call you Pard."

"My name is Blade."

"Oh. We're sorry, sir."

Blade leaned closer. "Tell me. Did you happen to see what happened to my friends?"

"No, sir," Tabitha answered.

"We did see Master Elphinstone going toward the front

of the great house," Selwyn disclosed and giggled. "He never saw us hiding in the weeds."

A frown creased Blade's lips. There it was again, a hint of immaturity or instability or a combination of both. The serfs knew they would be punished for their transgressions, yet they viewed the whole affair as a great game. "Why have you been following me?"

"Because we like you, sir," Tabitha said.

"Please call me Blade."

"Okay. Because we like you, Blade, sir."

"Do you know where we are?"

"Of course, sir. In the lowest level below the great house. There are a lot of rooms with many strange things in them, just like this one."

"More storerooms?"

"More rooms like this one, sir."

"On which level do the serfs live?"

"The next two up."

"Take me there."

"If you want, sir, but Master Morlock and Mistress Endora might be there. They'll punish us," Selwyn said.

"Take me."

Brother and sister turned and exited the room.

Cramming the third box of matches into a back pocket, Blade trailed them. He'd save the box until it was really needed. They passed more doors and once a branch to the right. "Where does that go?" he inquired.

"The bone room, sir," Tabitha said. "It's where Grell throws the bones of all the animals and such he eats."

The mention of the monster quickened Blade's pulse, but he didn't allow the panic to seize control again. "He saves bones?"

"Yes, sir. Likes to munch on them when the masts give him time to himself. The room is sort of his den."

"Keep going."

The serfs guided the youth to the central stairway and started up the steps. They slowed when they were halfway to the next landing and turned to the giant.

"We'd rather not go any farther, sir," Tabithaa said respectfully.

"That's right, Blade, sir," Selwyn started. "We're just not in the mood to be punished right now. We'd rather stay out until morning and take our medicine then."

"You don't need to worry. I won't let any of your masts harm you."

"I doubt you can persuade them not to punish us, sir," Tabitha said.

"There are ways."

Shrugging, the pair climbed higher.

Blade followed and could make out the landing and several forks. It wasn't pitch black, after all, and he attributed the reason to moonlight filtering in from outdoors. The matches would help, but any light on the lower levels would undoubtedly attract Morlock and company like a campfire in the open sometimes attracted murderous scavengers.

They reached the landing and halted, Tabitha and Selwyn hanging back, reluctant to advance.

"Please let us leave, sir," she begged.

"You have nothing to fear," Blade told them. He walked to the left-hand fork and peered down the corridor, then turned his back to the middle branch and smiled at his newfound friends. "I'll take care of you."

An express train hurtled out of the darkness and slammed into his back.

CHAPTER FOURTEEN

The impact knocked Blade prone, the breath whooshing from his lungs, and sent the Marlin skidding across the landing. He heard Tabitha and Selwyn laugh—laugh?—and then he frantically pushed to his knees and tried to turn. A naked foot caught him at the base of the neck and sent him down again, his surroundings spinning as if in a whirlpool.

The serfs laughed below.

Numb from the last blow, Blade feebly attempted to roll over. Iron hands closed on his shoulders, and he was bodily lifted into the air. He struggled weakly, but it wasn't enough to prevent his assailant from throwing him against a corridor wall. He landed on his left side and finally saw his attacker.

The hulking form of Elphinstone moved toward the youth, his mallet-like hands clenched into huge fists.

In a certain sense, Blade felt relieved. It was the apish brute, not Grell. At least he stood a chance. Since he'd arrived at Castle Orm, he'd been played a fool, beaten, treated like dirt, and experienced the supreme humiliation of stark cowardice. Now was his chance to show these bastards what Warriors were made of.

Elphinstone halted next to the youth's head and leaned down to grab him.

Not this time, Blade thought, driving his knees up and around, his legs bent, and succeeding in catching Elphinstone in the left temple.

The brute grunted and staggered backward.

Blade was up in a flash, in the on-guard stance. He considered resorting to his Bowies and promptly discarded the notion. His foe wasn't armed. Using the knives would be unfair.

Neither of the serfs were laughing.

Straightening, Elphinstone vented an inarticulate growl and charged, swinging his fists wildly, going for the youth's face.

This time Blade was ready. He ducked under a couple of punches that would have caved in his skull and delivered three swift jabs to the brute's ribs. When Elphinstone shifted to the right, Blade pivoted, pressing his initiative, burying his left fist in the apish man's stomach and following through with a right to the jaw that rocked Elphinstone on his heels.

Instantly, Blade closed in, kneeing his adversary in the groin. Elphinstone wheezed and doubled over, and Blade executed a flawless snap kick into the brute's nose that sent him tottering backward almost to the edge of the landing. "Had enough?" he asked.

Elphinstone recovered his balance and bellowed his enraged response. "No!"

Blade wanted to end the fight before Morlock or Grell showed up, especially Grell. As Elphinstone came toward him, he ran to meet the brute halfway. But instead of using his fists, he leaped into the air, performing a flying side kick, the yoko-tobi-geri, and struck Elphinstone full in the mouth.

As if smashed by a sledgehammer, Elphinstone catapulted head over heels onto his stomach with a loud thud. For a moment he lay stunned. His head slowly rose from the hard floor, his lips cracked and bleeding, and he spat blood. With a guttural growl, he started to rise.

Blade was ready. Instead of slugging it out with the brute, he must rely on the martial arts. Elphinstone obviously knew nothing of the science of self-defense, and while the brute might be stronger, his reflexes and coordination were no match for Blade's.

The young Warrior glided in and flicked a snap kick to his foe's head before Elphinstone could rise, rocking the apish man on his haunches. Another snap kick with the right leg was blocked, but a crescent kick with the left connected and sent the brute onto his back.

Elphinstone took longer to rise this time. Dark stains coated the lower half of his face and neck. He grunted as he propped himself on his elbows, then came off the floor in a surprising burst of speed.

Still in the on-guard stance, Blade retreated a step to give himself more room and leaped into the air, whipping his body in a spinning back kick that hit the brute at the base of the throat and lifted Elphinstone from his feet to sail to the edge of the landing and over it. He alighted on the balls of his feet and moved to the first step, expecting to see the apish figure barreling up toward him.

There was no one there.

Perplexed, Blade scanned the stairs below and saw no sign of his adversary. Yet Elphinstone had to be down there, somewhere. He doubted the brute was gravely injured. It would take more than a few kicks to put the Neanderthal out of commission. Pivoting, he looked at the serfs.

Tabitha and Selwyn were riveted in place, their expressions reflecting total astonishment.

Blade anticipated they would be elated at his victory

and walked up to them. "See? I told you I'd take care of you."

"You hurt him!" Tabitha declared angrily. "You hurt Master Elphinstone!"

"You had no right to be so cruel!" Selwyn added.

Bewildered by their passionate reaction, Blade blinked and jabbed a finger at the stairs. "He was trying to kill me," he said defensively.

"He was not," Tabitha disagreed. "He probably just wanted to put you in a cage."

"And you think I should have let him?"

"Certainly. He's one of the masts, after all. All of us should serve them gladly."

"I'm no one's slave," Blade snapped, "and I don't serve your masts. If I can, I'm going to put them out of business for good."

"What do you mean, sir?"

"I mean I'm going to put an end to their enslavement of the serfs."

The brother and sister looked at each other.

"You can't," Selwyn responded in horror, forgetting his usual excessive civility.

In exasperation Blade threw his hands into the air and both serfs flinched. "Why not?" he demanded.

"Who will watch over us?" Tabitha asked, on the verge of tears. "Who will protect us and clothe us and feed us?"

The implications of her questions shook Blade to the core of his being. He took a pace backward and gazed at them in blatant disbelief. "Let me get this straight. You *want* them to take care of you?"

"Of course, sir," Tabitha said.

"'We'd be lost without them, sir," Selwyn chimed in.

"But they take advantage of you."

Tabitha giggled. "How do they ever do that, sir?"

"They make you work for them, make you till the fields to produce their food, and they keep you cooped up during the day. You're little better than slaves."

"Oh, you have it all wrong, sir. We like working for the masts. They love us and treat us fairly."

"How can you say such a thing? They beat and tortured your friend Tweena until she died. And Grell *ate* a serf."

Tabitha nodded. "But Tweena deserved to be punished for disobeying the masts. And Cathmor deserved to be eaten for trying to leave the Domain."

The absurd illogic baffled Blade, and he pressed a palm to his forehead as he tried to make sense of it all. The serfs were enslaved and didn't even know it. Worse, they preferred the status quo. How could they? Didn't they realize how precious freedom was?

"Can we go now, sir?" Tabitha asked.

"Go where?" Blade responded absently.

"We'd like to find our friends and play before dawn, sir," Selwyn said.

"Or before the masts catch us," Tabitha stated and snickered.

Blade stared at their pale skin, at their pale features, at their pale eyes, and suddenly their very paleness offended him. Their personalities were as colorless as their complexions, devoid of all character, stripped of any semblance of conviction and independence. They were pale imitations of human beings, at best, puppets on a string who didn't want the puppeteers removed. "Go," he said harshly. "Get out of here."

The serfs giggled and danced down the stairs, and moments later they were swallowed by the inky shadows.

Good riddance, Blade reflected. He abruptly realized his rifle was missing and scoured the landing until he found it. As he stooped to retreive the Marlin he heard a little laugh behind him.

"I could have spared you a lot of trouble, boy."

Startled, Blade crouched and spun, leveling the rifle, his finger on the trigger. He saw the thin figure of the lord of Castle Orm standing at the junction.

"I'm unarmed," Morlock said calmly.

The youth hesitated, suspecting a trick. "Don't move or I'll shoot."

"There's no need for violence, boy."

"The name is Blade, remember? Come closer so I can see you."

Morlock advanced and held out his empty hands to demonstrate he posed no threat. "See? You have nothing to fear."

"How long have you been standing there?"

"A while."

"Where are my friends?"

"I have no idea."

Blade took a stride and aimed at the smaller man's forehead. "Tell me the truth."

"Or what? You'll shoot me? I think not." Morlock chuckled. "You won't kill a defenseless man, boy."

"Don't tempt me."

Morlock nodded at the stairs. "I saw your fight. If you were a born killer, you would have pulled your knives instead of trying to best Elphinstone with your hands and feet." He paused. "My compliments, by the way. No one has ever beaten him before."

"Where is he now?"

"How would I know? Probably nursing his wounds."

"And where's your wife?"

"My darling Endora is taking her nightly stroll."

Blade lowered his rifle barrel a few inches. Now that he had Morlock right where he wanted him, he didn't know what to do. By all rights he should put an end to the man's reign of terror by terminating him on the spot, but he couldn't bring himself to fire. Morlock was right, damn him. Blade wasn't a cold-blooded killer. "We need to talk," he said lamely.

"Indeed we do. That's why I'm here. I knew you entered the underground through the portal in the mausoleum and came down to meet you."

"How did you know?"

Morlock grinned. "That's my little secret." He shifted and gestured upward. "Must we stand here in the draft to discuss what's on your mind? Why not come upstairs with me where we can have our chat in a civilized fashion?"

"Lead the way," Blade said, keeping the Marlin trained on the thin man's back as Morlock led the way toward ground level. His every instinct told him not to let down his guard for an instant. For the time being, though, he had to play along, at least until he knew the fate of Hickok and Geronimo. "Where's Grell?" he asked.

"You know about him, do you?"

"Just answer the question."

"Very well. I'd imagine he's out trying to round up the serfs. Eventually they'll stop playing their games and let themselves be herded together."

"Just like cattle," Blade stated bitterly.

"In a way, they are."

"Where did they come from? What have you done to them?"

"I'll explain everything once we're comfortable."

Blade fell silent until they reached the ground floor. The sight of candles flickering in holders at regular intervals along the corridor prompted an observation. "I thought all of you can see in the dark."

"Our night vision is exceptional, but we're not completely weaned from a dependence on light. We usually keep a few candles lit after dark," Morlock said and began to climb the next flight.

"Where are you going?"

"The chamber I have in mind is on the third floor."

"What's wrong with one on this floor?"

Morlock paused to look down. "Not a thing, but the sitting room I have in mind is very comfortable and private. We won't be disturbed there."

Who would disturb them? Blade wondered, reluctantly following all the way to the third landing. He stayed on the small man's heels as they went right to the second door, which was wide open. Inside was a lavishly furnished room. Instead of candles, a kerosene lantern provided moderate illumination. "You must have a kerosene storage tank somewhere," he commented, crossing to a wooden chair.

"Take that one, why don't you?" Morlock suggested, pointing at an easy chair near the sofa.

Since it made no difference to the youth, he sat where Morlock wanted.

"And yes, we do have an underground storage tank," the master of the castle disclosed enroute to the sofa. "It's almost dry after all these years, so we conserve what little usable kerosene we have left. When I knew you were coming, I lit a lantern in preparation."

"How did you, by the way?"

"I'll get to that in a bit," Morlock said, taking a seat and folding his left leg over his right. "Would you care for refreshments?"

"Just information," Blade said, not knowing what to make of his host's continued civility. It must be a trick of some kind. At the first hint of hostility, he'd put a bullet in the bastard's brain. He was safe as long as he had the rifle and his Bowies.

"Very well. Where would you like me to begin? With the serfs?"

"That would be nice."

"I overheard enough to know you believe the darling creatures are little better than slaves. Am I right?"

"They *are* slaves."

"Correct me if I'm wrong, but I believe the definition of a slave is someone completely under the domination of another person, someone who is the property of another. Would you agree?"

"Sounds accurate enough to me."

"Then your accusation is unfounded. You heard Tabitha and Selwyn. Do they consider themselves slaves? Absolutely not. They like the life they live and have no desire to change. They're happy," Morlock said. "Would you begrudge them such a blessing?"

Blade disregarded the disquieting question and tried another tack. "Where did they come from?"

"The serfs have served the Morlock clan since shortly after the war—"

"Wait a minute," Blade interrupted. "Is Morlock your first or last name?"

"Morlock is the family name. Moray Morlock was the first lord of Castle Orm."

"Then what's your first name?"

"Angus," Morlock replied, smirking.

Why did he do that? Blade asked himself. "Okay. Back to the serfs. Who were their ancestors? Where did they come from?"

"As I understand it, a dozen survivors showed up here about a week after the missiles were launched. They were suffering from radiation sickness. Moray took them in and let them live in the lower levels. Eventually most of them recovered, and they decided to stay here and work for Moray in exchange for their lodging."

"So the current serfs are their descendants?"

"Aye. Over the years their skin has become paler and paler, and now they're strictly nocturnal."

The explanation was plausible, but Blade felt he was being deceived. He couldn't put a finger on the reason. Perhaps it was Morlock's smug expression and superior air. "And where did Grell come from?"

"Moray found him in the woods ten years after the war."

Blade sat up. "Impossible. That would make Grell close to ninety years-old."

"He is. The serfs even refer to him as the immortal one since three generations of them have known and feared him. Grell was just a pup when Moray stumbled on him hiding in a thicket. Moray liked the wee creature and gave it a home. Ever since Grell has been the Morlock watchdog."

"What kind of mutation is he?"

"I don't know. Moray believed a bear embryo underwent a radiation-induced transformation. If you've seen Grell, you know that no bear grows to such a massive size." Morlock shrugged. "Who knows what his parents were?"

Blade thoughtfully pursed his lips, debating whether to pry into another disturbing matter, and decided to try an oblique approach. "Did Moray ever marry?"

"Yes."

"Another survivor?"

"Aye. Bands of wanderers would travel through the area from time to time. His wife, Constance, was a refugee from the Twin Cities."

And what about your wife? Blade wanted to inquire, but couldn't bring himself to.

"Are you certain I can't entice you to take some refreshment? I took the liberty of having a tray of food set out in the next room."

"I'm not hungry."'

"Too bad. We have excellent wine and cheese."

Wine? Blade wondered if enough of it might loosen Morlock's lips. Perhaps a glass or two of wine was in order. He'd do anything to uncover a clue concerning his friends. "All right. Some wine can't hurt."

Again Morlock smirked and stood. He walked toward a closed door in the east wall. "Follow me. You can select whatever you want."

Blade held the rifle down low as he crossed to the doorway. His host went through first, and he took three strides himself before he realized he'd been suckered.

Displaying unexpected speed, Morlock darted to the left and grabbed a lever on the wall.

Taken unawares, Blade was sluggish in reacting. "Don't touch that!" he warned and began to bring the barrel up. Too late.

Morlock yanked on the lever.

Blade's finger was tightening on the trigger when the floor fell out from beneath his feet.

CHAPTER FIFTEEN

Gruesome visions of a pit lined with sharp stakes at the bottom filled Blade's mind as he plummeted straight down, enveloped by darkness, his arms above his head, the useless rifle clutched in his left hand. It took a few seconds for him to realize he was hurtling down a metal shaft toward an uncertain fate.

Damn his stupidity!

Anger supplanted the initial shock, anger at his gullibility. He'd waltzed right into the trap with both eyes open. Attila or any of the other experienced Warriors would never have let themselves be so blatantly duped. Being a novice was no excuse. Even novices were expected to exercise basic common sense.

The shaft angled to the right, then the left, in gradual curves designed to retard the speed of passage.

Blade's elbows and knees banged and scraped on the sides, and when he lifted his head and tried to see the bottom his forehead struck the top with a resounding crack. The descent went so long that he estimated the shaft must drop down into the underground levels. When he began to wonder if it would ever end, it did.

Shooting out of the mouth like a tongue out of a lizard, Blade plummeted over ten feet into an enormous tank of stagnant water. He hit with a loud splash and went under, instinctively holding his breath but unable to prevent the warm liquid from filling his nose and ears. A bitter taste filled his mouth, almost gagging him, and then his boots hit bottom and he shoved off, kicking desperately for the top.

He burst from the surface and inhaled deeply, grateful merely to be alive. Shaking his head and wiping his arm across his face, he blinked and looked about him, treading water to stay afloat. To his consternation he found himself imprisoned, enclosed on all four sides by clear glass or plastic walls rising over ten feet above the water.

It was like a gigantic fish tank.

Blade swam to one side and took stock. The depth was 12 feet. The length and width were the same, ten feet both ways. He reached out and touched the wall, deciding the substance must be a hard plastic. Never in a million years would he be able to climb so smooth a surface. And since he couldn't get a purchase for his legs either, he was ingeniously snared and effectively helpless.

The water had a brownish tinge and gave off a foul odor.

Abruptly realizing there must be a light source nearby, Blade surveyed the chamber in which the tank was located. It dwarfed all the others. Fifty feet high and seventy in length, the walls were composed of large, square stones, and the ceiling of immense wooden beams. More thick candles mounted on the walls provided marginal illumination. Far off on the right, at the top of a flight of wooden stairs, stood a broad wooden door.

He swung to the left and received a pleasant shock. Aligned against the wall were five metal cages, the bars on each spaced six inches apart, and two were occupied by unconscious figures.

Hickok and Geronimo!

Elated, Blade swam to the left side of the tank and stared happily at his companions until a horrifying thought occurred to him. What if they were dead? He licked his lips and called out. "Hey! Sleepyheads! Rise and shine!"

There was no reaction.

Intensely worried, Blade yelled louder. "Wake up, you dummies! It's me, Blade."

At last Geronimo stirred, groaning and rolling onto his back. His arms moved feebly.

"Geronimo, wake up!"

The insistent shout had an effect. Geronimo's eyelids fluttered, and after a few seconds he opened his eyes and sat up, gazing in confusion at his surroundings until his gaze alighted on the tank. Recognition brought a flood of awareness, and he suddenly rose to his knees. "Blade! What's going on?" He seized one of the bars. "Where in the world are we?"

"In an underground chamber below Castle Orm," Blade called out. His legs were beginning to tire and he wished he could rest for a while, but there was no place in the tank to gain a firm footing. "What happened to you? How did they catch you?"

Geronimo rubbed the back of his head and stood. "I'm not sure. The last thing I remember is running around the corner and not seeing any sign of Hickok or the serfs. I stopped and was turning when something or someone rose out of the shadows at the base of the wall and clobbered me but good." He paused. "I think it was Elphinstone."

"Morlock captured me," Blade revealed, without bothering to elaborate.

"Have you seen Hik—" Geronimo began and looked to his left. Beaming, he stepped to the side of his cage. "Nathan! On your feet, you goof."

The gunfighter didn't budge.

Geronimo reached through the bars and tried to grab Hickok's cage, but it was inches out of reach. He desisted and cupped his hands to his mouth. "Yo, Nathan! I know you need your beauty sleep, but don't go overboard."

Hickok finally moved his arms. His head bobbed, he licked his lips, and his eyes snapped open. "Where am I?" he bellowed, sitting up. "Where's the lowlife who hit me?" He saw the tank, did a double take and glanced in both directions. Discovering Geronimo, he did another double take, then chuckled.

"What can you possibly find amusing?" the Blackfoot inquired.

"Since you two clowns are here, it's a safe bet I'm not in heaven."

"You're still on Earth, dimwit. Under Morlock's castle."

The gunfighter shoved up, his hands falling to his holster—his empty holsters. "Hey! Where are my six-shooters?"

It was Blade who found them. He noticed a table at the end of the row of cages and distinguished a small pile of weapons. "Over there," he shouted, pointing.

Hickok looked and fumed. "Some hombre is going to pay for takin' my Colts. Nobody takes my guns—ever!"

"How did they manage to catch you?" Blade yelled so his voice would carry over the top of the tank.

"I was after those fairies, as I recollect. I ran into the yard, thinkin' I was about to catch 'em, but they were all gone. I didn't know if they went on around the blamed castle or lit into the trees, and then I saw one of those fancy tombs was open. So I just kept on going, right inside, and I was about to give a call and let you know where I was when the door swung shut and someone bashed me on the head," the gunfighter explained.

"Probably Elphinstone," Blade said. "He's been a busy bee tonight."

"Wait'll I get my revolvers back," Hickok snapped. "I'll teach that yahoo a lesson."

"How are we going to get out of this mess?" Geronimo asked.

Blade wanted an answer to that one himself. After all he'd been through, after the strain of the chase and the fight, his limbs were already weary. The sustained effort of staying above the surface only aggravated his condition. He found it hard to keep his grip on the Marlin.

"Are you holdin' your rifle, pard?" Hickok inquired in amazement.

"Yeah. Why?"

"Try to shoot your way out of that overgrown goldfish bowl. A couple of shots should crack one of those walls, easy."

"What if they're bulletproof?"

"Then the ricochet might hit you," Hickok said. "But what does a little scratch matter if it gets us out of this dungeon?"

Blade tapped the nearest wall with the Marlin, debating the merits of the gunfighter's suggestion. He still had no idea whether the substance was glass or plastic, but a few rounds might just do the trick. There wasn't enough water to do more than cover the floor to a depth of two or three inches, at most, so none of them need worry about drowning. His main concern was the wall. Would it break cleanly or with jagged edges? If the latter, he might be cut badly when the water poured from the tank. "I don't know," he said uncertainly.

"What's wrong with the idea?"

"I could be killed."

"Don't sweat the small stuff, pard. It'll be a piece of cake."

Geronimo snickered. "Easy for you to say, Nathan. You're not doing the slicing."

"And what the blazes is that crack supposed to mean?"

Their discussion was interrupted by the opening of the big wooden door. In strolled the master of Castle Orm bearing a five-gallon bottle in his hand. The bottle contained a brownish liquid.

"Ahhh, good. I see all of you are awake."

Hickok grabbed hold of two bars and shook them violently. "Let us out of here, you vermin!"

"Sticks and stones, boy," Morlock said chuckling as he walked toward them. "Are all of you comfortable?"

"Up yours," Hickok declared.

"What he said," Geronimo added.

Morlock glanced at the giant. "Enjoying your swim?" he asked scornfully and cackled.

"The guy is off his rocker," Hickok commented.

"Must be related to you," Geronimo stated.

Blade pressed his right hand to the wall, treading water with an effort, wishing he could throttle Angus Morlock's skinny neck. "What do you plan to do with us?" he snapped.

"It should be obvious, even to childish morons like yourselves."

"Give me my shootin' irons and I'll show you who's childish," Hickok declared.

Walking up to the tank, Morlock halted and grinned at Blade. "To answer your question, I plan to dispose of the three of you."

"Why?"

"Need you ask?" Morlock snorted. "Did you really think I would allow you to leave the Domain so that you could return to Humboldt and tell others all about us?"

"But you threw us out this morning."

"And you were watched every minute after that until night fell. Had you left the valley, I would have sent Grell and Elphinstone after you tonight. One way or the other, you'd never have reached Humboldt alive."

"Shows how much you know," Hickok said. "We're

not from Humboldt, yo-yo."

Morlock took the news in stride. "It doesn't really matter where you are from. By morning, all three of you will be dead."

Blade glanced at the top of the tank, then scrutinized the water. How did Morlock intend to kill him? Simply let him tire out and sink to the bottom?

"If you kill us, you'll be sorry," Hickok said.

"I won't regret my actions in the least," Morlock replied. "You're interlopers who threaten the peace and security of the Domain. I have an obligation to my family and the serfs to protect them at all costs." He deposited the bottle at his feet.

"Who are you trying to kid?" Blade said. "You have an obligation to protect yourself. You're afraid a group of survivors will learn what's been going on here and put a stop to it."

"To what? My alleged mistreatment of the serfs? We've already discussed that issue, and you know they're quite content."

"I'm not talking about your slaves. I'm referring to what you've done to everyone who has passed by your castle." Blade indicated the chamber with a sweep of his head. "This torture chamber must see a lot of business."

The diminutive man laughed. "This is my holding room. The torture chamber is in the next room on the right."

"How many innocent people have you killed over the years?"

"Those I've slain deserved to die," Morlork said. "And I don't keep a tally. Perhaps there have been three dozen."

The number appalled Blade. "Did you build this tank yourself?"

"Heavens, no. Great-grandfather Moray had this room built. From the information in his diary, he used the facilities much more than I do."

"So Moray started the tradition of slaying all outsiders?"

"Aye. He knew outsiders would never be able to appreciate our way of life."

"And Moray was responsible for having the secret passages constructed?"

"Aye."

"And those survivors you told me about, the ones who became the serfs, he didn't take them in out of the goodness of his heart. He probably forced them down here at gunpoint and imprisoned them, then tortured them until they were mental vegetables."

Morlock laughed. "You're not as dumb as you look, boy."

"I also know about your family tree."

Sudden anger tinged Morlock's cheeks crimson. "Yes, you definitely are a bright one. Not that the information can have any significance to you."

"You're sick."

"Who the hell are you to judge me, boy? What do you know about life? Our way was established centuries ago. The Morlock clan has always been close-knit."

"In more ways than one."

A malevolent sneer curled Morlock's mouth. "I'll enjoy killing you." He clasped his hands behind his back and walked close to the cages. "Please be patient. After your friend is finished, you'll each have your turns."

"You're making a major mistake," Geronimo said. "We have other friends who know where we were headed. They'll send a search party."

"Let them. By then I'll have the crack in the outer wall repaired, and they'll have no way to get inside. They'll learn nothing and leave empty-handed."

"Have it all figured out, huh?" Hickok remarked.

"I'm a Morlock. The males in our family have always enjoyed an extremely high I.Q."

"Does that include Elphinstone?" Blade interjected.

Angus shrugged. "There are exceptions to every rule.. He's an inferior idiot, useless for breeding purposes. I, on the other hand, am a genius."

"You're a madman," Blade corrected him.

Morlock returned to the side of the tank and smiled up at the youth. "Enough idle chatter. Are you ready to die?"

CHAPTER SIXTEEN

Blade watched Angus Morlock pick up the five-gallon bottle and walk around to the opposite side of the tank where the murky water concealed him from view. He glanced at his friends, neither of whom could see Morlock either, and started to dog-paddle across the tank. A metallic scraping noise caused him to stop, and a moment later he saw the upper end of a ladder being placed against the tank wall. The top rung came within inches of the upper edge.

"Be careful, Blade," Geronimo yelled.

"Use the rifle," Hickok urged.

The ladder bounced slightly as Morlock climbed above the water level and beamed at the giant. Secure under his left arm was the bottle. "Did you miss me?" he asked and tittered.

Blade arched his spine, letting his upper back float to relieve some of the strain on his tired legs. He hefted the Marlin, his eyes on Morlock.

"I wouldn't waste my time using the rifle, if I were you. This plastic in shatterproof. You could smash it with a sledgehammer, and it wouldn't crack."

"Has anyone ever tried?"

The question elicited another cackle. Morlock climbed laboriously to the top of the ladder, pausing every three or four rungs to adjust his grip on the bottle.

What was in there? Blade wondered. What was worth such effort? He glimpsed small, dark forms being swished about but couldn't identify them. Goose bumps broke out all over his skin.

Morlock was careful not to expose himself. He kept his head below the plastic rim and grinned. "You must be curious about my surprise package."

Blade wasn't about to give him the courtesy of a response.

"There is a stream about a quarter of a mile south of the castle. Quite by accident I discovered that a marvelous mutation inhabits its water. I went fishing one day, tossed in my line and pulled out one of these amazing creatures."

Lightly stroking the Marlin's trigger, Blade waited for the madman to lift the bottle above the rim.

"I had no idea what I'd caught and foolishly tried to remove it from my hook. The thing clamped onto me and wouldn't let go. I was forced to return to the castle and used a candle to burn it off. By then, of course, I'd lost a pint or two of blood."

Geronimo and Hickok were listening attentively, their countenances reflecting their worry.

Morlock grunted and tightened his hold on the bottle. "My research indicates this particular form of mutation once existed as common flatworms. As you might know, free-living flatworms exist in ponds, streams and oceans all over the world."

Blade's forehead knit in perplexity. Worms? The man had worms in there? What possible threat could worms pose?

"Some flatworms closely resemble leeches, which might explain these mutations. Of course, few grow as large or become aggressive, but radiation is notorious for drastically altering genetic traits," Morlock said, starting to raise the bottle toward the rim.

Blade held the rifle at water level, his stomach muscles tightening. The madman must not be accustomed to having victims fight back, he reasoned, or else Morlock wouldn't make such blatant mistakes.

The demented lord looked into the bottle and snickered. "Are you thirsty, my little ones?" He glanced at the giant. "They haven't been fed in days. I'd imagine they're famished."

A few more inches, Blade thought, his visage impassive.

"Time for the festivities," Morlock said and hoisted the container above the edge of the plastic wall. He held it steady in preparation for upending the contents into the tank.

Blade was ready. He snapped the Marlin to his shoulders, took a hasty bead on the middle of the bottle and fired. The booming of the 45-70 almost deafened him.

The slug smashed the bottle to pieces and sent a shower of glass, water and mutations spraying down on both sides of the wall. Most of it struck a shocked Morlock full in the face, and screaming, he brought up his hands to shield his eyes and lost his balance. Desperately he tried to grab a rung, but he plummeted from the ladder.

All this Blade barely noticed. He had problems of his own. Three dark forms had dropped into the tank and disappeared in the soup. He swam to the far corner and pressed his back to the wall, waiting for whatever they were to attack.

They didn't waste any time.

Something crested the surface and made a beeline for the youth, its slender shape visible as a dark brown blur, throwing off a narrow wake.

Blade levered a fresh round into the chamber, pressed the rifle to his shoulder and tried to track the speeding mutation. He squeezed off a shot when the thing was only inches from the end of the barrel, and the mutation promptly dived. He had no idea whether he'd scored or not.

"What are they?" Geronimo called out.

"Use the rife on the wall! Use the rifle on the wall!" Hickok stressed urgently.

Feeding in another round, Blade turned right and left, his legs kicking vigorously. He envisioned one of them going for his groin and involuntarily shuddered.

Suddenly Morlock appeared, his features a mask of fury, blood seeping from a half-dozen cuts on his face and neck. Dangling from his left cheek and his forehead were two of the mutations. He shook his right fist at the giant and bellowed, "Damn you! Damn you all to hell!"

Blade couldn't help but look.

The mutations were a foot in length and two inches in width, except at the center where they tapered to an inch. Their bodies were essentially flat, but their heads were round and the size of a grown man's fist. Somehow the creatures had latched onto Morlock and were sucking his blood.

"I'll be back!" the madman shrieked and ran toward the door, tugging in vain on his unwanted appendages.

Blade gulped and scanned the water. Where were they? Had the shot deterred them? Even more important, how could he get out of there before the things tried again?

He stiffened when he felt a nudge on his right ankle. It had to be one of the mutations! The nudge was repeated on his shin, then his knee and his inner thigh. The thing was working its way up his body, perhaps seeking naked flesh.

Blade stared straight down, transferred the rifle to his left hand and drew his right Bowie. He distinguished the rippling form of the bloodsucker several inches below his belt, writhing snakelike. Elevating the knife above his head, he froze until the thing was level with his belt, then speared the point into the water.

The Bowie connected, slicing the creature open, and black fluid poured from the wound. Instantly the thing angled toward the bottom and vanished.

Two down, or at least wounded, Blade congratulated himself. But he'd been lucky. He couldn't expect to hold them off forever. Had Morlock succeeded in dumping in the entire bottle, he'd probably have a dozen of the mutations gorging on his blood. He glanced up at the transparent walls, racking his brain for a way out. They were shatterproof, Morlock had boasted. A sledgehammer wouldn't crack them, which meant his Bowies were useless.

Another thin shape materialized on the surface eight feet away and swam toward the youth as if propelled by a rocket.

Blade saw it coming and braced to meet the slender monster, swinging his right arm on high and bringing the Bowie down again at just the right moment, trying to cleave the creature in two. He missed.

He glimpsed a circular head rearing out of the water, a head consisting entirely of a gaping mouth ringed by tiny, tapered teeth. From the mouth protruded a tubular tongue six inches long. And then the mutation smacked into his abdomen next to his navel, and an incredible pain lanced his gut. Those tiny teeth sank in and held fast. He doubled over, feeling as if someone was gouging his midriff with a scorching poker.

It was the thing's tongue!

Blade realized the creature was seeking a vein or an artery. With a supreme effort he straightened, stuck the knife in his mouth with the sharp edge outward and tried to seize the writhing horror. Its slippery body squished through his fingers again and again. In desperation he seized it near the head and finally succeeded in getting a firm grip. He yanked, but the mutation was locked onto his body.

"Use the rifle on the wall!" Hickok bellowed. "Use the rifle on the wall!"

In the back of his mind Blade wished the dummy would shut up. If a sledgehammer wouldn't do the job, what good would his rifle do? He wrenched on the flatworm, his right arm bulging, and his hands slipped off. There was no way he could remove it unless he got a firm footing. Which brought him back to square one.

He spied another of the creatures swimming slowly on the other side of the tank.

Dear Spirit, what should he do? He pounded the plastic in frustration, and then inspiration struck. Sure, a sledgehammer wouldn't work, but a sledge delivered its force over a broader area than a bullet. A 45-70 was one of the most powerful rifles ever made. Its thick, blunt bullet could plow through thick brush to bag a deer or an elk. At point-blank range, what would the effect be on the plastic?

There was only one way to find out.

Twisting, Blade jammed the barrel against the glass several inches below the water line. If he was wrong, the ricochet might well kill him. But it was either that or let the mutations slowly suck him lifeless.

He fired.

The shot was muffled by the water. His arms were driven backwards by the recoil.

Blade leaned closer and saw a dent in the plastic. The bullet hadn't penetrated. He guessed the slug had flattened and sank to the bottom. But the dent was encouraging. The creature's tongue fluttered around inside his stomach, adding incentive to his limbs as he worked the lever. He placed the barrel directly on the dent and squeezed the trigger.

The 45-70 did its job. The high-powered round drilled through the plastic, trailed by a stream of water that splashed onto the floor below.

One hole wouldn't suffice. Blade levered the fourth

round home, then groped in his back pocket and extracted three more shells. He quickly loaded and pressed the rifle to the wall again, only this time three inches below the hole. Once more he fired, expecting to dent the plastic.

This time the first shot bored through, producing a second stream, but it did something more. The concentration of pressure at the two holes as the water gushed out put an immense strain on the plastic between and surrounding the holes, and the pressure accomplished what the Marlin alone never could.

A resounding snap sounded, and suddenly a network of fine lines mushroomed in the wall. The next moment those lines became cracks, the water hissing and cascading from the tank.

Blade tried to paddle away from the wall, but he was too late. The whole section buckled and split, and an irresistible wave carried him through the gaping opening onto the chamber floor. He fell to his knees, nearly losing his grip on the rifle, and was buffeted by the escaping water. The reeking liquid enveloped his momentarily, then dispersed across the chamber.

"Blade!" Geronimo shouted.

His stomach on fire, Blade slowly stood and staggered toward the cages. The water was up to his ankles, and he had to be careful not to slip. He halted and stared at the repulsive thing hanging from his abdomen. Grimacing, he wrapped his right hand around it, squeezed with all of his might and wrenched savagely.

The upper edge of the mutation's mouth peeled off, but it still hung on.

Blade grit his teeth, closed his eyes and pulled like he had never pulled on anything before. For half a minute nothing happened, then abruptly the creature popped loose, its blood-covered tongue sliding out and flopping in the air. In a frenzy of rage, he repeatedly smashed the rifle stock on the thing until its body and tongue both hung limp. Disgusted by the violation of his body and still not satisfied the mutation was dead, he placed the flatworm under his boot and ground it into the stone until a sarcastic voice made him realize what he was doing.

"I think the sucker is a goner, pard."

Blade stopped grinding his heel and looked at his friends. "I guess you're right," he said softly.

"Why don't you find a way to get us out?" Hickok suggested. "And hurry it up before the runt and his ugly pals show up."

The reminder sparked Blade to action. He hurried to the cages and searched the nearby wall and the table for keys. There were none.

"You might need to get the keys from Morlock," Geronimo said.

"No," Blade responded.

"Then how do you figure to get us out?" Hickok asked.

Before Blade could answer, Geronimo extended his right arm between the bars and pointed. "Look!"

Turning, Blade beheld a sight that chilled his blood.

Most of the floor was now covered with water, and swimming about in search of prey were a dozen or so mutations, going every which way, their slim forms easy to spot.

"We don't have to worry about them," Blade declared. "They can't suck blood unless they touch flesh, and all of us have on footwear.

"But what if they can crawl as well as swim?" Geronimo remarked. "They could come right up our legs."

The idea intensified Blade's nausea. "Take this," he said, handing the rifle to Hickok.

"What are you fixin' to do?"

"Watch." Blade planted both feet firmly in front of the door and gripped the bar, one hand above the lock, the other below it. He winked at the gunfighter, inhaled and applied all of his prodigious strength to forcing the door open. His muscles rippled and contorted, his neck swelling and the veins expanding. Breathing in short, loud spurts, he battled the metal bar for a minute. Two. Then slowly, creaking noisily, the bar began to bend. Next the lock tilted outward. At last, with the sweat pouring down Blade's face and his chest aching terribly, the lock gave way with a grinding retort.

"Took you long enough," Hickok muttered, stepping out and surveying the chamber. "You work at freeing Geronimo, and I'll keep you covered."

Despite being weary to his core, Blade moved to the next cage and repeated the procedure. This door resisted longer, draining his flagging energy, and just when he thought he couldn't do it, the lock snapped, making him stumble backward. He caught himself and swayed.

"Are you sure you're all right?" Geronimo asked, emerging.

"Fine," Blade said. "Just give me a chance to catch my breath."

"We don't have much time, pard," Hickok mentioned and returned the Marlin. He ran to the table, picked up his cherished Colts and grinned. "Let's get to kickin' butt."

Geronimo went over to retrieve his weapons. "What's our first move?" he asked.

"We'll search this castle from top to bottom," Blade said, arching his back to relieve a cramp.

"And when we find the runt?" Hickok inquired, walking back. He twirled the Colts into their holsters.

"The Morlock rein of terror ends today," Blade vowed, glancing over his shoulder to check on the mutations. His eyes widened at the sight of five of the grotesque genetic deviations converging on him from all directions.

CHAPTER SEVENTEEN

Blade raised the rifle and aimed at the nearest creature, feeling sick again at the thought of one of those things inserting its tongue into his body. Try as he might, he couldn't seem to hold the barrel steady.

"Let me," Hickok stated, stepping past the giant, a grin curling his lips. "Eat these, bloodsuckers," he said and drew both Colts in a blur of ambidextrous speed. Five shots boomed in succession.

Blade was astonished by his friend's accuracy. With each shot a mutation flipped into the air or skidded backwards, its thin form neatly punctured, then thrashed wildly in its death throes, spraying water right and left.

"Let's skedaddle, pard," the gunfighter proposed. He began reloading the spent rounds, his gaze constantly roving over the floor.

No urging was necessary. Blade hurried to the wooden stairs and climbed them to the door. Surprisingly, Morlock hadn't bothered to lock it, but with those vile creatures sucking blood from his face, he'd probably been too preoccupied to give thought to the door.

"Let's clear up one detail before we step out there," Hickok said as Blade pulled the door open. "Do we shoot to kill on sight?"

There was no hesitation on Blade's part. "Yes."

Hickok chuckled. "Maybe you'll make a decent Warrior after all."

They entered a dark corridor. From somewhere came a fluttering sound, like the beating of bat wings.

Blade took the lead and advanced for dozens of yards before he noticed an unlit candle in a holder to his left. "Wait a second," he said and felt in his pockets for the boxes of matches. All three were soaked on the outside. Doubting he would find a match that wasn't drenched, he opened the boxes and felt for a dry one.

"Where'd you find those?" Hickok asked.

"In a storage room."

"Did you happen to see any dynamite?"

"No."

"Shucks."

At the center of one of the boxes Blade found five dry matches. He quickly lit one, removed the candle from the holder and applied the flame to the wick. "Geronimo, will you gather up the matches?" he requested. "If we dry them out, we might be able to use them."

"Sure." The Blackfoot squatted and put the boxes in his pockets. The four dry matches went in a separate one.

Blade resumed walking, holding the candle aloft to give them a ten-foot radius of dim illumination. He tried not to think of what would happen should they encounter Grell, but an image of the fiery eyed beast haunted his every step.

The corridor connected to the central stairs, where a whispering draft almost extinguished the flickering flame. Blade cupped the same hand holding the rifle around the top of the candle and started upward into the wicked heart of the festering evil.

At the next level they paused. There were four forks

extending on a line with the four main points of a compass. From the southern branch light laughter arose.

"Serfs, you reckon?" Hickok commented.

A few moments later six pale figures materialized and pranced gaily toward the three youths.

Blade smiled, relieved to encounter some of the innocents first. They drew close and halted, giggling childishly. Tabitha and Selwyn weren't among them. "Hello," he said in greeting.

"Hello, sir," one of the males responded.

"What are you doing?" Blade asked casually.

"We're waiting for the great mast to come back so we can play pincushion."

Only then did Blade see the knives in their hands. Shocked, he lowered his arm. "Pincushion?"

"Yes, sir." The male tittered. "Sometimes Master Morlock puts outers in a cage. We get to surround the cage, and when he opens the door we play pincushion with our knives."

Horrified, Blade glanced at his companions, then at the presumed innocents. "Do all of the serfs play pincushion?"

"Yes, sir. The masts gather all of us together for the treat. Master Morlock gave us these knives an hour ago and told us to wait on this level until the rest of the serfs come back. Then the fun will begin."

"How can you describe stabbing a human being to death as fun?"

"Oh, it's terrific," the male stated, and several of the others laughed. "The outers always scream and beg and whine while we poke them with our knives. Some of them put up a wonderful fight. In the end, though, they always fall down and go to sleep."

"Why don't you put those knives down and go play something else?" Blade suggested.

One of the women answered. "We can't do that, sir. The great mast gave us orders, and we must obey."

Blade stiffened when a harsh voice bellowed down from one of the upper levels.

"Felcram, do you hear me?"

"Yes, Master Morlock," the male answered, gazing all around as if he couldn't figure out where the voice came from.

"Kill the three outers!"

"These three?"

"Yes. Kill them now."

"Now, wait a minute—" Blade began, thinking he could persuade the serfs to let them pass in peace. Suddenly the six attacked, cackling with glee and swinging their knives maniacally. He swung the Marlin to keep a man and a woman at bay while holding the candle aloft.

Geronimo used the rifle in a similar fashion, fending off two males, blocking repeated swings. "I don't want to harm you," he said. "Please stop."

They only chortled.

Lacking a rifle, Hickok was twisting and dodging to evade a pair of women intent on burying their knives in his chest. "We don't have time for this," he said, blocking a fierce swing with his forearm, then slugging the woman in the jaw. She collapsed at his feet.

"Please stop," Blade pleaded. "You don't know what you're doing."

"Sure we do," one of the males said. "We're playing pincushion."

Blade knew the three of them wouldn't be able to evade the knives forever. There had to be a way to drive the serfs off without hurting them. As he side-stepped a lunge at his legs, he inadvertently lowered the candle and saw both males hastily back up, their eyes narrowed. He remembered how Tabitha and Selwyn had dreaded going near the campfire and grinned. Instead of using his rifle, he now swung the candle from side to side, keeping it at eye level, careful not to let the flame go out, and moved towards the serfs.

Both males shielded their eyes, whined and fled.

As if on an unseen cue, the rest of the band joined their fellows in flight except for the woman Hickok had decked.

"Good riddance," the gunfighter stated.

"Why did they run?" Geronimo asked.

"They can't stand bright light," Blade said. "Even a candle shoved in their faces is more than they can take."

"Too bad we don't have another torch," Hickok said.

Blade watched the retreating serfs until they took a left and disappeared. He gazed up the stairs and snapped. "Let's go."

They ascended quickly, alert for traps or an ambush, until once more they stood on the ground floor. The candles along the corridor caused intermittent shadows to dance and writhe like ethereal, inky demons.

A strident howl of glee echoed to their ears from above.

"It's Morlock," Hickok fumed.

In verification came a taunting shout. "Did you like playing with my serfs, boys?"

"Show yourself!" Blade yelled.

"And spoil all the glorious entertainment yet to come? You must be joking."

"You can't hide from us forever," Blade called up.

"I don't intend to, dear boy. You'll see me when you least expect it." Morlock paused. "It's so rare for us to have guests such as yourselves. This is a very special night, and we want to prolong the amusement for as long as we can."

"I can't wait to plug that cowchip," Hickok muttered.

"Never happen, boy," Morlock said.

None of the youths replied, and silence gripped the castle.

Geronimo was the first to speak. "How did he do that?"

"Do what, pard?" the gunfighter asked.

"How did he hear your last remark? He must be three floors above us, at least."

Blade mulled the same question. Earlier, Morlock had

claimed to know the moment he entered the underground through the mausoleum. How? Had Morlock watched him from a hidden passage? But a secret passageway wouldn't explain overhearing a hushed remark from three floors up.

"Maybe we should split up," Hickok proposed. "We can each take a floor and get this over with a lot sooner than if we stick together."

"No," Blade said. "We'll do this as a team, as if we were a Warrior triad."

"But Geronimo isn't a Warrior yet."

"Keep rubbing it in, why don't you?" Geronimo cracked.

"We'll start with the second floor," Blade suggested and went cautiously up to the next landing. There wasn't a candle lit along its entire length, so he raised the one he held and walked to the nearest door. Standing to one side, he nodded.

Geronimo gripped the knob and turned. The door swung inward to reveal typically well-preserved furniture and a thick red carpet.

"Empty," Hickok said.

And so it went. Room after room after room was examined, and in each they discovered furniture and nothing more. They finished with the second floor and moved to the third, where Blade stepped to the second door on the right and threw it open.

The lantern still glowed, but Angus Morlock was nowhere in evidence.

Blade crossed to the door in the east wall, which hung wide, and stared grimly at the square opening and the dangling trapdoor.

"What's this?" Hickok asked.

"Where Morlock pulled a fast one on me."

"I've got news for you, pard. That bozo has been jerkin' us around ever since we got here."

Blade retraced his steps to the hall and continued to search. Three more rooms yielded zilch.

"We're wastin' our time," Hickok complained. "He's likely sittin' behind one of these walls laughin' himself silly at our expense."

"We're not giving up."

The gunfighter snapped his fingers. "Hey, I've got a brainstorm."

"Uh-oh," Geronimo said.

"What's your idea?" Blade asked.

"Let's smoke the rascals out. We'll set fire to the place and wait outside for them to show their faces."

Geronimo pressed a hand to his cheek. "My, why didn't Blade and I think of that?"

"It's brilliant," Hickok bragged.

"Except for one small detail," Geronimo said.

"Like what?"

"The castle is made of *stone.*"

"Oh."

"But you keep thinking, Nathan. It's what you're good at."

"Was that a cut?"

Blade glanced at them. "Will you two clowns clam up?" He shook his head and walked toward a closed door. As far back as he could remember, Hickok and Geronimo had always been at each other's throat in an amiable sort of way. It always amused him that they could verbally rip each other to shreds time and again, but if someone else were to insult either one, then both would be on the offender's case in a flash. Hopefully, once all three of them were Warriors and they were confronted with the full responsibilities of their posts, the nonstop banter would cease. He looked forward to the peace and quiet.

A faint glow rimmed the next door.

Blade motioned for his friends to be ready and tried the knob. Unlike other doors, this one was locked. He stepped back, drew up his right leg and planted his boot next to the knob. The wood held firm.

"Allow me, pard," Hickok said, moving across the

corridor. He lowered his shoulder and ran straight at the door, striking it with a resounding thud that knocked him onto his posterior. The panel shuddered but wasn't even cracked.

Geronimo clucked a few times. "I could have told you that wouldn't work."

"Oh, yeah?" Hickok responded indignantly, rising.

"Yep. You should have used your head."

"How about if I use these?" the gunfighter retorted, and both Colts leaped into his hands. Two shots thundered simultaneously, and the wood above the lock splintered and blew apart. He stepped over and tapped the door with a gun.

Even Blade had to grin when the door swung inward. He entered and halted just over the threshold, astounded by the extraordinary furnishings.

"Wow!" Hickok said. "What is all this?"

"It's a weapons room," Geronimo speculated.

Mounted on every wall and displayed in numerous cases were scores of weapons—swords of every size and type; axes and pikes; dirks, daggers and knives; lances and shields bearing various crests; maces and spiked clubs. Ringing the room at ten foot intervals were complete suits a medieval armor braced by supporting stands. Occupying the middle of the floor were five tables bearing additional ancient arms.

Hickok walked over to the suit of armor and ran his fingers over the polished metal. "Where's Sir Galahad when you need him?"

"I'm impressed, Nathan," Geronimo said, moving to the first table. "I thought your knowledge of history was strictly limited to the Old West."

"I've gone through the same schooling courses you have," Hickok replied. "I'm not ignorant, you know. I remember readin' all about those Knights of the Oval Chamber Pot."

"They were the Knights of the Round Table, nitwit."

"Whatever."

Blade stood to the left of the doorway and admired the collection. Someone, undoubtedly Moray Morlock or one of his ancestors, must have spent a fortune to accumulate such fine, authentic weapons. Perhaps the Morlock clan collected diligently for generations.

The gunfighter knocked on the breastplate and asked, "Is anyone home?"

Geronimo chuckled. "What would you do if it answered?"

"Head for the hills."

"We should keep looking for Morlock," Blade said, motioning at the corridor.

"What's the big rush?" Hickok responded, stepping to the next display of body armor, a huge suit suitable for the Biblical Goliath. "There might be something here we can use."

Blade was about to argue but changed his mind. Technically, he had no authority for bossing the gunfighter around, and he'd rather save his energy for when it was really needed. He absently glanced at the door, at the shattered wood above the lock, then at the source of the light, a lantern resting on a case near the huge suit of armor.

Something about the door and the lantern bothered him, but he couldn't determine the cause. So what if one of the clan left a lantern in the room earlier? So what if the door had been locked? Morlock probably didn't want them to get their hands on any of the weapons.

Geronimo had picked up a weapon resembling a short lance topped by a spike and an odd hatchet. "What were these called?"

"Thingamajigs," Hickok said.

"Thank you, Mr. Middle Ages expert."

"It's a halberd," Blade told them. "They were used in the fifteenth and sixteenth centuries by knights and foot soldiers alike."

"No wonder you always got A's in school," Hickok said. "You have a knack for recallin' all the diddly details that no one else does."

"You remember them," Blade stated. "You just pretend you don't so you can act dumb."

Geronimo looked up. "Why would he want to *act* dumb when it's his natural state?"

"Same to you, turkey," Hickok said. He started to reach toward the visor on the huge armor.

Blade stared at the door again, jarred by an unsettling thought. What if the latern was there because someone had been using it? And what if the door had been locked from the inside, not the outside? He turned to voice his concern to the others.

The gunfighter rapped on the visor and repeated the same question. "Is anyone home?"

From within the armor came a guttural reply that shocked all three youths. "Yes." And with that, the knight attacked.

CHAPTER EIGHTEEN

Hickok was the first to fall. Dumfounded by the development, his lightning reflexes were unable to prevent the knight's right gauntlet from striking him a heavy blow on the left temple. He crumpled with his hands almost to his Colts.

"Nathan!" Geronimo cried and rushed in with the halberd upraised, neglecting to use his rifle in his concern for his friend.

The knight shifted to meet the Blackfoot. When the halberd arched toward his helmet, he blocked the blade with his right vambrace and delivered a left fist to Geronimo's jaw that felled the youth in his tracks.

Leaving only Blade. Too late he'd noticed there was no supporting stand bracing the huge suit. He released the candle and jammed the Marlin to his shoulder. "Don't move!" he warned.

But the knight paid no attention. He clanked to one side and lifted a mace from the wall. Pivoting, his armor creaking loudly, he advanced and elevated the weapon.

"Your armor won't protect you from a bullet," Blade

said and then wondered why he bothered. The person in that suit was an enemy. Hickok and Geronimo were already down. What did it take to get him to do what had to be done?

"Kill," the knight declared gruffly. "Kill."

Blade sighted on the knight's visor and touched the trigger. "Try this on for size," he said and was about to fire when intervention from an unexpected source ruined his aim.

Endora Morlock materialized out of nowhere and batted the barrel upward with her arms just as the Marlin boomed. "No!" she shouted, trying to pull the rifle free.

Angered by her interference, Blade faced her and tried to tug the Marlin from her desperate grip. "Let go," he demanded.

"No," Endora replied passionately. "Don't hurt him."

The scraping of metal joints almost at Blade's left side made him look and jump back, relinquishing his hold on the Marlin to preserve his life. A heartbeat later the mace cleaved the air at the spot where he'd stood.

"Kill," the knight vowed and turned ponderously to keep the youth in the limited field of vision afforded by the slots in the visor.

Blade retreated a yard and assumed an on-guard stance. His Bowies would be useless against armor designed to render its wearer impervious to edged weaponry.

Endora grabbed the knight's elbow. "Leave him alone, Elphinstone!"

"Go away," the brute snapped, jerking his arm loose. "Must kill bad man."

"He's not bad. Please, Elphinstone. Don't fight him."

"Must fight. Father says must kill."

Endora darted around in front of her brother, her face a study of emotional turmoil. "Please," she begged again. "For me, Elphie. For *me*."

The visor fixed on her earnest visage, and Elphinstone's dull eyes met her beseeching eyes. "For you?"

"Yes. I don't want either of you to be harmed."

"Bad man hurt me."

"But there's no reason to keep on hurting each other."

"Bad man kicked and hit me."

Endora placed her right hand on the breastplate. "We've always been close, Elphie. There's always been just the two of us. You know how much you mean to me. Please don't fight this man any more."

Elphinstone contemplated her appeal in stony silence.

With the rifle held loosely in Endora's left hand, Blade couldn't resist the temptation. He lunged, grasped the barrel and tried to tear it from her hands.

The instant the youth sprang into action, so did Elphinstone. He swung the mace at Blade's arms, forcing the Warrior to skip out of the way empty-handed.

"No!" Endora wailed, but she was rudely shoved aside.

Like a great, mad, lumbering elephant, Elphinstone bore down on Blade, furiously swinging his mace. He clipped Blade's shoulder but failed to connect with a death stroke. Relentlessly he pressed the youth, driving him all the way back to the east wall.

Blade felt the wall bump against his shoulder blades. He looked both ways. Mounted to his left was an axe, and in two strides he had it in his possession.

Undaunted, his brute intellect focused on the sole task of slaying the youth in the leather vest, Elphinstone relentlessly closed in.

Axe met mace in a savage cadence of metallic clanging, a primal pounding of weapon on weapon, the room ringing to their resounding blows.

Blade braced his legs and fought with all the skill at his command. He swung overhand, underhand, from the side and in figure-eight patterns, striving to break through his foe's defenses. Twice he struck Elphinstone's helmet, yet neither blow seemed to have any effect.

Off near the door stood Endora, her left hand covering her mouth, her eyes wide with fear for her brother's life.

Blade's fatigue slowed his movements. He had to fight on two fronts—one with himself, the other with the apish Morlock. Every clash of their weapons jolted his arms to the bone. After a minute of sustained combat he reluctantly gave ground, backing up slowly, on the defensive and not liking it one bit.

On Elphinstone's part, he fought as five men even though encumbered by the weight of the armor. Like a tireless machine he swung and swung and swung, his dull eyes never blinking.

Blade accidentally backed into a standing suit of armor. He stepped to the left, continuing to block a hail of fierce blows, when an idea blossomed that he immediately implemented. Suddenly bounding out of his adversary's reach, he sent the suit of armor crashing to the floor at the brute's feet.

Elphinstone had to tilt his head and stare straight down to avoid tripping over the obstacle, and in that costly moment of distraction he failed to keep his guard up.

Blade whipped the axe in an overhand loop, putting all of his strength and weight into the strike, the blade smashing onto the helmet just above the visor and rocking Elphinstone on his heels. Again Blade struck, this time hitting the helmet on the right side.

The brute staggered.

Both blows had dented the helmet but not pierced the metal. Eager to end the conflict quickly, Blade drew his arms back as far as he could, then drove the axe around and in, slamming it into the visor.

Elphinstone toppled, dropping the mace as he fell and landing on his back with a crash that rattled every weapon and suit of armor in the room.

Stepping closer, Blade lifted the axe on high for the *coup de grace*.

"No!" Endora screamed. "For the love of God, don't!"

Blade hesitated, conscious of the sweat caking his body and his aching muscles and joints. He glanced at her. "Why shouldn't I? He tried to kill me."

"You can't blame him. He doesn't know what he's doing. Haven't you noticed he's feeble-minded?"

Lowering the axe, Blade frowned and moved to his friends. First he checked Geronimo, then Hickok. Both were breathing, simply unconscious, the gunfighter sporting a nasty bruise on his temple.

Endora ran to Elphinstone and pried the visor open with difficulty. She placed her ear to his lips and exclaimed in relief, "You just knocked him out. He'll live."

"And what will happen when he revives?" Blade snapped. "If he comes at me again, I'll be forced to kill him. Which reminds me." He saw the Marlin lying on the carpet and quickly retrieved it, flung the axe aside and levered in a new round.

"If you leave now there won't be more violence," Endora said. "Wake your friends and get out of here."

"We can't leave."

"Can't or won't?"

"Both," Blade said. "We know all about what has been going on here, and we mean to put a stop to it."

Endora's features clouded. "You don't know everything," she said softly. "There are things too horrible to mention."

"Such as the fact your husband is actually your father?"

Stark consternation rippled across Endora's face. She gasped and clutched at her throat. "Who told you?"

"No one."

"Impossible! Someone had to tell you. I'll bet it was one of the serfs. A few of the older ones know our secret," Endora said, her cheeks flushing crimson. Her expression abruptly hardened. "I'll kill every one. I'll have them skinned alive."

"You'll do no such thing," Blade stated. "The Morlock family has caused enough sorrow and comitted too many atrocities as it is."

"Who are you to judge us?"

"Like father, like daughter."

Endora took several steps toward him, her fists clenched in anger. "What the hell is that supposed to mean? And what do you really know about our family history, about the incredible hardships the Morlocks have endured? We were cut off from the rest of the world. To survive we had to resort to incest."

"Don't lie to me," Blade said sternly. "The Morlock clan has practiced incest for centuries."

Astonishment made Endora blink. "How did you know that?"

"I can add two plus two."

"You're smarter than you look. Angus underestimated you from the beginning. He thought he could play with you, have a little fun before he finished off the three of you."

"Where's your father now?"

"I don't know."

Blade made as if to strike her with the rifle. "What did I tell you about lying?"

Recoiling in fear, Endora licked her lips. "Honest. I don't know where he is at this very minute. Probably in the control room."

"The what?"

Realizing she'd given away too much, Endora shook her head. "I won't say another word."

"We'll find him with or without your help," Blade said, walking to Hickok's side. Kneeling, he gently shook the gunfighter's left shoulder. "Nathan, get up."

Slowly, groaning in pain, Hickok opened his eyes and

gazed in confusion at his surroundings. "Where am I, pard?"

"In Morlock's castle, remember?"

The mention of the madman sufficed to bring Hickok around. "Yeah," he said, sitting up and touching his temple. "Where the heck is the tin man who clobbered me?"

"It was Elphinstone, and he's out cold," Blade said, pointing at the unconscious brute.

The gunfighter spied the Blackfoot's prone form. His eyes widened, and he scrambled over on his hands and knees. "Geronimo!" He looked anxiously at Blade. "Is he hurt bad?"

"No. He should wake up shortly."

Hickok glared at Elphinstone. "I get first dibs on gorilla puss."

Endora stepped in front of her brother, put her hands on her hips and adopted a stance like a protective hen. "You're not to touch a hair on his head."

"Don't fret none, lady. His hair will still be in one piece when I'm done with him."

"We didn't ask you to come here," Endora said, incensed. "Why can't you go away and leave us alone?"

"You already know the reason," Blade said. "We can't turn our backs on the serfs and overlook all the atrocities your family has committed. We'd never be able to live with ourselves. And your family will never let us leave in peace, anyway." He paused. "What happens next is inevitable."

"Nothing is inevitable."

"You're wrong. It's inevitable that all of us must live with the consequences of our acts, and the Morlock clan is long overdue to reap the results of decades of tyranny and savagery."

Endora cocked her head. "How old are you?"

"Sixteen. Why?"

"You must be older than that."

"Don't let his fancy words fool you, lady," Hickok interjected. "He talks that way every now and then, usually after he gets through readin' one of those books by the Greek guy who ran around dressed in a towel."

Geronimo moaned, and his eyelids fluttered. "Nathan?"

"Right here, pard," Hickok said, leaning over his friend.

"That's what I was afraid of."

"Another cut. That's two I owe you."

The Blackfoot's eyes opened, and he struggled to sit up, still woozy from the blow. "Where's the—" he began, then saw their attacker lying on the floor. "What happened?"

"The big guy took the tin man down. Elphinstone is the one wearin' the armor."

"Let's find something we can use to tie him up," Blade proposed, surveying the room.

"I won't let you," Endora stated.

"You can't stop us," Blade said. "And we're not leaving him loose to sneak up on us when our backs are turned."

"I'll keep him right here."

"Not good enough, Endora. We can't trust you, either."

"Then why don't you tie me up, too?" she asked scornfully.

"We will."

The patter of dozens of feet filled the corridor, accompanied by much giggling and tittering. A general commotion ensued with pale figures jostling to see who would stand the nearest to the doorway.

"It's the wimps again," Hickok remarked. "What the dickens do they want now?"

"Oh, outers!" came a high-pitched taunt from a pale

throat. "Come out and play with us, won't you please?"

"Yeah," chimed in another. "All of us are here to play pincushion, and this time you won't scare any of us away. So be nice and come out and die."

CHAPTER NINETEEN

Blade stepped to the doorway and saw dozens of smiling serfs packing the corridor, blocking any possible escape. Every one carried a knife. None made a move to harm him—yet.

"Hello, Pard."

The youth glanced to the right and recognized a pair of friendly, beaming faces. "Tabitha. Selwyn. Not you, too?"

"What do you mean, sir?" Tabitha responded. "We like to play pincushion as much as everyone else."

"But pincushion isn't a game. All of you could be killed."

Tabitha chuckled. "Not us, sir. Why, unless we're eaten or chopped into itty-bitty bits, we just curl into little balls for a couple of hours and wake up as good as new."

The full extent of her insanity staggered Blade. He sadly shook his head and scanned the rows of fragile, thin figures. "You don't understand about dying. You don't know the first thing about pain and suffering, Please,

please, put down your knives and go have fun in the forest."

"But we can't sir," Selwyn said. "The great mast wants us to play pincushion with you, and that's what we must do."

"What if my friends and I don't want to play?"

"You must, sir."

"We don't want to hurt you."

The serfs laughed, exchanging amused looks, and then, all at once and all together, without a signal to spur them forward, they attacked.

A glittering knife almost ripped Blade's left arm open as he stepped backwards and tried to shut the door. Fists and blades rained down upon the wood, and the press of bodies kept the door a foot from the jamb, preventing him from doing more than temporarily thwarting the serfs.

Hickok and Geronimo rushed to his aid and added their weight to the fray.

The serfs laughed, giggled and snickered the whole time. As they pounded on the door, as they pushed against the panel in a compact mass, as they slashed at the space between the door and the wall, they did so with the utmost hilarity, and the harder they fought, the more mirth they expressed.

Blade's muscles were taxed to their limits. He pushed on the door until he was red in the face, but after all he'd been through he was in no condition to withstand the combined strength of dozens of determined serfs, no matter how weak they might be individually. Even his finely sculpted physique wasn't made of iron.

"They're gettin' through!" Hickok declared as the door slowly inched inward and the serfs were able to extend their reach.

In the end it was the knives that made Blade acknowledge the door couldn't be held. A razor edge sliced into his left forearm, not much more than a prick, but he realized it was only a matter of time before they inflicted a grievous wound. "On the count of three," he told his companions. "We let go and fall back. Spread out and take as many with you as you can."

"I don't much cotton to gunnin' nymphs," Hickok grunted.

"It's either them or us. We can't afford to go easy on them or we'll never see the Home again."

Standing near Elphinstone, Endora Morlock cackled and mocked them. "You're not so tough now, are you, boys? In a few minutes you'll be lying on the floor, and I'll be dancing in your blood."

"One," Blade said, ignoring the barbs. To think he'd once felt sorry for her!

The nonstop drumming on the door continued, mingling with the laughter and the tittering to create an insane din.

"Two," Blade stated. If nothing else on this trip, he'd learned never to take potential enemies and circumstances at face value. Hidden motives and meanings always lurked beneath the surface, and they had to be diligently peeled off like the layers of a rotten onion to expose the putrid core within.

"Kill them, my little darlings!" Endora cried. "Show them how foolish they were to cross the Morlocks."

"Three," Blade barked and leaned backwards. He held the Marlin in his right hand, leveling the barrel as his friends swiftly backed up and the door crashed inward.

Serfs jammed the doorway in their eagerness to plunge their knives into the youths, beaming inanely, bloodlust animating their eyes.

The Marlin boomed, and two serfs dropped. Blade fired twice more, wishing there was some other way he could stop them, overcome with guilt.

Geronimo's Winchester cracked five times in succession, and with each shot a pale, smirking fury fell.

"Kill them! Kill them!" Endora shrieked.

Doing their best to accommodate her, the serfs pressed inside without a spare glance at their fallen comrades. They were about to crest into the room like a tidal wave breaking on a shore when a lean youth in buckskins barred their path.

Hickok had held himself in reserve for just this moment. A lopsided grin creased his lips as he slapped leather, both Colts clearing leather in a streak of movement too fast for the eye to follow. He thumbed off two shots and bored two slugs through two atrophied brains.

The serfs concentrated their attack on the gunfighter. A male lunged with his knife extended.

Unflinching, Hickok sent a round into the male's nose, then shifted and blasted two others. More took their place, and he gunned them down, a single shot apiece, invariably going for a head shot, firing until both revolvers were empty and a pile of corpses choked the doorway.

Over the pile came the rest of the serfs, their enthusiasm bordering on fanaticism, those in the front laughing the hardest.

Blade saw the gunfighter trying to reload, and he grabbed Hickok's shirt and propelled him backward. Discarding the Marlin, he drew his Bowies and advanced to meet the serfs head-on. Suddenly they were swirling around him, cutting and hacking and cackling, always cackling, thoroughly enjoying themselves. He blocked and countered and stabbed, matching their madness with a frenzy of sheer desperation, becoming a tornado of whirling limbs and flashing Bowies, only dimly aware of Geronimo battling on his right, of the twin tomahawks weaving a lethal tapestry to rival his own.

Incredibly quick, the serfs fought like spitfires, prancing and lancing and thrusting and dancing, always in motion, always laughing.

Fury seized Blade, a fury at these creatures—for they could hardly be called human—who had no regard for life, their own or anyone else's. All that mattered to them was fun, fun, fun, having a good time at the expense of everyone and everything. Work became a game. Killing became a game. Existence was a giant game presided over by an insane games master.

His flesh was pierced and gashed and nicked, but he fought on. His arms flagged and his legs complained, but he endured. The sight of so much blood and gore sickened him, but he let self-preservation take its course and took on all comers.

After a while individual foes no longer existed. In their place was a pale demon of many guises who cackled and popped up here, there and anywhere, wounding him in a score of spots, decorating his clothing with crimson streamers. He killed and killed, and still they came on.

Blade ripped a male from gut to sternum, then severed a woman's neck with a single swipe. He deflected an overhand swing and gave a thrust to the throat in return. A knife bit into his side and he bit back. On and on the combat raged, until all of a sudden he found himself standing alone with a carpet of corpses all about him.

"We did it, pard."

The weary voice drew Blade's attention to the right, where Geronimo and Hickok were back to back, the Blackfoot holding gore-spattered tomahawks, the gunfighter a red-stained axe. Bodies ringed them.

There wasn't a serf alive. They were sprawled in all manner of positions, many coated with blood, ripped and torn and cleaved. And every one, every male and every female, smiled even in death, as if they had played a monumental joke on their slayers, a joke only they comprehended.

"Dear Spirit," Geronimo said softly, "is this what it's really like to be a Warrior? Is this the price we'll pay for protecting our loved ones?"

"I am a mite tuckered out," Hickok confessed.

Blade swallowed and surveyed the slaughter. He spotted Tabitha and Selwyn a few feet to his left, dead side by side, and realized, in horror, that he must have slain them.

"Thank goodness there wasn't any more of those rascals," Hickok said. "A few more minutes and we would have bit the dust."

"I wonder if I should become a Warrior?" Geronimo asked, a question meant more for himself than his friends.

Blade looked down at the wounds he'd sustained and the blood seeping out. One knife had cut his vest right above the heart but missed the skin. His cuts weren't life-threatening, but they hurt terribly.

"You murdered our babies, you fiends!"

The youths turned to find Endora Morlock gazing in shock at the serfs.

"You bastards will suffer for this!" Endora raged. "I'll torture you personally."

"Shut your face, bimbo," Hickok snapped, dropping the axe. He began reloading both Colts.

Endora stepped over several bodies and shook her fists at all three of them. "Why couldn't you leave us alone? We were perfectly happy until you butted in. You barged into our castle, sat in judgment on our lives and decided we were evil, decided you had to meddle in our personal affairs." She trembled in her fury. "You had no right."

Blade licked his dry lips and tasted blood on the tip of his tongue. "We had every right. Evil must be exterminated wherever it's found."

"Who the hell are you to say what's evil and what isn't?"

It was Hickok who answered. "We're Warriors, lady."

"And what is that supposed to mean?"

"It means we know the difference between loving, decent folks and perverts who go around preyin' on people who can't defend themselves. It means you can have one minute to make your peace with your Master."

Both Blade and Geronimo glanced at the gunfighter. "Don't," the giant said.

Endora Morlock snorted in contempt. "My Maker? There is no God, you fool. We are what we are, and that's all there is to it."

Hickok nodded once. "And I'm a Warrior." His right hand swept straight out.

"No!" Blade cried, taking a stride toward him.

The weapons room thundered to the retort of another gunshot, and the lady in white sprouted a hole between her eyes, eyes that conveyed a flicker of astonishment a millisecond before she spun in a graceful pirouette and sank to the floor.

Geronimo dashed over to her and uselessly felt for a pulse. "She's dead."

"What did you expect?" Hickok asked.

"We had no right to kill her," Geronimo said. "How could you, Nathan?"

"Piece of cake," the gunfighter replied. "And we had every right to kill her. She wanted us dead, didn't she? She was goadin' the nymphs on to tear us apart."

"But Warriors aren't supposed to be cold-blooded killers."

"And what do you think Warriors do for a living? Grow flowers? We're trained to kill. That's our purpose in life. Oh, I know we do it to protect the Family and the Home, but when you get down to the nitty-gritty, we kill scumbags for a living."

"There's more to being a Warrior than that," Blade said, staring at Endora's oddly composed features.

"Like what, pard?"

"Like adhering to higher ideals of duty and purpose."

"You've been listenin' to Plato again. Ideals are fine and all, but when those nymphs came through the door at us I'll bet you didn't spend one second thinkin' about ideals, duty and purpose. All you were thinkin' about was stayin' alive and killin' as many of those crazies as you could. Am I right?"

"Of course, but—"

"I rest my case."

"You didn't let me finish. Yes, we kill for a living, but only when the need arises. We can't go around blowing people away for the hell of it. There must be a reason."

"How about savin' the lives of lots of innocent folks? Is that a good enough reason for you? The Morlocks have been torturin' and murderin' people for years. All we're doing is puttin' a stop to it."

Blade dropped the subject. He knew better than to waste his breath trying to persuade the gunfighter to change his mind. Also, the sentiments Hickok expressed matched his own in many respects, but he still disliked the callous way in which Hickok had slain Endora Morlock. It had beem more like an execution than a necessary act of preservation.

"Let's go find the brains of this outfit," Hickok suggested, walking toward the doorway, carefully stepping over the many bodies in his path.

Blade and Geronimo started to follow him.

Unexpectedly, Elphinstone sat up, the armor rasping loudly, then heaved himself erect and surveyed the room. His gaze lingered on the dead serfs and finally on his sister. "Endora?"

The three youths simply watched as the brute sank to his knees and lifted Endora's head into his metal lap.

"Sissie? Talk to Elphie."

Blade could barely stand the sight. Shame saddened his soul, and his broad shoulders slumped dejectedly. Should they just leave Elphinstone to his misery? If they did, he might come after them. Perhaps it would be best to reason with him. "Elphinstone?"

Those dull eyes snapped up, peering through the dented visor, and locked on the youths. "You!" he growled. "You did this to her!"

"Please, Elphinstone," Blade said. "Stay calm."

"Kill!" the brute bellowed, surging to his feet, his sister's head hitting the floor with a thud. "Kill!" he repeated, raising his enormous fists, and charged.

CHAPTER TWENTY

Blade had the Marlin halfway to his shoulders when Geronimo's Winchester cracked twice.

Both rounds were aimed at the visor, one of them flattening against the metal with a distinct ping and not quite penetrating while the second went through the right eye slot, bored through the brute's brain, and pinged a second time when it struck the back of the helmet.

Elphinstone halted, his arms sagged, and he swayed. Although his brain had ceased to function, his body hadn't quite gotten the message. His fingers twitched, as if he wanted to grab something, and his left knee jerked forward as if about to intitiate another step. Then, like a towering tree in the forest, he toppled with a tremendous crash.

"Two down and two to go," Hickok said, departing without a backward glance.

Geronimo slowly lowered the rifle and looked at Blade. "I didn't want to do that."

"I know."

"There was no other choice."

"I know."

"I don't think being a Warrior is all it's cracked up to be."

Blade wheeled and stepped into the corridor where the gunfighter was waiting. "Endora mentioned something about a control room. If we find it, we'll find Morlock."

"A control room for what?"

"I don't know."

A reserved Geronimo joined them and fed new bullets into the Winchester. "Let's get this over with as quickly as possible."

"What's the matter, pard?"

"I may not become a Warrior."

Hickok's mouth dropped. "Why not?"

"I'm not like you, Nathan. When I kill someone, I feel a hurt inside."

"And you think I don't?" Hickok responded, his tone betraying bitterness. "I feel it too, but I don't let it get to me. I control it. I tell myself it has to be done." He turned and walked toward the stairs.

"Nathan?" Blade said.

"What?"

"Why did you shoot her?"

"One of us had to do the job, and it might as well have been me," Hickok said and kept walking.

Blade glanced at Geronimo, whose melancholy visibly intensified. "He did it so we wouldn't have to," he stated in a whisper.

"Me and my big mouth," Geronimo remarked.

They hurried to catch up, and the three of them were soon climbing the steps to the next floor. There were no candles lit, no sounds indicating any of the rooms were occupied, so on they went to the next level, and the floor after that, until eventually they reached the uppermost one, ten stories above the ground. An arched, open window gave them a view of the glittering stars and the inky expanse of countryside and explained the breeze they always felt on the stairway.

A sole candle burned next to a partly open door along the left-hand corridor.

"He's mine," Hickok said, leveling both Colts and stalking forward to the door. He kicked it open and darted inside.

Blade and Geronimo were right on his heels. The giant marveled at a large chamber illuminated by two lanterns that revealed banks of electronic equipment aligned along all four walls. There was no sign of Angus Morlock.

"The crud has skipped," Hickok guessed.

"What is all this?" Geronimo asked, moving to a console and studying a series of switches and knobs.

When Blade noticed a dozen blank squares of glass arranged in three rows on the far wall, curiosity impelled him closer to study them. Their shape prompted vague memories of photographs he'd once seen in a book in the Family library, but he couldn't put his mental finger on the exact photos. Two knobs were positioned under each square.

Hickok walked to a piece of equipment and flicked several toggle switches. "I wonder what these do?"

"Maybe we shouldn't touch anything," Geronimo said. "Morlock might have this room booby-trapped."

"No way, pard. He wouldn't want to damage all this stuff," Hickok said and worked another toggle.

Suddenly, from a speaker mounted on the north wall, came the sound of leaves being stirred by a stronge breeze, the distant wail of a coyote and the croaking of tree frogs.

"Where the blazes is that coming from?"

"Outside somewhere," Geronimo said. "But how?"

An answer formed unbidden in Blade's mind, and with it came comprehension. "A microphone."

"What?" Hickok said.

"A microphone. It's a device that can hear sounds and relay them elsewhere. There must be a mike planted outside the castle walls connected to this room by an underground wire, or else the equipment in here operates on battery power."

"How do you know all this?" Hickok asked.

"I remember reading a book about the electronic age, as it was called, and all the wonderful devices available before the Big Blast. The people had devices for playing music, washing clothes and cooking food in a minute flat," Blade said, indicating the blank squares of glass. "And unless I miss my guess, these are monitors used to keep watch on the grounds." He twisted one of the dials.

A screen in the upper row crackled to life and showed one of the gloomy underground passageways.

"See what I mean," Blade said.

"But how could this gear work after so many years?" Geronimo wondered. "Electricity is a thing of the past."

"Not if the Morlocks have a stockpile of rechargeable batteries," Blade said. At least he understood how Morlock had known he entered the castle from the mausoleum.

"Keep turnin' those dials," Hickok advised.

Blade did so, going from monitor to monitor, and one by one corridors and rooms were dimly depicted, all empty. When there were only three screens left, the weapons room materialized with its grisly carpet of pale, grinning corpses.

"Morlock must have seen the whole thing," Geronimo said.

Blade twisted the second to last dial, revealing yet another corridor, and was disappointed at not finding Morlock. Where was the madman? From the number of monitors, he concluded only the main corridors and some of the rooms were part of the surveillance network. There weren't enough to cover the entire castle. "If the runt saw the whole thing, why didn't he try to help the serfs or sic his walkin' fur rug on us?" Hickok brought up.

"He probably believed we'd be no match for the serfs," Blade guessed. "And I doubt he expected us to kill Endora and Elphinstone. Like Endora said, he's been taking us too lightly all along."

"His mistake," Hickok said.

Blade twirled the last dial and stiffened.

The last scene depicted was the roof. And there, standing on a rampart and staring grimly directly into the camera, stood Angus Morlock with a shotgun cradled in the crook of his left arm. Somehow, he knew he was being observed because he nodded and made a beckoning motion with his right hand.

"He wants us to go up there," Geronimo said.

"Let's not disappoint the crumb," the gunfighter stated.

Blade didn't like the setup one bit. Why would Morlock blatantly challenge them to go onto the roof unless it was a trap?

"Are you comin?" Hickok asked, moving to the door.

"Yeah," Blade said. He stared at the monitor for a few seconds, then went into the passageway with his friends.

"The stairs stop on this floor," Geronimo noted. "There must be another way up."

"Each of us will take a door," Blade directed.

The youths separated. There were seven doors all tolled and it wasn't until Geronimo opened the fifth one and called out, "Here it is!" that they found a spiral metal staircase to the top.

"Well, this is it," Hickok said, inspecting the chambers in his revolvers to be sure the guns were fully loaded.

"I'll go first," Blade volunteered.

"Be my guest," Geronimo said.

Blade went up a step at a time, tilting his neck so he could cover a wide door above. Once there, he tested the knob, found it rotated easily, and looked over his right shoulder. "Are you ready?"

"I was born ready," Hickok said.

"No, but go ahead anyway," Geronimo said.

Tensing, Blade flung the door open and threw himself outside to roll on his shoulder and rise to his knee with the Marlin sweeping the flat area before him.

Morlock had vanished.

The central section of the roof was level except for the doorway leading to the spiral staircase, which had been constructed as an isolated, elevated island in the very middle and fronted the northern battlements.

Blade glanced at the top of the door and saw the camera mounted on a sturdy bracket, so he knew Morlock had been within ten feet of the door a minute or two ago.

There were four ramparts connected to four turrets, one at each corner, and those turrets were the only hiding places on the roof.

"He must be in one of those beehive kind of things," Hickok whispered.

"Spread out," Blade said. "We'll check the turret at the northwest corner first." He rose to a crouching posture and advanced warily. A cool breeze caressed his face and brought to his nostrils a peculiar, pungent animal scent unlike any other he knew. He surmised the wind had carried the scent from an animal in the woods below but immediately realized such couldn't be the case. And if the smell didn't come from below or above, then there was only one explanation. The thought made him slow up, and his friends passed on by.

It couldn't be! Blade told himself, staring at the turret in mounting apprehension. He would have smelled it before now, wouldn't he?

Hickok was the closest to the three steps leading from the rampart into the shadowed turret. Both Colts were out and ready.

Blade moved forward, chiding himself for letting his imagination get the better of him. The thing was in the forest. Had to be.

The gunfighter had two yards to cover when a blood-curdling roar rent the night and the monster squeezed through the turret entrance, all ten feet of hair and muscle and unbridled ferocity.

"Grell!" Geronimo yelled.

Hickok squeezed off four shots so fast they sounded like one. But none stopped the gargantuan mutation. He was lifting his arms to fire at the beast's eyes when a swipe of a brawny arm sent him flying over five yards to crash onto his back, dazed.

"Try me," Geronimo bellowed, lifting the Winchester. Quick as he was, Grell was quicker, and a second swipe tumbled the Blackfoot head over heels to lie in a stunned heap.

Blade felt his blood turn to ice. He gazed into those hellish red orbs and felt as if his life force was being sucked from his body. Fear—total, dominating, terrifying—rooted him in place. He wanted to shoot, but couldn't make his hands move.

Grell snarled and lumbered toward the youth.

A tidal wave of panic engulfed the youth. Never had he been so outright scared. His dearest friends were down, perhaps severely injured and needing his help, and yet he couldn't get his limbs to cooperate with his mind. He saw Grell's long white fangs exposed and Grell's right claw sweeping at his head, and he reacted automatically, spinning and running toward the safety of the doorway and the stairwell, his heart pounding, thinking only of escaping with his life. His spine tingled, and he shivered as he ran.

Somewhere, Morlock laughed.

The sound brought Blade up short in midstride, shocked at what he was about to do. He was fleeing, running away, being a coward. Worse, he was deserting his two best friends, leaving them to suffer a horrible fate at the hands of the madman or the mutation. Tremendous revulsion welled up within him, revulsion at his own behavior. He spun.

Grell had halted and coldly regarded the youth.

How could he be so base, so spineless? Blade asked himself. He'd let instinctive fear get the better of him, but fear could only maintain its grip if the person afraid allowed it to dominate their being. And he wasn't about to have fear override his personality, have it supplant his will. He was a *man*, damn it, a man endowed with the power of choice. He could choose to let instinct win, or he would exercise his free will to do what had to be done.

At that moment, as he stood there confronting the monstrous, growling beast looming above him, he came to grips with his innermost being. His spiritual inheritance triumphed over his animal heritage and in the process forged a soul tempered in the adversity of supreme danger.

Blade smiled.

"Kill him, Grell!" came a shout from the darkness, and the creature stalked forward.

Whipping the Marlin up, Blade went to fire, then paused. No. He wouldn't take the easy way out. If he wanted to truly conquer fear, he must face it fully. The triumph must be total—spirit, mind and body. He threw the rifle to the roof and drew his Bowies.

Grell lifted his massive arms and snarled hideously.

Blade ran straight at the mutation and leaped into the air, his back arched, his hands overhead, the big Bowies held with the blades pointed downward. At the apex of his leap he was only a foot from Grell's head. He could almost feel those baleful red orbs boring into his brain and smelled the beast's fetid breath. For an instant panic tried to reassert control, until he grit his teeth, tensed his steely sinews and swept both knives in a flashing arc, burying a Bowie in each crimson eye, sinking the sharp blades all the way to the hilts.

Grell stiffened, roared and swung his arms, catching the youth a glancing blow that knocked him aside. He staggered backwards, clutching at the Bowies and snarling, and managed to yank both knives out.

Blade gasped when his left side smacked into the hard

stone roof, and he lay still for a few seconds, recovering, then pushed to his feet and dashed to where he'd thrown the rifle. He'd proven his courage to his satisfaction. There was nothing to be gained by further heroics. And without a weapon, slaying the monster would be impossible. He scooped up the Marlin and aimed at the thing's head.

"Put down the gun."

The youth froze at the gravelly command.

"You heard me. Put down the gun, and do it real slow."

Blade estimated Morlock was not more than ten feet to his left and slightly behind him, just out of the line of vision. He could try to nail the madman, but even if he hit Morlock the shotgun might go off, and at such close range it would blow him in half. Reluctantly, he lowered the Marlin.

"Good. Now turn around, boy. I want to see your face when I kill you."

Blade complied, his arms at his sides.

A malicious grin curled Angus Morlock's lips. "At last I have you right where I want you. Any last words?"

The youth refused to give the madman the satisfaction.

"Very well. But I want you to know how much I hate you for what you've done. My daughter and my son, both dead. Poor little Grell, blinded for life. And why? All because I didn't have you slain right away instead of toying with you."

The scraping of calloused soles on the stone surface made Blade twist his head slightly so he could see the mutation. Grell was shuffling toward him, those hairy hands pressed over his ruptured eyes, hissing like an enraged viper.

Morlock glanced at his pet. "Look at him," he said morosely. "Look at what you've done."

Blade shifted, saw that he stood directly between the pet and its master, and instantly took the initiative. "You bloodthirsty brute!" he shouted. "You deserve to die!"

Grell lowered his arms, roared again and charged wildly in the direction of the youth's voice.

"What are you doing?" Morlock exclaimed.

In three great bounds the monster was almost upon Blade. He dived to the right and felt the creature's side brush his legs as it went past, glancing at the madman as he did.

Angus Morlock comprehended the ruse too late. "No, Grell!" he yelled, but his pet paid no heed. He already had the shotgun leveled, and he fired into the mutation's chest. The explosive impact stopped Grell for just a moment, and then the beast's swinging hands fell on Morlock's shoulders.

"No!" the madman screeched. "It's me, you dumb animal."

Blade would never know whether Grell recognized the voice of his master. He saw those immense fingers wrap around Morlock's head even as Morlock struggled and bellowed frantically. He saw Grell wrench sharply to the right, then the left. And he heard the snap, loud and clear.

A moment later yet another unfortunate victim crashed lifeless on top of the true beast of Castle Orm.

CHAPTER TWENTY-ONE

The youths watched the flames lick at the pile of four corpses located on the roof near the north battlement and gazed in silence at the black smoke curling into the bright morning sky.

"It's fitting the Morlocks are being burned together," Geronimo commented thoughtfully.

"How do you figure, pard?" Hickok asked.

"Their destinies were intertwined from the start."

The gunfighter chuckled. "If you say so. But you worry me."

"I do?"

"Yep. You're startin' to sound like the big guy."

Sighing, Geronimo stared at their somber friend. "Are you all right?"

"Fine."

"You sure?"

"Drop the subject."

"What's with you?" Hickok asked. "You should be happy, not down in the dumps. We won, didn't we? We took care of these bozos so they'll never kill another innocent wanderer.''

"Did we win?" Blade inquired softly.

"We're still alive, ain't we?"

"And what about the serfs?"

"What about 'em?"

Blade glanced at the doorway, his features profoundly troubled. "What happened to their bodies?"

"Who knows?" Hickok said and shrugged. "There must have been a few off playin' somewhere when we killed the rest, and while we were up on the roof they came and dragged the dead nymphs off."

"We weren't up here long enough for all the bodies to be removed."

"You don't know that for certain,." Hickok said. He stretched and crinkled his nose. "Boy, the Morlocks and that hairy critter aren't exactly roses, if you get my drift. Let's skedaddle. I want to get back to the Home."

They turned and walked to the doorway, two of them deep in contemplation, the third grinning at the fitting conclusion of their adventure. At the doorway all three abruptly halted when they heard the sounds wafting up from far, far below, the sounds of giggling and tittering.

EPILOGUE

Plato closed the file and leaned back in the wooden chair, his brow creased, his blue eyes narrowed, and absently ran his right hand through his long gray beard. An unexpected knock on the cabin door curtailed his reflection. "Come in," he called out.

The door swung inward to reveal a seven-foot giant wearing a black leather vest and green fatigue pants. Around his waist were strapped two Bowies. "Hi, Plato. Sorry to bother you."

"Nonsense, Blade. How may I be of service?"

The giant's eyes strayed to the Family Leader's lap. "The Chronicler told me you have a certain file I need."

"This one?" Plato asked innocently, tapping the blue cover.

"Yeah. Are you done with it?"

"Sure am." Plato said, holding the file out. "Be my guest."

"Thanks." Blade walked over and took it, his gaze lingering on the older man's face. "Any particular reason you were reading this one?"

"No," Plato fibbed.

Blade turned to go. "Well, I'll see you later."

"How is Gabe doing?"

The giant stopped and glanced at his mentor. "You heard, huh?"

"I would imagine everyone in the Family knows the story by now."

Blade frowned. "You're probably right."

"No one blames him for what happened."

"He blames himself."

A kindly chuckle issued from Plato's lips. "When you're five years-old and you see a slavering, mutated black bear bearing down on you, your first reaction is to run. He has nothing to be ashamed of. Especially since, as I understand it, he only ran a dozen yards or so, then went back to get Tommy."

"That's what happened," Blade confirmed. "Tommy was so scared he just stood there. They were both lucky that Ares heard Gabe screaming for Tommy to run and got there in time to kill the mutant."

"So all's well that ends well."

"Not quite. Gabe is upset because he ran in the first place. He thinks he's a coward and can never grow up to become a Warrior like me."

"I take it a bedtime story is in order?"

Blade nodded. "I'm hoping it will help."

"If he's anything like his father—and I know he is—Gabe will recover quickly. We all do when we're that young."

The giant smiled and stepped to the doorway. "Thanks again."

"Say, Blade?"

"Yes?"

"Did anyone ever go back to Castle Orm?"

"No."

"One of these days we should go there."

"One of these days."

DAVID ROBBINS
BACK IN PRINT AT LAST!
Don't miss this opportunity to order these special Collector's Editions of the *Endworld* series!

#1: The Fox Run. Savage barbarians called the Trolls are enslaving women from scattered settlements throughout the burned-out land. If Blade and the Warriors can't defeat them, they'll lose their women, their honor, and the world they risked their lives to save.
_3105-1 $3.50 US/$4.50 CAN

#2: Thief River Falls Run. On a mission of mercy to get much-needed medical supplies, Blade and the Alpha Triad are attacked by heavily armed renegade soldiers. Their lives in the balance, Blade and his comrades must fight as never before—or the blood of hundreds of innocent people will be on their hands.
_3106-X $3.50 US/$4.50 CAN

LEISURE BOOKS
ATTN: Order Department
276 5th Avenue, New York, NY 10001

Please add $1.50 for shipping and handling for the first book and $.35 for each book thereafter. N.Y.S. and N.Y.C. residents, please add appropriate sales tax. No cash, stamps, or C.O.D.s. All orders shipped within 6 weeks via postal service book rate. Canadian orders require $2.00 extra postage. It must also be paid in U.S. dollars through a U.S. banking facility.

Name _____
Address _____
City _____ State _____ Zip _____
I have enclosed $_____ in payment for the checked book(s).
Payment <u>must</u> accompany all orders. ☐ Please send a free catalog.

BLADE DOUBLE EDITIONS
By David Robbins
A $7.00 VALUE FOR ONLY $4.50!

The action-packed series that set the genre on fire is now in Giant Double Edtions. It's twice the mayhem at one low price!

First Strike. In the remote California wilderness, a genetic mistake called Spider is producing an army of inhuman spawn that will conquer mankind—unless Blade and the Freedom Force can destroy his web of terror. *And in the same volume...*

Outlands Strike. Led by a diabolical fiend with a taste for human flesh, the Reptiloids round up all the people in the Outlands of Oregon as preparation for a great feast. But Blade is coming to dinner—and the special of the day is lizard stew.

_3257-0 $4.50

Vampire Strike. Murderous fiends called the Vampires are kidnapping young girls for their deadly rituals. It is up to Blade to drive a stake through every one of their vicious hearts. *And in the same volume...*

Pipeline Strike. When the Federation learns of a man who claims he can reactivate the Alaskan pipeline, they send Blade and the Force into the Arctic Circle to search for him. Blade and his comrades are looking for a source of energy that will save the world—what they find is a madman bent on destroying it.

_3310-0 $4.50

LEISURE BOOKS
ATTN: Order Department
276 5th Avenue, New York, NY 10001

Please add $1.50 for shipping and handling for the first book and $.35 for each book thereafter. PA., N.Y.S. and N.Y.C. residents, please add appropriate sales tax. No cash, stamps, or C.O.D.s. All orders shipped within 6 weeks via postal service book rate. Canadian orders require $2.00 extra postage and must be paid in U.S. dollars through a U.S. banking facility.

Name_____
Address_____
City _____ State_____ Zip_____
I have enclosed $_____in payment for the checked book(s). Payment <u>must</u> accompany all orders.☐ Please send a free catalog.

A $7.00 VALUE FOR ONLY $4.50!

Pirate Strike. Thriving in the waters off the Pacific coast are vicious buccaneers more barbarous and savage than the pirates of legend. And the sea wolves will continue to rule the waves—unless Blade and the Force can drive them to a watery grave.

And in the same action-packed volume....

Crusher Strike. From the human cesspool called Shantytown, Crusher Payne and the most ruthless degenerates alive lead an attack to annihilate the civilized zones. And they'll succeed unless Blade can single-handedly penetrate Crusher's operation and wipe Shantytown off the face of the planet.

_3371-2 $4.50

L.A. Strike. When Los Angeles falls victim to an incursion of mindless savages, it is up to the Force to lift the siege. Matching violence with superviolence and death with megadeath, Blade and his comrades blow into the City of Angels like devils out of hell.

And in the same red-hot volume....

Dead Zone Strike. When deadly mutants start terrorizing the Dakota Territory, Blade and the Force track them to the heart of the Dead Zone. There the Force must destroy the marauders—or die in the infernal depths that have spawned them.

_3446-8 $4.50

LEISURE BOOKS
ATTN: Order Department
276 5th Avenue, New York, NY 10001

Please add $1.50 for shipping and handling for the first book and $.35 for each book thereafter. PA., N.Y.S. and N.Y.C. residents, please add appropriate sales tax. No cash, stamps, or C.O.D.s. All orders shipped within 6 weeks via postal service book rate. Canadian orders require $2.00 extra postage and must be paid in U.S. dollars through a U.S. banking facility.

Name_____
Address_____
City _____ State_____ Zip_____

I have enclosed $_____in payment for the checked book(s). Payment <u>must</u> accompany all orders.☐ Please send a free catalog.

SPEND YOUR LEISURE MOMENTS WITH US.

Hundreds of exciting titles to choose from—something for everyone's taste in fine books: breathtaking historical romance, chilling horror, spine-tingling suspense, taut medical thrillers, involving mysteries, action-packed men's adventure and wild Westerns.

SEND FOR A FREE CATALOGUE TODAY!

**Leisure Books
Attn: Customer Service Department**
276 5th Avenue, New York, NY 10001